D.N.A.

Book Two in the
Acroname Series

By

Jack & Sue Drafahl

© 2016

"DNA is the crossword puzzle of life"
Jack Drafahl

i

D. N. A.

Jack and Sue Drafahl

Published by
www.earthseapublishing.com
Copyright © 2016 by Jack and Sue Drafahl
All Rights Reserved

ISBN: 978-1-938971-02-0
10 9 8 7 6 5 4 3 2 1
February 2016

This book is dedicated to
our two favorite scientists:

Our daughter Dr. Kristy Drafahl, Ph.D.
and
her husband, Dr. Chris Veazey, Ph.D.

Chapter 1

Fifty-five-year-old police detective, Frank Ridge looked down at his watch and saw that he was behind schedule. He was never late for work, but had completely miscalculated the storm's impact. He reminded himself not to trust the weather forecaster. He still had more than five miles to go on the slow-moving freeway before he could escape to side roads leading to Seattle's ninth precinct.

Frank had been a detective now for twenty years, but recently had started to wonder if it was really worth continuing. His black hair was starting to show streaks of gray, and his daily uniform of a tweed suit was starting to wear thin in several areas. He was a very handsome man with a slight dimple, but sported a scar on his forehead from a previous gunfight. For the past five years, he spent his evenings working out on a treadmill and was in great physical condition, but that had not always been the case.

His wife, Ann, had died from cancer ten years earlier, and he'd been devastated. He became very depressed, and for several years came close to becoming an alcoholic. When he finally hit rock bottom, his boss and friend, Captain Mark Carson, was there for support.

His comrade had worked his way up in record time from a beat cop to become one of the first black captains in the precinct. The captain was a short stocky man who could yell loud enough for everyone in the building to hear him. Over the years, Mark and Frank had become very good friends, and Frank was always welcome at the captain's famous family barbecues.

Frank would now have to push that friendship a bit by arriving at least a half-hour late for the morning briefing. The captain was strict and the only acceptable excuses for missing briefings were vacation leave, being undercover, or getting shot.

Frank watched as the downpour tried to overwhelm the windshield wipers. Even at full speed, the wipers were starting to lose the battle. Traffic was almost now at a standstill. As his old beat-up Ford Mustang slowly crept along, he saw flashing red and blue lights up ahead. A Washington State Patrol officer had stopped someone for a traffic infraction, and Frank was sure it wasn't for speeding. He had a lot of respect for the troopers because they never knew if a traffic stop would produce an irate businessman or a drug addict. Department protocol required that the officers keep their weapon holstered until they were sure they needed it. Problem was that the time it took to draw a weapon was more than enough for an armed driver to use theirs. Such events were rare in the Seattle area, but not unheard of.

The driver hadn't pulled completely off the road and was blocking part of the right-hand lane. This made navigation for the officer very dangerous as he confronted the driver, ticket book in hand. Frank thought something didn't look right. The brake lights of the stopped car were erratically blinking off and on, indicating the driver was nervous. As the officer started to talk with the driver, the brake light blinking increased its pace. Frank finally couldn't stand it anymore. As he started to get out of his car, a muzzle blast of gunfire came from the driver's window, hitting the officer square in the chest.

Frank got back into his car and radioed in a code 510; Officer needs help, and that he required an ambulance by air. He gave his mile marker location, dropped the mike, and ran for the downed officer. The driver was already out of the car and running into the ditch. Frank pulled his gun but there were too many cars and people in the line of sight to take a shot. The officer was in bad shape, and Frank's concern was to help him first, and then go after the driver of the car. When he reached the officer, he could tell that whatever he could do, it wasn't going to be enough, and the medics would never reach him in time. Frank knelt down and watched the officer cough up blood. The officer tried to say something, but Frank couldn't hear him, so he put his ear to the officer's lips.

Again, the officer spoke. "Get that son of a bitch."

More blood came out of the officer's mouth, and his eyes started to glass over as he died in the pouring rain. Frank checked for a pulse and found none. The two slugs had hit him square in the chest. Frank was amazed that the officer had even spoken, as most people would have died instantly from such wounds.

He looked up to locate the suspect. He'd already crossed a short field and was headed into a grove of trees, almost out of sight. Frank knew that he needed to stay with the dead officer, but any shred of evidence was being washed away in the rain.

"Can I help? I'm Doctor Phelps. I work in emergency at the local hospital."

Frank looked up at the man who had just spoken and saw he had a doctor's bag in hand.

"Can you do me a favor? I tested his pulse and got nothing. Check to confirm, and then can you wait until police or medical personnel arrive? I have to go document the scene before the rain washes everything away."

The doctor opened his bag and took out a stethoscope.

"Not a problem, go do your job, and I'll do what I can here. My job is the same whether it is on the side of the road or in the emergency room; it really doesn't make a difference."

Frank nodded and ran to the other side of the suspect's car. His clothes were now soaked from standing so long in the downpour. His phone was in his wet pocket, and he hoped it was still working. It looked fine, so he quickly checked to make sure he had the WORM (Write Once Read Many) card in the phone. He got this new phone a couple of years back, but had never used it for a crime scene because the CSI team normally did the documentation.

Truth be told, he hadn't ever used the phone to take a picture, but after going through several menus, he found the camera function. He turned around to the suspect's car and pressed the capture button. The image didn't look great, but it was an image. He looked down and saw the suspect's footprints in the mud. He knew he had to hurry because with this rain, the footprint would soon be lost in the growing puddles of water. He wiped the rain off the lens and pressed the capture button. The resulting image wasn't very clear. He turned the phone over to find several more drops on the phone camera lens. He wiped the lens and turned the phone around, but he was too late. Water had broken through a small mud dam near the top edge of the road and washed the footprint away. He slowly worked his way down the side of the ditch, but no other footprints were visible.

Convinced he'd done his best in this downpour, Frank headed back up the hill, but slipped and fell. His phone skidded into a muddy puddle. He quickly grabbed the phone and immediately took out the battery, and shoved the wet phone safely into his pocket.

When he reached the downed officer, the doctor looked up with the *"I'm so sorry"* expression, that Frank assumed the doctor had relayed many times before. The rain started to taper off so the two stood next to the suspect's car, waiting for the helicopter.

Two hours later, Frank sat in the front seat of his car as the on-site investigators took his statement. The body had been removed, and the CSI team was preparing the suspect's car for transport back to the lab. More than two dozen cops were searching the woods where the suspect had escaped, but he was long gone.

Frank gave his phone to the investigating team. They told him they would try to salvage it and replace the WORM data card with a new one. The card he'd used to document the footprint had been added to the small amount of the evidence they had collected.

Frank was surprised when Captain Carson walked up behind the CSI investigators. He reached out and shook Frank's hand.

"How are you holding up, Frank? Sorry about the WSP officer. I knew him. His name was Jim Monney, and he had a wife and two kids."

Frank looked down to the ground and then back up to the captain. "This whole thing is crap. I knew a couple of seconds before that something was wrong. There wasn't a thing I could do. Damn it. He had two kids; that's too bad. Do you want me to talk with the wife as I was the last one to see her husband alive?"

The captain leaned over to Frank.

"Frank, I know you mean well. I've been in your shoes more times than I want to count. I'll talk to her and if she wants to contact you later, that's fine. Right now though, you need to go back to the department, fill out a report, and then go home. Take tomorrow off. Don't even think of arguing with me, because that's an order. Just know that you did your best. The detectives on the case will get back to you later today. Just make sure you write down everything in your report, because even the slightest thought may help later. You know the drill."

Frank glanced over to the woods.

"I just hate this injustice, but don't worry, Captain, I'll do as you say. I won't argue about a couple of days off, but right now, I am looking forward to a very long hot shower. So, if you don't need me any longer, I'll head back."

Several hours later, Frank signed the report and put it on the captain's desk. As he walked through the department, he could see everyone's eyes were following him. He just wasn't sure if they were expressing sympathy, or disgust for not getting the bad guy.

For the last six months, Frank was without a partner. Most of the detectives his age retired or moved to another precinct. Those that remained had tried working with Frank for a couple of months, but then requested another partner. Frank was one of those people who adapted slowly to new technologies. He was in favor of the old adage of "if it ain't broke, don't fix it." He had done well in his career until some of the new-fangled CSI technologies had come along. The captain had warned him that he was going to have to adapt because the higher ups were putting pressure on him to retire Frank.

An hour later, Frank sat in his La-Z-Boy drinking a large glass of orange juice, and listening to the Carpenters oldies but goodies CD. He couldn't get the shooting out of his mind. He kept replaying the scene, trying to figure out if there had been any way he could have saved the officer.

He was about to change to a different CD when his doorbell rang. He looked through the peephole and saw it was his only child, Debra. She was thirty-seven, very beautiful, tall, blonde, smart, and still unattached. This was probably because she'd become the driving force in the district attorney's office. She held the position of assistant district attorney (ADA) but in fact, did most of the work for which her boss took credit. The bottom line was that she was a workaholic and had only two things that mattered in her life - her job and her father.

She and Frank had a standing date every Thursday for dinner where they talked about everything but work. It was a rule she had laid down and Frank gladly agreed. They would eat together, watch an old movie, and talk about family issues. She always stayed overnight in her childhood bedroom which Frank had never changed. She stored a full set of work clothes and extras, so she could go directly to work in the morning.

On the other six nights, she stayed in her condo located just a couple of miles from where she worked. That made it easier to go back to work when an emergency came up, and she seemed to have plenty of those. What little time off she had, was devoted to maintaining good physical shape. She alternated between jogging and bike riding, or working out on her exercise gym when it rained.

Debra had a steadfast rule never to date anyone in law enforcement, which left out just about everyone she met. She had a great deal of respect for her dad as a detective, but that wasn't what she was looking for in a possible mate. She had this idealistic notion that she must separate work from her personal life.

When she heard about the shooting, she had rushed over to see her dad.

Frank opened the door, and she hurried in and put her arms around him.

"Are you okay, Dad? I just heard about the shooting. I'm so sorry."

Frank was never so glad to see Debra.

"I'm okay, just really bummed about the dead officer. He was married and had two kids. It's such a damn shame."

"I know, Dad, but you did what you could to help. I'm just glad to hear you're taking a couple of days off."

"Just where did you hear that, young lady?"

"I have my sources inside the police department."

"It's Captain Carson, right?"

Debra nodded and pulled her left hand from behind her back where she held a bag of take-out food.

"How about Chinese tonight? I knew you wouldn't want to cook, so I hope you don't mind."

Frank smiled and walked into the kitchen and opened the cupboard.

"You know, Sweetheart I'd never turn down a Chinese meal on any night."

She smiled as Frank reached up and took down two of the three plates in the cupboard. When Frank's wife had died, he downsized the house to a point where he had just what he needed to survive. The extra plate, glass, and additional set of silverware were reserved for his absent wife, as his way of honoring her memory.

Debra had asked him what he was going to do if he had more than two guests since he had only three place settings. His simple answer was that it was a sure sign they were meant to go out for dinner. She couldn't convince him otherwise, so she gave up the fight.

They had one of the best father/daughter relationships possible. She knew that he would do whatever it took for her well-being, and she would do the same. Although they agreed to never talk about work, tonight was different. Debra knew her father needed to talk with someone about his feelings and get them out in the open. So, they talked long into the night, causing her to be late for work the next day.

Chapter 2
(Two Months Later)

Frank hated courtrooms, especially when he was there to testify in the case. The shooting of the State Patrol officer that he had witnessed had taken a positive turn a week after Frank returned to work. A routine traffic stop in downtown Seattle had netted Jesse Carr. Mr. Carr had a rap sheet covering more than a dozen different offenses ranging from burglary to assault. When the car was searched, the arresting officer found a weapon that matched the one used during the WSP shooting.

Frank's phone image of the footprint found next to the suspect's car sealed the case. It had been determined that Carr had been on a camping trip a few weeks earlier and had gotten his shoes wet while wading through a stream. Carr had set his shoes next to the fire to dry them, and one of the shoes had fallen next to a hot ember. The ember had burned a unique pattern in the sole of the shoe, making it easy to identify. The phone photo of the footprint showed the same rare pattern.

During the first two days of the trial, Prosecutor Dana Bennet laid out the circumstances that led up to the shooting and the events that resulted in the suspect's arrest. Ballistic experts testified that the slugs that had killed the officer were a perfect match to the weapon in Carr's possession. Two witnesses who had seen the suspect run from the scene were put on the stand. Although their testimonies were weak, the prosecutor remained confident that the bullet match and the footprint photo would be enough to convict.

Frank had a very uneasy feeling about how the case was progressing. Carr's Defense Attorney, Linda Galleon, was not putting up much of a battle. She made a few objections, and those were very weak. This case seemed to be a typical slam-dunk that prosecutors love, but Frank sensed something wasn't right. The closer it came time for his testimony, the more he was concerned that the case was going to hinge on his photo.

The third day of the case, Frank was called up to testify. The prosecutor ran through the circumstances that brought Frank to the location behind the suspect's car and the eventual shooting. Finally, the prosecutor came to the crux of the case for Frank.

"Detective Ridge, can you describe what happened when Officer Jim Monney approached the suspect's car."

Frank looked at the defense attorney for an objection, but none came.

"Traffic had come to a standstill, and the rain was coming down hard. I saw Officer Monney approach the suspect's car. When the officer faced the window, two gunshots came from the driver's side of the car, striking the officer directly in the chest."

Again, there was no objection from the defense. Now Frank knew something was very wrong. The prosecutor was pushing the limits of the law and getting away with it.

Frank continued. "I radioed for help, and then headed for the suspect's car. I tried to get a clear shot of the suspect with my weapon as he ran away, but there were too many civilians in the way. I didn't discharge my weapon. I checked the downed officer, and saw he was barely alive, but he said nothing."

Frank hated lying on the stand, but he felt it would accomplish nothing to bring out what Jim Monney had said to him before he died. Frank looked at the defense attorney. She was letting him say whatever he wanted, so he continued.

"Officer Monney died less than a minute later, which I confirmed by checking his pulse. A doctor volunteered to verify that fact and stayed with Officer Monney while I went after the suspect who had headed for a wooded area next to the freeway. I realized he had gotten too much of a head start on me, and it would be useless to search the woods by myself, so I returned to the downed officer. The rain was still coming down hard, and I realized that any evidence was being eroded, so I used my phone to photograph a single footprint made by the suspect as he fled the scene. Before I could get a second photo, the footprint was washed away. I then waited with the body of Officer Monney until the medical teams, CSI, and detectives arrived on the scene."

Frank looked at the prosecutor and then over to Defense Attorney Galleon. It appeared that he was done with his testimony, so he began to get up and return to his seat in the back of the courtroom.

As Frank stood up, so did the defense attorney.

"Detective Ridge, could you remain seated as I have a couple of questions to clarify some of your statements. Specifically, I have questions about the photo you took with your phone. What kind of memory card did you use to record the photo?"

Frank knew now why the defense attorney had been so lax about the rest of the case. There was something amiss with his photo. What had he missed? The prosecutor had gone over his testimony step-by-step to make sure Frank was up to speed on anything that the defense attorney would throw at him.

"My phone uses two cards - a standard SIM card which stores phone numbers etcetera. The second card slot is designed to hold a WORM data card which my phone uses to record photos."

"Detective Ridge, can you tell the jury what a WORM card is?"

The prosecutor would normally object to this question, but it was to her advantage for Frank to answer. The judge looked at both the prosecutor and the defense attorney. He sensed something was amiss.

Frank took a second for the sounds in the courtroom to settle. He hated some of the new technologies. The only reason that he knew about the WORM card was that he had to attend a mandatory evidence lecture given by the CSI division of the Seattle Police Department. It was one of the few new technologies he knew by heart.

"It's a new type of data card that records data once and is never used again. The WORM stands for Write Once, Read Many. Each card used to document a crime scene is kept in the case evidence file. The cards were originally designed for digital cameras, but have been adapted to phones that have two card slots. The CSI team investigating the shooting of Officer Monney took my card and added it to the evidence they had collected."

Defense Attorney Galleon straightened her skirt as she picked up a single sheet of paper and looked it over. "Detective Ridge, how do you get the data cards for your phone?"

"We pick up new cards from the evidence locker. Each card is signed for, and a case number is written on the card when the card is used for a specific case. We're required to initial the card before we turn it over as evidence to the CSI team."

Galleon looked over the paper one more time and then to the jury. She smiled. She picked up the remote that turned on the large LCD monitor to the side of the jury panel.

"Is this the photo that you took with your phone?"

Frank looked at the photo. It was the photo, and yet it wasn't. It looked a lot better on the big screen than on his phone, which didn't make sense. "Yes, that's the photo I took of the footprint."

"Detective Ridge, are you aware that every WORM card has an embedded serial number?"

"No, I was not."

"Detective Ridge, can you explain how it is that you signed out card #3SEDEAET345 for your phone and yet the card we reviewed had serial number #3SUWIEWD643?"

The audience started to sound like a flock of geese. They knew something was up. Judge Lawrence Bender brought down his gavel, and looked at Prosecutor Dana Bennet.

"I want to see the prosecutor, Detective Ridge, and the defense attorney in my chambers immediately! Court is adjourned until tomorrow at 10 a.m."

Frank looked at Prosecutor Bennet. The expression on her face told him that the two of them were in big trouble. What in the hell had they done to his WORM card?

Everyone gathered in Judge Lawrence Bender's chambers along with the head of the CSI department. Judge Bender looked over to Prosecutor Bennet. "This better be good. If you can't explain the discrepancy in serial numbers, I'll have to call a mistrial. Let's hear it."

Prosecutor Bennet looked over to the CSI head and then back to the judge.

"Your honor, I wish we could, but to be honest; it was a major screw up. I didn't know about the switch of the data cards, and we're now in the process of investigating the reason for the switch. The best I could do on such short notice is to ask the head of the CSI team, Morgan Teller, to explain it to you."

Fifty-year-old Morgan Teller was a short wiry man who looked too fragile to ever be in the field. Teller proceeded, but was choosing his words carefully.

"Judge, I take full responsibility for what the prosecutor calls a screw up. Over the last few months, the budget cuts have forced us to downsize some of the more experienced CSI agents and bring in less-expensive new blood to the department. The technician working on the case was trying to impress me with his expertise and took it upon himself to edit Detective Ridge's photo. The image was very poor quality, so the technician enhanced the image in Photoshop and somehow managed to transfer the image to a new card, and change the timestamp date to match the original date and time of the photo. Unbeknownst to me, the technician even forged Ridge's signature. He destroyed the original card to cover his tracks. We're not sure how he could get around the safeguards built into the WORM card, but are in the process of putting in new safeguards to prevent this from happening in the future. I fired the tech as soon as I learned about the problem from Prosecutor Bennet, and we're now filing charges against the man."

The room was silent for at least ten seconds. Prosecutor Bennet knew she'd lost the case and wouldn't push the issue with the judge. Defense Attorney Galleon smirked and waited for the judge to make his ruling. Judge Bender's face turned from rose to bright red. He was pissed because this CSI screw up had wasted a lot of valuable court time and was forcing him to make a decision he was going to regret for a very long time.

"I have no choice. The chain of evidence has been tainted with illegal lab procedures. The lab tech that altered the photo also processed the weapon, so both the photo of the footprint and the weapon will be disallowed. I'm going to have to call a mistrial. If the D.A.'s office wants to re-file, it will have to be without this disqualified evidence. We're done here, and I don't want to see any of your faces for a long time. The justice system took a big hit today people. Get out there and fix the problem, because I don't want to see this kind of thing ever happen in my court again."

Frank was devastated. Jesse Carr was going to walk, and there was nothing he could do about it. It was all because of that stupid photo. Why in the hell did they mess with his photo? They could have convicted Carr on the poor photo and an enhanced version next to the original. It was such a stupid mistake, and now a cop killer was walking.

An hour later, Frank walked into the precinct, and everyone's eyes were on him as he walked down the aisle of cubicles. He knew deep down that he was partly at fault for the case's failure. If he'd been more adept at taking photos with his phone, the CSI tech wouldn't have messed with his photo. Frank was about to check his messages, when the captain called him in to see him. He felt like a schoolboy going to the principal's office. The captain motioned for him to close the door, and take a seat.

"Frank, we have a serious problem. We lost the case due to a CSI screw up, but not everyone sees it that way. The mayor thinks that you're partly responsible. We're taking a lot of heat from the press, and everyone is looking for someone to blame.

Half the detectives out there think Carr got off because you screwed up. I looked at your record and see that you haven't taken a vacation in three years. Here's the deal. Take a month off and use up all your vacation time and let things cool off."

Frank started to say something, but the captain continued. "Frank, this is not a choice; it's an order. This should give the press time to give up on this, and then you can get back to work."

The captain continued, "Frank, do me one other favor. I know how much you hate some of the new technologies, and I understand because we're both old school. You're still one of the best profilers in the department and can read the bad guys better than anyone I know. You know where to look for motive, method, and opportunity. Your aversion to these new technologies is getting you into trouble, and that has to change if you want to come back. I don't care how you do it. Take some criminology courses from the local college, go online, or visit the CSI down in Portland. I don't care how you do it, but you have to get up to speed on these new forensic methods."

Frank was about to respond, but the captain held up his hand. Frank knew that was his signal to leave. He pulled an empty box from the storage closet and ten minutes later, he had cleared all his personal stuff from his desk. As he headed out the door, box in hand, everyone in the squad room assumed that it was a permanent situation. In a month when he returned, they would be in for a surprise.

An hour later, Frank sat in his La-Z-Boy, lights low, orange juice in hand, listening to music, contemplating what he was going to do next with his life. Just when he was beginning to relax, his doorbell rang. He figured it was one of two people - his daughter, Debra, or the captain. After his confrontation today with the captain, he was hoping it was Debra. He set his glass of orange juice down and slowly walked to the door. A second ring sounded as he looked out the peephole and saw it was Debra. He opened the door, and she rushed in.

"Dad, I just heard, and I'm so sorry. I can't believe the CSI technician screwed up your photo."

Frank motioned for her to come in and sit down. He held up his glass of orange juice and then pointed it to the kitchen.

"There is a little left if you want. Did you catch any flack for my screw up today?"

"Dad, you did nothing wrong. The CSI technician is totally to blame. Don't worry; I can take care of myself. If anyone says anything about you or me, I'll become their worst nightmare."

Frank laughed. "I know you can take care of yourself. I just hate you having to defend me."

"Dad, I wouldn't have it any other way. Now what's going on with you?"

Frank went on to explain the captain's plan of a forced vacation. When he was done, Debra took it all in and thought about it a few seconds before commenting.

"You know, Dad, the captain's right. You need a break. Maybe this is the time to consider what you want to do in the future. It might just be the time to hang up your gun. I'd be fine with that, but it's ultimately your decision."

Money was never a problem for Frank as he had been socking money away ever since his wife had died. He had amassed over $100,000 in the last eight years and could easily retire if he wanted. The problem was that he loved being a detective. He loved getting the bad guys and putting them behind bars.

Frank finished the last of his orange juice, and set the glass down on the coffee table.

Debra moved over to the refrigerator, looked in, and saw there were a couple of beers. She knew her dad didn't drink anymore, so they must be for guests. She opened one and sat down on the couch next to her father. "If you're interested, I have a couple of ideas that may turn things around."

Frank said, "I'm not sure I'll like what you have in mind, but what the hell. It's better to hear it from you, than someone in the department."

"I don't know if you remember, but a couple of years back I had a couple of dates with a guy who was getting a degree in acting. Anyway, to make a long story short, he roomed with Dennis Andrews, a real nerd then, but who now works as a civilian scientist in a special military science center. This Andrews is supposedly a wiz with new forensic technologies. I've never met him, but the guy I was dating told me that Andrews was very good at explaining new terminologies to the layman. Maybe you could talk to this Andrews fellow and see if he can help you, or at least point you in the right direction."

Frank put his hands behind his head and tried to massage the muscles in the back of his neck. "You really think a guy who probably has an IQ twice mine is going to give me the time of day, especially when he's never met me before?"

"Dad, what do you have to lose? Things can't get any worse than they are now, right? You need to start looking at other ways to solve crimes, or maybe you'll have to retire. You're a lot smarter than you give yourself credit for, and you can adapt better than anyone can in your department. You've just gotten too comfortable with the crime-solving tools you've used for the last twenty years. I'm sorry, I love you very much, but that's the way I see it."

"Okay, you're right. Maybe I do need to change. If anyone else had suggested this, I'd have told them to go to hell. For you, I'll give it a try. So, where do I find this Dennis Andrews?"

Chapter 3

Frank slept in, which he rarely had the opportunity to do. He and his daughter talked late into the night, soul-searching about their futures. As usual, she stayed overnight but scooted out early for work. The aroma of coffee, eggs, and bacon caused him to stir. Breakfast was a luxury for him as he never had time and usually just grabbed something on his way to work.

When he got down to the kitchen, he found a note. *Dad, loved talking with you last night. Everything is going to work out. Don't worry about me. You just need to reheat the eggs and bacon. You'll have to make your own toast. Love you, Debra.*

Frank grinned. Everything else could go to hell, as long as he still had his daughter. He just wished she would find someone special. His biggest concern was that she was putting her father before her own life too much. That was going to have to change, starting today.

After leisurely reading the newspaper, he got dressed and headed to the local electronics store. The first thing he was going to do was to buy a GPS unit for his car. He was familiar since similar units were installed in the patrol cars. He picked out the unit that Debra had told him to buy and spent the rest of the afternoon reading through the instructions. He mounted the unit in his car and drove around testing the system. He was very impressed, and wondered why he'd waited so long to get one.

Tomorrow he would tackle the phone store and upgrade his cell. Debra mentioned that there had been some big advancements in phone features in the last few months, and Frank should take advantage of them.

The next morning, he got up early, worked out on his home exercise equipment, and then headed to the phone store. The young salesman had colored, spiked hair and pants twenty percent longer than his legs. He proceeded to talk down to Frank, as though he had no brain at all. He ignored the kid as he rambled on about the different features, and selected a phone just like Debra's. That way, she could help troubleshoot problems while he became proficient using it. By late afternoon, he felt comfortable enough with the new phone to call Debra. He pressed the icon on the speed dial for his daughter and waited.

"Dad, is everything okay? You never call me at this time of day. Is something wrong?"

"Deb, I'm just testing out my new phone. I got the GPS working great, but it will take a little longer getting used to this new phone."

"That's great, Dad, but you still need to go see Dennis Andrews. There are plenty of more technological advancements to learn than a GPS unit and a new iPhone. Promise me."

"Don't worry. That's my plan for tomorrow. Are we still on for dinner next week?"

"Wouldn't miss it, Dad. Love you, but I've got to go back to work."

Frank clicked the end button. He was now ready for the next big step. After his progress the last couple of days, he wasn't sure he needed to go, but he'd promised Debra.

He plugged the address to Advanced Nano Devices into his GPS. The company was located in an industrial park Frank had never been to before, so the GPS would be a big help. He put it on charge and set it next to the picture of his wife and daughter. He smiled. His late wife, Ann, would be so proud of his progress. He went into his closet, picked out one of the usual work suits, locked his gun in the nightstand, and was asleep by 10 o'clock.

The morning dawned with bright sunlight and a cloudless sky, a rarity for Seattle. The air was a little crisp, but that was fine as the heater in his car still worked. He chuckled as he mounted the GPS in his dated Mustang. The young would be leading the old today, in more ways than Frank could imagine.

Frank realized that he was going to arrive too early, so he decided to play around with the GPS. He followed its instructions

19

to exit the freeway, but when it told him to go right, he went straight ahead. The unit blinked and presented a recalculating message. In seconds, a new route appeared on the screen. Frank was impressed. A mile from the destination, Frank analyzed the businesses along the street. Most were warehouse types with a small access door near the loading dock. A few blocks from the destination, the scenery changed to grassy knolls with glass entrances and office windows facing the street.

When the GPS indicated that he had arrived, he was looking at a security gate. Frank stopped and rolled down his window to talk to the guard. Neither he nor Debra had called Dennis in advance, and this was looking like this might be a waste of time. The short, overweight guard set his Danish down and leaned over to the driver's window.

"I'm Detective Ridge and I'm here to see Dennis Andrews."

The guard looked over at Frank's car. "What's your business?"

Frank hesitated, but then pulled out his badge. "It's police business, and none of yours. Are you going to let me in, or am I going to have to call someone?"

The security guard looked around and said, "Go ahead. This place will be closed down in another couple weeks. There's not much to worry about guarding anymore."

Frank put his badge away and put his car into gear as the barrier came up. He pulled into the parking lot, and wondered if it was a holiday, and he'd missed it. There had to be fifty parking places, and only five or six were being used.

He locked his car, and slammed it shut, but it bounced back open. He was about to walk away anyway, but then realized that he now had something of value in it, his new GPS. He went back, kicked the door hard, and it closed and locked.

The front of Advanced Nano Devices had tinted glass that sloped up to a second floor and then angled back out to the roof. He'd never seen such a design before and found it quite attractive. As he opened the front door, he ran into another guard. He started to pull out his badge, but the guard held up his hand.

"It's okay. I just got a call that you were coming. We don't have many visitors, especially police detectives. Just sign in, please. Dr. Andrews's office is through those double doors and down at the end of the hall."

Frank signed with a flare that even a doctor couldn't read and headed off without saying a word to the guard.

This company was touted as some kind of research center. The building construction indicated that this company once had a lot of money. There were expensive floor tiles, thick solid-core doors, and stainless steel everywhere. Once he reached the end of the hall, Frank hesitantly entered a set of double fire doors, not sure what to expect. The room was large with dozens of cubicles, but they all appeared to be empty. As Frank walked slowly down the row, he noticed there was one large glass enclosed office at the end of the cubicle corridor. He approached the glass office, and noticed the person inside was wadding up papers and throwing them into a wastebasket.

He knocked on the door and stuck his head inside. "Are you Dr. Andrews?"

Thirty-five-year-old Dr. Dennis Andrews slowly turned with a note of surprise on his face. Frank immediately sized the man up - not short, but not too tall, not fat, but not thin. He had a face that looked like millions of other 30-35-year-old men with light color skin, brown hair, and hazel eyes. He wore a T-shirt, jeans, and Nike tennis shoes. Dr. Andrews was a normal-looking fellow who could easily get lost in a crowd.

"Hi, I'm Detective Frank Ridge. I was wondering if we could have a little talk."

The look on Dennis's face immediately turned to fear. Dennis felt his life had already turned to crap, and now there was a detective in his office asking questions.

Frank realized from the look on Dennis's face that he'd used the wrong approach.

"Don't worry Dr. Andrews, you're not in trouble. My daughter, Debra, used to date your college roommate and asked me to come see you on some personal business. I was actually looking for some help from you."

Dennis dropped the last crumpled piece of paper in the trash and stood up to shake Frank's hand.

"I've never actually met your daughter, Detective. My roommate always picked her up at her work when they were dating. I haven't seen my roommate in a couple of years, so what could I possibly do to help a police detective?"

Frank looked around the deserted office and continued. "It's a long story, and you may think I'm totally crazy. Especially since you've never seen or heard of me before. All I ask is that you hear me out. Besides, your roommate told my daughter that you were a sucker for sad stories. The truth is, I want to hire you to help me with a personal project. I can pay you five thousand dollars for a couple of weeks work."

Dennis froze and looked at Frank, trying to size him up. The man didn't look like a police detective, nor did he look like a man who had that kind of money. Previously, Dennis had been getting more money than that, but in a couple of weeks his project would be over.

"Okay, Detective, I don't know what kind of scam you are trying to pull, but I'm not doing anything illegal. You don't even know what I do here."

Frank pulled up a chair next to the desk turned it around and sat with the back toward his chest.

"It really doesn't matter what you do here, or should I say did. I don't want to hire you to do something like you do for this company. I want to hire you to educate me on some of the new forensic technologies in use today."

"You really are crazy."

"My daughter said that would be your reply. Just hear me out, and then if you don't want the money, I'll never bother you again. I told my daughter it was a stupid idea coming to see you, so for once I can tell her she was wrong, and I was right."

"Okay, you've got my attention. Do you want a cup of coffee, Detective...what was the name again?"

"I'm Frank Ridge and my daughter is Debra Ridge."

"Okay, Frank. Let's hear this crazy story of yours."

For the next hour, Frank laid out the whole story about the shooting, the phone photo of the footprint, and the screw up by the Seattle CSI. When Frank completed his yarn, Dennis set his empty coffee cup on his desk.

"You know, Frank, I thought I was having a bad month, but I really think you beat me. Normally, I'd have told you that I was too busy, but you can see that's not the case. This project is at an end for me, so I'm looking for something new to do. You have given me a crazy idea, and I think I may be able to help you, in more ways than you can imagine. Are you doing anything else the rest of the day?"

"Not really, what do you have in mind?"

Chapter 4

Frank and Dennis walked out to the parking lot, and Dennis pointed over to the silver BMW and clicked the opener for the door locks. As Frank climbed in, he noted that the car was loaded with every feature and gadget you could imagine. With this nice a ride, he was happy to come back later for his car.

Dennis was very quiet until they had cleared the front guard station. He even looked in the rear-view mirror before saying anything.

"I didn't want to say anything until we were clear of the compound. You have to understand that not everything was as it seemed. That building and everything inside it were financed by the military. The project I was working on was classified, so I have to be careful what I say to anyone in the building as they have eavesdropping devices everywhere. The project was shut down a couple of weeks ago, and we're in the process of cleaning up loose ends.

"In case you're wondering, we're headed to my mother's house about twenty-five minutes from downtown. I've been living there for the last three years, and most of my personal research is done in her lab. She's a biochemist and guest lecturer at universities all over the world. Most of the time she's out of the country, so I usually have the house to myself."

As they drove south from downtown Seattle into the hills, the space between the houses increased until all you saw was land. As the BMW slowed in front of a large gate, Frank looked at the acres of lawn sprawling beside the never-ending driveway. Frank had been on a couple of high-profile cases in neighborhoods like this, but was shocked to see a castle-like home in the distance.

"Next, you are going to tell me that your name is really Bruce Wayne."

Dennis looked over to Frank with a questioning face. "Who's he?"

"Come on; don't tell me you've never heard of Batman?"

"Oh, you're into superhero movies, right?"

"Not really, my father ran a market downtown many years ago, and he sold comic books to the local kids. I used to read them all. It was one of the reasons I wanted to be a cop. I knew I'd never be a super hero, but I could still catch bad guys as a cop. Didn't you ever read comic books?"

Dennis pressed a button on the car's visor, and the gate opened.

"Not really, I never had much time for comic books or even movies. My research consumed most of my time."

"That's too bad, because some of them were pretty good. I haven't read one in years. We sure could use a couple of super heroes on the police force. The criminals today are getting smarter, even though we have better tools with which to catch them."

Dennis grinned as he slowed the car in front of the house. "Maybe together we can do something about that."

As they approached the house, the front door opened and a housekeeper welcomed them. Dennis pointed towards the large living room to the right.

"Why don't we talk in the living room? Would you like something to drink?"

"Coffee would be fine."

"You don't want anything stronger?"

"I don't drink."

"Really, I thought all cops drank to some extent."

"I guess I'm the exception."

Dennis gave instructions to the housekeeper, and the two sat in a room that was bigger than many houses.

"How big is this house, if I may ask?"

"Twenty-six thousand square feet, not counting the lab."

"You mean the Batcave?"

Dennis paused for a second. "Oh, right, Batman. You really are into that stuff."

"Not anymore, but it's just that this place is right out of one of the comic books. Look, I don't want to be rude, but you mentioned that you might be able to help me in some way?"

Dennis waited until the housekeeper had served the coffee and left.

"I have to be honest, Frank. The reason I agreed to help you is that your problem overlaps a project that has been my life's work. I thought I'd lost everything when they shut down the plant, until you showed up."

Frank took a sip from the coffee. It was excellent.

"What exactly are we talking about with your project?"

"It's a new way to fight crime, and we're not talking about super heroes."

"Is it legal?"

"I'm not really sure, because it's so new. I'm breaking half-dozen federal laws telling you this, but I have nothing to lose, so here goes. About four years ago, the government hired me away from my research position at a local college and put me in command of a new forensic project used by the Army. The device was called a Molecular Laser Analyzer, or MLA. You have to understand that this device doesn't upgrade present day forensic science, it totally replaces it."

Dennis took a sip from his coffee and continued. "The device is about the size and shape of a postal drop box and weighs about two hundred pounds. It has a built-in computer that uses the power of the Internet and thousands of workstations to which it can connect. The device uses a laser that can analyze data down to the molecular level. It can scan an object at various depths like a medical CAT scan. The device can scan biological or chemical compounds, and that data can be compared to numerous databases around the world. When the unit starts up, it can scan a room, create a 3D image of the room, and collect data from any small trace elements in the room. If there's evidence in a room, this device can find it and identify it."

Dennis looked to see Frank's reaction before continuing. "Best of all, the process is non-destructive. It doesn't have to touch the sample or break it down to analyze it. It can look at the molecular structure from a distance and give results in minutes. Many of the CSI shows on TV make it look like they can analyze DNA in minutes, but in truth, it takes a lot longer and usually destroys the sample during the process."

Frank finished his coffee and poured a second cup, taking a moment to try to digest all this unbelievable material.

"There has to be a downside, or every police department on the planet would want one, right?"

"Yeah, there is, and that's why the project was shut down. The power source used to run the device in the field couldn't be nuclear, so we had to use a capacitor storage device. It's a little like an electronic flash on a camera. This device can store enormous amounts of power in a small container, and then release it in an instant. We figured a way to build a capacitor the size of a beer barrel and discharge it at a constant rate. The problem is that if you overload it, it becomes a large bomb that could easily take out a city block. We built two of these units for the Army, and one of them blew up during a field test, killing three of my fellow scientists and friends. The Army deemed the project not feasible, and shipped the second MLA device to a storage depot and labeled it 'Top Secret'."

Frank listened patiently but couldn't see where the conversation was going. "Sounds like a dead end to me. The device was so dangerous that one blew up, and the other was shipped off so no one else could use it. How does that help either one of us?"

"Well, that's because there's a third device - the prototype. The Army never even knew about it. I wanted to make sure the whole concept was valid before I built any for the Army. The prototype proved my theories, so I built two for the Army. I took the prototype apart, took it home a piece at a time, and then put it back together. It still works great."

Frank took another sip. "This coffee is great. What is it? I could drink this all day."

"I get it from a company in Oregon called Longbottom Coffee. It's low in acid and a little pricey, but it's great."

"So, you have a third unit. How does that help if it's basically a bomb?"

"That's the good news. The reason the Army's unit blew up was that they insisted on adding defensive and offensive weapons, which overloaded the device. My prototype doesn't have those features, and has worked perfect every time I've tested it. Do you want to see it?"

Frank nodded, and Dennis was up strutting like a proud father who just had his first child. They headed down a long hall and after a couple more turns, encountered a large steel door with an electronic lock. Dennis punched in several numbers, and the door opened. The two entered a small elevator and then descended one floor. When the doors opened, it no longer resembled a home, but rather looked like Advanced Nano Devices.

Dennis walked into the middle of the room and moved his hand around in an arc. "This is my world, Frank. Now let's go meet Medusa."

He picked up a remote control and when he pressed a button, the door to a small closet opened revealing a strange-looking device.

Dennis walked over to the device and pressed a button on the front. A few lights came on, and the device rolled forward a few feet.

Frank stepped to the side and tried to get a handle on what he was viewing. "Medusa, huh? I thought you said the device was called an MLA?"

"The military labeled the device as MLA - Molecular Laser Analyzer. I never liked it because it was too impersonal. When the device starts to operate, snake-like arms come out of the top and scan the surrounding area. I thought it sort of looks like the mythological Medusa head, thus its name. The other two units I called Stheno and Euryale, which were Medusa's sisters. In Greek mythology, the three sisters all had snake-like heads. I just thought it would be more appropriate that they had real names. I guess I could have called them Larry, Moe, and Curly, but it just didn't seem right."

Frank moved around the unit to get a better view. "So how much did one of these things cost, or do I really want to know?"

"Well, that's probably why no one in law enforcement will ever see one. They each cost about one billion dollars. The entire project was a little over five billion, and I don't know how the Army could hide such an expensive project, but they did. Now they're covering their tracks and spreading the loss over other projects that had a better success rate."

Dennis pressed another button on the device, and a few more lights came on.

Frank watched as the snake-like sensor arms started to poke out of the top of the device. He stepped back as one of the arms moved up and down in front of him. Another scanned Dennis and a third stretched out and panned around the room. Before Frank could say anything, a computerized voice came from the device.

"Good afternoon, Dr. Andrews. Is there a task you would like me to accomplish? I have identified your visitor as Detective Frank Ridge."

Frank leaned over and looked closer at the device.

"Okay, it talks. You can have conversations with it?"

Dennis smiled and put his hand on the top of Medusa.

"Yes, she can talk, but the other two didn't. The Army didn't want that feature, so I removed it from their versions. Medusa can respond to most questions you ask."

Frank scratched his head in amazement and responded, "I'm still not sure how this will help me with my problem."

Dennis reached over and picked up the trash can under the shredder.

"How about a demonstration of what Medusa can do? These are all the documents that the Army asked me to destroy. I'm sure you've run across this problem with crooks all the time. They shred all the incriminating evidence before you get to a crime scene. Then you have a bunch of guys in the department try and piece them together. By the time you find out what they shredded, the information is no longer valid. That's all about to change. Medusa, please assemble the documents I'm dumping on the floor."

Dennis turned the trash can over and slowly dumped the contents on the floor. When the trash can was empty, Dennis picked up the pile of shredded documents and threw them in the air a second and third time.

Dennis reached over and pressed a button labeled document recovery. Medusa's arms passed over the pile and immediately pages and pages of text scrolled down the display screen.

Dennis turned back to Frank and smiled. "I bet the guys in your department would have taken days to do what Medusa did in thirty seconds. That's just the tip of the iceberg. She can read all the bar codes in a room, or index every book, and magazine in seconds. If there's an identification to be made from the data, or an unusual pattern, she can do it."

Frank picked up the pile of shredded newspaper, and then looked at the screen.

"This is amazing, but I'm still not sure how this helps me. I can't show up at a crime scene with a civilian, and a machine called Medusa. There would be tons of questions, and to be honest, we'd both be in a lot of trouble with our bosses. As incredible as Medusa is, I'm not sure how we could put the two of you to good use."

Frank paused a minute, then continued. "Even if we could work something out, why would you help me? I've just met you, and I find it strange that you would trust me without really knowing who I am. I'm not sure I'd trust me if I were in your shoes. I could be someone from the government trying to trip you up."

Dennis reached over and started the shutdown process on Medusa.

"To be honest, Frank, I do know you in a roundabout way. I told you that I never met your daughter, but I did have long discussions with my roommate. Your daughter must really care about you because she was always talking about you to my roommate. Although they didn't date for long, I got to know about you. It was obvious that you were a kind and honest cop, who treated everyone with respect. When you came to see me today, it was like an answer to my prayers. I hated the direction my project was headed with the Army, but I still wanted it to work. You handed me a solution right out of the blue. I believe we can make this work, and I really want to see what Medusa can do."

Chapter 5

A couple of days later, Frank and Debra had their weekly dinner together. Frank was quiet when she first arrived, and it was driving her crazy. She brought Chinese again and set the table with napkins, drinks, and candles. Frank smiled as she worked, but kept the conversation to small talk. Finally, Debra couldn't stand it any longer.

"Okay, Dad, what gives? Did you go see Dr. Andrews like I suggested, or are you going to keep me in the dark for the rest of the evening?"

Frank opened the first box and used the chopsticks to pick up his share.

"Yes, I did meet with Dennis. He seems to be a nice guy. He's smarter than you indicated, definitely way out of my league. We do have some common ground, so we'll be working together on a couple of projects."

"What kind of projects?"

"I wish I could tell you, Honey, but it would be better if we kept this between Dennis and me right now."

"You're kidding, right? Is it something illegal?"

Frank took another helping from one of the boxes. He loved this innocent torture.

"No, it's not illegal, but it wouldn't be a good idea for you to know about it just yet. Call it a conflict of interest or something. I wish I could tell you more, but there's a good chance this idea will fizzle. This is my one last chance to finish what I started with my career. Don't worry, as I'll let you know as soon as I can. Are you going to be pissed at me?"

"Never, but I may be somewhat irritated just like mom used to get when you were secretive about your work."

"I promise I won't do anything stupid, and let you know when the time is right. That's enough about me, how are you doing at work?"

Debra wasn't surprised when Frank changed the subject. Just when things were getting interesting in her dad's life, he suddenly wants to know how she's doing. If she didn't give him something, she wouldn't get any more information about Dr. Andrews.

"I have to tell you, Dad, getting convictions is getting harder every day. Criminals today are really milking the system. If there's the tiniest crack in our case, the bad guys will exploit it. I hate to bring this up, but Jesse Carr is back in the system. He was picked up for a bar fight. It seems he was bragging about how he beat the system. A couple of friends of the trooper he killed were in the bar, and took great offense to his bragging. He was arrested, but we had to throw it out. He found himself a bottom feeder lawyer that used the police vengeance angle, and the judge bought it. As he left the court, he told everyone he was untouchable, and he would get even with everyone who ever tried to put him in jail. It made me want to get a gun and shoot him myself."

The veins in Frank's forehead started to pulse with anger.

"If he comes after me, he'll be dead before he can say a word."

"Dad, you can't do that. I know you believe in the power of the law too much. Carr will screw up again, and we'll put him away for good. Promise me that you'll leave him alone."

"If he comes after me with a gun, I can't promise that."

"Fair enough, Dad, but I worry about you."

"I love you too, Honey."

Two weeks later, Frank Ridge opened the door to the detective department. Everyone in the room stopped talking, and Captain Carson looked up to see what caused the silence. As Frank slowly walked by each desk, he smiled at the dumbfounded detectives. The look in their eyes told Frank that they were sure he'd never come back, and yet he had. The captain motioned for him to come into his office. Frank sauntered down the gauntlet of blue suits, knowing that everyone in the room wasn't happy to see him back, but he really didn't care. This was going to be his last shot at solving cases, and he couldn't give a shit what they thought about him coming back. Frank closed the door and pulled up a chair. He smiled, but said nothing.

The captain stood up, looked through his glass windows, and yelled to the troops. "What are all of you staring at? Get back to work. Immediately, or I'll have you all handing out traffic tickets."

The captain's voice was so loud it carried into the next room and down the hall. When the muffled chatter started again, he looked back at Frank with anger, and then a smile emerged.

"Damn it, Frank, I thought I told you to take a month off. That means four weeks, not two and a half. Everyone is still pissed at you. Okay, now that I have that off my mind, how in the hell are you doing?"

"Sorry, Captain, I should have called first, but I had an idea, and I needed to present it in person. I don't plan to come back to the department. I don't think any amount of time is going to change their opinions of me. I was wondering if you could transfer me to the cold case division? I know it's small and underfunded, but it's what I really want to do, and I think I can make a difference."

Captain Carson looked out into the outer office, and then back to Frank.

"Are you serious, Frank? The two detectives working the cold cases from our department would give anything to get back in the office out there. In some cities being part of the cold case division is an honor, but not so here. The lack of budget has made it almost impossible to solve any of the cases down there. Are you really sure this is what you want to do, Frank?"

Frank opened up a briefcase and took out a couple of sheets of paper.

"I know the solve rate right now is less than five percent. There hasn't been a break on any of the cases for the last six months, but I want that to change. However, I do have a request. If you allow me to transfer to the cold case division, I'd like to bring onboard a civilian CSI specialist. I'll pay him out of my own pocket, so don't worry about budget. I know this isn't the norm, but just think of him as my snitch."

Captain Carson couldn't believe what he was hearing. It was just about the last thing he thought Frank would ever want to do.

"To be honest, Frank, the guys upstairs would love to see you move to the cold case division. That would put you out of the mainstream police department, and no longer a news story. You know they'll expect big things from you and that if you don't solve a case within a few months, they'll have their reason to boot you out for good. Is this really what you want to do, because you're handing them exactly what they want?"

"Yes, Captain, I thought it over long and hard, and it is exactly what I want to do. I know the risks, and I think I can do this. If I can't, I'll resign without a fight. The key will be your approval of the CSI civilian. I'll need a special police pass that can get him legally into cold case crime scenes."

"Frank, I can pull in a couple of favors. It's the least I can do, but I just hope you know what you're doing."

"So do I, Captain, so do I."

Frank reached over, shook the captain's hand, and closed his briefcase. They talked briefly about old times and as Frank closed the office door, the detective's room quieted again. He nodded to each detective as he retraced his steps through the office. When he reached the outer door, he turned and waved, knowing that would throw them off their game. Frank felt so good about himself right now. As he opened his car door, an old detective's saying came to mind —"the game is afoot."

Chapter 6

It took a couple of weeks for Frank's transfer to the cold case department to become effective. The captain also came through with the credentials for Dennis. Before they left the cold case division, the two detectives met with Frank to go over their current case load to make a smooth transition.

Now he had the entire department to himself. He'd told Dennis to wait until he was sure that they would be the only ones in the department before coming down, but now the coast was clear. The cold case department had a loading dock, which was essential for moving Medusa into the work area. Frank was trying to log onto the department's computer system when Dennis knocked on the door. Frank cussed the keyboard and opened the door.

"You got here just in time. I was about to shoot this damn thing. It's as old as my car, and doesn't work any better."

Dennis reached out and shook Frank's hand.

"Thanks for getting me the pass. The computer is no problem. I have a couple of brand new powerful laptops at my house. I'll bring one in tomorrow, and we can transfer everything to the new system. We can store the old one in the closet and hook it back up at night. I'll then take the new one home with me and lock it up."

Frank looked back at the blue screen of death now appearing on the computer. "That sounds like a great idea. Did you bring Medusa?"

"Yep, backed up to the loading dock. Let's go get her and introduce her to her new work space."

Frank got up, and the two walked down the long hallway to the loading dock. Dennis had parked sideways along the dock so that they could put a board from the panel truck and roll Medusa right out of the vehicle. After a few minutes jockeying the device, the two were whistling their way down the hall pushing the billion-dollar analyzer. They pushed Medusa into the small gun locker that was the size of a broom closet. The two sat down at the work table and toasted to their new adventure with a couple glasses of orange juice.

Frank reached over to a box sitting on the edge of the table and pulled out a folder.

"Do you want to hear about our first case?"

"Damn right. Let's see what this new technology can do to help truth and justice."

Frank pulled out a single paged synopsis of the case.

"Two years ago, five-year-old Sarah Widen was taken from her home while her mother worked in the garden behind the house. There was no ransom demand and no sightings of the little girl. The CSI went through the girl's bedroom with every trick they knew, and came up with nothing. A search through the rest of the house uncovered nothing. The parents, Vernon and Martha Widen, went on TV and pleaded for the return of their daughter. Nothing substantial came in.

"Finally, they got a tip and the police obtained a search warrant for the father's car. Some of Sarah's bloody clothes were found in the trunk. A more intensive investigation into the father's background discovered that he was having an affair with his secretary. The mayor was under tremendous pressure to get the situation resolved, so he forced the D.A. to file charges, even though the case was weak. Vernon's wife kicked her husband out of the house, and he ended up in a fleabag motel downtown. Some vigilantes found out where he was staying and killed him. The case went cold after a couple of months, and nothing has turned up since.

"The only thing we have to work with is one evidence box, and by going back to the little girl's bedroom. I can tell you right now, this is going to be a hard one. The two guys who operated this department may not have liked working cold cases, but they were still good at their jobs. If they couldn't find anything, it will be a challenge for us."

Dennis looked over the sheet that Frank had read, just to get a feel for how the reports were written.

"The best place to start is to spread all the evidence from the box out on the table. Then let Medusa have a look and see if she can come up with something that human eyes cannot."

Dennis got up and went over to where Medusa was stored, opened the door, and turned the power on. At the same time, Frank put on a pair of latex gloves, opened the evidence box, and laid the parts out on the table. It contained a sealed bag with bloody clothes, hairbrush, toothbrush, one torn stuffed animal, a single broken crayon, and several small evidence bags with lint and dirt from the bedroom floor.

There was also a small child's walkie-talkie that Sarah used to talk to her girlfriend. Frank picked up a second investigation sheet about the walkie-talkie and realized that it wasn't Sarah's, but rather belonged to the neighbor. The investigators questioned the neighbor and found out that the child had left it behind by accident. The investigators then assumed that Sarah had taken the other unit with her. For days, one of the detectives drove all over Seattle calling into the walkie-talkie, hoping that Sarah would answer, but there was never a response.

Dennis had Medusa up to full power and moved her over next to the table. Frank opened the bag of bloody clothes and laid them on a special evidence pad.

Dennis typed in a few last commands that allowed him to use verbal commands. "Medusa, scan the bloody clothes on the left corner of the table. Basic scan first, and then a super scan until I tell you to stop."

Frank stepped back as the snake-like appendages came out of the top of the unit and moved across the bloody clothes. In thirty seconds, the first diagnosis was displayed on the viewer. *Blood from clothes belongs to Sarah Widen. No contamination of other blood types or tissue from other suspects. The amount of blood indicates a small cut. Now ready for next diagnosis.*

Frank looked at the screen. "You're kidding. Medusa could determine all that, in less than a minute? You didn't help her along, did you Dennis?"

Dennis saved the information into a new folder labeled Sarah Widen, and cleared the screen. "Actually, Frank, Medusa matched the DNA to a file saved on the police evidence server."

Frank looked at Medusa. "How did you access the police server? I haven't cleared you for that yet."

Dennis scanned the rest of the evidence on the table.

"Sorry about that, Frank, I should have told you sooner. Medusa has a military stealth status that allows her to move from one network server to the next without having to use different logins or passwords. It was necessary for the military to move around cyberspace without coming up against firewalls. The system that penetrates the different servers costs more than 750 million dollars, and no one knows about it except those people working with the project. She does this by accessing millions of documents in seconds and pieces together administrator passwords and backdoors from the initial programmers. If any of the other departments within the government found out what we have, they would want the program destroyed or keep it to themselves. Either way, Medusa can hack just about anything on the planet."

Frank was getting a nervous twitch in his face. "No one can track it back to us?"

"Nope. Medusa is very good about bouncing off dozens of locations in milliseconds. If anyone tries to track her, she leaves a nasty virus in their path that can shut them down for hours. So, the answer, Frank is that we're perfectly safe from prying network eyes."

Frank picked up the broken crayon. "What do you make of this?"

As soon as Frank set the crayon down, one of the snake-head sensors moved over the crayon. A second report was immediately displayed. *Crayon is a Crayola basic red crayon made five years ago and purchased three years ago on the Widen's MasterCharge card. The DNA on the crayon matches Sarah and an unknown person. The sample from the unknown suspect was found on the broken surface of the crayon and is undetectable to present day CSI testing. Recommend testing of other evidence to see if there's a match to the unknown DNA.*

Frank looked at the printout that Dennis had just printed out. Seconds later, Medusa brought up a new update screen. *The unknown DNA belongs to Sarah's friend next door.*

Dennis looked at the updated screen. "Sorry, Frank, the unknown DNA belongs to Sarah's friend. I don't think a six-year-old would mastermind a kidnapping."

"You might be surprised, Dennis. I've seen a lot of weird stuff in the last twenty-five years."

For the next three hours, the two set out one sample at a time and analyzed each with a basic scan, and then a more advanced scan when necessary. Once it was all completed, Medusa's analysis screen showed nothing new. It looked like they were at a dead-end.

Frank kept out the walkie-talkie, but packed up the remaining parts and sealed them in the evidence box.

"I'll call the mother of the missing girl tonight and get her permission to come into the house tomorrow. Hopefully, we'll do better there. I know it was a bust, but that's how it goes sometimes. If they were always easy, detectives would be out of a job, and all the bad guys would be in jail. I'll come over to your place at 9 a.m., and we can go from there."

Dennis shut down Medusa and the two pushed her back out into the panel truck. They shook hands, and Dennis headed home. Frank returned to the office and put the evidence box back where he retrieved it. As he sat down and looked around the room, he heard a sound from down the hall. He ran to check it out, and as he rounded the corner to the hallway exit, he saw a dark shape through the frosted glass. He pulled his gun and slowly opened the door. There was nothing. He heard a car engine start in the distance, but there was no way he could catch up. Maybe he was just imagining things. Everything about this new life was making him a bit jumpy. He turned off all the lights, locked up and headed home.

Chapter 7

Frank arrived at Dennis's place at 8:45. As he approached the gate, it opened without him having to slow down or stop. Dennis was already pushing Medusa onto the loading platform that extended out from the panel truck. Frank got out of his car and walked over. Dennis reached around to the side of the truck and picked up two cups of Longbottom coffee. Frank took one of the cups, and took a sip, trying to get his tired old body going.

"Dennis, I have to say it again, that this is great coffee. I talked to the missing girl's mother last night. She was surprised to hear from anyone. From what I gathered, the two cold case detectives had prepared her for the worst, and she was trying to get her life restarted. She hesitated at first, but I told her we were using new technology. She's going to wait for us to come, but doesn't want to be there when we go through Sarah's room, and I can understand that. We need to get in and out as quickly as possible."

"Frank, it doesn't work that way. What you saw Medusa do yesterday was child's play for her. Scanning an entire room at the molecular level could take hours."

"I was afraid you were going to say that. Oh well, my career might be over sooner than I thought."

Dennis closed the door and walked to the driver's side. "Frank, give Medusa and me a chance. If there's a clue, she'll find it."

Frank got in the passenger's side and leaned over to type in the destination address into the GPS. A computer voice gave them directions, and the two were off on a new journey. Forty minutes later, the GPS confirmed they'd arrived at their destination located in a mid-income neighborhood with several ranch-style homes.

Dennis was about to exit the panel truck, but Frank stopped him. "Remember that you're my partner, but I'm in charge. There're always many twists and turns you don't expect in this kind of investigation, so just follow my lead. We'll leave our snake-head friend in the truck right now and go introduce ourselves first."

Thirty-seven-year-old Martha Widen opened the door before Frank could even knock. She had on a kitchen apron, and it looked like she'd been baking. Frank was surprised at her stature. She was tall, thin, and looked older than her years. He noticed that she'd been crying.

Frank pulled out his badge with his left hand and reached to shake her hand with his right. "I'm Detective Frank Ridge, and this is my partner Dennis Andrews. We're so sorry to bother you at this time, but we have some new type of CSI technologies that might shed some light on the case. We're not sure how long it will take, but my partner hopes to run all the tests in less than four hours. Is that okay with you?"

Martha shook his hand and then reached around to shake Dennis's hand. "I really didn't expect anyone to follow up on Sarah. I was prepared for the worst. I've seen too many shows about what pedophiles do with children, and I just couldn't handle it anymore. Sarah's room is in the back. Take your time, as it's all I have anymore. I'm going out for a couple of hours, so if you need to leave, just lock the door behind you. Do whatever you have to do, but please, find out what happened to my little girl."

Frank and Dennis walked back to Sarah's bedroom. He pulled out two pairs of shoe covers and handed one set to Dennis. "We don't want to leave anything from our clothes that may slow down our analysis."

Dennis quickly put on the covers. "Great idea. Medusa would have eliminated us from the search, but this does help."

Frank opened Sarah's door and it was just as he expected. Nothing had changed since Sarah had been abducted. The bed was made; toys were in their place, and dozens of school drawings were pinned to the bulletin boards.

Dennis looked around the room and tried to estimate how

long it was going to take. He was worried that four hours wasn't going to be enough. The 220-volt connection in the garage was going to help boost the power on Medusa, so that might cut down some of the time. Ten minutes later, they moved Medusa to the middle of the room, and Dennis connected the 220-volt line to his pride and joy.

Frank watched as Dennis started to power up Medusa. "So, how does this work, Dennis? The scanning of the evidence I understand, but how do you do an entire room?"

Dennis flipped the last switch, and Medusa was alive again. "First, she'll do a 3D scan of the room. Once that file is created, we can review the room later at the office. She'll then scan for large biological samples - skin tissue, fingerprints, or hair. She'll place markers in the 3D image as to their location, eliminating everything not human. The fingerprints will be run through every available database and grouped by importance to the case.

"The remaining samples will be scanned at a higher level to determine the type of tissue, DNA, and any other biological markers. These scans work much like a CAT scan in a hospital, but at the molecular level. Any DNA is identified and listed in the order of importance. A second scan around the room will determine if there are any unusual chemicals in the room. This test rarely turns up anything unless it has to do with Meth labs, weapons, or bomb-making materials. The last scan will look for all types of data in the room - bar codes, numbers, any visible text, or drawings, and then she will form an opinion if anything seems out of place."

"Wow! You have to be kidding," said Frank as he watched Medusa start her scan.

Dennis motioned for Frank to move back. "It's best if we leave the room so that she can have full access to all the areas."

Frank backed out of the room. "That's fine with me. We don't have to do anything, but wait for results?"

"Nothing at all, that's why she cost a billion dollars."

The two sat out in the backyard looking at the high fence separating the different lots. The two were thinking the same thing. The kidnapper had to come through the front door. It had to be someone Sarah knew, or she would have yelled. It didn't make any sense.

Dennis looked down at the ground under the swing set. The worn area was now starting to fill in from lack of use. "Mind if I ask you a question, Frank?"

"Let's hear the question."

"You never said much about your daughter. How does she fit into all this?"

"She works for the DA's office as an assistant. She does most of the work as far as I am concerned, but those are the politics of this city. She seems to be running into the same problem as I am. The bad guys are getting a lot smarter and much harder to put away. We get together once a week to talk about what we're doing that week. My wife Ann died ten years ago, and Debra saved me from falling into a really bad place. We don't have any other family, so neither one of us is very sociable."

Frank was quick to turn the tables. "So, what about your mother? What's her story?"

Dennis wasn't prepared for this one. Up until now, he was private about his personal life. "Well mom loves to travel, and she's a great lecturer. Her professional name is Dr. Sandra Alexander, and she has Ph.D.'s in Biology, Marine Biology, and Biochemistry. If you ever meet her, she'll bore you to death with her latest research project."

"What about your dad?"

Dennis swallowed and looked down. This was hard for him, even after so much time had passed. "My dad, Carl, was killed when I was six. Mom was away lecturing, and someone broke into the house and shot him while he slept. I heard the sounds, but was afraid to find out what happened. I don't remember much after that, but the police told me later that they found me sitting in his bedroom on the floor with the phone in my hand. I was the one who dialed 911."

"Did they ever get the killer?"

"No, it was one of those cold cases."

Frank looked straight at Dennis. "That explains a lot that I couldn't understand before. You built Medusa so that you could get some payback, right?"

"Yes, in a way I did. At first, I planned on using the prototype to find my dad's killer, but now I realize too much time has passed."

Frank kicked a clod of dirt towards the fence. He understood what Dennis was going through. "I understand how you feel, but I wouldn't give up just yet. Let me find out if there's anything on file about your dad. It's the least I can do."

A beep came from a small device in Dennis's pocket. "Medusa has finished. Let's go see what she's found."

The two got up and headed back into the house. Almost two hours had passed, which surprised Dennis. When they entered the room, Medusa was silent. Dennis moved over to the main screen and started to scroll through the analysis documents. Everything seemed normal. There were more than a couple of dozen DNA identifications, but nobody with a record or reason to grab Sarah.

Dennis turned to Frank. "There's nothing out of the ordinary. The DNA is from family, friends, kids from school, and a couple of Sarah's teachers. I'm sorry, Frank."

Frank wasn't prepared for this defeat. "So that's it. A billion-dollar machine that's supposed to be the world's best CSI technician comes up with nada."

"Frank, I made no guarantees. There's one other thing we haven't tried yet. Medusa, did you find anything odd in the data from Sarah's room?"

There was silence for a few seconds, which Dennis interpreted as a no.

"*Yes, there's one item at the bottom of the report that has some inconsistencies,*" Medusa said.

"Go on."

"Sarah has many school pictures on the wall and most show her with school friends and her teachers. There are nine pictures of what appears to be a teacher instructing her class. Eight of the pictures show the teacher in brightly-colored clothes, and the teacher is smiling. One picture shows a teacher in black clothes with a sad face. That alone is not enough to form a theory, but a single hair found under the bed has DNA matching to that teacher who substituted at her school. The teacher quit two weeks before Sarah was abducted. A search for the teacher produced nothing. I searched for teachers applying for jobs on the West Coast, and found a dozen that fit her description, but only one had a little girl the age of Sarah. That's the end of my report."

Dennis and Frank where euphoric when they heard the news. Dennis was about to ask Medusa more, but Frank put his hand up. "Medusa, do you have an address for that one?"

"I do if you quit calling me snake-head. I researched it, and it doesn't have good connotations. The woman is teaching in a small grade school just outside of Stockton, California. I'll print out the specifics, so that you can follow up."

Dennis reached over and picked up the single sheet that had been printed out. At the bottom was a picture of the daughter of the teacher in Stockton. The two looked at the picture and compared it to the pictures on Sarah's dresser. They were a match. Dennis shut Medusa down, and the two pushed her back out and quickly loaded her into the panel truck. The mother had not yet returned, so Frank wrote a short message thanking her for letting them in, and locked the front door. On the way back to Dennis's house, the two argued about who was flying down to Stockton.

Frank was the first to make his case. "There's no need for both of us to fly down. I'm only going for research because I want to make damn sure we have this right before we fork over the evidence to the captain. Besides, airplane tickets on a moment's notice cost an arm and a leg. I know you may have a lot of money, but no need to throw it away."

Dennis stopped the panel truck in front of his house before responding. "What makes you think I was going to buy a ticket, when we can fly down in my jet?"

"You're kidding, right? You have a jet? What was I thinking?"

Dennis grinned as he lowered Medusa to the ground. "Frank, why go through security, when we can come and go whenever we want. I'll call the pilot, and we can leave this afternoon."

Frank shook his head from side to side. He had no idea who this Dennis really was, but this kid was starting to grow on him.

Chapter 8

Frank hated flying - dealing with security, gate changes, seats that were too small, and the awful food they served. The trip down to Stockton was a completely different experience. Frank had comfortable chairs, a long couch, drinks of choice, a large-screen TV, full Internet access, and the food was wonderful. Even the female pilot was very easy on the eyes. He could really get to like this.

He looked at an old Architectural Digest magazine. "So, Dennis, I don't mean to pry, but the detective in me wants to know where you got all your money. You can tell me it's none of my business, and that'll be fine. Curious minds just want to know."

Dennis pointed to the front cover of the old magazine in Frank's hand. "I kept that magazine to remind me about my father. He was an outstanding architect, and designed the building on the cover. The money really started with the success of his father, who was also a fine architect, but my dad took it to a new level. He designed many of the buildings in Seattle, Chicago, and New York. He was very good at creating unique structures that could withstand extreme earthquakes. When the quake hit San Francisco in 1989, many of the buildings still standing were his designs. One of the reasons my mother can travel so much and lecture is because she doesn't have to worry about a paycheck. She just loves the lecture tour. She's due to come back in a month, so we should all get together."

Frank started to thumb through the magazine, looking at the bylines on the article and photos. He stopped on one that was written about Carl Andrews. The buildings were gorgeous.

"Dennis, the bottom line is that you don't really need to be working with me. You have more than enough money to party and never work another day."

Dennis took a sip from his coffee cup. "When I was younger, a lot of my friends from similar backgrounds did just that. Most of them today are in drug rehab centers, jail, dead, or flat broke. I wanted to do something with my life that has meaning. The money just helps me get there faster."

The pilot came over the speaker system and asked them to buckle up. A few minutes later, the jet came to rest in a private section of the airport. Frank grabbed the briefcase full of printouts on the case. He knew Dennis had a digital version on his device that links to Medusa. It looked like an Apple iPad, but it had a large flat screen, was more sophisticated, and much more expensive.

A limo was waiting for them at the bottom of the staircase. The driver opened the car door, and Dennis gave him instructions. Thirty minutes later, they were slowly driving by the school where Kristen Maples worked as a grade-school teacher. Dennis instructed the driver to find a spot next to the playground. When the car stopped Dennis started to exit the car, but Frank reached out and stopped him. "That's not the way we do things. We have no idea what we're walking into, so we observe first."

"Why not go in and talk with the principal of the school? Let them know everything is in confidence?"

"Look, Dennis, I appreciated the plane ride and the help from Medusa, but I'm still the detective with the experience. Miss Maples may be watching everyone who comes into the school. Her classroom may be on the front of the building. She could be watching us right now and rabbit in the next thirty minutes. She could also be having an affair with the principal, so there are too many possible variables."

Just as Frank was about to continue, a black-and-white pulled up parallel to the limo. Frank rolled down his window and held out his badge. The cop on the passenger side exited and looked at the badge. "What's your business down here?"

"We're working a cold case. We'll move to a more discreet location, Officer."

"I would appreciate that. They don't take too kindly to cars they've not seen before parked out next to the playground."

Frank put his badge away. "I understand. Thanks for the information that we've been spotted. We have nothing on our case so far, but if we do, my captain will call yours before we proceed."

As the cop got back into the car, he looked at Dennis sitting next to Frank. "We would appreciate that very much. You have a good day now."

Frank told the driver to move down a couple of blocks. He opened his briefcase and pulled out a mirrorless SLR camera with a long telephoto lens attached.

Dennis leaned over to look at the camera. "What's that? It looks like a point and shoot camera."

Frank turned the lens to expand it to its full focus range. He reached into the case again and pulled out flesh colored latex gloves. He pulled them on and then turned on the camera. Everything seemed to work. His daughter had taught him well. She had taken several photo classes in college and convinced Frank that a much smaller nonprofessional camera would blend in better when he was on stakeout. It took them a couple of hours one night for him to get the hang of the system. He grabbed a small evidence bag out of the case and shoved it into his pocket. He pulled his tie off and removed his jacket. He was ready. He opened the door and looked back at Dennis.

"You stay put. Two new people in the area might stand out. One tourist taking pictures might not. I'll be back in a couple of hours. Relax; I'm sure you have something on that DVD player I saw in the ceiling."

Before Dennis could respond, Frank slammed the door.

Three hours later, the door opened again and Frank got back in. He had an evidence bag containing a drinking cup.

"We really lucked out on this one, Dennis. I just can't believe it. Sarah came out for recess with a drink cup in her hand. When she was done with the cup, she went over to the

51

trash can, tripped, fell onto the concrete, and skinned her knee. The playground teacher told one of the other kids to go inside, and a minute later Miss Maples came out and helped Sarah back inside. I took pictures and videos of everything. Even better was the fact that the trash can was just out of view from the front of the school. When recess was over, I dashed over, grabbed the drink cup, and took a swab of the blood on the concrete. We have all we need."

Dennis watched as Frank scrolled through the images on the back of the camera. He was impressed with how Frank had collected the evidence. Dennis had underestimated him. As Frank was removing the latex gloves and putting them into the evidence bag, the black-and-white came from behind and stopped.

Frank got out to talk to the driver, as they often are the lead cop. "We're just heading back to Seattle. Captain Mark Carson will be calling your cold case people and letting them know more about the case we're working on."

"Next time it might be a good idea to go through channels and let us know you are coming."

Frank looked down at the ground and then back up to the driver. "This is one of those cases that came to a dead end, and we didn't want to get anybody's hopes up just yet. We were trying to keep the circle of those in the know to a minimum. We're sorry to tread on your turf without any advance notice."

The driver seemed to back off. "I understand, Detective. Is there anything else we can help you with?"

We're good for now, thanks."

The car sped off, and Frank walked back to the limo. As he entered, he told the driver to head out to the airport.

"Dennis, that was close. We're really supposed to go through the chain of command when we're in somebody else's backyard. Good thing that cop has been around for some time, so he seemed to understand. They could've taken us down to their precinct and called our department to find out what was happening. It seems to be our lucky day."

The ride back to the airport was quiet as Frank and Dennis didn't speak. Once the jet lifted off the runway, Dennis wanted to say something, but was holding back.

Frank glared at him and said, "Kid, it's obvious you have something to say about how this all went down, so spit it out."

Dennis's face turned red. "Look I'm not a kid. I'm just younger than you are. I thought you handled everything perfectly. I couldn't have done any better, but I do have one question."

"Shoot."

"When you present the evidence to Captain Carson, are you going to wear that same suit? If you really want to shake up those detectives in your old department and send a message, I can help. You won't believe this great tailor that I know!"

Frank started to say something, but Dennis put his finger up to his lips and shook his head. The remainder of the trip, the two dozed as the plane headed back to Seattle.

Chapter 9

Captain Mark Carson was having a bad Monday. He'd been chewed out by the mayor about the mishandling of two cases the week before. One was almost as bad as Frank's CSI screw up. Right now, he needed a miracle, or a stiff drink at ten in the morning.

His prayers were answered as the door opened and in strutted Detective Frank Ridge. At least, he thought it was Frank, but this wasn't the normal Frank Ridge. Frank's suit was classy, shoes impeccable. He sported a new haircut, and had an appearance of royalty. The room was dead quiet as Frank walked toward the captain's desk.

Captain Carson looked up and smiled. He waved him in and said, "Damn, Frank. What the hell happened to you? I hope you didn't bill those new duds to the department?"

"No, Captain, it's out of my pocket. I wanted to come and update you on my progress in the cold case department."

"Hey, Frank, I told you that it wasn't going to work in your favor by transferring. You may never solve a case, and that's not because of your lack of experience. Those cases are tough, and can really get to you. If you want out, I can try to transfer you to some other department."

"Actually, Captain the reason I'm here is because we've solved the first case."

"What? Which one?"

"Sarah Widen. The missing little girl a couple of years back."

"You found her body? Where?"

"No Captain, we found her alive and well, living in Stockton, California."

Frank opened his briefcase, pulled out an iPad, and started to scroll through the images of Sarah in the playground. Frank then pulled up pictures of the drink cup, matches for fingerprints, and a DNA printout.

The captain was in shock. First, that Frank was using an iPad, and secondly, the evidence definitely pointed to a solved case. "So, Frank, this is definitely going to help fix your reputation. You quickly dug yourself out of a hole, and I'm amazed. We need to meet with the guys out there and bring them up to speed. Are you okay with that?"

Frank continued to pull evidence out of his briefcase. "Not really, Captain. I don't want any credit for this one. I would prefer going back to work on the next cold case and let the guys out there take it from here. I understand a couple of them are in hot water with you. Give the case to them, and let them get the credit."

"You're kidding, Frank. You don't want me to say anything? They're still going to hate your guts. If you give them this one, they'll lord it over you even more. Are you ready for that?"

"Captain, this isn't about me. It's about solving cold cases. All the basic evidence is there. You can tell the detectives that the tip came from an anonymous informant, okay?"

Carson reached out and shook Frank's hand. "Damn, Frank, I don't think I would've been that nice to those guys out there. I would've taken the credit because sometimes you have to watch out for number one."

"I am, Captain, don't worry. I'm fine, actually better than fine. I haven't felt this good since before Ann died. Oh, one other thing. You need to contact the precinct captain in Stockton and bring him up to speed. I may have stepped on a couple of toes, so they need some of the credit too. You know, one of those joint task force things where everyone comes out smelling like roses."

"That's not a problem, Frank. You take a couple of days off before you start again, okay?"

"I plan to do that. In fact, I think I'm going to spend some extra time with my daughter."

"Good for you, Frank. You did a great job. Good luck."

Frank exited the captain's office and walked slowly back to the entrance, getting the cold shoulder along the way. He really didn't care, because they didn't have a clue he now had a secret billion-dollar crusader on his team. Frank knew he was doing the right thing, working to get the bad guys, one at a time.

On his way home, Frank stopped to pick up some supplies to restock his kitchen, and rent a couple of movies. Driving along, the top news story on the radio was about two detectives who had broken down the wrong door looking for drugs. The reporter clarified that the error was made by the clerk who sent the detectives to the incorrect address. It didn't help though that the detectives arrested the old woman and child in the room. Frank hated the media. Today those detectives were described as idiots and in a couple of days, the same detectives would be heroes, and the media would be praising their work. He smiled thinking this was the captain's problem, not his.

He turned the radio off and called Dennis to let him know that they wouldn't start again until Thursday. Dennis said he was fine with that as he had some personal errands to run.

Frank parked his car in the driveway, and started to unload his groceries. A cantaloupe rolled out of the back seat, and he caught it just before it hit the ground. He bent back up and found himself looking directly at the barrel of a .38 revolver. He started to say something, but the gun fired six rounds point blank. Frank fell back and landed on one of the bags of groceries. The shooter looked down to see the results of his work. A large pool of blood was starting to run out onto the driveway. He smiled, but was distracted by a siren in the distance. A dog started barking, and someone was yelling from across the street. He ran down the side of the driveway, jumped over a fence and got into his car. As he pulled away, he looked into the rearview mirror, but saw no one chasing him and thought, payback was so sweet.

Chapter 10

Frank tried to focus his eyes, but everything was a pulsating blur. He kept hearing strange sounds like geese squawking. Someone was calling his name. "Frank, can you hear me?" Then he remembered the gun being fired at him, and everything went black again.

An hour later, it was the same thing as before, bright lights and strange sounds. Then he felt something in his throat. He was starting to put it together that he was in a hospital. His vision was getting better, and he focused harder to see. He moved his head a little, and he heard the voice again. "Frank, you can do it. You're too stubborn to die on us now." Then he passed out again.

Frank went through longer waking moments before slipping back into dreamland. By the end of the day, he could stay awake long enough to focus on everyone in the room. The captain, Debra, two nurses, and a doctor were all standing around him. The nurse and the doctor were busy removing the breathing tube. He coughed a couple of times, and he could see Debra straining to come to his rescue. When the doctor and nurse were done with the tube, they took some vitals and then told the captain and Debra they had ten minutes and no more.

She walked over to the edge of the bed and held Frank's hand. "I'm so glad you're alive. I don't know what I would've done without you, Dad. You're always there for me."

Frank squeezed her hand. "The opposite is the truth. I couldn't have made it without my one and only daughter. I'll be fine, but I have a feeling that wouldn't have been the case without my Kevlar vest. Just how many shots got through?"

Debra squeezed his hand and said, "One came very close to your heart. There were three in the vest, and two into the garage wall. Dad, it could've been a lot worse. Promise me you'll never go anywhere without that vest."

Frank looked over to the captain. "Honey, I have to talk to Mark for a few minutes. Don't worry, I'm not going anywhere for a while. Go get some coffee while we talk police business. I don't want a conflict of interest with you in the room."

Debra squeezed his hand again and backed away. As she left the room, Mark leaned over, but Frank held up his hand to stop the captain from saying anything.

"Jesse Carr shot me. He thought I was dead. I hate that damn vest, yet I still wear one. After those two cop killings last year, I live in that vest. I'd never want my daughter to lose both parents."

Mark looked around to see if anyone was behind him. "Frank, that's one of the best things you've done for this department. Several of those bozos in the department go out on assignments without vests. They think they're supermen. Now they're all wearing them. Those that didn't have one, put in requisitions for one. Several spouses have called in to make sure that I make their loved ones wear vests. Are you sure it was Jesse Carr?"

"Absolutely, there's no doubt."

"We took the slugs and ran them through the ballistics database. Either the gun isn't registered or never had a ballistic test run on it. Sorry, Frank, but I need to go back and put out an all-points bulletin for that scumbag. There's a Dennis Andrews trying to see you. Is he the private CSI tech working with you? I never did see the name on the form."

Frank coughed and took a sip of water. "That's him, but I really would like to meet with Dennis privately, with no one else around."

"Why all the cloak-and-dagger stuff, Frank?"

"I don't need the news media picking up on the fact that a police detective has his own private CSI tech. They would dig deep very fast, and expose the department to all kinds of conspiracy theories."

"Good point, Frank. I'll personally call this Andrews fellow and clear it with the hospital, so he can see you later tonight."

Debra came back minutes later, and the two of them talked for fifteen minutes before the nurse instructed her to leave. He reached out to squeeze her hand and said, "Promise me you'll go home and get some rest. I'm in good hands here. Come by before you go to work tomorrow, and then tomorrow night. Okay?"

"Are you sure, Dad?"

"I'll be fine, and I'm sure the captain has an officer stationed outside, right?"

"Yes, Dad there is."

"So, go home and that's an order young lady."

"Okay, Dad. I love you."

Frank turned on the TV and saw he was the main event for tonight. "*We interrupt your program to bring you this Breaking News. A local police officer was gunned down in front of his house. We'll bring you further details on a special report tonight at 11 that you can only see here on Channel 8.*"

Frank switched to a couple of other channels, and they all said the same thing. He wondered how every channel could tout an exclusive report on a news event.

He was about to switch to another channel, when an updated report started with Captain Carson standing in front of the mike.

"Late this afternoon, Detective Frank Ridge was gunned down by a man who has now been identified as Jesse Carr. Mr. Carr boasted to several of his friends that he was going to get even with those trying to put him in jail. It appears that he has made that attempt. If you see the man shown here on your screen, don't try to apprehend him. Call 911 or the number listed below. Consider Mr. Carr armed and extremely dangerous. Detective Ridge was severely injured in the chest, but is expected to make a full recovery. We'll update you when we have more information about the shooting. Thank you."

Captain Carson shut everyone down before they could get one question out. He knew that the press would now go back to the trial transcripts and attempt to place doubt on the guilt of Jesse Carr. Everyone in the department knew that it was just a matter of time before Carr made another mistake and this time he would either be dead, or in jail for the rest of his life.

Frank was very tired. He turned off the TV and was about ready to shut his eyes, when the door opened and Dennis peeked in. "Is it okay if I come in, Frank?"

"Since you got by the officer, I'd say that's a yes. What brings you here?"

"You've got to be kidding, Frank. Someone shot and almost killed you."

"It happens all the time, Dennis."

"Are you okay? I just saw the news, and they say you'll survive. I'm worried if you're really all right."

Frank pushed up in the bed a little to get a better view of the room. "I'll be out of commission for a couple of weeks, just enough time for me to select our next case. I have a question for you. Have you ever fired a gun? I don't mean a BB gun, a real gun."

"My dad hated guns and wouldn't allow one in the house. Where are we going with this?"

"Slow down a second, because these drugs make my thinking a little clouded. If we're going to work together, we have to plan on the worst-case scenario. That's a situation where you may have to defend yourself, or me. This is a non-negotiable item. When I get out of here, I'll take you to the range, and we'll find out what weapon best suits your needs."

Dennis was fidgeting with his answer. "No way am I going to shoot a gun. That's what killed my dad."

"No, Dennis, the man who had the gun is the one who killed your dad. You want me to get another hit like this?" Frank pulled his sheet back to show the large amount of dressings across his chest. "I'll be happy to show you pictures if you need, because they took lots of great angles. I know this is very distasteful to you, but if you want to fight crime, you need to know how to use all the weapons. When I get out, we're going to the range, and that's the end of this discussion."

Dennis was about to bring up another argument, when Debra came rushing into the room.

"Debra, what are you doing back here?"

"Sorry, Dad, but I couldn't stay away. I was so worried."

Frank looked at her and then to Dennis, who was standing out of view. "Debra, I'd like you to meet Dr. Dennis Andrews. He's my new partner."

Debra turned to Dennis. "So you're the one who got my father shot. What kind of idiot scheme did you drag my dad into?"

Dennis looked helpless. He was trying for a comeback but lacked the words.

Frank beat him to it. "Stop it, young lady. Dennis had nothing to do with me being shot. The scheme, as you call it, has nothing to do with Jesse Carr. You have it all wrong, and I'll stand against you on this one. I love you very much, but you crossed the line."

Debra could see that she had. Her frustration with the situation had brought up so many emotions, and she had taken it out on someone she'd just met.

She turned to Dennis and stuck out her hand. "I'm sorry, Dennis, I guess I got carried away. Can you forgive me?"

Dennis shook her hand. "I'm glad to finally meet you. Frank has told me a lot about you, and believe it or not, it was all good."

Frank laughed and then coughed. "Dennis, you told a joke. There's hope for you after all. Debra, maybe you can help me. I think Dennis should learn how to shoot a gun, but he objects. What do you think?"

"Dad, what the hell are you talking about? You just were shot and now you are arming your friends to join the posse.

Come on, Dad; let's take this one step at a time. Maybe later he could learn how to shoot, but maybe I should be the one to show him. I know you would be showing him something Dirty Harry would use. Right now, let's just get you better."

Frank slid back down in the bed. "Okay, maybe I pushed the issue a little. Dennis, if you want something to do, you might start compiling all the data from the cold case folders into your database system, and have snake-head take a look at them."

Dennis gave Frank a dirty look but understood why he didn't mention Medusa. "Okay, you take it easy, Frank, and I'll talk to you tomorrow. It was nice finally to meet you, Debra."

Frank waited until he was sure that Dennis was gone. "So what do you think of Dennis?"

Debra sat down in the chair next to Frank. "Well, he's sort of cute."

"That's not what I meant. I don't even want to go there. I meant as my new partner."

"He seems awfully young to be your partner."

"Hey, Deb, you're the one who connected us together. Now you're saying that it's not a good idea?"

She turned her chair and moved it closer to the bed. "Dad, I just wanted him to help you upgrade your technical skills, not be your partner. How's that possible anyway?"

"I got it approved with the captain. I just call him my informant. That seems to work with everyone so far, and Dennis is fine with it. He's really a nice guy once you get to know him."

"Dad, I just met the guy. It's not like we're getting married."

"Thank God for that," said Frank in a relieved voice.

"So you think he's good enough for you, but not for me? What a double standard."

Frank's head was spinning. "Hey, we're getting way ahead of ourselves. Let's talk about something else."

"Okay by me. You're the one who started it."

The both started laughing so hard the nurse came in and told them to tone it down.

Frank reached over and grabbed Debra's hand. "Look, I know all this is hard for you, but it's going to work out fine. Both of us will wear vests, and will call for backup whenever we're in trouble. How much trouble can you get into when you work on cold cases? Most of the time everyone's dead and buried."

"I know Dad, but you seem to get into more trouble than most."

Chapter 11

Two weeks had passed, and Frank had been released from the hospital. Jesse Carr had done a Houdini act, and vanished without a trace. The department had assigned Frank around the clock protection, but it would have to end soon because of the department's limited budget.

Frank sat back in his chair and turned on the news. The captain had called earlier to tell him that today was a good day to watch the news. As he surfed the channels, he spotted a "Breaking Story" showing the news reporter standing in front of his old office. Captain Carson stood in the background, waiting to make an announcement.

The blonde reporter, who looked more suited for a Playboy cover, started her report. "We've just learned that Sarah Widen, who was kidnapped over two years ago, has been found safe and returned to her mother. The combined efforts of our local police department and the Stockton police used a tip from an informant to track down Sarah and her kidnapper. The suspected kidnapper is being held without bail."

The reporter was interrupted as Captain Carson approached the microphones to make a statement. Standing next to him was the mayor, taking full advantage of the situation to help his re-election.

The captain unfolded a single sheet of paper and proceeded. "I would like to make a quick statement. Sarah Widen has been found safely living in Stockton, California. It appears her kidnapper wanted to keep her as her own child. She was discovered through hard work from our detective bureau, and our counterpart division in Stockton. Sarah seems unharmed, but somewhat disorientated. She's been returned to her mother. We have a suspect in custody, and she'll be arraigned tomorrow. For now, the suspect is being held without the possibility of bail.

"Before I go any further, I need to emphasize that this little girl has gone through a lot. I don't want to hear about any of you trying to get an exclusive from the family. They're totally off limits. I understand the freedom of the press, but please show these people some respect. Remember this is an ongoing investigation, and we don't want some ambitious reporter slowing us down or contaminating our investigation. My assistant has a handout for every reporter here, providing everything we can legally tell you at this point. If you have any questions after reading the report, contact our press department for any updates."

Frank turned off the TV and picked up the phone to call Dennis. "Frank here, did you see the news report? Dennis, are you okay with getting no credit? ...Good, I have something new planned for today if you're free. ...Okay, I'll pick you up at 10 a.m. and be sure to wear some old clothes. ...Great, see you then."

Frank opened his gun safe and loaded an assortment of weapons into his traveling firearm's case. He relocked the safe and headed out the front door. He informed the black-and-white watching his house that he was headed to the gun range. He released them from duty and informed them that he would be back in three to four hours.

He turned on the radio, and the news was no longer about him, but about Sarah Widen. In the back of his mind, he kept wondering where Jesse Carr was hiding. He had a feeling that if Carr met up with any local police officers, the report would read that he resisted arrest and was killed in the resulting gunfire.

When he reached Dennis's house, the sky was a deep blue, and the temperature was already up to sixty-five degrees. There was virtually no wind, which made it perfect for the range. Dennis was standing outside in an old ratty shirt and blue jeans. Frank laughed and realized he was really getting to like this guy.

Dennis buckled up and noticed the large gun case in the backseat. "Where are we headed today?"

"I know you're not going to like this, but we're going to the gun range. You said you don't like guns, but give it a shot, no pun intended. You don't have to shoot today, just watch me do my yearly qualification. Our department requires that anyone shot in the line of duty has to re-qualify on the range before going back on active duty."

Dennis looked back at Frank. He wasn't pleased that Frank had tricked him into this trip. "I don't care what you say, I don't like guns, and you know why."

"I'll give you that, Dennis, but you can't let the past dictate your future. The reason you don't want to have anything to do with guns may get you killed by one. Just follow me around today. If you change your mind, let me know. Remember, guns don't do bad things. People do."

The two were quiet as the car weaved its way up into the hills above Seattle. When they reached the gated entrance, Frank showed his badge and a paper the captain had signed authorizing one guest to shoot on the range. Frank had been here enough times to know which day had the fewest shooters. He figured fewer people would cause less stress for Dennis. He grabbed the gun case, and the attendant assigned him a spot on the range. Frank handed a headset to Dennis, who quickly put it on.

Frank pulled out his .38, checked the chamber, and loaded it. He set the weapon down on the special gun table in front of him and pressed the target recall button to bring the target clips to him. He attached the target and sent the target to the halfway position. He put his headset on, picked up the .38, and shot in rapid fire until the gun was empty. Dennis's eyes were huge. Frank had made an impression on him.

Frank then pulled out his Glock and repeated the entire process of loading and setting a new target. A few minutes later, the target displayed a nice pattern in the center. Dennis seemed to be interested in the whole process. Frank put the Glock away and pulled out an old Colt Revolver he'd restored.

Dennis came over and looked at the antique gun. "Is that a six-shooter from the Old West?"

"Yes, but most of the guns like this aren't from the 1800's. Most of them are replicas made today for people who can't afford to buy the real thing. This gun though is the real McCoy, a Colt from the late 1800's, used by a U.S. Marshall in Kansas City. I picked it up at an auction and had to do some work on it, but isn't she a beauty?"

Frank loaded the Colt with the ammo and took careful aim at a new target. Instead of rapid fire, he slowly squeezed off all six rounds almost all dead center on the target.

Frank took out the empty shell casings and loaded in new ammo. He looked over to Dennis and said, "You want to try a few shots? I won't force you to buy a gun, but you should at least know how to fire one."

Dennis started to balk at the request, but then surprised Frank by saying, "Okay, I'll try it. However, I want to shoot the Colt. I don't feel comfortable with the other two."

"Great, but first some rules. Never point a gun, loaded or not, at anyone unless you plan to shoot them. Always point the gun at the range, or down to the ground in front of you. Now watch how I pick up the gun and then slowly squeeze the trigger. The gun will jump if you try to force the trigger, and you'll miss the target completely."

Dennis moved over to the center position and picked up the gun. He was surprised it was so heavy. He used the sight on the top of the gun, and slowly squeezed the trigger. The gun jumped back, and he quickly set the gun down. The shot hit the outside edge of the target. Once the target was back in place, he picked the gun up again. His second shot was two inches closer to the center. The rest of the shots were dead center.

Frank was in shock. "Are you sure you've never shot a gun before?"

"No, but I understand the physics of shooting. It's just a matter of recalculating the recoil, movement of my hand, and timing as I squeeze the trigger."

Frank was about to say something when the range supervisor came over. "Who's your hotshot friend, Frank?"

Frank quickly tried to think of a safe answer. "He's a cold case consultant from the private sector." That sounded good and wasn't a lie, but rather an extension of the truth.

The manager looked Dennis over. "Frank, I'd like to see him take another round with that gun.'

"Sure, why not. Are you all right with that, Dennis?"

Dennis looked at the two and decided to give it another go. If that's what it took to get back to work, then that's what he would do. Frank started to reach for the Colt, but Dennis picked it up, opened the chamber, and loaded six more rounds. With a new target in place, he took a stance and placed all six shots dead center.

The manager's mouth dropped. "What the hell is going on, Frank? Who is this guy?"

Frank took the gun from Dennis. "I think it's time to leave, Dennis. We've got to get back to work."

Dennis wasn't sure what he'd done wrong, but found he actually liked shooting. As Frank put each weapon away, he showed Dennis how to load and unload the respective weapon, and the use of the safety. Twenty minutes later, they were on their way to the cold case department.

Frank was very quiet and Dennis finally couldn't stand it any longer. "What did I do wrong? You wanted me to shoot a gun, and I did. Now you won't even talk to me. What gives?"

"Are you sure you've never used a gun before? It takes years for some cops to learn to shoot like you just did. How in the hell did you do that?"

"I swear I've never used a gun before, but it just takes an understanding of projectile physics. I studied that when I was doing my doctorate in physics. Once you eliminate the variables causing the projectile to miss the target, all the shots should be dead center. I don't understand why you seem mad at me."

"To be honest, Dennis, I'm jealous. It took me forever to get to where you are on the second set of shots. There are very few people on the planet to which shooting comes naturally. You're one of a dozen people I know who fit in that group. The other reason I was upset was that the range manager recognized your talent right away. The word could get out and draw attention to ourselves. I don't want anyone to know about snake-head yet."

"Will you quit calling her snake-head?"

"If I call her by her real name, someone might connect it to your machine. No, I prefer snake-head."

"Okay, but please call her by her real name when you're around her."

"Give me a break Dennis, are you telling me *IT* has feelings?"

"Did you ever wonder why Medusa cost over one billion dollars? She uses AI, or Artificial Intelligence. She can absorb information and form an opinion. She also has some limited responses. When you called it snake-head, she researched the name and found out that most references have a negative connotation. You're lucky she doesn't have offensive weapons."

When they arrived at the office, Frank turned off the alarms, and the two went inside. He immediately noticed a single box on the table and several stacks of organized folders. "What's this, Dennis?"

Dennis picked up the top folder and said, "Our next case. I looked over several of the cases and selected ones I thought had a 50/50 chance of us solving."

"Hey, I'm the detective in command. I thought I decided which case we'll work on next." He smiled and then said, "So, tell me about it."

At first, Dennis didn't know for sure if Frank was teasing him or not. "I think I'm getting the hang of how these things are written. Two years ago, Nancy Limen was found tortured and murdered in her home. When she didn't show up for work at a local finance office, the manager became worried and called her friends. No one had heard from her in two days, so he called the police, and they found her body. The house had been ransacked, and several items were stolen. Surprisingly, all the stolen items were found in a dumpster a few blocks away. The CSI team worked the scene, but came up with nothing.

"A couple of weeks later a company audit was completed, and several million dollars were found missing. The money was transferred by an unknown party using passwords to access various larger accounts. Miss Limen's computer was searched, but nothing was found. The only deleted files were some pictures taken at an office party. The files had been overwritten, and the images couldn't be recovered. The case went cold and although a recent follow-up had been done, nothing surfaced that would help point to her murderer."

Frank looked at the evidence box with Nancy Limen written on the side. He was about to open the lid when his cell phone rang.

"Frank Ridge here. ...You're kidding, right? ...No, we'll be right there."

Frank closed the lid and put his phone in his pocket. "Put everything away. We have to go right now."

"What's going on, Frank?"

"Someone set my house on fire!"

Before Dennis could say another word, Frank grabbed his jacket and was heading out the door. Once Dennis was outside, Frank locked the door and ran for his car. Dennis jumped in the passenger side and didn't even get his seat belt fastened before Frank burned rubber. Frank turned on his siren, and most cars yielded as his car raced through traffic. He barreled down the street doing sixty through the green lights and only slightly slowing for the red ones. Dennis had never experienced anything like this, and it was new and scary. Minutes later, Frank's car screeched to a halt in front of one of the fire trucks.

The fire chief had known Frank for years, and said, "I'm sorry, Frank. We didn't get to her in time. Someone set two other fires a couple of blocks over, and they were called in first. When we got to yours, it was already gone. I wish I could let you in, but the arson squad is in there right now sifting through the debris. Someone was really sending a message to you, because it was definitely arson. Do you think it could be Jesse Carr, that guy who shot you?"

Frank looked at the burned-out house and said, "That would be my best guess. He must be pissed that I didn't die. Did your guys see anything in there that could be saved?"

"There's only one thing so far. I guess Carr was so pissed at you that he turned everything over in the living room, including the couch. We did find something that had fallen underneath it."

The fire chief opened the fire truck door and pulled out a picture of Frank's dead wife, Ann. He handed it over to Frank. "I know that I should give this to the arson team, but I don't think it would help them as much as it will you. What are you going to do, Frank?"

Frank took the picture and gently wiped off the black soot. "My insurance will cover the house, and my daughter has most of my personal photos. There was a gun safe in the bedroom, so your guys should check on it. I'll get a hotel until I find an apartment. Don't worry, I'll be fine."

The chief motioned to one of the firefighters to move a hose and then looked back at Frank. "Your gun safe wasn't there. It looks like Carr took it with him. You can stay at the fire station if you want. The guys are great cooks, and it's cheaper than a hotel."

"I appreciate your generous offer, Chief, but I'll be fine. Besides, I'm somewhat of a loner."

The chief shook Frank's hand and looked at Dennis in the background. "If you change your mind, Frank, just you let me know. Again, sorry we couldn't save her for you."

"I'll let you know, Chief. Let me know what you find in there and if anything can be salvaged, I'd appreciate it."

Frank turned and motioned for Dennis to follow him to the car. Dennis looked back at the burned-out house and then jumped in and buckled up. Frank just sat in the driver's seat not saying a word. He was about to turn the key when Dennis put his hand on the key stopping him.

"Look, Frank. I don't really know you all that well, but I know you're the kind of person who hates charity. I think a hotel is a bad idea, because Carr won't give up. He'll find you, and no amount of fire power will stop him. I think you should stay at my house."

Frank started to respond, but Dennis was on a roll. "Up to now, you've made all the decisions. I'd like to make one to protect my future. My mother has been paranoid ever since my father was killed, so our house has all kinds of security measures. If anyone tries to enter the house when the alarm is set, steel doors come down and a special security company is called along with police."

He hesitated before continuing. "I also have a personal reason for your staying, and you might call it selfish. I want to continue working on the cold cases with Medusa, and can't do that if you're dead. You would have your own private guest quarters that my mother built for visiting scientists. The space is larger than your house, and has a living room, bathroom, kitchen, and an office. I'm not going to take NO for an answer."

Frank pushed Dennis's hand off the car key. "Are you done, yet?"

Dennis quickly pulled his hand back. "Don't be stubborn, Frank."

Frank turned to Dennis and grinned. "You convinced me, Dennis. I'm not stupid. I see your logic and it makes sense, but what about your mother?"

"She doesn't get back for at least another month or two, and I'll let her know in advance. Besides, she doesn't invite guest scientists much anymore. She only did that when she taught at the college."

"Well, in that case, let's go look at my new digs."

Chapter 12

With his housing situation solved, Frank seemed more relaxed as they made the trip back to Dennis's house. As the gate swung open, the gardener working near the entrance waved at the two as they drove up the driveway. The housekeeper was on the porch cleaning the front door and looked up as they parked the car.

Dennis got out of the passenger side and reintroduced them both. "Mrs. Henson, this is Frank Ridge. He'll be staying in the guest quarters for several weeks or more."

Frank shook Mrs. Henson's hand. "I understand you run the place. I'm a quiet person, and I don't smoke, drink, or make life difficult to those who are providing me a safe haven. Just let me know if I'm doing something wrong, and I'll correct it."

Dennis smiled and thought this was going to work after all. The two men walked into the main entrance, and Dennis pointed down a hall to the right. "The guest quarters are located at the end of this hall. Mrs. Henson keeps it ready for any unannounced guest."

When they reached the end of the hall, Dennis opened the door that opened into a spacious living room. Frank scanned the room and was amazed that it was so much bigger than his burned-out living room. It hosted two couches, an easy chair, coffee table, a full bookcase and landscape paintings covered most of the walls.

Dennis opened another door to the left of the living room, and Frank saw a king-sized bed and a walk-in closet that was bigger than his original bedroom. Frank shook his head in awe. Dennis moved over to the full kitchen, which adjoined the living room. He opened the refrigerator and found it was fully stocked with food.

Dennis looked back at the bewildered Frank Ridge. "If you need any groceries, just make a list and put it on the fridge. Mrs. Henson will pick it up for you when she goes shopping."

Dennis opened the door and said, "There's one more room, that I'm guessing you'll really like." This was Frank's dream room. There was a large flat-screen TV, pool table, desktop computer system, and a bar surrounded with comfortable lounge chairs and couches.

Dennis could see that the guest quarters weren't exactly what Frank had expected, so, he said, "I'll tell you what, I'm sure that you could find a cheaper place, but how about $1,000 a month because I think the added security makes it worth it?"

Frank looked around the room. "Dennis, if you had offered the quarters for free, I'd have refused. You know that don't you?"

"I wouldn't have offered it to you for free, because I know you would've turned it down."

"Are you trying to profile me, Dr. Andrews?"

Dennis smiled and was about to respond when Frank's cell phone rang. It was his daughter, Debra.

"Calm down, Honey. I'm fine, although the house is gone. I was able to salvage your mom's photo. Right now, I'm sure glad that I took most of my personal stuff to your house."

Frank was quiet as he listened to his daughter vent her anger at what had happened to her dad. When she finished, he did his best to calm her down. "Look, I'm fine. I'll be staying with Dr. Andrews at his home. He has really nice guest quarters that he's willing to rent to me at a very reasonable price."

Dennis could see that this last piece of information didn't sit well with Debra. From what he could decipher, Debra was accusing him of taking advantage of Frank's situation. Frank gave her his new address, and they exchanged a couple of personal comments, before he disconnected.

Frank sat down in one of the overstuffed chairs. "I don't know why she doesn't seem to like you. She thinks you're taking advantage of the situation. I invited her over tomorrow night, so she could see for herself. I hope that's all right?"

Frank looked straight at Dennis with a very serious face. "You really don't need the rent money for the guest quarters do you?"

"No, Frank, but I knew you wouldn't have taken it any other way."

"You're right about that Dennis. Let's get back to the cold case office, and maybe we can still salvage this day."

The two returned to the office and rehashed the case that had been interrupted by the fire. When they were sure that they understood every aspect of the case, Frank called the company where Nancy Limen had worked. He talked to the company president and arranged for the two of them to visit Nancy's work area in the evening when everyone else had gone home. The president had objected at first, but changed his mind when Frank asked if there was something he was hiding. The security guard would let them in, show them Nancy's workstation, and then leave them to do their work.

When Frank hung up, he suggested they get a bite to eat before heading to the crime scene. They loaded Medusa in the panel truck and headed out to Frank's favorite hamburger joint.

Frank saw that Dennis had juice running down the side of his mouth from his burger, and said, "Dennis, do you mind if I ask a personal question?"

Dennis set the burger down, and wiped his mouth. "If I did object, would you still ask?"

"Yep."

"Then go ahead and ask away."

"How come you don't have a girlfriend? Someone like you should be fighting them off, or should I be asking a different type of question?"

Dennis choked on the last comment and had to take a sip from his soda. "Normally, I'd say it's none of your business, but the truth is that I'm so wrapped up in my work that most girls tire of me after a couple of dates. And NO, I'm not gay."

"I'm just asking. Detective partners generally know more about their associates than their spouses do. You just don't fit the mold of a typical rich kid. Sorry for asking."

"That's all right, Frank. I understand. My mother is always harping at me to get a social life, and only when I turn the tables on her, does she shut up. Maybe after a couple more solved cases, I might have some free time."

Frank tossed the finished burger wrappers in the trash and fifteen minutes later, they were talking with the security guard. After showing the guard his badge, Frank headed back to the panel truck to help Dennis unload Medusa. They pulled a cover over the device so prying eyes couldn't see the third member of their team. Once Medusa was loaded into the elevator, the guard pressed the level three button. When the doors opened, they were greeted with total silence. Frank looked over the drawings taken from the evidence box and motioned to Dennis. The area where Nancy Limen's workstation was located was empty.

Frank looked back at the guard. "Okay, where is her workstation?"

The guard said, "As soon as we discovered that Limen was dead, we cleaned out a storage room, and the police locked her workstation inside. New locks were installed, and a security camera monitors anyone entering the room. The SEC and a couple of other financial agencies were interested in what was on her computer. I never understood why they just didn't take it to their labs, until I saw representatives from two different agencies arguing over jurisdiction. All I know is that everyone who looked into the system wore gloves and those funny white paper slippers over their shoes. I'm supposed to give you some too if you want to look inside the room."

Frank grabbed the gloves and shoe slippers from the guard and said, "I think you're probably right. I see jurisdiction disputes all the time. That's good for us though because we don't have to jump through all their hoops, and it sounds like they protected the evidence."

The guard looked up at the camera and then took out two keys to open the door. He looked down at his watch. "Hey, I have to be on the other side of the building to check some other offices. How long are you going to be?"

"Probably a couple hours or so. We'll come find you at your front desk when we're done."

The guard was gone in seconds, and Frank gave a sigh of relief. "I never thought he was going to go. We couldn't let him see our other team member."

Dennis set Medusa next to the workstation, while Frank removed all the police tape. Before long, Medusa was up and running. Frank and Dennis stood back as the device created a 3D image of the workstation and then proceeded to scan for all DNA surrounding the area. Once that was completed, a scan for fingerprints, unusual chemicals, and all barcodes was made. Frank knew that Medusa was much better than a normal CSI team, but she had little to work with in this case.

As Dennis monitored the data screens, Frank wandered around the many cubicles in the office outside the storeroom. He shook his head and decided that he could never work in this type of environment. It was too 9 to 5 for his taste. He liked the excitement of not knowing what each day would bring.

He looked out the window and down toward the parking lot. A man in a hooded sweatshirt was standing next to their panel truck. At that moment, the man glanced up at Frank, and immediately walked away and out of view. Frank was about to run down to see who it was, but realized he would be long gone. The hairs on the back of his neck rose as he realized the man was about the same height and weight as Jesse Carr. Sweat started to roll down his forehead. He turned around to see Dennis standing next to him.

Dennis was surprised at the fearful expression on Frank's face. "Is everything okay, Frank?"

"Fine, it's just a little warm in here."

Dennis knew that was an outright lie, because if anything, it was a little chilly. "Okay, Frank, Medusa has performed the first-level scan. The workstation is clean. The DNA scan shows two users on the keyboard. Ninety-nine percent are Nancy Limen's, and there's a trace of someone else who didn't work on this floor. Nancy's DNA is on all the keys because she did a lot of typing on the system, but the other DNA is only on a few keys. Medusa ran the keystroke combinations and found several possibilities."

Frank looked at the screen to see what Dennis was sawing. He scanned down through the list until he hit an email address. "Who's dreadnot66@hotmail.com?"

Before Dennis could respond, Medusa responded in a computer voice. *"I've scanned all the Hotmail records and found that the email address belongs to a Vince Duncan. He works in the computer section of this company. The company records indicate that Duncan quit his job at the same time Limen was killed. One of his keystrokes was the delete key."*

Frank scratched his head and decided they were finally getting somewhere. This was almost too easy. "Okay, snak... uh, Medusa. Can you hack into Duncan's personal records?"

Medusa's response was out before Frank had barely finished his sentence. *"I've already done that. If there had been anything pertaining to the case, I'd have indicated such information."*

Frank smiled as he looked over to Dennis. "Touchy isn't she?"

Dennis didn't respond to Frank, but instead asked Medusa another question. "Can you tell me if there were any attachments to the email sent to dreadnot66@hotmail.com?"

"I was going to ask that," added Frank as he looked over Dennis's shoulder at the display.

"*Two pictures had been attached to the email, and the file names match the images deleted from Nancy Limen's computer,*" remarked Medusa.

Frank took out his iPad and typed in the file names. "So, where does this guy live?"

The response was immediately presented on Frank's iPad screen. "Hey, Medusa, are you hacking my iPad?"

Dennis started the shutdown process for Medusa. "Frank, you still don't understand what Medusa can do. Keep in mind that Medusa's original task was to track down terrorists and gather as much information as possible. That meant she had to break a few laws, no rather, a lot of laws. If you don't want her to update your iPad, tell her next time she's working."

"No, that's fine Dennis. I have no objection because I probably would have typed the information incorrectly anyway. Those keys on the iPad are so damn small that I keep hitting the wrong one and have to keep backing up. Right now, I have to call a judge and get a search warrant. Tomorrow we're going to break this case. I can feel it."

Chapter 13

The two sleuths were tired when they arrived back at Dennis's house. Frank was still amazed with his new lodging. His bed was one of those with various comfort settings. He found his setting within minutes and had one of the best night's sleep in ages.

Dennis awoke to a wonderful aroma. He quickly dressed and rushed to the main kitchen to find Frank busy with two pans on the stove.

Frank turned when he heard Dennis come in. "Hi, I gave Mrs. Henson the morning off. She had some errands to run, and I wanted to try out your kitchen. Sit down; I have waffles, eggs, and hash browns coming up."

Dennis was about to say something, but decided to let it go. The breakfast smelled great. Mrs. Henson was a superb cook, but her meals never smelled this good. "Hey, Frank, where did you learn to cook?"

"My wife loved to cook, and then she passed away. I still wanted to enjoy her cooking, so between her recipes and the cooking channel, I tried my best. I never was as good as she was, but close."

Dennis sat down, and Frank loaded up his plate. Neither one spoke for the next ten minutes, other than sighs of contentment.

As Dennis got up from the table, Frank motioned for him to pick up his plate.

Dennis looked down at the plate. "That's okay, Frank. Mrs. Henson will clean it up when she gets back."

Frank grabbed his plate and Dennis's. "That's not the way I was brought up. Mrs. Henson is a very nice lady, and you should treat her with more respect." Frank cleaned off the plates and placed them in the dishwasher. Dennis was in shock. Just when he thought he was getting to know Frank, something new would pop up.

"Frank, what about the search warrant?"

"It's already done. Load up sna... sorry, Medusa, and let's get going."

Dennis gave him a glare, but Frank just ignored him.

An hour later, the two stood in front of Vince Duncan's front door.

Frank pulled out his badge and the search warrant. When the door opened, a bewildered man looked at the two. "I'm Detective Frank Ridge. We have a search warrant to look at your computer."

Duncan was not impressed. He was sure the warrant was bogus until he completely read it through. "What's this all about? What are you looking for?"

Frank pushed his way inside the front door. "We'll know when we find it. Where's your computer?"

Duncan pointed to the room beyond the living room. Frank led the way as Dennis followed. The computer wasn't turned on. Dennis reached over and pressed the power button. Duncan kept yelling in the background about the whole process being illegal. In less than a minute, the log on screen came up.

Duncan smiled and chanted, "You can look all you want, but I don't have to give you the password, and the warrant states that you can look at the machine, but not remove it, unless it is part of a crime scene."

Dennis reached over and whispered into Frank's ear.

Frank grinned. "Okay, Duncan. You're right about that point. Therefore, if you don't mind, I'm going to stand here and just look at the computer, which is within the parameters of the search warrant. Dennis, why don't you go work on that other problem while I try to figure this one out?"

Duncan became bolder. "You know that if you type in the wrong password three times, the whole system is wiped clean. I mean entirely and nothing can be recovered."

"Really," was Frank's sarcastic answer.

Frank stood watching the log in screen blink a few times, and then shut down.

Duncan looked at the computer. "What did you do, Detective?"

"Nothing. You saw me. I was just looking at the screen. It's not my problem if you're using a temperamental computer. Hey, I know a guy in our department who can come and look at it for you."

Duncan's face was turning turnip red. "Get out, Detective. I don't know what you did, but I'm going to call your supervisor."

"Go ahead, Duncan. That will give them an excuse to look at you even closer."

Frank walked out the door, slamming it behind him. He opened the door to the panel truck and went inside. "So, what do we have?"

Dennis selected a couple of menus to bring up the results.

"Duncan thought he had a strong password and firewall. Medusa was through it in seconds. We found the two photos Duncan emailed to himself. They were just standard images with nothing hidden in the pictures. It looks like just office party fun."

Frank wasn't happy with what he heard. "All that bullshit with Duncan, and it was for nothing."

Dennis pulled up another menu. "Frank, I said the image itself had no hidden embedded picture. The metadata is another story. Every digital camera stores all kinds of shooting information for every picture it takes. Data like shutter speed, ISO, f/stop, flash firing, and more. What most people don't know is that there's a special area to add in personal information about the photo, such as where it was taken, copyright, or notes about the scene. It takes a more advanced editing program, such as Adobe Photoshop or Lightroom, to add this information.

Interestingly, Medusa found a series of Duncan's passwords and his offshore transfer account numbers in the file. Medusa has already frozen the account until we can notify the authorities."

Frank looked back at Duncan's front door. "Got you dirt bag."

Chapter 14

Captain Carson was having another bad day. One day, his life smelled like roses and the next day it was horseshit. The paperwork was getting out of hand and driving him crazy. Internal Affairs was on his back, and the mayor was pushing for a lower crime rate in order to boost his political aspirations.

He heard his office door open and was about to chew out whoever had stepped into his domain without permission. It was Frank, so he stood up to shake his hand.

"Damn, Frank, I didn't think I was going to see you for a month. With Jesse Carr still gunning for you, I thought you might take more time off. You know that no one will ever team up with you again after the shooting. They're worried they might be collateral damage when Carr comes back."

Frank shook the captain's hand with force to show him that he was back, better than ever. "It's nice to see you too, Captain. Are you going to write me off as well? I don't need a partner, as I have my own private CSI consultant. I'm living in a house with some intensive security, so Carr won't get me at home. Maybe on the street, but not where I live. Enough about that, let's get to the point of my visit."

Frank pulled a file out of his briefcase and slid it over. The captain sat down and reviewed the file for a few minutes, then responded, "You've got to be kidding. The original detectives looked over everything and found nothing. Yet, you are shot several times, your house burns down, and you still manage to solve an unsolvable case. Frank, how's this possible?"

He closed his briefcase and leaned onto the captain's desk. "Trust me, Captain; you don't really want to know. I don't want any credit or mention that I had anything to do with the case. Give the credit to someone else who needs it. Now I'm going to take a much-needed week off as my chest still hurts like crazy. I want to take some time to regroup and re-evaluate what I want to do from here. With Carr still out there gunning for me, I don't want to put anyone else at risk."

The captain closed the file and stood up. "Frank, that's the best idea I've heard from you yet. I'll support whatever you decide, because you've paid your dues. After you were shot, most of the guys out there sort of changed how they feel about you. They respect you, but they just don't want to work with you."

"I understand, Captain. I'll give you a call in about a week."

As he headed for his car, he noticed the same man he'd seen before was now standing across the street. As soon as the man realized he'd been made, he sped off. Traffic was congested, so there was no way Frank could've followed. He dismissed the man as his mind was on a long hot shower and a large glass of orange juice.

When he arrived at Dennis's gate, he punched in the security code and drove up to the front of the house. There were no cars around, and the front door was locked. He unlocked the door, checked the alarm, and found it was off. He yelled out for Dennis, but there was no answer. He looked in the kitchen, the library, and the game room, but found nobody. He thought this was strange, but headed down the hallway to his quarters, and looked around. He checked each room, but nothing looked amiss. This Carr thing was really making him jumpy and putting him on edge.

He turned on the shower to be hot, stripped down, and grabbed the shampoo bottle. For the next ten minutes, he was in heaven as he let the showerhead beat on his aching shoulders. He didn't want it to end, but the water temperature started to drop. He turned the water off, grabbed a towel and started to dry himself. He heard a sound and looked up to see a woman he assumed was Dr. Sandra Alexander, staring at him with extreme anger in her face. She was almost as tall as Frank, very thin, and extremely well dressed in a light-blue pant suit. She had dark-brown short hair, wore very little jewelry, but appeared to be a classy lady.

"Who in the hell are you and what are you doing in my house?"

Frank rapidly adjusted the towel as he was trying to compose himself. He wasn't fast enough because she quickly responded.

"There's no need for that. What I see doesn't impress me, so just tell me who in the hell are you?"

At this moment, Frank would have felt better facing Carr because this woman wasn't cutting him any slack, and he was getting chilled.

"Your son arranged for me to stay in the guest quarters. He and I are working on a project together, and my house burned down. He was just helping me out."

Dr. Alexander's anger pulled back a notch when she heard the last part.

"What do you do with my son? Work at that son-of-a-bitch place they call a government lab? I hate the idea that my husband's design was used to build that lab. You still didn't give me your name."

"Detective Frank Ridge, and your son and I are working on cold cases together with his snake-head friend."

She leaned toward Frank. "Did my son hear you call Medusa snake-head?"

"Actually yes, and he wasn't impressed."

"Well, I'm not either, and I'm also not impressed that he's working with the police. I hate the police, and anyone who has anything to do with the police. Therefore, that means I hate you, and you'll have to leave my house. Get dressed and get packing."

Frank stood with the towel wrapped around his waist waiting for her to leave, but she didn't budge.

She put her hands on her hips and stared straight at Frank's face. "I suppose you want me to leave while you get dressed?"

He nodded, but the two stood in a standoff with neither one moving.

"What's going on here, Mom? I didn't know you were getting home so soon."

They both looked at Dennis, and Frank gave way to Dennis's mother.

"My last lecture in Austria was canceled, so I decided to cut my tour short. I needed some time at home. Dennis, this man has to go immediately as I won't have a policeman in my house."

Dennis looked like a drowning man. "Mom, my grant was canceled. Everything is shut down. Frank came to me with an idea to help prove that my project works and has value. We've already solved two cold cases together."

Dennis's mother looked back at Frank and scanned him from head to toes. He felt like he was being inspected in a meat locker. She turned back to Dennis. "I don't care, Dennis. It didn't help your father, because the police did nothing to solve his crime. His case was cold before it got warm. I'm not going to budge on this one. He goes."

Dennis took a deep breath. He rarely stood up to his mother, but this was one time he felt the need. "Mom, here's the deal. Frank's a good man. He's nothing like the policemen who handled dad's case. He represents the epitome of what a police officer should be. If he goes, then so do I. You need to trust me, otherwise I'll pack up tonight and never come back. Mom, you're wrong on this one."

His mother turned and stormed out without another word.

Dennis looked over to Frank. "Did I put it on a little too thick about your sainthood?"

"Just a touch, Dennis, but thanks for the thought. Does this mean I am okay to stay here?"

Dennis smiled. "This is one of the few times I've seen my mother back down on an argument. She'll never verbally give in, so the best option is what we just got from her. I think you're fine to stay, for now anyway."

"I think I should find a hotel until I can work something else out."

"Frank, you're fine here. Don't undo what just happened. A year ago, she wouldn't have given in. Something happened in Europe, and it has made her let her guard down."

"There's another problem. My daughter Debra and I always get together once a week for a family meal. Her place really has no kitchen to speak of, so she eats out most of the time. Normally, she comes to my house, but it seems I'm one house short right now."

Dennis thought about the problem a second. He analyzed all the possible ramifications of his mother meeting Frank's daughter. "You know, Frank, this may be just what my mom needs is another woman in the house. She rarely entertains, and most of the time it is professional people, generally men. I think this might just work."

Frank reached over and picked up his cell phone. "I think I'll give her a call right now."

Dennis started laughing. "Frank, you might want to get dressed first. I can't guarantee that my mother isn't going to come charging back in here for another round."

"Right. Clothes first, then a phone call."

A few minutes later, Frank was sitting in a comfortable lounge chair sipping his orange juice. He let the phone ring a couple of times, and then Debra's voice mail came on the line. He debated and finally left a message.

"It's Dad. Hey, about our dinner this week on Thursday, why don't you come over to Dennis's house? He was kind enough to say it was all right, so make it 7 p.m., and you don't have to bring anything but yourself. The address is 3614 8th Street in the

Lincoln Heights area. Dennis said he would send you a map link with driving instructions. See you then. Love you."

He set the phone down and debated. He wasn't going to put it off any longer. He had to face his enemy now before he became too entrenched in her home. Sure enough when he reached the living room, she was sitting on the couch reading her Kindle. She didn't look up as he came into the room. He cleared his throat, walked over to her, and held out his hand. "We were never formally introduced. My name is Frank, and yours?" She just looked at him, not offering her hand in return. He looked around for the best place to sit and found a love seat at the opposite end of the room. He sat down and reached for the newspaper. As soon as he opened it up, she took another shot.

"My name is Sandra Alexander, but you can call me Dr. Alexander. You move into my guest apartment, and now you're making yourself at home in my living room. That happens to be my newspaper."

Frank realized this was a losing battle and was about to leave when Dennis came across the room.

"Hey, Frank. Is everything all right in your quarters?"

"It's fine, Dennis. Actually, it is better than fine. You have a lovely home."

Dr. Alexander set her Kindle down and glared at Frank. "What gives you the right to come into my house and take advantage of my son?"

Dennis walked over between his mother and Frank. "We've already gone over this, Mom. Frank is my very good friend. Forget for a moment that he's a police officer. He's no different than any of the guests you've had here in the past."

Dr. Alexander picked up her Kindle and pressed the next page button. "I have to argue with you on that one, because he's nothing like my friends. He's..."

She stopped talking and started reading. Dennis looked over at his mother. Something was different. She was arguing with them, but lacked that bright fire in her eyes as before.

Something must have happened in Europe, and it wasn't just a canceled lecture tour. Then it hit him that she must have found someone special, and he'd broken her heart. She wasn't mad at Frank. She was just infuriated by men in general.

"There's one other thing, Mom. Frank's daughter, Debra, will be joining us for dinner tomorrow night. If you don't want Frank and his daughter to eat with us, then they can eat in the guest quarters, but I'll be joining them, and you can eat by yourself."

Dr. Alexander looked up at Dennis with a look that could kill. "That'll be fine, Dennis. We can all eat in the main dining room. I'll let Mrs. Henson know."

"I've already done that, Mom. Excuse us as Frank and I have a few business things to discuss. We'll go to his quarters and give you some peace and quiet. See you at dinner."

The two worked their way back to Frank's quarters, and they sat down, each commandeering a couch. "You know, Dennis, despite all her hatred of police, I like your mom. She's a strong woman, just like my wife, Ann."

This statement caught Dennis completely off guard. "Really, Frank? Why would you still like her after the lousy way she's treated you?"

"Hey, I understand. Anyone who loses a spouse instantly makes them very hardened on life in general. I was lucky enough to be with my wife to the end. We talked about a lot of things - our past, my future. Even though I never got over her dying, I was still somewhat prepared for her death. Your mother didn't have that opportunity. She was never able to say her good-byes. Everything was gone in an instant. I can understand how she feels. It had to be much worse than I had losing Ann. Dennis, I'll deal with it and try to control how I respond to her aggressiveness. Okay?"

Dennis was impressed. He didn't totally understand Frank giving his mother a break, but it was a nice change to the alternative. "So, Frank, what do we do now?"

Frank reached for the remote. "Not a damn thing to do with work. What's your pleasure - a game or a movie?"

Three hundred feet away in a van, a pair of high-powered binoculars were focusing on the Alexander home. The prying eyes had been watching the house for the last three hours. When the lights in the house finally went out, Jesse Carr put his binoculars away. He admired himself in the rearview mirror. His facial reconstruction was worth the pain because it gave him a completely new identity. Too bad for the man who'd done the work, because he was now cemented in the foundation of a construction project downtown. No one would find him for several decades. Jesse Carr's rule number one – leave no witnesses behind. Tonight another one would be crossed off his list.

Chapter 15

Frank was awakened at 5:00 a.m. with a call. He let it ring three times to clear his mind.

"Frank Ridge here and you better have a good reason to call me this early."

He waited for the response. Even when he heard the information, it took him a couple of seconds to decipher it all. "Are you sure it was Carr? …Okay, I understand. Thanks for the heads up."

Frank grabbed a bathrobe and headed toward Dennis's room. He knocked, and it took a minute for him to get an answer before barging through the door.

"I just got a call from the captain. Jesse Carr was busy last night. I don't know if you remember one of the witnesses in Jesse Carr's case, a Brian Schlemmer. He was murdered last night, shot point blank when he answered his front door. Internal Affairs wants to see me pronto, so you can sleep in, and I'll be back later today."

Dennis rubbed the sleep from his eyes. "Are you sure, Frank?"

"Absolutely. Besides, I don't want the guys in IA asking you questions. They can be relentless when they smell something's not just right. Spend some time with your mom, and see if you can find out what's bothering her. I'll be back later today."

Dennis pulled his blanket over his head and rolled onto his side.

"You know what's best, Frank. Don't worry about my mother, because she can get really moody."

"Oh really, Dennis. I never noticed."

Frank took his time driving downtown. He didn't have a clue why IA wanted him. When he arrived, the captain was waiting for him in the parking lot. This wasn't a good sign.

"Frank thanks for coming so quickly. When they pulled the slugs from Brian Schlemmer's body, they got a match. The slugs came from two guns - both yours. Carr is definitely sending you a message. The guys in Internal Affairs didn't know about your stolen gun safe because they never got the paperwork. They're pissed that they jumped the gun by putting out a warrant for your arrest, because twenty minutes later, the report surfaced. For some reason, they thought you had something to do with the report's delay. I told them I drug my heels, and you had nothing to do with it. You've already been cleared, but I don't know when you'll ever get your two guns back."

Frank looked over the captain's shoulder to see if anyone was watching. "Which two guns?"

"There were four slugs from the .38 and four from the Glock. You can kiss those two guns good-bye."

"That's fine with me as I can always get new ones, but the Colt was something special. I really want that one back. Do I have to go up to IA or am I done?"

"I'm sorry, Frank, but you still have to go up and talk to them. Meanwhile, we're putting together a list of anyone we think Carr is gunning for. I know you're at the top of the list, but I think it will be some time before he comes back for you."

"Why do you say that, Captain?"

He looked both ways before proceeding. "I shouldn't tell you this, but Jesse left you a message. It read, *one down and several more to go, Frank. Their deaths are on your head, and I'll be using your guns to clean up this mess. See you soon, Frank.*"

Frank thought about what he'd just heard. This was a no-win scenario. "I'll go up to IA and talk with them, but I'm not going to give them shit. They'll have to pry it out of me."

The captain dropped his head in despair. "I figured as much. Take it easy because whatever you do falls back on our department. Don't let them get to you."

Four hours later, Frank drove down the freeway listening to an old country-western station to sooth his nerves. At the overpass before his turn off, he glanced up to see Jesse Carr looking down with a gun pointed straight at him. Frank swerved but Jesse never moved a muscle. As he exited the freeway, he called 911 to report the sighting. As he circled back to the overpass, there was no sign of Carr.

Minutes later, he was surrounded with patrol cars. Teams searched the area, but found nothing. A detective from his office took a report, and Frank was done in a half an hour. By the time he was home, it was all over the news about Carr's latest victim.

As he opened the front door, he was greeted by Dr. Alexander. "Detective, do you have any guns in your room or anywhere in my house? I won't tolerate having guns in my house."

"No, ma'am. The only guns I had were lost in the fire. If I did get a new one, I'd leave it at work or lock it in the trunk of my car. Is that satisfactory?'

She nodded and added, "Just so we understand each other, Detective. I still don't like having you here or working with my son, but he seems to have taken a liking to you. I don't exactly know why, because I thought I brought him up to recognize good stock."

Frank's face started to turn red in anger. Dennis came up from behind his mother and said, "What's going on here, Mom? I thought we were clear about this?"

"Maybe as far as you're concerned, but I don't like it one damn bit."

As soon as Dennis's mother left, Frank headed for his room and motioned to Dennis to follow. Frank opened the fridge and pulled out a new bottle of orange juice. "So, Dennis, how did it go with your mother today? Wait, let me guess - it sucked, right?"

Dennis pulled out the last beer. "You're right about that one. The Austria lecture tour wasn't canceled by the university, but rather by my mom. I asked her why, and she told me it was none of my business. I started to leave when she said something strange. She indicated she couldn't read people correctly anymore, and that she was going to quit the lecture tour, stay home and write a book. That's plain weird because she loves teaching, and now she acts as if she hates it. I tried to find out if she'd met someone, and she just clammed up. All I can tell you is that she's in a really bad mood, and that's not going to change any time soon."

Frank took another sip of orange juice. "I'm sorry to hear that. Is there anything I can do to bring her out of it, other than leaving?"

"No, Frank. The problem is my mom's and mine. I hope that she'll tell me someday, I just hope it's soon. So what happened today?"

Frank went over every detail of his day from when he got the early-morning call to his drive home. Dennis listened intensely from start to finish.

"The bottom line is that Jesse Carr is trying to kill everyone he thinks has ever done him wrong. Everyone involved in the case is now under police protection. The captain wants me to keep a very low profile for a while. He prefers that we work on the cold case files at home. He gave us permission to take the evidence, one case at a time to your lab. We'll still need to log in the chain of evidence showing where it was taken, when, how long, and what was analyzed from the evidence. He asked me to pick out a case, and an officer will bring it to our doorstep. Until then, we're sort of in a lock down."

Dennis finished off his beer, and threw it into the trash can. "This isn't going to go well with my mom. If she finds out that there might be a killer outside waiting for you or me, she'll have a meltdown."

Frank got up, removed the empty beer bottle from the trash, and put it into a recycling container. "Dennis, don't you have any respect for the environment? I guess all your money makes you exempt from being a little green."

"Sorry, Frank. It won't happen again. You know you're not what most people would consider as a typical cop."

"Is that bad?"

"No, it's just that you're different. You would be a great role model for kids. After Carr is caught, you should consider visiting schools and talking to them about being a detective."

Frank closed the cap on the orange juice and put it back into the refrigerator. "No, I'm not very social, so I'd be a lousy role model."

"I don't agree. You'd be a hit. I bet you were a great father."

"Dennis, let's change the subject. We really need to let your mother know what's going on. If she finds out everything from the news it will look like you're hiding something from her."

"Actually, I was already ahead of you. While you were gone, I told her that we needed to sit down and go over a few things. She hesitated at first, but I told her that it was very important to me. She agreed. There's never going to be a better time than now, so let's go."

They found Dr. Alexander sitting on a couch reading her Kindle and drinking a very large glass of red wine. She looked up and then pressed the sleep mode on the Kindle. "What's so important that we have to have this meeting?"

Dennis looked at the wine bottle. He'd seen the full bottle on the shelf early this morning, and now it was close to empty. "Look, I know you don't like having Frank here, but the situation has now changed."

Dr. Alexander took a sip from her glass. "You mean Jesse Carr and the fact that he's gunning for everyone having to do with

98

his most-recent incarcerations? I watch the news, Dennis, and I think I have a handle on what's going on. The police don't have a clue where he is, do they?"

"No but he'll screw up eventually," Dennis proclaimed.

Dr. Alexander glared at Frank. "How many bodies will it take before they get him?"

Frank was about to defend himself, but Dennis was on a roll. "That's not fair, Mom. We never did anything to force Carr to kill anyone. We have orders from the department to stay here until things settle down, or Carr is caught."

Before anyone could continue, the gate buzzer went off. Dennis went over to the camera viewer and saw it was a police officer in a patrol car. He opened the gate and went to meet them at the front door.

Frank piped up saying, "Someone from our office is bringing our most recent work case."

A couple of minutes later, Dennis came in and set a cardboard box down next to Frank. He looked at the name on the top of the box - Judy Narland. He was about to take the box to his room when Dr. Alexander commented on the delivery.

"So, you're now bringing murder cases into my house. I knew this was going to happen. Once someone has a foot in the door, who knows what'll follow. I don't want to see any of that stuff in the main part of the house. Keep it in your guest quarters and I don't want any visitors from the police department. If you need to see someone about a case, it will be outside of my house."

Frank looked at Dennis and then back to his mother. "That seems like a very fair request to me, so consider it done. I'm sorry that I have invaded your space. I know how much you hate the police, and I'll try to keep that part of the equation to a minimum."

Dennis picked up the box and was about to say something back to his mother when Frank touched his arm and shook his head back and forth. Dennis knew that he needed to back off.

"Okay, Mom. We'll work until dinner. Tomorrow Debra is coming over, remember?"

Dr. Alexander picked up her Kindle and woke it up. "That'll be fine."

Dennis and Frank rushed back to his quarters and had the box quickly opened. Frank pulled out the summary sheet on top of the evidence and sat on the couch reading aloud.

"Four months ago, 42-year-old Judy Narland, an employee of a local tea company, was found murdered in her home. There was no apparent motive for the murder, and nothing was stolen. Her money, credit cards, jewelry, and electronic devices were still there. Her car keys were on the key rack in the entranceway, and nothing seemed disturbed.

"The detective in command of the case had the victim's daughter see if anything seemed out of place. She commented that her mother was a neat freak, and the only area disturbed was the coffee table in the living room. Normally, all the books were stacked with the upper left corners lining up and one coaster at each end of the table. They were now all stacked together, very unlike her mother's way. The detective collected everything off the coffee table and put them in this box.

"The CSI team took more than a thousand pictures covering every room, and every shelf. The detective in charge was convinced that they had missed a significant clue, key in the case. A thumb drive was used to collect and sort all serial numbers, labels, and ID numbers to everything the team could find around the house. A small bag of lint and carpet debris was collected using a CSI evidence vacuum cleaner.

"Everyone at her workplace was interviewed, and those were added to the daughter's interrogation. In addition to being a neat freak, Mrs. Narland was a coupon collector, bought extensive online merchandise, and had a passion for game shows. She was widowed, had no boyfriends that anyone knew of, and was a loner. Most of her neighbors knew her, but never came into her house or had her visit theirs. Everyone commented that she was a quiet neighbor and didn't cause any trouble. She hired local handymen and high school boys for repairs and yard work. They interviewed those who knew or worked for her, and ran background checks. The detective in command concluded that they had no suspects or motive for the murder, and the case went cold a month after the murder."

Dennis put on a pair of latex gloves and opened the box. He immediately saw there were hundreds of items with matching tags. "I think we need to take all this to the lab and have Medusa take a look. That should quickly narrow down our search."

Dennis put the lid back on the box, and the two headed for the elevator in the basement. Normal evaluation procedure dictated that an investigator takes out one item at a time, inspects it, and returns it to its tagged envelope. When they reached Medusa's area, Frank opened the box and laid all the evidence on a large research table, carefully removing each piece of evidence and setting it next to the tag containing its pertinent information. Medusa was a very unusual CSI agent, and she required different analyzing methodology.

Dennis turned on the last sensor and motioned for Frank to move to the side of the table. "Frank, let's put her to work. I programmed her to analyze each item separately, and then analyze similar groups as a single item. The estimated time on the screen indicates about an hour. I suggest we go back up and get some coffee. I ran out in the lab, and had Mrs. Henson get some of the Longbottom Coffee you enjoyed yesterday."

Frank watched as the sensor arms extended out from the top of Medusa and passed across the debris collected from the carpet. "Are you sure that's a good idea? Your mom is still probably in the living room."

"Frank, are you afraid of my mother?"

"Yeah, I would rather have the captain chew me out, although she's prettier."

"Wow, the big bad detective is afraid of an old woman who can't lift a large bag of cat food."

Frank walked into the elevator and as the door closed he commented, "I didn't think she seemed old, and I didn't know you had a cat."

"Yes, we have a Bengal cat."

"A Bengal tiger?"

"No, Frank, not like the Bengals in the zoo. It's a breed of house cat that's called a Bengal. We happen to call ours Tigger. When people ask me if I have a pet, I tell them that I have a Bengal Tiger, and then move on to other conversations. You would be amazed at how many people think nothing of it and let it slide. A few ask for an explanation and then want to see Tigger."

"My wife Ann loved cats. Her favorite one, Patches, died a week after she did. It was an older cat, but it held on as if it were waiting for its master to die first. It stayed by Ann's side until the very end. A few days later, I found it lying next to my wife's favorite rosebush in the garden. It died peacefully during the night. So, where is Tigger? I'd like to see him."

The doors opened, and Dennis pointed to the back of the house. "Tigger has his own house in the garden, complete with automatic food dispenser, heated blanket, and filtered water dish."

Dennis opened the French doors to the back patio, and pointed to a large greenhouse about fifty yards away. "His house is the greenhouse. There's a small cat door, and if it gets too hot, he has a second house in the lower branches of the tree behind the greenhouse."

As the two walked toward the greenhouse, Dennis called for Tigger, but got no response. Dennis opened the greenhouse door, but no one was home. Dennis pointed toward the tree house, and the two started walking around the greenhouse. As Dennis walked under the branch that held the cat house, Frank noticed a miniature staircase that led to what looked like a large dollhouse.

"Whose cat is it, yours, or your mother's?"

"Tigger was my mom's cat, but she traveled so much that Mrs. Henson and I spend more time with him now. The funny thing is that the cat now has little to do with my mother and has adopted me as his master. He's a little picky, so don't be surprised if he'll have nothing to do with you."

As if on cue, Tigger came out of the door, stretched and walked down the staircase. Dennis reached over expecting him to come into his arms, but the cat had a mind of its own. Tigger ran over to Frank and moved back and forth against his legs purring so loud it could be heard from several feet away. Frank reached down and picked him up, and Tigger responded by pushing his head under Frank's chin. Dennis reached out to pet Tigger, but the cat took a swipe at Dennis.

A sound from behind made the three look back toward the house. Dr. Alexander stood with her hands on her hips. "Well, that confirms it. I knew that cat was a little screwed up. Look at the company he picks. So, Detective, do you have a cat?"

Frank set Tigger down, but he came back demanding more attention, so Frank picked him up again. "My wife had a cat we called Patches. She died a week after my wife did."

For the first time since Frank had met Dr. Alexander, there seemed to be a small crack in her armor. Her demeanor mellowed considerably and she said, "I'm sorry about your wife, Detective. I apologize for the nasty crack about Tigger's choices."

Dennis was in shock. He'd never heard his mother apologize to anyone. She always walked away when she'd lost a round. Dennis was about to break the silence, but Frank bailed him out.

"You don't have to call me detective. Frank is fine with me."

"That's fine with me, Frank. I hate the word *detective* anyway. In return, you can still call me Dr. Alexander."

Dennis and Frank couldn't decide if she were joking or not. Before they could decide, Dr. Alexander continued. "I'm just kidding. My friends call me Sandra. You can too, but if you want to talk police business, it's still Dr. Alexander."

The pleasant conversation was interrupted by a beeping sound from Dennis's pocket. His mother continued her conversation. "I assume that's Medusa calling. Do you have her working on the case file that was delivered earlier?"

Frank set Tigger down and looked back to Sandra. "Dr. Alexander, you are correct in your assessment of the situation."

Frank stopped the conversation. Why had he said that? It was a stupid, but an official way of saying yes. "We'll need to go look at the results. We're two for two so far, and I'd like to think that your son's creation will net us a third."

Sandra didn't respond, but instead reached down to pick up the cat hoping to prove that she was still in command. Tigger quickly moved over to Frank and swayed back and forth again against his legs. Sandra said nothing but turned abruptly and headed for the rear of the garden.

As Frank and Dennis headed back to the house, Tigger trotted behind, closely following Frank. He stopped, reached down, scratched the cat's head one last time before the cat turned, and ran toward his tree house.

Dennis put his tablet back into his pocket. "You know you didn't make any points with my mother. A long time ago, Tigger used to be her best buddy. She may have apologized, but she's still really pissed at you."

"I know, Dennis. There was nothing I could do. You know the saying about cats. They don't live with you; you live with them. They pick their master and their enemies. Tigger was just checking out a new source of head scratching and petting. Patches was that way. Right now, I'm more interested in what Medusa found out."

The two were quiet during the rest of the trip to the basement. Medusa sat idle, and everything on the table was exactly where it was when they left. Dennis scrolled down the list of items scanned and their results. The list was huge.

Dennis stepped back from Medusa. "Medusa, can you give a condensed report about your findings?"

The two waited for a couple of seconds before Medusa started. *"I first reviewed all the photos taken by the CSI team and found nothing that would help the investigation. Each of the other items inside the box was scanned for biological, chemical, and material clues to a possible solution. Again, the results were negative. The last scan was of all data records in the box and in the pictures. Only two items produced possible leads. The arrangement of the objects on the coffee table may be connected to a missing page in a Consumer's Digest magazine. My assumption is that the intruders searched the coffee table and removed one page from the magazine. They were interrupted by Mrs. Narland, and the person or persons shot her point blank. This completes my report."*

Frank looked at the magazine on the table, and picked it up. He started to page through the magazine, but was stopped by Medusa.

"Detective, go to page 66."

Frank looked at Medusa and then back to the magazine. He turned to page 66 and pulled the pages apart. He saw a small strip of a serrated edge in the binder of the book. He reached into his pocket and took out a magnifier. Scanning the center binding, he confirmed what Medusa had found. Page sixty-seven followed page sixty-six. The insert had to be some kind of ad that is printed on heavy paper so that when you open the book, it automatically goes to that page. "Okay, Medusa. What was between these two pages?"

"There was a contest run by the magazine. The page was a renewal page inserted in every issue of the magazine. This month was special because anyone who renewed using the missing forms was eligible for a million-dollar cash prize drawing."

Frank set the magazine down and picked up the *Consumer's Digest.* "I don't understand. Aren't those prizes connected to the subscription label on the front of the magazine? The organizers already know ahead of time who's won."

A couple of seconds processing the new data and Medusa continued. "*That's true with most of the contests in subscription magazines, but in this case, it was a blind contest. No one except the computer programmer knew anything about the winner. The winning prize number was encrypted by the programmer and stored in a company safe. The programmer didn't know who the winner was, only that it was encrypted, and where it was stored.*"

Frank set the *Consumer's Digest* down, and looked at some of the other magazines. "Did you scan to see if anyone won the million dollars?"

"*A Claudia Stedmont in Florida was the winner.*"

"Okay, I don't see the connection. If no one knew who the winner was, why did the killer take the page out of Mrs. Narland's copy of the magazine? If the winning number was in her copy, how did someone in Florida get the number? Is there any connection between Mrs. Narland and anyone at the company?"

Dennis felt left out of the conversation between Medusa and Frank, and finally broke into the conversation. "Medusa, can you tell us who the programmer was and does he still work for the company?"

"*Bill Greene, and he still works for the prize company who ran the contest. His bank accounts haven't seen a notable change, and he has no connection with Claudia Stedmont. I'm making a deeper search of the two to see if there's any remote connection.*"

Dennis sat down in his chair. "We can't win them all, Frank. I know you thought we might be on the right track with the contest, but it appears that's not the case."

Frank stood with a blank stare on his face. Something wasn't right. "Medusa, is Claudia Stedmont her real name?"

A few more seconds went by. Several lights on Medusa indicated that some intense processing was going on. "*Stedmont* is her husband's last name. Her maiden name was Claudia Denson."

Frank smiled. "Okay, now go back to high school records. Does...

This time Medusa was faster. "*They went to high school together. I checked her phone records. She made several calls to the Seattle area. Most were to phone booths near Bill Greene's house. She has booked a flight to Seattle for next week. It matches up with a class reunion.*"

Frank sat down in a chair next to Dennis's desk. "If these two did it, they're very clever. They must have put the money in some offshore account, and are waiting it out. My guess is that Claudia's trip here next week is to pick up her accomplice, and then they'll leave the country."

Medusa confirmed Frank's theory with some new information. "*It appears that Greene is leaving on a scheduled vacation next week. He indicates that his destination is Australia. I checked flight records and Claudia also bought a ticket the day before Greene. It appears the two will be meeting there and recovering the money from an unknown bank account.*"

Dennis plugged a thumb drive into the side of Medusa and transferred the case to the drive. "I don't see any way we can get them. If Greene was the killer, he must have worn gloves and a head mask to keep from leaving DNA. If he left any DNA, the CSI team never picked it up. Going back to the murder scene won't help. Records indicate that an aunt of the murder victim cleaned out the house and sold it to someone else. A remodel is already in progress."

Frank looked at the call log that Medusa printed out. "What if we sent an email to Greene from Claudia that would force him to check on the money?"

Dennis put the thumb drive in an evidence cabinet they had set up. "I'm not sure what you would say in the message, and there's always a chance that Greene would call her to confirm."

As Frank started to put the evidence back in the box, he laid out the plan.

"First, the email would indicate that Claudia is pissed that Greene had turned her in. She would indicate that she'd found a way to transfer the stolen money to a different location. The wording would be vague enough to cover real cash or a bank account. She would indicate that she would tell the police that she was forced to do what Greene wanted, or he'd have an accomplice in Florida kill her.

"Medusa could then go into Claudia's email account and terminate the account along with her phone service. If Greene tried to contact her at work, Medusa would break the connection. This should make him very nervous. He'd start to wonder if the money was really safe. Medusa could monitor all communications, and you and I would watch Greene on a stakeout. Either way, we should be able to find out where the money went, and what access codes were necessary to hand over the case to the captain."

Dennis closed the data log on Medusa. "Is that legal?"

"It's not illegal to send an email. Besides, once we have the account information, we can have Medusa send a virus to wipe out his emails for the day."

Dennis was still uncertain about how this was going to work. "What about Carr? He could be following us to the stakeout. What's to stop him from going after us while we watch Greene?"

"Look Dennis, there's always a risk when you are a police detective. We constantly have to keep an eye out for someone watching us. I'm not going to hide in your house just because someone has threatened to kill me."

Chapter 16

The email had been sent, but now they would have to wait for Greene's reaction. It was a little past 9 a.m. and there was still no action. They'd been sitting in Frank's car for the last couple of hours a block down from Greene's house. Dennis had turned on Medusa in the lab and was in direct contact. Medusa was monitoring Greene's phone, his email, and any access to his laptop. Frank had turned on the CD player in his car, and was listening to an oldies but goodies CD.

Simultaneously, Frank's phone and Dennis's iPad started to ring with incoming messages. Dennis turned his iPad sound off and started to read the message from Medusa while he partially listened to Frank's phone call. The expression on Frank's face was pure despair. From what Dennis could discern, the caller had to be his daughter.

"Are you sure? ...When did it happen? ...What did the message say? ...Are you okay? ...I'll call the captain to make sure someone from the department remains near you. ...I know, baby. I'm so sorry. ...No, we left the house a couple of hours ago. We're on a stakeout. You be careful. I'm afraid you're on his list. I'll talk to you tonight. I love you."

Dennis looked up from his iPad. Medusa reported that nothing had happened yet. "Is something wrong, Frank? You're as white as a ghost."

"That was Debra. Her boss, Pamela Tornence, never showed up for work this morning, and she had several critical meetings today. They sent a couple of detectives to her house and found her in her bathtub fully clothed. She'd been shot eight times. The police team said none of the neighbors heard the shots, and never saw anyone enter the house. The security camera in the back of the building didn't showed any entry from the back either. The killer had to gain access from the roof. The building next door is close enough for someone to jump from one rooftop to the next.

"The preliminary report indicates that the entrance wounds points to two guns. A message was pinned to her blouse. It read; *Your turn is coming soon, Frank. I like your guns. They're great for killing your friends and associates. I'm saving the Colt to kill you.*

"The coroner places her death around midnight. She normally comes to work at 6:30 a.m. When she didn't show up by 7:30 for the first meeting, someone called the police. The state's attorney has appointed Debra as temporary D.A. until things get sorted out, which makes her a prime target. She's not going to come tonight as she needs time to deal with things. She wanted to know if we can do the dinner tomorrow night?"

"That's not a problem, Frank. I'm sorry about her boss. This is getting scary. I'm a little concerned about who's next, and maybe we shouldn't pursue any more cold cases until Carr is found and put away."

Frank took one last look at his phone, and put it back on vibrate. "If we don't see any action soon, we need to turn what we have over to the captain."

Dennis checked his iPad one more time and found nothing new. "I agree. I think we need to quit right now. Your family is more important than solving cold cases. I'll check one more time when we get home, and tomorrow you can give the captain everything we have so far. I can keep Medusa monitoring all the traffic cameras in this area. If Greene tries to make a move, we'll know about it. That's the best we can do for now."

"Concentrating on the cold cases and Carr at the same time is making us weak," said Frank. "We need to focus on how to stop Carr. We must figure out where Carr is going to hit next, get off the defensive, and try some offensive tactics."

Frank turned the key in the ignition, and the two rushed back to the Alexander estate. The gate opened right away, but when Dennis unlocked the front door, the alarm started blinking.

He entered the code and rushed into a TV room situated to the living room. Sandra was watching the *Breaking News* report on the killing of the D.A. Dennis sat next to his mother and Frank on the nearby love seat. No one said anything as the news story was unfolding. The newscaster had very little information other than the D.A had been murdered. An update was going to be made at the top of the hour.

As the station went to an advertisement, Sandra turned to Dennis. "Did this Carr guy do this?"

Dennis looked at Frank for help and then back to his mother. Frank indicated he was on his own right now. "Yes, it was Carr. He left a message for Frank indicating that his turn was coming. The D.A. was his daughter, Debra's boss. We're not sure who's next on Carr's list, but the police are working on it."

Sandra stood up, grabbed the remote, and turned the TV off. "I knew this was going to happen. You invite this man into my house without my permission, and now a killer with a real hard-on for Detective Ridge is coming after us."

"Mom, I've never heard you talk crude like that before."

"It got the point across, didn't it?"

"Yes, you made your point. If Frank is in danger, so are we. I'm sorry about that, but we can't turn back the clock. We have to live with the cards we've been dealt."

Dennis was about to add more when a message came onto his iPad. Greene had left his apartment. A traffic camera at a corner of the street picked up Greene's car. Dennis turned the iPad so Frank could see the results.

Frank wanted to go see where Greene was headed, but didn't want to leave the present conversation unfinished. "I'm sorry all this came down on you and Dennis, but I can't control Carr. I think the best solution is for me to check into a hotel. It will take Carr's focus away from this place and put it back on me. I can take care of myself."

Before Dennis could respond, his mother picked up the pace. "Sounds like a good plan to me, Detective. For once, I agree with you. It was never a good idea for you to stay with us in the first place."

Dennis looked at the two. Both were stubborn enough that when put together were unstoppable. "Frank, if that's what you want, okay, but I don't agree. We need to go check Medusa first, and then maybe we can figure out what to do about Carr."

Frank nodded, and the two headed for the elevator leaving Dr. Alexander glaring at them.

As they got in the elevator Frank broke the silence. "She hates my guts, doesn't she?"

"Pretty much."

"Is there no way to fix it?"

"It would take more than a rocket scientist to figure it out, and I'm pretty much a rocket scientist. I don't know what you're going to do. Sorry, Frank, I thought this was going to work out, but I think I made things worse."

"Don't beat yourself up. I don't blame you or your mom. She has scars that don't heal easily. We just opened them back up."

"You mean my dad's murder?"

Frank smiled and said, "I guess, you really are a rocket scientist."

The elevator door opened, and the two could see several lights on Medusa blinking. Two computer monitors were showing traffic camera images. Dennis pulled up a chair for Frank and sat down at the chair already in front of the computer monitors.

"Medusa, please bring us up to date."

"*Mr. Greene left his apartment thirty-seven minutes ago and drove six blocks to a local Internet café. I hacked into the system at the café and monitored what he was doing. He logged onto a bank in Australia using a password and checked his account, which had just fewer than one million dollars. From the expression on the traffic camera, he was happy when he realized that the money was safe. Then his expression turned to anger as he turned his computer off. He tried to make a call to Claudia, but I blocked the call. He headed toward Claudia's work and parked outside the building. He talked to someone inside the lobby and then came back outside. A few minutes later, Claudia came out and the two had what appeared to be a big argument. Eventually, Claudia was pushed out of the car, and Greene drove back to his apartment. A few minutes later, I detected a change in his airline ticket to this afternoon instead of next week. That ends my report so far."*

Frank grinned, and turned to Dennis.

"From what I can tell, Claudia is going to roll over on Greene once we tell her we have everything we need to convict them both. Divide and conquer is always the best way to go with these types. Although there's a problem because Greene can still access the money."

The screen showing traffic camera images changed to a bank routing screen.

"That's not a problem, Frank. Once Greene logged off, I logged on with his password, changed it, and transferred the money to a new account I set up in Claudia's name."

Frank reached over and patted Medusa on the top. "You know, I'm really getting to like you. I promise that there'll be no more snake-head comments."

He looked over to Dennis, and continued. "When Greene gets to Australia, he'll find out that the account has changed. If he's good, he might be able to detect that the money was transferred to Claudia's account. When he can't reach her, he'll fly back right into the arms of the Seattle Police Department. All I have to do now is give this information to the captain. I probably won't give him all of it, but just what they need to nab the two. I'm going to pack a few things and head downtown. You need to lock this house down tight. Until Carr is caught, he could come after you and your mother. I don't want that on my head. Are we clear, Dennis?"

Dennis pressed a transfer button and sent the data to his iPad and to Frank's phone.

"I understand, Frank. However, I still think we can work it out so that you can stay in the apartment. We just pushed my mother too much, and extremely fast. She didn't have time to adjust. I'll talk to her, and see if she'll reconsider."

"No, if she wants to offer me the apartment on her terms, then I will reconsider, but that's between us. If she wants to charge me more for the apartment, then so be it. I just don't want her to be forced into letting me rent the apartment. I hope that's crystal clear. I don't want any interference; just let nature takes its course."

"So, what about Debra and tomorrow night's dinner?"

Frank looked down at his phone and saw a text message from Medusa. He looked back to Dennis, who was waiting for an answer. "I'll call her as soon as I see the captain. Then I'll call you back and let you know about the new plan."

Frank grabbed a small suitcase and threw in enough to last three days. He latched it shut and left Dennis to make some adjustments with Medusa. In less than a minute, Frank was out the front door, and racing down Main Street toward his old department.

Debra Ridge's life had just become more chaotic. In fact, it was a total mess. She never agreed with how the D.A. ran the department, but she sure didn't wish her dead. Her appointment as the temporary D.A. really didn't change her responsibilities, but rather just added a few unsavory ones. In addition to managing her own assistants, she now had three assistants to the D.A. asking her what to do.

The first thing on her agenda was to set aside all court dates until she could get everything under control. This meant she would have to make a trip to the courthouse and personally visit each judge. Her request would clog up the judicial system for weeks.

In addition to all her problems, her father was in Jesse Carr's gun site. She really hoped that he was being careful. She always liked to think of him as a super cop, but even super cops die when they get careless. She also wasn't thrilled with Dr. Dennis Andrews as her dad's new partner. She knew her dad would keep one eye on Dennis and the other looking out for Carr. She wished he had a partner who would be better at keeping her dad safe.

She was in the process of packing up all the cases to be heard in the next two days when her assistant, Danny Melcan came in.

"There's a cop down in the lobby waiting to take you to the courthouse. I checked his badge, and his orders were signed by the police chief. He said to take your time, and that he'd be with you the rest of the day."

Debra packed the remaining files in her briefcase. It had to weigh thirty pounds. She looked around the office one last time, then to Danny.

"Go down and tell him that I'll be there in twenty minutes. I have to check scheduling to see if there's anything I missed."

She pulled out her phone and sent a text message to Frank indicating that her police escort had arrived, and she'd be in the court building most of the day redoing schedules. All eyes were on her as she walked toward the elevators. Danny gave her thumbs up, and she really hoped it was going to be that easy.

Chapter 17

Captain Carson was having one of the busiest days in his life. The chief had called down to make sure that all vacations and time off was canceled until Carr was caught. He wanted around-the-clock protection for the newly appointed D.A. right away.

The last thing he needed was for Frank Ridge to walk into his office. "Look, Frank, I don't know why you're here, but Carr is out gunning for you. That man's a nut job, and you're supposed to be hiding, so there better be a good reason why you're here."

"It's nice to see you too, Captain. I just wanted to check and make sure that Debra was protected."

"Don't worry, Frank. I already sent a couple of guys down to escort her the rest of the day."

"Are these guys good?"

"Not as good as you, Frank, but they'll do a good job. Debra called and said she was going down to the courthouse to meet with the judges to put everything on hold until her office could regroup. Don't worry, we have it covered."

"I'm not too sure about that, because Carr keeps getting by us somehow. His picture is plastered all over the news, and yet no one has seen him. I'm not sure how that's possible."

He grabbed a folder and said, "The other reason I came down here involves the cold case we're working on. We found out who killed Nancy Limen and why. Don't even ask how we got all this stuff. Some day after you retire I'll tell you, but for now, you'll just have to trust me."

Frank laid out the short version. "Bill Greene, a programmer for a consumer magazine, discovered what address the winning number to a million-dollar contest was sent. He broke into the house and found Judy Narland had come home early. He became impatient, killed Narland, and carefully tore out the winning number from the magazine. He then contacted an old girlfriend in Florida and sent her the number. A couple of weeks later, she collected the money and put it into a special bank account set up by Greene. He then transferred the money to a new account in Australia. The two made arrangements to leave the U.S. and settle down in Australia together and live on the one million dollars."

The captain leaned back on his chair. "Wow. In the middle of all this Jesse Carr mess, you tell me you've solved another cold case. What the hell is going on, Frank? You're good, but not that good. Three for three isn't possible. I'm sure as hell not going to ask you how you did all this because I want to keep my job. Just send me enough data to get these two and not break any laws. I'll figure out how to handle it from there. You need to concentrate on keeping yourself and Debra safe. No more cold cases, and if I catch you working on them, I'll suspend you, Frank. Now get the hell out of here, and be safe."

"Yes, Sir."

Frank slowly walked back to his car. The captain was under a lot of pressure from his bosses. They hated Frank Ridge and now his daughter had taken over as acting D.A. That must have really stuck in their craw. The captain was right about one thing though. Solving three cold cases in a row was going to send up a red flag. It was time to shut the Medusa project down for a while, and Dennis wasn't going to be happy. He was becoming addicted to solving cold cases. What he didn't realize was there's a never-ending supply of them. New ones will keep showing up just as old ones are solved.

A car beeped. Frank realized he was sitting at a green light and had lost focus. He stepped on the accelerator and headed toward a couple of large hotels downtown. He'd randomly would pick one he felt had the best security, and then call the captain and disclose its location.

As he slowed, his phone rang and vibrated. He picked it up. It was a text message that read. *Look at the video*. He pulled over to the curb and stopped. He clicked on the small

117

video icon and immediately saw Debra sitting in a chair, tied up with a gag over her mouth. The camera panned to the left and next to her sat Dennis and his mother, also tied to chairs. He noticed that Dennis had blood running down his shirt. The video then panned back to Debra and stopped. A few moments later, his phone rang. The display said it was from an unknown caller, but Frank knew exactly who it was.

"Hi, Frank. Did you like my video?"

"You bastard."

"Come on, Frank. We're best buddies. We have a connection. Here's the deal. I know how the police department works. If I hear a siren or car doors slamming, I'll shoot one of these nice people. I have nothing to lose Frank, so killing one of them is going to be easy and actually fun. You should keep in mind that I've already killed four people just trying to get to you."

"Four?"

"Oh, you may not have heard, or maybe they haven't been found yet. Those two cops the department sent down to escort Debra, well, they ain't no more." He gave a sadistic laugh. "They never knew what hit 'em. They thought I was just another cop from a different precinct. Even your pretty daughter never caught on. It makes sense that if a cop comes to pick her up in a black-and-white, why not trust him?

"Now I really don't know these other two well, but I figured they're important to you too. I've seen the fellow riding around with you, and you've been spending time at their house lately. That's probably because yours burned down huh, Frank? The old lady was just in the way, but it makes my game a little more interesting. If you want to save them, Frank, go to the phone booth at Market and Seventh. When the phone rings, pick it up, count to five, and hang it up. Catch the bus marked Route 7 and get off at 28th Street. Wait for the phone in the booth to ring there. I'll only call that phone once. If you don't answer, one of them will die. It's that easy."

Carr continued confidently, "You can call your captain if you want, but keep in mind that I have someone in the department who'll call me as soon as you do. You know what will happen then, don't you, Frank? Well, here's your chance to be a hero. On your mark, get set, go."

The line went dead before Frank could respond. He was sure that Carr was bluffing about having someone on the inside, but what if he wasn't lying? He wasn't about to take a chance, but he knew he should call somebody. He began remembering all those TV cop shows where the main character always does the wrong thing. He never calls for help and tries to rescue the kidnapped person alone. It was stupid, so why was he thinking about doing the same thing?

He had plenty of time to get to the first phone booth, so now was the time to use some of that new technology he learned. He selected the captain's phone number and began to type a text message:

Captain, you may have a mole working with Carr in your dept. Carr has Debra. He'll kill her if I call you. Don't tell anyone unless u trust them. Put GPS trace on my phone. I'll leave it on and stall as long as I can.

Frank arrived at the booth with five minutes to spare. As he walked over to the booth, a woman with several shopping bags raced him to the phone. He put his hand in front of her and held out his badge. She objected at first, but finally relented. The phone rang. He picked it up for five seconds, and then hung up. Three minutes later bus #7 pulled up to the curb. He got on, showed the driver his badge, and sat down. He prayed that the captain would do the right thing, because Debra's life depended on it. Frank got off the bus at 28th Street as directed and waited for the next call.

Captain Carson had just hung up the phone from the chief when he saw he had a new text message. He read it quickly, started to look up but decided to read some of the paperwork on his desk as a cover. He gathered some random paperwork into a folder and told his assistant that the chief wanted to meet with him right away. If there was a mole in the department, the slightest hint that Frank had called might kill Debra. He kept it business as usual.

Three floors up, he headed for the chief's secretary. She was about to stop him, but he told her that the chief had called him about a new strike that was about to hit the department. He went into the chief's office and closed the door.

Sixty-five-year-old Chief Norman Kinsey worked his way up through the ranks as a beat cop, detective, captain of the detectives, and most recently, chief of the division. He was as tough as nails when it came to police business, but a push over when it came to his grandchildren. He'd planned to retire at the end of this year, but this Carr thing may force him out early. The news media was always looking for a scapegoat to blame, and this month it seemed to be him.

"Captain, what can I do for you?"

The captain held out his phone with Frank's text message and then held his finger up to his lips. "I wanted to talk with you about the strike that might happen next month."

Dennis couldn't believe how stupid he'd been. Carr had called him saying that he had Debra and Frank captive and would trade them for one million dollars each. All Dennis had to do was bring his laptop and transfer the cash to Carr's account. Once that was done, he would lock them up and let the police find them after Carr left the country. Carr also stated that he had a mole in the police department and that if any calls were made about the kidnapping, the two would be dead.

Dennis talked it over with his mother, and to his surprise, she agreed to pay the ransom, but with one condition. She wanted to come along to make sure the tradeoff really happened. Dennis told her that there was a good chance that Carr would shoot all of them and just take the money. He suggested that they call the captain because he trusted him, but she disagreed. He gave in because he realized arguing with her would just be a waste of time.

When they arrived at the warehouse, they found Debra tied up in the middle of a large storage room. As they started to untie her, Carr came out of a small room, and pistol-whipped Dennis. He had a large gash across his face, a broken nose, and swelling in his left cheek. Sandra ran to help her son, but Carr insisted that he do it on his own. Dennis struggled, but eventually could sit in one of the chairs. Carr ordered Sandra to tie him up, and demanded she sit down and then Carr tied her up too. He then used his phone to videotape the three, and sent it to Frank.

Carr's last instructions for Frank told him to set the phone down with the line open. That way, he could be sure that he didn't make any other calls. He was instructed to walk down to 37th Street, make a left, and enter a warehouse with the number 1173 over the door. Frank knew this was a bad idea, but had no other choice. He hoped that Carr's ego would help stall things. He expected that Carr would expound on how much better he was than Frank, and how he'd outsmarted the whole police force.

Hopefully that would play in Frank's favor. He took out a piece of paper and wrote the address of Carr's final instruction. He put the paper under the phone and started running toward his daughter.

Ten minutes later, he arrived at the 1173 door in a very sketchy neighborhood. He took out his gun and set it just inside the door. He knew that Carr would immediately take it once they made contact. Carr had all the trump cards at this point, so Frank needed a couple of diversions. He took off his shirt, pants, shoes and socks, stripping down to just his underwear. It was the last thing Frank wanted to do, but he was desperate. He reached into his pocket for all the loose change and found three quarters, four dimes and three pennies. He ignored the quarters, but slipped each dime and penny between two fingers and held his fingers tight together.

The building hadn't been occupied for years. The dust was thick and Frank could see several sets of footprints across the floor. He followed them down a long hallway toward the main storage area. As he approached the end of the hallway, he could hear Carr in the distance. His first view into the room showed Dennis in a chair, next to Dr. Alexander. Carr held a gun against Debra's head. She had a gash running across her forehead and was almost unconscious. Anger sped through every pore in Frank's body, but he took a deep breath and stepped into view.

"Frank, Frank, Frank. You are so predictable. I was going to tell you to strip down, but you just saved me the time. Where's your service revolver, Frank?"

"I left it in the car. I didn't want to give you another one for your collection."

"That's funny, Frank. I really like your guns because you take such good care of them. It makes them so easy to kill with."

Frank looked beyond Carr to see his .38 and Colt were sitting on a table just beyond Dennis.

"Frank, you haven't said anything about my new look? Did you even recognize me?"

"Carr, your evil soul is impossible to miss."

"So, Frank, who do you want me to kill first?"

Frank was getting frantic. He was running out of time and had no prospects for help. He glanced at Sandra and saw her eyes were darting toward Dennis. Then he saw the opening he needed. Whoever tied Dennis up did a lousy job. His hands were free, and the rope was almost on the floor behind him. He sent a visual message to Dennis and then worked on distracting Carr.

"You know Carr; you're no different than any other criminal. You talk about how great you are, and your ego makes you lose all track of time. How do you focus your thoughts with your mouth continually flapping? Leave these folks alone. I'm an easy target, Carr. Take your best shot."

Carr's face turned red with anger. He wasn't done with Frank.

"Frank, you know what your problem..."

As Carr was mid-sentence, Frank released his fingers and the coins hitting the floor were enough to distract Carr. In that split second, all hell broke loose. Carr pushed Debra and her chair to the floor, so he had a clear shot of Frank.

The distraction gave Dennis enough time to grab the Colt. Carr heard the sound of the gun dragging across the table and turned back toward Dennis. Dennis didn't hesitate and fired one shot. Carr dropped to the floor with a single bullet hole in his forehead.

Frank rushed over to Carr and kicked his gun away. He winced with pain as he forgot he was barefoot. He reached down to check on Debra, but she was out cold. He reached down and undid the knot holding her to the chair. He looked over to Dennis, who was already working his way to Debra, waving the Colt.

"Dennis, give me the Colt."

Dennis handed it over to Frank, who then turned and fired another shot into the ceiling.

He set the Colt down, picked up Debra, and set her up against a wall. Her breathing was shallow. He needed to call an ambulance, but had no phone. He remembered Carr had one, so he searched his body and found the phone. As he called for an ambulance and the captain, Dennis came over and sat down next to Debra. Frank looked and saw that Dennis should be in shock, but was more worried about Debra. Frank walked next to Dr. Alexander and untied her ropes. She got up, rubbed her wrists, and walked over to Dennis. Sirens could be heard in the distance, so Frank realized he only had minutes before everything would be set in stone.

"You both need to listen to what I am saying. I killed Carr. No one will have a problem with that, they'll have a problem if they find out Dennis made the shot. We really don't want the detectives looking into the Andrews background. Does everyone agree?"

The two nodded in unison. Dennis looked at Frank's bare feet.

"You might think about getting dressed before anyone else arrives."

Frank looked at Dr. Alexander with a sheepish grin, and then ran back to where he had ditched his clothes. As he returned fully clothed, the sirens were approaching. Debra was now lying in Dennis's lap, and he was tending to her head wound.

Dennis looked up as Frank approached. "Frank, what was the deal with ditching your clothes?"

"Hey, I was winging it. I needed as many distractions as possible, so we might stand a chance. He was expecting me to come fully clothed, so I was hoping it would catch him off guard. Once he saw I had nothing to hide, he had to figure out where the sound came when I dropped the dimes and pennies. That gave us the needed distraction, and I was counting on you to throw me the gun. I never expected you to shoot him. Are you handling that all right? Very few civilians would've done what you did. Just remember, I shot him. That second shot put the necessary gun residue on my hand and arm to confirm that I fired the gun. Do you understand?"

Dennis nodded, but his mother said nothing. She was the one in shock. Thirty seconds later, a SWAT team entered the building and approached Frank. One team member checked Carr, while another looked after Debra. Another collected all the weapons and bagged them for evidence. Finally, the ambulance arrived and two EMTs headed straight for Debra. As she was placed upon a stretcher, the captain came into the room and looked down at Carr.

"Now there's my wish granted." He looked up at Frank and started to shake his hand, and then realized Frank was part of a crime scene. He looked over at Debra, and one of the EMTs gave him the thumbs up.

The captain turned back to Frank. "I'm sorry, Frank, but you can't go to the hospital with Debra. She'll be all right and needs some rest anyway. Carr shot the two officers who were supposed to escort Debra, and the detectives here want to wrap this up fast. Right now, we need you to close the lid on this case."

They looked over to Dennis and Dr. Alexander, who were waiting their turn for the EMTs attention. Dennis had his arm around his mother as she was still in shock. One of the EMTs came over, checked her vitals, and put a couple of loose dressings on Dennis's wounds. The EMTs then loaded all three into the ambulance, and the CSI team began processing the crime scene.

A CSI team member came over to Frank and handed him a new set of clothes so that they could process his. He undressed again, and put everything into the evidence bag. Then he realized there would be no evidence on his clothes. He explained to them that he had ditched his clothes right down to his underwear.

Frank waited until he, and the captain were alone. "Captain, Dennis and his mother had nothing to do with this case. Carr grabbed them because they knew Debra, and he wanted as much insurance and collateral damage as possible. I can fill the detectives in on everything that happened."

The captain looked over to the detectives and then back to Frank. "You have to go with the detectives, so they can debrief you, and quickly clear this up. The mayor has been on my ass all day, and I want to go home, ulcer free. Once you're done with them, go see Debra. I'll call the detectives and fill them in on Dennis and his mother. Come in tomorrow and we can sort the rest of this mess out."

Chapter 18

It was late afternoon before Frank finished his debriefing. He'd been careful to stick with the truth as much as possible. The only difference in his story was who actually shot Carr. He hoped Dennis, and his mother would stick with the story too. When he reached the hospital, Dennis and his mother had been sent home, but Debra had been kept overnight.

When Frank reached her room, he found Officer Tim Carson, the captain's son, stationed outside. Frank held out his badge and Tim looked at it very closely. As they shook hands, he said, "I'm sure glad your dad put his best man on duty protecting my daughter."

Frank entered the room and found Debra carefully drinking water through a straw. She stopped and looked up. "Hi, Dad. Are you okay?"

"The question is how are YOU doing? That was a pretty nasty hit you took from Carr."

"I'm fine, Dad. It just looks worse than it really is. How are Dennis and his mother?"

"They're fine and have already gone home."

"Sorry I got duped by Carr. I should have been more cautious, but he looked and acted like a cop. His badge looked real, and his face wasn't like his old self."

"He had plastic surgery, so don't beat yourself up about it. It just happened, and it worked out in the end."

Debra set the cup of ice water down. "What happened? The last thing I remembered was falling to the ground in that chair. The captain came by earlier and told me that you shot Carr. How is that possible? You obviously didn't have a gun. I don't even want to know why you were in your underwear. The captain told me that Dennis threw the gun to you, but I think you were too far away. Something doesn't smell right. So, what gives?"

"Does it really matter? Carr's dead, and you're alive. That's all that matters to me."

"But what really happened <u>does</u> matter to me. Carr could've killed us all he was so crazy. Another thing I don't understand is why Carr brought Dennis and his mother into this?"

"Carr saw Dennis and me together, and followed us to the Andrew's house. Carr wanted to hurt everyone I was associated with. He was as crazy as anyone could get. His focus on me was his undoing. Dennis and his mother are fine, and you'll get better in time. That's all that matters right now."

"Okay, I'll let it go for now, but I want to talk more about it later. I do have another question. How were you ever able to work with Dennis? He seems like such a mama's boy."

"Hold it right there. You don't know anything about either one of them. It may seem like he's a mama's boy, but that's far from the truth. Dennis is a nice guy, and a rocket scientist wrapped up into one. Just because he lives with his mother doesn't make him a mama's boy. She's never there, so he pretty much lives alone except for the housekeeper. After Carr was shot, the first thing Dennis did was rush to see if you were all right. He held you in his arms until the EMTs arrived. He never once asked how his mother was handling things. Having someone killed right in front of you put both of them into somewhat of a trance. If you only knew everything, you'd never have said that."

"Wow, I didn't realize. I trust your judgment, but what about his mother? She appears to hate your guts. I think she would have rather seen you dead on the floor."

"Actually, she hates me and anyone having to do with the police force. Trust me when I tell you she may have a good reason. I don't hold it against her. I actually understand her resentment. Just give both the benefit of the doubt. Now, let's talk about something else. Are you going to be the D.A. on a permanent basis, or do they conduct a special election?"

Debra hesitated for a second. She had been mulling it over in her mind for the last few hours. The idea of being the D.A. excited her and yet scared her at the same time. "The mayor called me an hour ago. A special election is too cost prohibitive when a normal election is just right around the corner. He's pushing me to run for D.A. in the next election. I think his motive is purely political. He realizes that I'm in the public eye right now, and everyone is on my side. He just wants to ride on my coattails and have me indebted to him at the same time. The truth is I don't care about his motives. I want the job because that's what I really want to do, at least for right now. In the future, I may regret it."

"Fair enough, but there's one other thing that I need to talk to you about, but now is not the time. I need to take care of a couple of things first. The hospital said you need to stay overnight, but they'll release you tomorrow afternoon. I'll come by and take you home to your apartment, and then we can talk some more."

"You sound very mysterious. What's going on?"

"Look, Honey, I have to be honest. I never like keeping secrets from you, but I have, and that's not right. I haven't told you everything, but I will tomorrow. Right now, I have to wrap up some loose ends."

Frank leaned over and kissed Debra on the cheek. She wrapped her arms around him. "I love you very much, Dad. After a couple of days rest, I'll be back as the new D.A. Go now and do what you have to do."

"I love you too," Frank said as he made his exit from the room. Once in the hall, he shook the officer's hand and said, "Watch out for her."

The officer nodded agreement, and Frank headed toward the parking lot. When he reached his car, he pulled out his phone and called Dennis. Mrs. Henson, the housekeeper answered the phone. Frank asked to talk to Dennis, but was told that Dennis and his mother weren't taking any calls. He asked if she would kindly tell them that he was stopping by in the early afternoon to pick up his things, and he would like to talk to them for a few minutes. Mrs. Henson indicated they may not want to talk to him, but she would try. Frank thanked her and ended the call.

His next destination was a hotel downtown near the precinct. He stopped by and picked up a few food items and the afternoon newspaper. His picture was on the front page along with Debra and Carr. Dennis and his mother were mentioned but there were no pictures, so that was good news. He asked about a room at the top of the hotel, as he wanted to look out at the city at night. It was so beautiful, and he needed the distraction. He had told Debra that it was all right that Dr. Alexander hated him, but deep down, it really bothered him. He wasn't the evil man the doctor portrayed him to be, but he would have to address that issue later. Right now, he had to plan for the big day tomorrow.

Chapter 19

It was just past 9:00 a.m., and Captain Carson was still dealing with the fallout from the shooting when Frank Ridge walked into his office wearing a Hawaiian sport shirt. Frank closed the door as the detectives' eyes in the next room followed him across the room. Carson closed the folder he had been working on.

"Okay, Frank. What's going on? I've never seen you in that shirt before."

"This isn't going to be easy, Captain, but here it is." Frank pulled out a folder from under his arm, opened it, and removed a stapled group of papers. "I'm taking an early retirement, starting today. Don't try to talk me out of it as I've gone over it repeatedly. It's the right thing for me to do."

The captain was in shock. This wasn't what he had expected. "Is this all because of Carr?"

"Yes and no. I've been thinking about it for some time, and Carr just pushed me over the edge. I love working as a detective in this department, but I really don't fit in anymore. It's not anyone's fault. It just happened, but I'm fine with the decision. I know your bosses will love it, so you'll benefit from my early out."

Carson looked at the papers. Everything had been filled out and signed. Frank was serious. "Okay, Frank I think I understand. What the hell are you going to do? I can't picture you tying fishing flies or collecting stamps."

"Actually, Captain, I do have something else in mind. I want to go the "Rockford" or "Magnum Private Investigator" route. I still want to be a detective, just not a public one."

"Come on, do you really think you can make that change? It takes some PIs years to build up a reputation. You're starting from scratch. If you were younger, I might agree, but now, Frank?"

"The truth is that over the years, I've had offers to work as a consultant for several large corporations that I encountered while investigating robbery cases. Some of those offers were in the six figures, and that was for just a six-month project. I always politely turned them down and recommended a couple of PIs I know, but now I'm going back and refresh some of those contacts."

"Wow. I'd have never in a million years thought of you as a private dick. I can't talk you out of it, can I?"

"Nope. I've already made up my mind."

"Is there anything I can do to help?"

"Actually, there's one thing I need."

Frank leaned over and whispered his request in the captain's ear.

Carson leaned back in his chair. "You're kidding, right? You really want me to do this? It could get me in a lot of trouble. If it had been anyone else, I'd have told you no. Come back later this afternoon, and I'll have it ready. Are you sure you really want to do this? You can't come back once you go down that road. It sounds really crazy to me."

"Captain, you've been a great friend, and I really hate to ask, but there's no other way. Does this mean I can't come to your barbecues anymore?"

"You're always welcome in my house, Frank. Now get the hell out of here. We both have a lot of work to do today."

As Frank walked down the aisle between the detective's desks, a good feeling washed over him. It was as though a big rock had been lifted from his shoulders. He knew in that moment that he had made the right decision.

His next stop was HR where he would spend two hours processing out. He handed over his badge, guns, and all official items that he'd collected as a police detective. The only item listed to be returned to him later was his Colt firearm. As a retired cop, he could still go to the range and keep in practice. Getting a PI permit would be easy, and a gun permit should be even easier. Although his next stop was going to be the most difficult one of the day.

As he pulled up to the Alexander estate, he waited for the gate to open. For a second, he wasn't sure that it would, but then it slowly unlocked allowing his entry. He knew that Dr. Alexander hadn't pushed the button, and Dennis was now a 50/50 chance. No, it had to have been Mrs. Henson. He really liked her because she was so down to earth. Everything was cut and dried to her, right or wrong, with nothing left on the fence.

He parked his car next to Dennis's and waited at the front door. A minute passed before Mrs. Henson opened the door. "Frank, so nice to see you again. Dennis and his mother are waiting for you in the living room. She didn't want to see you, and I don't know about Dennis. I told them that the only way to move past this horrible experience was to see you today, and that seemed to do it."

"Thank you for that. I know how hard that was for you."

"Not really because I don't put up with any crap from either one of them."

Frank chuckled. She was something else. She led Frank into the living room where Dennis was staring up at the ceiling and his mother was reading a book. He took a seat on the couch opposite them.

"I'm really sorry to intrude, but I needed to pick up the rest of my belongings and talk about yesterday."

Dr. Sandra Alexander laid down her book. "Go pick up your things and never come back. You've done enough damage to our family. There's nothing more to say about the subject, other than leave Dennis alone."

Frank was so close to losing it. He knew this was going to be difficult. He looked directly at her as he stood up. "I don't give a rat's ass what you think about me or the police. The only thing I'm concerned about is my daughter, Debra. Your son saved her life and for that, I will always be indebted to Dennis.

So don't hand me any of this bullshit about it being my fault. It just happened. It's over, and thankfully, my daughter and all of us survived. Don't worry, I'll go get my things, and never come back to this house. Thank you for taking me in when I needed the help, even though you hated me. I'm ready to move on, and so should you."

Frank turned and started to head down the hall when he saw Mrs. Henson pointing to two boxes near the front door. Dr. Alexander had packed his stuff, which just made things easier. He picked up the two boxes and headed out the front door. No one made a move to follow him.

As Frank got into his car, it dawned on him that Dennis wasn't acting the way he had in the past. Either something had happened between him and his mother, or the reality of killing a man had finally sunk in. Frank was opting for the second reason, and hoped he could get past it.

After leaving the estate, he headed to the hospital to take Debra home. They drove to the local fast food restaurant and picked something up for them to eat. After a quick meal in her apartment, Frank got her comfortable and told her to rest for the afternoon. He said he'd be back later with dinner, and then they'd talk about everything. She nodded and waved good-bye.

He headed back to the captain's office. When the captain saw him, he merely pointed down to a box on the floor. Frank opened the door, picked up the box, and left without saying a word. If any questions were asked later, the captain wouldn't have to lie about helping Frank pick up the box. It was flimsy, but it would have to do.

Once Frank reached the parking lot, he opened the lid and looked through the top folder, and found the address he needed. Twenty minutes later, he was driving by the house. It had a For-Sale sign in the yard, which was a big break for Frank. He pulled out his phone and called the local realtor. She was more than happy to show Frank the house in a half hour. He walked around the yard as he waited. When the realtor drove up, Frank locked his car and walked over to her.

"I like the house a lot. I hope it's as nice on the inside as it is outside."

The realtor's eye lit up with the comment. "Oh, yes it is. No one has lived in it for a couple of years. Before that, there were a few renters, and one couple leased it for a couple of years. It just came on the market. The neighbors are pleasant, and it's very quiet. I shouldn't tell you this, but in all fairness, I feel it's necessary."

"What, the house is haunted?"

"Well, that's close. You need to look at this background report on the man who built this house. Look at the bottom of the page."

The realtor handed Frank the folder, he opened it, and quickly scanned down the page.

The realtor leaned on one foot and then the other in a nervous stance. "I'm telling you now because everyone eventually finds out, and it changes their minds. I hate doing the paperwork over and over."

"I have no problem with this report. I'm a retired detective, so I'm used to seeing all kinds of crazy stuff. This doesn't bother me at all."

"Really? Let's go see the inside of the house."

"Lead the way. Do you also handle leasing business properties?"

Four hours later, Frank was on his way to Debra's place with dinner. As soon as the door opened, she reached out with her arms, and Frank gave her a big hug. He closed the door and walked with her to her living room.

"So how are you doing, Honey?"

"I would feel better if I was back at work. I hate sitting around waiting while things are going crazy at the office. So what's with the wild shirt?"

134

Frank motioned for her to sit down on the couch. "I'll dish up some dinner for you, and you can eat it sitting on the couch. We've a lot to talk about, and you're not going to like some of it. You want me to get you a stiff drink before we start? You may need it."

"No, Dad. I'm fine. What is it?"

Frank dished two plates for them, came back, and sat in the chair facing Debra.

"I turned in my papers for early retirement today."

"What? Is this because of the Carr thing?"

"Maybe a little, but I've been considering it for some time. Now is just the right time. There's another reason, but before I tell you, I have a question."

"I don't think I'm going to like this am I, Dad?"

"No, but here goes. In a hypothetical situation where a detective lies about a shooting to protect someone else, what would the D.A.'s office do with that detective?"

Debra squirmed in her seat for a couple of seconds. She was trying to figure out where this was going. "Well, my initial reaction would be that the detective would be terminated from the department, and charges may be filed against the detective if the shooting was criminal."

"What if it wasn't criminal?"

"There would still be a termination. Where's this going? Are we talking about a detective you know or is it you?"

"What do you remember about Carr when I arrived at the warehouse?"

"He knocked me over and when I came to, the EMT was working on me. Carr was dead. Tell me. What's this all about? I'm getting nervous."

"One of the reasons I took an early retirement is that I didn't shoot Carr, and I lied to the detectives about it. Dennis shot Carr. There was no way for him to throw me the gun and for me to shoot Carr, so Dennis did it himself. The important thing is that someone shot him before he killed you. I was trying to protect Dennis and his mother, and not put your job in jeopardy. I was considering early retirement anyway, this just pushed up the schedule."

Debra got up from the couch. "I DO need a drink. What the hell were you thinking? Dennis shot Carr. Why would he do that?"

"To save you. He knew that I couldn't save you, so he did."

"Why not tell the truth? It was a self-defense."

"That's the rub. You know that Dennis and I have been working together on some special projects. Well, if his name was front and center in the headlines, there are people in the Federal Government that wouldn't be too happy. Think of him as being in the witness protection program. The law is the law unless it can harm the innocent. Then we have to bend the law. I don't like it any more than you do, but I had no choice. I had two minutes to make the decision, right or wrong. I made it, and I have to live with it. If you want to turn me in, I'll understand."

Debra opened a beer and took a long swig. "So why didn't Dennis or his mother tell the truth about the shooting?"

"Because they knew that putting Dennis front stage put them both in the gun sight of a bigger fish than Carr. They're both intelligent people and when they weighed the consequences, they had no qualms about not telling the truth. I'm sorry, Honey, but you owe your life to Dennis. I was proud of him and sorry that he had to do what I should have done in the first place. I'll never be able to repay him for saving your life."

"Is this why Dennis's mother is so pissed at you?"

"Partly, but more because I was a cop."

"Let's get back to the lie. What do you suggest I do? I'm the acting D.A. My first action is to cover for my dad. Is that what you want me to do?"

"Well, I really didn't break any criminal laws. Okay, maybe I did, but what the hell. I'd do it again. I know that now, so that's why I quit. I still want to do the same type of work, but without the restrictions of the department."

"What did you two do on the special projects?"

"Believe it or not, it's classified. I wish I could tell you, but it would put you in further harm's way. One of the reasons I lied was to protect Dennis, who's the project head. However, that doesn't really matter anymore, since we no longer work together."

Debra took the last swig on the beer, and went to get a second. "You forgot one thing though. What if the press asks me how I know Dennis and his mother? They're going to want to know why Carr took the three of us."

"That's easy. You dated Dennis's roommate in college and when it ended, you started to date Dennis. It didn't last, but you remained friends. Since you're my daughter, I'd also know Dennis and his mother."

"That's another lie. I really don't know if I can do this."

"I'll make it easy. I won't be seen in public with you for a while. Let the press tire of this story. They have such short attention spans these days. A couple of days and you can bet some senator or representative will be in some sex scandal. Magically then we're off the hook, and on page 25."

"Okay, just for now let's say I go along with your story, what are you going to do with your life?"

"I'm going to be a private detective. I'm leasing a small office, which will be available in a few weeks. I also bought a house on the edge of the city."

"You've got to be kidding - a private eye, no way. That'll really make it difficult for me as a D.A. We'll be on the opposite sides of the legal system. I won't be able to help you with your cases. You'll be treated no differently than other PIs."

"I know and I wouldn't have it any other way."

"Have you thought about a name for your new company?"

"I thought Ridge Detective Agency would work."

"Well that's original, Detective Ridge," she said sarcastically.

"Okay, maybe I should work on the name a bit more. I'm really sorry, but I have to run. I have plenty of loose ends to clean up. There's one last thing I need to ask. Could you please consider going over to see Dennis? You know he did save your life after all. I think the horror of killing another human being is starting to set in. He needs to know that some good came from it. You owe him that much."

"I'll consider it. I love you, even though you make my life crazy."

Frank walked out to the street and looked up. The sky was clear, and the air was crisp. He looked at his beat-up Mustang. It was going to need some repair. Maybe "Rockford" could get away with using an old car and make a living as a PI on TV, but that was Hollywood. He was going to have to clean up his act, as appearances are everything. He tried to open the door, but it was stuck. He kicked it just below the handle, and it opened. A new dent appeared and he mentally added it to the growing list of repairs. As he headed toward his hotel, he started to plan out the next couple of weeks. His life was about to take a full ninety degree turn, so he hoped he had made the right decision.

Chapter 20

Debra Ridge's life was in a quandary. She had just taken over as one of the youngest District Attorneys in the city's history, and now her dad was asking her to bend the rules. After her dad had delivered the bad news and retreated, she mulled over the problem. The bottom line was that if Dennis hadn't shot Carr, she would be dead. Maybe that was all there was to it. The department would always have to make some small compromises to ensure that justice persevered.

She tossed and turned the entire night with indecision. It was not until morning that she knew what she had to do. Her dad had been right that she needed to confront Dennis and his mother about these recent events. She poured herself a bowl of cereal and called the Andrews house. Mrs. Henson answered the phone and told her that both Andrews would be in for the day. She asked Debra to wait while she asked them about a time.

A couple of minutes went by before Mrs. Henson was back on the phone. "I told them that you wanted to come over. They wanted to know what the visit was concerning. I said you were the D.A. and didn't need a reason. They'll see you at ten this morning, if that is all right."

She was surprised that the housekeeper had such control in the Andrews household. She agreed to the meeting time and hung up the phone. She thought to herself that it was going to be a very interesting day.

She cleaned up the kitchen, showered, and put on a brown pant suit and matching flat shoes. She wanted to keep a low profile for this visit. Her plan was to be in and out as fast as she could. Forty minutes later, she was sitting in front of the Andrews gate, and was about to press the call button, when the gate opened. She headed up the long winding driveway that was beautifully adorned with well-manicured landscaping.

Mrs. Henson greeted her when she got out of the car. "It's nice to meet you, Debra. Both of them are waiting in the living room. I have to warn you though; Dennis's mother is not very keen on this idea. Dennis seems a little bit lost, and I'm not sure why, but maybe you can help."

"What have they told you about the Carr shooting?"

"They've said nothing really. They were kidnapped by Carr, and Frank saved them. That's about it. Is there more that I should know?"

As the two headed toward the front door, Debra considered her options, and what she should tell Mrs. Henson. "I think that you should hear the rest of the story from them. It's not my place to interfere with family matters."

"Really, then why are you here?"

"Good point. Maybe I'm here to stir the pot a bit."

"Atta girl, go for it," Mrs. Henson said and led her to a very well decorated living room. There were unique 3-D art form sculptures on several marble stands. Beautiful landscape paintings adorned all the walls. Dennis was busy working on a laptop while his mother was reading a Kindle. The two looked up when Debra was ushered into the room. Before Debra could thank Mrs. Henson, she was gone. Dennis closed his laptop and got up to meet Debra, although his mother made no effort of greeting.

Debra positioned herself in front of Dennis. "I want to thank you for letting me come into your beautiful home. My dad told me it was something to see. I now understand what he was talking about, and I wanted to personally thank you. Dad told me the whole story. I'm so sorry that you had to be the one to shoot Carr."

"Frank told you everything?"

"Yes, and it was very hard for him to tell me. He was concerned that it would jeopardize my job and our father/daughter relationship. He was so concerned that he retired from the department yesterday, which caught me totally off guard."

Up to now, Dennis's mother didn't move or comment. This new information made her put down her Kindle and look at Debra for the first time since she arrived.

She questioned, "He quit? Why would he do that?"

"I'm not totally sure, but part of the answer is that his position in the department was somewhat tenuous. He no longer felt comfortable in public service. The other reason he seemed very vague about. It has something to do with a project that he and Dennis worked on."

Dennis was about to answer, but his mother continued with her thoughts. "He never told you what he and Dennis were doing?"

"Nope. Just that it was classified, and it would be better for me not to know."

"I don't agree with your father on much of anything, but I do agree on that," quipped Dennis' mother.

"Wait a minute," said Dennis. "It's really up to me to decide who knows about the project."

Debra turned to Dennis. "So you're going to tell me what the project is all about?"

"No, as it would compromise your job."

"Now I'm really confused. Your project is related to my job as D.A.?"

"Yes and no. Do you want to go out to dinner tonight?"

"No, and you're changing the subject."

Dennis's mother got up and headed for the kitchen. "I believe this is my cue to leave. Dennis, you're on your own."

Dennis moved closer to Debra. "You know, you owe me for saving your life. All it will take to repay me is a dinner, and I'll even pay."

"I thought you saved my life just out of the kindness of your heart, and no reward was necessary."

"That's true, but I thought I'd give it a shot. That wasn't nice of me to put you on the spot."

"Are you really giving up that easily?"

"You'll go?"

"What the hell, it's just dinner."

"Give me your address, and I'll pick you up at six this evening."

She wrote the address and added her phone number, just in case. She handed it to Dennis, and he put it into his wallet. "If you change your mind, you really don't owe me anything."

"Are you dumping me before we even go to dinner?"

"You know, you're a lot like your dad, and it's very frustrating."

"I know."

Dennis walked her to the door and in a couple of minutes, she was on her way home. When she got home, she sat on her couch, trying to take stock of what had just happened. She'd gone over to the Andrews house to thank Dennis, and now she was going on a date with him. This wasn't normal for Debra Ridge. The longer she was around Dennis, the more he intrigued her. At first, it was idle curiosity, but as she talked with him, she could see a romantic interest growing. He was handsome, smart, had a strange sense of humor, and she felt very comfortable with him. He was what most women were looking for, and here she was treating this date as just a thank you. Her mind started to wander into areas reserved for a serious relationship, but her thoughts were interrupted when the phone rang.

The caller ID indicated it was her dad.

"Hi, how are you doing?"

"I'm fine, Dad. What are you doing today?"

"Looking for furniture and household supplies. My insurance check came in, and I can apply it to the house I just bought."

"You really did buy a house?"

142

"Did you think I was going to live at a hotel the rest of my days? It's a nice place. I'll email you the address, and I can move into it in less than three weeks. The escrow sailed through when the seller found out I was paying cash."

"I went over to see Dennis and his mother. Boy, she's something else. I do like the housekeeper a lot. She's a hoot. Anyway, we talked about the Carr shooting, and why you quit the force. I still don't understand what the deal is about the project you two worked on, but I'm going to have to trust your judgment on that one. Someday you're going to have to tell me what's really going on."

"So, you worked everything out with Dennis? Are the two of you all right with what went down with Carr?"

"I'm fine with it, and so is Dennis. He's even taking me out to dinner tonight."

"You really think that's a good idea? I wanted you to go and work things out, not go on a date. You don't know anything about Dennis."

"You don't trust him?"

"You're twisting my words. I do trust him with almost everything, except my daughter."

"It's just dinner. I'm not jumping into bed with him. Remember, he did save my life."

"Okay, I guess so, but I still don't like the idea. You're mixing business and pleasure."

"What part are you against - business or pleasure?"

"Let's change the subject. When are you going back to work?"

"I have to get through the date first. I'm just kidding. I'll probably go tomorrow or the next day at the latest. So, tell me about the house."

"All in good time. Wait until I move in. It'll be a surprise."

"What's with all the secrets?"

"Life would be boring if we knew everything. Some things should come as a surprise. Look, I have to go. I have another call. Love you."

She set the phone down and stared up at the ceiling. Something was going on with her dad. He was acting very strange. He seemed happier than he'd been in years. Maybe quitting the force was the right thing to do after all.

She walked over to her closet to select an outfit for the evening. Red was too much and black was always mysterious. She slid the outfits from side to side on the rack. One dress kept popping up, and she finally pulled out the lavender low cut evening dress. She held it up to the mirror. It looked very sexy and would probably send the wrong message, so she hung it back on the rack. Then she pulled it off again and thought about why she'd never worn this dress before. She'd bought it for her last date, which felt like a million years ago. The date was canceled, and she was stuck with this dress. She stripped down, slipped it on, and turned in front of the mirror. Yes, it was definitely sending the wrong message, but what the hell. She took it back off and headed for a shower.

As the time approached 5:30, she paced in her apartment. She was acting like a giddy high school girl. Nothing was making much sense. This wasn't love at first sight. These feelings had crept up on her slowly and grabbed her heart before she could understand what had happened. So, why him? He was a super nerd. He was handsome; she would give him that, but the rest was unknown. Maybe that's what excited her the most. She held her hand to her chest. What the hell was wrong with her? It was just a dinner.

The sound from the doorbell saved her from having an anxiety attack. She opened the door, and was pleasantly surprised. She expected him to be in a stuffy suit, but he wore light-colored pants, turtleneck sweater, and a very expensive jacket. Now she knew she was really in trouble.

Dennis held out his arm and escorted her to the long limousine. He opened the door and introduced her to his mechanic, who doubled as the chauffeur. Dennis complimented her on her outfit and asked if she would like a glass of wine on the way. She started to say no, but she realized that is what the "*old*" Debra would do. She needed a change in her life to match her new job as D.A. Her reign might not last long, so she needed to enjoy the limelight while it lasted.

Dennis looked out the window and then leaned forward to talk to the chauffeur. "Please take us to the jet."

"Jet? You said nothing about a plane."

"You agreed to dinner. I didn't say where. There's a very nice Italian restaurant in San Francisco. In a couple of hours, we'll be sitting in one of the best restaurants in San Francisco. My mother knows the owner. We have a standing table invitation anytime."

"I'm not so sure about this."

"Come on, Debra, take some chances. Your life is going upside down right now. Enjoy some new experiences. The flight time will give us time to talk."

"Talk about what?"

"Isn't that what a first date is about?"

"You make it sound like there'll be a second date."

"You know that in some cultures if you save someone's life you're responsible for them from that point forward. The only way that can happen is if there's a second date."

"Let's slow down, Dennis. I don't know anything about you. You know all about me from your roommate when you were in college."

"What makes you think he told me anything about you?"

"You know that answer, Dennis."

"Okay, so we agree that he couldn't keep secrets."

"If we have to kill a couple of hours, tell me about yourself."

"You make it sound like you are being forced. We can turn around and go back or anything you want. I haven't been on a date in months, and I like you. Let's make the best of the evening. We'll just be two people enjoying an evening out without any commitments. Let's wait until we're in the air before we talk about each other's past, present, and future aspirations."

Debra was about to respond, but the limo had stopped. The chauffeur got out and opened the door. Dennis escorted Debra up to the steps of the Learjet. She stopped and looked at the sleek looking jet. There was a lot more to Dennis than her dad had told her. He had the toys of a playboy but didn't fit the role. She looked up at the captain of the jet to see a beautiful blonde that could easily have been a super model. She looked back at Dennis and grinned.

"Is she one of your playmates?"

"No way. She's married and has two kids. Besides, she's my first cousin."

"Sorry, Dennis. That was out of line. I have this distrust of men with expensive toys."

"Let's get moving. Are we going to dinner or what?"

She headed up the stairs with Dennis close behind. Once they were seated, the pilot closed the door and told them to buckle up. Debra sat in a seat facing the front, while Dennis sat across the table from her. Dennis motioned for the pilot to take off.

"Now, where were we? Oh, yes. I know more about you than you know about me, so I'll begin to even the information pool between us. Let's see, where do I start? My childhood was normal with one exception; my father was murdered. I'd rather not talk about that period in my life.

"Just like my mother, I attended multiple colleges and have several doctoral degrees in the sciences. I hated the college life. Everyone partied while I killed myself trying to please my mother. She can be a pain in the ass sometimes. I love her very much, but she can be pushy. For some reason, she really hates

146

your dad. I wish I could fix that, but some things are outside this known universe.

"Not long after I got my final doctorate in Nano Technology, I was hired away by the Army on a special project. I worked on it for several years, but it really never panned out. The system I worked on was so cumbersome that it was more dangerous than its designed purpose. It was just too big and complex to work in a practical sense."

"Is that the special project you and dad were working on?"

"Yes and no. Your dad was helping me resurrect the project after it had failed for the Army."

"Maybe you're looking at the problem wrong. Whenever the government gets a hold of a project, they add layers of expensive bureaucracy that really has nothing to do with the original project's intent. Maybe you should strip the concept back to the original design and start over using only what is necessary to make it work. Of course, I don't have a clue what it is you are working on, so my input may be way off base."

Dennis was quiet for more than a minute. Debra waved her hand in front of his face. She could tell he was in a trance, and his mind was somewhere else.

"Earth to Dennis. Is anyone home?"

"Sorry, you may be onto something. I was so wrapped up with the status of the current project; I never considered starting over from scratch. You're wonderful! All those brains around me made worthless suggestions on how to fix it, and you come right out with the perfect solution without even knowing the extent of the project. Debra, you don't owe me anything for saving your life, because you just saved mine."

"So, does this mean that I have to ask YOU out for the second date?"

"No woman has ever done that before."

"Really? Well Dennis it looks like there's going to be a lot of firsts between us in the future."

"So, there's a possible future for us?"

147

"Not if my dad has anything to say about it."

"I don't have that problem. My mother has been pushing me into marriage for as long as I can remember. The only reason we get along is that most of the time we're never home at the same time. In truth, the last couple of weeks have been the most time we've spent in the house together in years. I couldn't live there if she was home all the time. The only reason I stay is because of the lab in the basement, and the house is very comfortable. We both use the lab from time to time, and building a second lab would be very costly. The design was one of my fathers."

"Have you always lived there?"

"No, we had a smaller house at the edge of the city. It was also very nice, but we moved away when my father was murdered. I've never been back to that house, because it stirs up too many bad memories."

"I'm sorry about your dad. Let's talk about something else."

"How about your dad? You know for an old coot, I really like him. He comes across as a dumb detective who hates technology, but I see someone different. He's actually very smart and has a likeable personality. I wasn't very fair to him after the shooting. I think I was in shock, and when he came by I barely said two words. After everything he did, I should have been more understanding. I can't believe he quit the force. He did that to protect you and I both didn't he?"

"Yes, but you know I think he's fine with it. He seems much happier now that he's out on his own. I'm not sure if being a PI is the way to go, but time will tell. Once he puts his mind to it, he can do anything."

"That was my opinion of him also."

Debra took a sip from the second glass of wine that Dennis had poured. "Can I ask you a question about the shooting? I know you don't want to talk about it, but I have to know."

Dennis glanced down with a sad look on his face. He was still in some shock over the shooting. "Okay, but make it a short conversation."

"I don't understand how you could take one shot and hit Carr in the head. I know it sounds so hideous, but remember, I see a lot of this in the office. You just don't strike me as the type of person who could make that shot. Dad could, but I just can't see you doing it."

Dennis took a deep breath. "Your dad talked me into going to the shooting range. I'd never shot a gun before. He talked me into it, so I tried the Colt. It appears that I'm some kind of shooting savant. At least, the shooting range attendant and your dad think so. I'm not proud of it, because it just seems natural to me. I don't ever want to pick up a gun again, and I still have nightmares of the killing. I don't know how anyone can live with it. That's enough on that subject. Let's talk about growing up in high school. That's something we both can relate to."

The two hours went by rapidly for the two as they laughed and cried over stories of their childhoods. Debra came to realize that Dennis was using his mother as a shield to scare off potential serious relationships. He was always wrapped up in his work, and when a woman became interested in more than just a couple of dates, he'd throw the mama's boy in her face. There actually was quite a bit of friction between those two, and he was far from being a mama's boy. She wondered why the other women didn't see that. The more she listened to him, the more she liked him. There was definitely going to be a second date.

When the jet landed, a second limo pulled up to the jet. Twenty minutes later, they were sitting at one of the best tables in the restaurant. Debra was afraid that they'd used up all the possible conversations on the plane, but it continued effortlessly. She was so impressed when he listened intently to what she had to say, and contributed too. For most of her dates, the guy would spend hours talking about himself. Dennis seemed to feed on what she had to say. Conversations jumped from her work to what she did to relax, and to where she'd traveled. The evening seemed too short for them both.

They boarded the jet late in the evening, and Debra was asleep minutes after takeoff. Dennis draped a blanket over her and then proceeded to pull out his laptop. She truly inspired him. Tomorrow he was going to start over, and give Medusa a makeover.

Chapter 21
(Three weeks later)

Frank closed the car trunk and carried in the box that contained the final touches for his new domain. He took out a sculpture of a sea turtle that he decided would look great on the coffee table in the middle of the room. Thanks to the insurance check and some additional tapping into his bank account, he completely furnished the house, including two extra guest rooms.

He'd been dividing his time between setting up the house and assembling the office of the Ridge Detective Agency. He already made several calls to potential clients he had previously worked with as a detective. A couple of them indicated they could use his services, so he set up follow-up appointments.

He looked around his new domain. It felt cozy and comfortable, so it was time to have Debra over for dinner. He'd missed her, but with all the attention in the news about the Jesse Carr shooting, they had restricted themselves to just phone calls.

Frank's decision to limit contact with Debra was well founded, because the press had taken the shooting into a new direction. Several reporters were stating that shooting a victim in the head wasn't an acceptable method for stopping an "alleged" killer. They felt Frank should've have shot Carr in the shoulder or leg and brought the criminal to justice. One newscaster even had a psychologist stating that most people believed a shot through the heart was more acceptable. Frank couldn't understand the controversy because the bottom line was that Carr was dead and no longer a threat to him or his family.

His biggest concern was that Dennis was watching every newscast, and it was probably taking its toll. Dennis was a good man, and Frank was sure that he would need some counseling to get past this. He hadn't talked to Dennis or his mother since he picked up his belongings. He only received a few bits and pieces of information from Debra.

After her first date with Dennis, the two had talked some on the phone, and then tried to go on a second date. It was foiled when a reporter and a photographer spotted them in a restaurant. The next news story was about the temporary D.A. out on a date with the man who'd been abducted with her. The newscaster kept referring to the fact that her father, a now-retired police detective, had shot the suspect in the head. The reporter then speculated that something more was going on because Frank had resigned the day after the shooting. Whenever she left her office or made an appearance in public, the press was constantly there asking questions about her father. They just wouldn't leave it alone.

Debra called right after watching the most-recent newscast, and cried to him on the phone saying she was sick of it all. She wanted to resign from her temporary position and hand it over to someone else. Frank convinced her that if she did, the media would put even more pressure on her department. He told her to hold her ground, and the press would eventually give up, but she wasn't convinced.

When he asked her about Dennis, she indicated that the two had agreed to put their potential relationship on hold for a while. Frank could tell by her voice that it wasn't her wish. She indicated that no one had seen Dennis for several weeks, as he hadn't left his house. Frank wondered what in the hell had Dennis been doing the past few weeks?

Dennis told her that his mother went back on tour a week after the shooting, and was now in Europe lecturing on the biological changes between the Pacific and Atlantic oceans. Before going to Germany, she had visited the Caymans, Bonaire, and a couple of other islands to research the lionfish problem. Frank had seen a couple of these fish in a pet shop, and couldn't imagine how they could be such a big problem. Then he remembered that this was exactly why Dr. Sandra Alexander was doing her research. He sure wished that they had a better relationship, and weren't always at odds.

Dennis sat in front of his laptop reviewing the most-recent data from his experiment. The week after the shooting, he was a lost soul. Every time he ran into his mother, she would bring up Frank and how he'd ruined their lives. He got tired of defending him, and was very happy when she left on tour. He talked with Debra a couple of times and could tell by her strained voice that the whole event was taking its toll on her too. He hadn't had a good night's sleep since the shooting. The idea of killing someone was eating away at him, and increasing day by day. He didn't understand how cops handled it.

When his mother left, he decided to concentrate on Debra's solution to his problem. He re-read all the research he'd done for the Army, and then he went back to his initial proposal. Debra was right, because he now saw his original idea had been encrusted with layers of bureaucracy by the Army.

He opened up his original designs and started to rebuild the device from scratch. His concern this time would be controlling the device's size, and that would mean a drastic change to Medusa. In fact, Medusa would no longer exist. He removed what he needed for the new, improved version and shoved the remaining bulk into a storage space. That left only one original MLA device and it was stored at the Army warehouse.

As each day went by, he worked longer hours until his schedule was twenty hours of labor and four hours of sleep. He was obsessed with the new project, working beyond the point of exhaustion. Thinking about his first date with Debra was what kept him going. He wanted to see her again, but he had to finish this project first. Dennis wanted to show her the results of her idea, and then they could both move forward. To exactly what end, he had no idea, but just imagining it brought a smile to his face.

Senator Bob Welding kept looking at the most-recent article about the Seattle Police Department. Even though he was in Washington DC, the news was big enough to hit the local papers. He didn't like the idea of Dennis Andrews's name being mentioned. A lot of time had passed since the failure of the MLA project, but he had hoped he'd never hear about Dennis Andrews again. However, here it was front and center. He picked up his private phone and punched in a number.

General Martin Harrison was in the middle of chewing out a major when he saw his private line blinking. He waved the major out of the room.

General Harrison had been through several Middle East wars and was starting to show wear from his years of command. He was a gray-haired man, six foot two with a strong muscular build that hid much of his excess weight. He kept telling himself that he needed to resign, but the money was just too good to quit, so he continued as long as it was in his best interests.

"General, we may have a problem."

"Senator, what can I do for you?"

'Have you seen all the articles and news reports from Seattle about that cop killer being shot and killed?"

"Are you referring to Dennis Andrews? Yes, I've been following the stories."

"Any chance that the MLA project is connected?"

The general reflected for a moment. Andrews, the brains behind the project had warned the general that the device was never designed to handle the addition of offensive and defensive weapons. They argued continuously about adding the weapon's aspect to the device, and ultimately, the general had the scientist barred from the field tests.

"Senator, the project is dead and gone. I don't think we have anything to worry about."

"Well, a lot could happen to both of us if anything about the MLA came out. I don't feel good about Andrews being in the news so much."

"What do you want me to do?"

154

"Verify that we have nothing to worry about. Use your resources to check on our friend Dr. Andrews, and see if there's anything under that smoke. If there's a fire, put it out. Do you understand what I mean, General?"

"Loud and clear, Senator, but we're in this together. If I go down, so do you.

"Is that a threat, General?"

"No, I'm just stating a fact. Whenever you work with people like Dennis Andrews, there's always a risk of exposure. I'll find out what our friend is doing, and if there's a fire, I'll extinguish it, but you'll owe me, Senator." He smiled as he realized he could retire on the bribes he had collected so far from the senator.

"I've already overpaid you, General, so don't give me any more bullshit. Take care of the problem if there's one, and I don't want to hear any more about this. I can cut off your funding anytime I want, and I have many friends in the CIA. Just do what you're told."

The senator slammed the phone down on the cradle. The MLA project was coming back to bite him in the ass. He could feel it in his bones. The more he thought about it, he realized he was going to have to do more than rely on just the general to take care of it. It was time to put a backup plan in place. He picked up the phone and made a call to an old CIA operative.

Chapter 22

Debra had been excited about becoming the temporary D.A. until she realized all the crap her boss had been handling. She assumed that she was handling the bulk of the work as Assistant D.A., when, in fact, her boss had been buried in work. She wished now that she'd let someone else step in. She had no idea that the D.A. handled so much in the political arena. The press wasn't helping as they continued to pressure her, using her father as the catalyst.

Her head was full of lingering thoughts of her first date with Dennis, which further complicated matters. She had such a good time that night. Debra hated the idea that she had to limit her conversations with Dennis to short phone calls. She wanted to talk to him in person. She picked up her cell and pressed his number. After a half dozen rings, it then went to voice mail. She left a short message, but was now more frustrated than ever.

This had to stop right now. She picked up the phone and called Captain Carson.

"Captain Carson here."

"This is Debra Ridge. Can you come down to my office? We need to talk."

"Sure, Debra. Give me fifteen minutes to clear my calendar for the rest of the day."

"Thanks, I'll see you then."

Captain Carson hated what was happening to Frank and his daughter. The media was relentless. He thought they would have given up by now, but most reporters considered the Carr shooting a Seattle Watergate, thinking there had to be more under the surface. He couldn't count the times he'd answered calls from newspapers and TV stations about Frank and Debra. He had a hunch that Debra had reached her limit with the media. He wasn't sure what she had in mind, but he was willing to go the extra mile for the Ridge family.

Thirty minutes later, Carson walked into her office. She asked him to close the door, and then called her secretary to tell her she wasn't to be disturbed for any reason.

Debra reached over and refilled her cup. "Thanks for coming, Captain. Would you like a cup of coffee?"

"Sure, black is fine."

Debra picked up a second cup, filled it, and handed it to Carson.

"You know why I asked you to come here?"

"I've got a good idea, but enlighten me."

"I can't leave the office without someone from the press tailing me and asking stupid questions. I need your help because I'd like to see a couple of people without every newsperson in Seattle following me and taking photos. Do you have any ideas?"

Carson took a sip from the cup. "My guess is that one person you want to see is Frank. Is the other Dennis Andrews?"

"Yes on both counts. I need to resolve some unanswered questions with Dennis and see my dad without everyone putting us in every tabloid in the city."

"Are you willing to break a couple of rules to make it happen?"

"I guess that depends upon the rules."

"I was considering using department resources for personal reasons."

"Fine, what do you have in mind?"

"Well, I have a female cop in vice right now who could easily double for you. She needs a break from her job because her husband hates her working vice. I'd be doing her a favor by transferring her to your department for a couple of weeks. She can come into your office looking like a prostitute snitch. She can then do a quick change of clothes, and presto, she's you. We can put her into a car in an area behind the garage that's off-limits to the press. When she exits the garage, she can take them on a wild goose chase and lose them. Meanwhile, the real Debra has escaped. What do you think?"

"I like it. How much trouble could we get in if the press figures it out?"

"Hey, right now I think the public is even starting to get tired of the press's obsession with you and Frank. I can set it up as soon as I get back. When do you want this to happen?"

"Tonight if that's possible. I want to see my dad, but I don't know where his new place is located."

"That's not a problem, because I do. I should warn you not to tell anyone because Frank is trying to keep a low profile. He has the same problem as you, but on a lesser scale. The last time I talked with him, he told me that it took forty-five minutes to get home when it should have only taken twenty. A couple of times they got close, but he's almost as good as the vice detective who'll be working with you. They used helicopters a couple of times, but he parked downtown and resorted to public transportation to lose them. Therefore, if you want to see your dad, it should be soon. The press will eventually find him."

Debra finished her coffee and set the empty down, debating if she wanted another.

"Can't the press do a search for his phone number or mailing address and find him that way?"

"They could, except he bought the house through a lawyer and is using an alias as the buyer."

"Really, he goes by another name? What is it?"

"Let him tell you. I'm going back and set this up. Clear your schedule for this afternoon and evening. I'm so glad I can help."

"Thanks, Captain. I owe you."

"No you don't. Friends don't owe friends. They just help when needed."

Debra smiled at the captain as he exited the office. She walked out and told her assistant, Danny, that all appointments would be moved to tomorrow, and that a vice cop would be up to see her. He was to show the vice cop right in and not make any passes at her. Danny gave her a quizzical look and wondered what was going on with his boss.

Debra picked up her phone and pressed her dad's number on her cell.

Frank answered on the second ring.

"Hi, Honey. How's it going?"

"Hey, Dad, I'm coming to see you tonight. Is that okay?"

"Sure, but what about the press?"

"Captain Carson is helping me. No one will follow me. You don't mind if I show up looking like a hooker, do you?"

"What kind of crazy stunt are you pulling?"

"Hey, just put the dinner together, and I'll be there without any press. I miss you and love you, Dad. See you soon."

Frank stood in the living room looking at his cell. He started to talk to himself. "What the hell are you doing, girl?"

The next couple of hours Debra frantically worked to tie up any loose ends that might prevent her from leaving her office early. She had just finished reading and signing off on the last report and assigning all the new cases to the Assistant D.A., when Danny beeped her on the intercom. "There is a...well, she calls herself Buttons...out here to see you."

"Show her in, please."

Buttons entered and Debra had to restrain herself from breaking out laughing. If there was anyone who looked like a hooker, Buttons was it. The vice cop held out her hand. "Karen Palmer at your service. The captain tells me you need some help. Whatever it is, thanks because you've saved my marriage. My husband was about to kill me over my last assignment. I told him I had a desk job for a couple of weeks. He was so happy. Thank you."

"Don't thank me yet. It won't be easy losing the press."

"Hey, that's not a problem. They all think in two dimensions. X and Y. I think in four; X, Y, Z and time itself. I've never had anyone follow me to a destination, unless I wanted them to. So, what do you want me to do? The captain told me to bring a duplicate of my outfit. I assume you'll be wearing it to leave through the front door, and I go out the back dressed as the D.A."

"Just so we understand. This isn't some clandestine operation. I only want some time with my family without the damn press sticking their noses in my business. It's nothing illegal, just some much-needed time off."

"Hey, I can relate. Here's the outfit."

Karen handed Debra the outfit, and the two of them laughed at how ridiculous it looked. She then pulled out the last item, a small fancy purse. "The captain told me that another cop from vice would come and transport you to wherever you want to go. He suggested that you use the hotel room downtown where we monitor most of the vice operations. You can change into another disguise that's different from what you're wearing now. Several changes of hair, clothes, and makeup are necessary. You can never tell when someone from the press could pick you out of crowd and follow. It's best to keep out of the limelight and not draw attention to yourself, so you see, going as a hooker wouldn't be a good idea."

"Damn, I was hoping to see the expression on my dad's face when I showed up."

"You can still do it if you want, but I don't recommend it. Let's get started. It takes some time to put all this stuff on. It's supposed to come off and on fast, but in reality, it doesn't."

Thirty minutes later, the male vice cop knocked on the D.A.'s office door, came in, and escorted the new "Buttons" to his car. Karen pulled on a hair wig that was identical to Debra's hair, and was wearing the pant outfit that Debra had discarded. Debra had told Danny that as soon as the hooker had left, she would be going out the back to her home and would return tomorrow. Danny waited ten minutes and opened Debra's office door. It was empty. He closed and locked the door, and started to reschedule any further appointments.

Frank had planned to use the new laser-measuring device to check each room dimension down to the inch, but that would now have to wait until tomorrow. He needed to run out and buy some food for the dinner that evening. When Debra told him that she was coming, he became rejuvenated. He missed their weekly visits.

At 6 p.m., a car Frank hadn't seen before drove up his U-shaped driveway. A woman he'd never seen before got out and looked at the front of the house. He opened the front door and was about to tell the individual that whatever they were selling he wasn't interested. Then he realized it was Debra. He ran out, put his arms around her, and gave her a hug.

"I was expecting a hooker."

"Really, Dad. Are things that bad?"

"Hey, you told me you were coming as a hooker."

"The plan changed."

"I don't care. I'm just glad to see you. Come on in, I've been working on dinner."

She took off her coat, pulled off the wig, and looked around the living room. "This is a nice place, Dad. How did you find it?"

"The captain pointed me to it. Promise not to tell anyone where I live. Right now, my new clients prefer that I stay as low-key as possible, and that includes my home address."

"What kind of clients are we talking about?"

"The kind of clients who are worried about industrial espionage. They have many technical secrets to hide, and someone is always ready to steal them. So, how are you doing as the new D.A.? Let me guess, that it's not what you thought it would be?"

"Why did I ever take this job? I hate all the political shit. Pardon my French. I really enjoyed the job I had as the Assistant D.A. Now all I do is play games. I don't know how long I can last."

"Just a first observation, but maybe the job isn't for you."

"So what can I do? There aren't too many job openings for an unemployed D.A."

"Well, I do have an idea, but let's talk about your job after dinner. Besides, I want to know what's going on with Dennis. He was different than most people I've worked with before, and I sort of miss the kid."

"So, I finally come over after all this time, and all you want to know about is Dennis?"

"No, I want to know everything about you, but it appears to be a touchy subject. Let's go a different direction. Would you like a tour of my new house?"

"Sorry, Dad. I seem to be a little jumpy about everything, don't I?"

"That's okay. I've had some rough spots in my past too. We'll get through this together."

"So, what made you select this house?"

"It just looked like the right house for me. It has two guest rooms, just in case you and a friend come over."

"Do you mean Dennis?"

"No, anyone."

"Be honest, you meant Dennis."

"Yeah it would be great if it were Dennis. I told you he grew on me."

The two wandered from room to room with Frank giving a blow-by-blow description of all the upgrades he'd made. When they finally reached Frank's home office, Debra noticed a strange-looking device.

"What's that thing?"

Frank picked it up and turned it on. A bright-red beam shot out the end. "It's a laser ruler. It can measure down to less than a millimeter."

"What do you need that for?"

"It's part of my new work."

Debra looked down at the paperwork on the easel and saw it was a blueprint of the house. Each room measurement had a second set of numbers next to the original measurement arrows. She pointed down to the blueprint. "What's this?"

"It's a hobby I picked up. It helps me with my investigations."

"What kind of cases?"

"The kind where someone is hiding something in a hidden safe or behind a wall. Industrial thieves can be very clever. I was just practicing on my house."

The two finally migrated back to the kitchen. Frank had put a roast in the oven several hours before, and the marvelous smell was driving them crazy. Debra opened cupboards until she found a full set of plates and then opened a drawer for the silverware. Frank pulled out a bottle of wine from the refrigerator. He grabbed two glasses and poured wine into them both.

Debra looked up at her dad in wonder. "Wine, Dad? I thought you swore off all alcohol?"

"The people I'm working with expect me to drink with them. I don't do the hard stuff or beer, just wine. Don't worry; I have it under control. If I can't drink a couple glasses of wine and stop when I want, then I have no self-control at all. Besides, I think we need to toast your mom. She'd be proud of how far we've come."

The two sat down and slowly devoured half the roast. After dinner, they worked together to clean up and put the kitchen back in order. Frank gathered up the two wine glasses and moved them into the living room. Debra came in, took her glass, and sat down. "Okay, you want to talk about Dennis? What do you want to know?"

Frank took a small sip from his glass and smiled at Debra. "Let's talk about your job first. That's the most important thing to me. The way I see it, you've moved from a position you liked, to one you don't. I don't think there's any way they'll let you go back to your Assistant D.A. job. So, tell me what you liked about your old position?"

No one had ever asked her that question before. "I'm not sure it matters any more, but what the hell. The main purpose for the Assistant D.A. was organizing and keeping the cases on track. That meant lining up witnesses, making sure the chain of evidence was observed, working with the judges, and overseeing case assignments to all the Assistant D.A.'s in our department. There was more, but in a nutshell, I kept the department running on track. The best part of all was that I could still prosecute some of the more difficult cases."

"What if there was another position that had similar management opportunities, but paid at least triple what you make now?"

"It probably wouldn't be located in this state."

"Actually, it's right under your nose."

"I don't understand. What're you talking about?"

"I'm talking about working as the manager of Ridge Detective Agency. You would be the boss without all the political bullshit, and make a pile of money."

"You're kidding, right?"

"I'm dead serious. I'd love working with you on cases. Just think about it – we would be Father-Daughter detectives. You know how bad I'm at managing accounts, and I know the clients would love having you in command. In fact, a couple I couldn't sign would immediately change their minds if they knew you were at the helm. I could really use you, but no pressure. All I ask is that you consider it. Either way, I'm still your strongest supporter, whatever you decide."

"All right, Dad, I'll consider it, but give me a week to decide. I should know what I want to do by then. Now, as far as Dennis is concerned, I unintentionally did something to him on the first date. We were conversing about a lot of stuff, and then he started to talk about his Army project. I made a simple suggestion; he immediately became lost in space, and I almost had to slap him to bring him out of it. He never told me what the project was exactly, but when I made the suggestion, it seemed like I had just given him the keys to the kingdom."

"What did you tell him?"

"He explained that his project was never going to work because it was too big and cumbersome with all the layers of technology the Army had added. I told him the answer was simple. Start over using the basic concept, but build it the way he wanted. That's when I lost him."

"Shit. No wonder we haven't heard from him. Do you have any idea what you did?"

"I just made a simple suggestion. What did I do?"

"You changed his entire life. That's why you need to work for me. Your perspective on things like that is just what we need. I'll bump up my offer to four times your salary."

"Are you serious? Are you really going to get paid that kind of money?"

"Yes, but there's one other small problem. If you come to work for me, I'm also going to need Dennis. Now, before you say anything, let me tell you that Dennis has a lot to offer in areas neither one of us can fathom. It's mandatory that we have him as part of the team, even if his mother does hate me."

"Well, for the first dinner we've shared together in a long time, you sure have given me plenty to think about. You know that the press is going to go crazy when they realize they can't find the D.A. They're like obsessed hound dogs."

"That's all the more reason to consider a new career. You know, I thought I was making a big difference catching criminals. When I first started, I loved it, but now I have to say it's a losing battle. No matter how much evidence you have against a bad guy, he almost always gets out the revolving door of justice. I'm happy with my new career choice. My clients appreciate me, and don't hand me a bunch of crap. I don't care, one way or another, if you keep your job or try something new, as long as you're happy. Now you probably need to get some sleep. I have a feeling you'll have a very busy day tomorrow."

Chapter 23

Debra felt someone shaking her arm. She opened her eyes. It was her dad trying to wake her.

"Did I miss work? Am I late?"

Frank turned the clock, around so she could see it. It read 7:00 a.m., which was about the time she would normally get up. "What's going on, Dad?"

"Well it looks like the shit hit the fan."

"What's going on?"

"I got up early to make us breakfast and was watching an early morning news show. The top story was how the new D.A. had swapped places with a hooker to avoid the press. They ran down the whole story of how you swapped places and then you both lost the tails following you. They never mentioned that the hooker was a cop. I'm not sure if that's better or worse."

She threw on her bathrobe and took the cup of coffee Frank had made for her. "I don't understand. The only people who knew about the switch were the captain, Buttons, and I. The other two cops at the hotel didn't know about the switch until I got there. The captain swore that he trusted them with his life. How did they find out? The only good thing was that I did lose my tail. It wasn't easy, but Buttons gave me a few tips yesterday before we split. I just don't understand how they found out."

"Is there any chance that anyone overheard you?"

"No, we were very careful."

"I hate to say this but there's another solution - your office is bugged."

"Oh come on, Dad, do you really think it's bugged? You watch too much TV."

"Actually, I've seen a lot of bugs lately because that's one of the biggest problems for my clients. They constantly have to make bug sweeps when they have a new product, or if in the middle of a merger. Using bugs is a very efficient method for the bad guys to collect data. In fact, I would go directly to the captain, take him outside away from the building, and tell him your concern."

"Dad, do you really believe all this spy stuff? All right, I'll talk to him, but he'll think I'm crazy. Fortunately, I can just blame you."

"Anytime, Honey - that's a dad's job. I'm going to make you a quick breakfast. You need to get ready to go see the captain."

The two split and Debra headed for the shower. Twenty minutes later with coffee in hand and toast on the car console, she raced toward the captain's precinct. She pressed the Bluetooth command and yelled, "*Call the captain.*" She made it very brief, just in case her dad was right.

As she pulled into the parking lot, the captain came over and opened her passenger door. He picked up the piece of toast. "Are we in a hurry today? My guess would be a little newscast that broke a couple of hours ago. I have to tell you that there was no leak at my end, and I know you said nothing. It really pisses me off. We were so careful and now the other stations are picking it up too. They're making it seem like it was some kind of big crime. I hate the press."

"Good morning to you too, Captain. Frank has another spin on this. Do you want to hear it?"

"I'll bet he told you that it was a bug."

"Did he call you this morning?"

"No, but there's a saying that when you have eliminated the impossible, whatever remains, however improbable, must be the truth. I think it was Sherlock Holmes who said that. Anyway, I put a call into a friend at the FBI. I wanted someone from the outside to help us. If there's a leak, we can't depend on anyone in your department or mine to find it. They'll be in your office by the time you get there. They're undercover, and will represent themselves as part of the police union. No one knows anyone in that group, so it will be a perfect cover. When they're done, they'll be headed over to my office checking to see if I have any of those pesky critters hiding. You know that if they do find some, all hell is going to break loose."

"Captain, do you have any idea how many criminal cases we discuss in a week in the D.A.'s office? You don't even want to know what will happen if the court finds out that someone had an inside ear on all the most-recent cases."

"Shit. I never even considered that. Wow, this could be really bad."

"Sorry to kick you out, but I have to go."

Before she put the car into reverse, she looked down at the missed calls. The mayor had called four times, several newspapers, and various numbers she didn't recognize. As she pulled through the parking garage entrance, the press crowded around her car and started to stick mikes against her window. Once she was clear of the reporters, she parked as quickly as possible. Debra rushed into the elevator, stabbed the up button, and tried to compose herself. When the doors opened, Danny was waiting. "Good morning, Debra. Before you go into your office, I have to tell you that two police union representatives are waiting for you. You also have at least fifty calls to return. What do you want me to do?"

She looked around the room and noticed all eyes were on her. "Please hold all my calls and appointments until I talk to these union representatives. Tell everyone, including the mayor, that I'm in an emergency meeting."

Danny nodded, and knew it wouldn't do any good to say anything. Debra opened the door, and the two men stood up from their chairs and nodded. They said nothing, handed a piece of paper to her. It read, *your office is definitely bugged. Don't say anything that would give us away*. She handed the paper back and picked up a blank sheet off her desk. She wrote, *what do I do?* She made small talk as she wrote. One of the agents wrote one word on her sheet - *Outside*.

As she walked out of her office, Danny started to say something, but she held her hand up telling him to wait. Debra and the two agents said nothing as they worked their way toward the large open area at the center of the building. At one time, it had been a small garden with Plexiglas windows and was used for smokers. Now that smoking wasn't allowed anywhere in the building, the site had been converted into an inside garden park where people could take a break or have lunch.

When they were clear of her office, the two pulled out their badges. "The only reason we're here is because Captain Carson called us. We normally don't get involved in local affairs, but people above your mayor are concerned that such a minor incident has caused so much press. Your office had at least six bugs, and they've been there for some time. We were careful not to touch them, but could get an ID off two. We found a third that had a fingerprint on it, so we disabled it. These things fail all the time, which is why they had so many. One failing won't send up a red flag to whoever planted them. We already had a courier pick it up, and we're running it through every database we can find."

"What can I do? I can't go on with business as usual. I'll be afraid to say anything that would damage a case or be the next article in the news."

"We agree, and that's why you need to cancel all your appointments today. Just tell everyone that you have to meet with the mayor and explain that little switch you made yesterday, which, by the way, was pretty cute."

"If I cancel today, the press will go into an even bigger feeding frenzy."

"It's the best thing to do."

"All right, but then what?"

"By tonight, we should have all the pieces put together. Whoever did this is an amateur. They made many mistakes, and we'll get them. Then it will be up to you to decide what you want to do. I can tell you right now, going through the front door isn't a good idea. The press is camping out there. Can you meet with us right here tomorrow morning at 9 a.m.?"

Debra agreed and the three split. She used her cell to call her office and told Danny to cancel everything for the day. She then walked out a back door on the lower floor and across a park at the rear of the building. It was her lucky day because a taxi came by right away, and she snagged it. No one saw her leave. If she had realized that getting by the press was this easy, she never would have made the switch with Buttons.

The up side was that they'd discovered the bugs. When she reached her apartment, several news trucks were camped out. She rushed in screaming "No comment," and closed all her blinds. She poured herself a glass of orange juice and tried to process the situation. She sat on the couch and watched one news story after another speculating on something evil going on in her office. She fell asleep and early in the evening, she felt someone pulling a blanket over her. She opened her eyes to see Frank staring down at her. Her first thought was what about the press.

"Dad, did the press see you come in?"

"Sure, but they don't know where I came from. I can see my daughter anytime I want. There's no law against that. Besides, I think you need a friend right now."

"Thanks. I really do."

The two sat and talked about everything that had happened and then watched a couple of old movies. They both knew they were just trying to pass the time until the next big challenge.

She had a hard time getting any sleep the rest of the night, and kept watching the various TV stations for any new developments. A lost Alzheimer patient and a cat trapped in a sewer pipe dominated the news. Then early in the morning, one station announced a breaking news report. The reporter was standing in front of her office stating that new information had come to light on the D.A. switching places with a hooker. The

171

reporter had confirmed that the hooker was a vice cop and proceeded to give her real name and her full background. Debra knew that this information would make it impossible for her to work vice anytime soon. Lots of money had been spent setting up the vice cop, and now all that was lost.

When the report finished, Debra quickly showered, grabbed a cup of coffee, and headed for her office. They had decided that Debra should leave first, and that most of the news crews would follow her. The remaining few, Frank could lose easily.

By the time she arrived at the front of her building, she was surprised that the news crowd was not as large as the day before. Maybe it was true that the press did eventfully tire and move on to another topic. She could only hope. She walked straight through the lobby and found her two FBI agents sitting on a bench drinking coffee waiting for her. The lead agent reached out and shook her hand.

"We have good news and bad. I'll make it quick, as I know you'll have to make several decisions in the next few hours. The good news is that your little swap with the vice detective will become history, because a bigger story has surfaced. The bad news is that we found the bugs were planted by one of the cleaning crews. We did a background search and found out he was a brother to a news reporter at a local TV station. We brought the man in last night and after a few threats of long jail time, he confessed that he placed the bugs for his brother. After a bit more pressure, he disclosed that his brother was selling information to several defense attorneys. On occasion, the reporter would feed a tip to his station so that he could work his way up his company ladder. The group is actually very small and includes the cleaning man, the reporter, and three lawyers.

"Normally, we would go ahead and make the arrests right away, but my boss wanted to coordinate with any announcement you might make. The key is that we make the arrests at the same time as your announcement. Usually, your department would take over the investigation, but we think you would look better to the public eye if an outside agency made the arrests. That way, there would be no cover-up theories flaring up."

"So, what do we do about the bugs?"

"We'll remove them at the same time the announcement is made. We suggest that you arrange for a scan for bugs every day until the dust settles. I have to tell you though; this is the first time I've ever heard of a D.A.'s office being bugged just to get a leg up on criminal cases. How will it affect past cases that were overheard by the reporter?"

"I'm not sure at this point, and nothing may come of it. If it had been the defense attorney's offices that were bugged, all the cases tried by those lawyers would have to be reviewed or retried. If the system was going to take a hit, the present scenario offers the least damage. The biggest problem is the fact that the press is well protected by the first amendment. Do you have solid evidence against these men?"

"Yes, and the announcement that the hooker was a vice cop just added to the rock-solid evidence. We were very careful since we're dealing with the press. I think the first amendment was trumped when they bugged your office. It was illegal as hell, no matter who they are, or behind what kind of constitutional law they try to hide. So, what are you going to do?"

Debra had already started to go over it in her mind. She had to turn this situation around. Then a great idea came to mind.

"Can you wait until 4 p.m. today to make the arrests? I'll arrange to make a public statement at that time. I'd appreciate it if someone from the FBI stands next to me to answer questions that relate to your investigation and arrests. I can tell you one thing, if I do this right, the press will take a big hit today. You know what happens in the animal kingdom when a single member of a pack of predators becomes injured. They all turn on the weak member and kill it. I'm hoping that the same happens today. Thanks for all your help."

As soon as the two FBI agents left, Debra called the mayor and explained the situation. She told him in detail, and that she would make an announcement at the same time the arrests were being conducted. He wasn't thrilled with that explanation and wanted her to run her announcement by his assistants. She told him that she had it under control, and the city would be off the hook by early evening. She reminded him that he'd taken a beating from the press, and this was going to be a good time for payback. He liked the idea, as long as she was sure it was going to work. She hadn't told him the entire plan, or he would have tried to stop her. She headed up to her office, called Danny into her office, and had him close the door.

"Danny, the rest of today is going to be a little crazy. Ignore everything you hear, unless it comes directly from me. There'll be a press conference today in front of the building at 4 p.m. For the next few hours, I'll be preparing that announcement. If I need something, I want you alone to get it. No one else, do you understand?"

Danny nodded his head affirmatively. "Is this about the news reports this morning? I don't understand why they're making such a big deal about you skipping out for a day. Politicians do it all the time. The press should care less because it's just part of the political process."

"First, they have nothing else to report about. It's been light news days for the press, sort of a letdown after all the coverage on the Jesse Carr shooting. They see smoke, and they think there's a fire underneath. The key is that it will all end today and evolve into a new story, and that's why I need your full attention. Today, you work for me and no one else. Understand?"

Danny nodded and set down all the documents and messages needing her attention. As soon as Danny left, she scanned through the stack and decided that most of the items could be put off. She read and signed a couple of the impending items. Once her mind had cleared, she started to work on her announcement. Before long, it was starting to take shape.

By quarter to four, most of the press had arrived at the front of the D.A.'s office building. They had all staked out their vantage points and placed mikes in positions to record the best sound. Reporters were standing in front of the cameras making their initial statements about why the press conference was being conducted. A couple of minutes before four, Debra stepped out in front of the press. Several reporters started to ask questions, but she held up her hand, and they quieted.

"I need everyone to wait until I've made my statement, then I, and the FBI agent next to me, will field questions. First, my switching with a vice cop was so that I could safely visit my father without everyone from the press following me. There's no other reason for the switch. I just wanted some family privacy, which the press feels I'm not allowed. No one in my office, and only a couple of trusted friends, knew about the switch.

"This brings me to my next subject of discussion. We assumed that there was a leak in my office when the switch became a nightly news item. After some help from the FBI, we discovered that a reporter from High Mountain Press had his brother plant bugs in several offices in our building. High Mountain Press owns two newspapers and has a controlling interest in Channel 14 news.

"After an intense investigation by the FBI, they discovered that the reporter was also selling gathered information about cases to defense attorneys. This individual was using the information to work his way up the corporate ladder. The FBI is making arrests of the reporter, his brother, and the defense attorneys involved right now. Since the press is always interested in news stories that most affect the public, you might consider looking at the way you handle business. I say this because I don't think the public would approve of your tactics. If you need more information about this invasion of the public trust, the FBI agent, standing next to me, will field questions relating to this crime. Before I turn it over for questions, I have one last statement to make."

Debra paused a few moments. The press was in shock. They weren't saying a word. She looked at her notes and proceeded to the last item.

"Because of these new developments, I regret that I'm stepping down as interim D.A. I feel my position has been compromised to the point that I can no longer work effectively as D.A. I'll be leaving the public sector and accepting a position in a private company. The state's attorney has been asked to step in and appoint a new D.A. from outside the district until another election can be held."

She continued with resolve, "I would advise the public to question the news media and how they report the news. It's true that they're protected by the first amendment, but that doesn't allow them to break the law in an attempt for a breaking news story. The justice system took a big step backwards today and the pubic now has a chance to fix it. Next time you turn on the television and hear an announcement of a breaking news story, remember that the driving force behind the story isn't always the truth. Getting people to watch the story is ultimately their top priority."

She fielded dozens of questions fired at her and the FBI agent. She allowed the agent to handle the initial questions about the crime, and then she answered questions relating to the case information overheard in her office. She avoided questions about what she was considering for her future. Fifteen minutes later, she was sitting in her office waiting for the FBI agents to remove the remaining bugs, and sweep the area one final time.

She started to pick up a report on her desk when her cell phone rang. It was Frank.

"Hi, Dad. Did you see the press conference?"

"Yep, and that's a hell of a way to tell me that you accepted my offer. At least, that's what I assumed you were saying. Am I correct?"

"You are, but it will take me at least a week to untangle myself from this mess. There're some things that I have to resolve. Can I talk to you later tonight?"

"You bet and I'm not going anywhere. I'm between jobs right now, so if you need my help, just give me a call. You made me proud today. I love you."

Debra hung up the phone. Danny came in with a stack of calls that would take most of the day to return.

Dennis had been working nonstop for days with almost no sleep. He couldn't remember when one day ended and the next started, and he had completely lost track of time. The good news was that he had accomplished in just a few weeks what had previously taken years. The new Medusa makeover was almost complete. He was about to start the next step in the process when Mrs. Henson came in to talk. Dennis looked up at the worried expression on her face.

"Is something wrong, Mrs. Henson?"

"Dennis, have you looked at the news lately?"

"No, I've been too busy on this project. Is there something I should know about?"

"It's Debra."

Mrs. Henson gave Dennis the look he used to get from his mother when she knew he'd done something wrong. Whatever was going on, it was serious. He reached over and turned on the TV that had been silent for days. The first thing that came on was an announcement by the D.A. He came in on the second half of the announcement, and had to change channels to get the whole story. Once he heard everything, he turned off the TV and sat down. He'd been so wrapped up in the project that he never considered that anything could go wrong with Frank or Debra. Since the whole Jesse Carr thing was over, he assumed that

177

everything would go back to normal. He wanted to call Debra, but knew she was up to her neck in problems right now, and he didn't want to burden her further. He'd been such a jerk in the last few weeks. He knew he should have called her, but he was torn between Medusa and all the political stuff going on with Debra. The one thing that stuck in his mind was the final comment his mother made the last time they spoke. It was simple and to the point. *"It's for the best, Dennis. They're not our kind of people."*

Then it really started to sink in. How could he do better? Debra was the first woman with whom he had ever felt at ease. They'd hit it off right away. She was so different, and he'd wanted that night to never end. Yet, he'd avoided her for several weeks. Why had he done that? Was it really about Medusa? Not really, because when he wasn't thinking about the Medusa project, he was constantly remembering his date with Debra. He realized he was torn between his two loves. He suddenly realized that he was only using Medusa as an excuse to stay away from Debra. Then it hit him why he was avoiding Debra and smiled. He pressed the intercom button.

"Mrs. Henson, do you have the number to a good flower shop?"

"It's about time, Dennis. I'll be back down in just a minute."

Senator Bob Welding scanned through the national news updates. He set it to flag any reference to Dennis Andrews. In the past five days, his name appeared every day. The whole MLA project could resurrect and come apart the more Dennis Andrews appeared front and center in the news. The first thing reporters would do is a background investigation on Andrews. If they were any good at researching, the MLA project would surely surface. The senator needed to know where he stood. He picked up his encrypted phone and punched in his CIA contact.

"Senator Welding, what can I do for you?"

"Is there anything yet on Andrews?"

"He hasn't made any calls to the D.A. or anyone else for that matter. We've monitored his house, and no one other than his housekeeper has left the property. We're not totally convinced he's even there. It's been weeks since we've had any sign of him. If he's in contact with either Ridge, we have no record of it. I'd say that he's out of the picture. We'll continue to watch as long as you keep our budget intact. Let us know when you want us to stop surveillance."

Chapter 24

Frank had just finished making a second measurement on the inside of the garage when his cell phone rang. He set the laser down and looked at the number. Wow, it was Dennis.

"Hi, Dennis. Long time since I've heard from you. Are you all right?"

"Not really because there may be a problem with M. Can you come over right away? We need to talk."

"Sure. Give me a half an hour. I'll button things up here and be on my way. Do I need to bring anything?"

"No, just get here quick."

Frank hung up the phone. Dennis didn't sound happy. Frank wondered what could be the problem with Medusa? He was about to close the front door, when he remembered his gun. He went back to his gun safe and pulled out his new Glock. He checked the clip, locked the box, and he was on his way.

As he approached the gate, it started to open and then closed almost on his bumper. When he reached the front of the house, Dennis was standing outside pacing back and forth. As Frank approached, Dennis motioned for him to come in as quickly as possible.

Frank looked around to see if the housekeeper was about. Dennis was the only person visible. "Dennis, what the hell is so important?"

Dennis pulled out a piece of paper with a note written on it. *You may be bugged. Let's get to the lab. Leave your phone on the coffee table.*

Frank read the message a second time. He motioned an affirmative, set his phone on the table, and the two headed for the elevator. When the door closed, Dennis pressed the elevator stop button, and waited a couple of seconds. He held up his hand and pulled out a remote control. He flipped the power on switch, and then activated the buttons.   Ten seconds later, Dennis pressed the elevator down button.

"Sorry, Frank. I had to be sure you were clean. After all the problems with Debra, I'm a little paranoid. I had a special device built into the elevator. When I pressed the buttons, it wiped out every electronic device inside the elevator walls. I know you have a mechanical watch, but your phone would have been toast. Sorry I haven't called lately, but I've been very busy. However, that's not exactly why I called."

The elevator doors opened, and Frank looked around. Parts of projects were everywhere, and the place was a mess. "What's going on, Dennis?"

Dennis motioned for Frank to grab a chair. The two sat down, and Dennis tried to compose himself. "Well, as you can see I've been occupied working on a new project. So busy, in fact, that I almost missed a critical security notice on my video surveillance system. It monitors both the inside and the outside of the upper floor of the house. It's one of those smart systems that can do both object recognition and repetition. It has a secondary function that does facial recognition and records objects that occur in the same place more than three times."

Frank was trying to understand where Dennis was going, and started to look around the room.

Dennis took a deep breath and continued. "Well today, the system indicated that the same car has been down the street more than six times this week. The system does checks on license numbers and throws out those for the locals that live here. This one doesn't live within the neighborhood. I started to look back over the surveillance footage and found a clip showing a man surveying the house through a pair of binoculars."

"It probably is just a news reporter."

"No, Frank. The license number is not registered with the DMV or any official agency. The number doesn't exist in any system, and I checked them all. I also ran the man's face through all the facial recognition files, and found nothing again. I don't like it, Frank. With everything that's happened lately, I'm not too sure that we hid Medusa well enough when we were out on those cold cases."

"Yeah, it does sound a little suspicious. Have you had Medusa out of the lab since the last time we took her on a case?"

"No, but it really doesn't matter anymore as I disassembled her. Medusa, as you knew her, no longer exists."

"Really, just when I was getting to like her. So, what are you doing now?"

"I took Debra's suggestion and started all over. I took the basic processing system out and junked the rest."

"You junked a billion-dollar machine based on my daughter's suggestion? You must have had a hell of a date. No, I don't even want to know about it. So, what are you doing now?"

Dennis reached over to a device that looked like one of the new computer tablets, but it was larger and twice as thick. "Frank, meet the new and improved Medusa. When we first started to build the original MLA, technology was still in the dark ages compared to today. I was able to reconstruct the system into this much smaller computer. It is totally wireless and taps into dozens of network systems within the area. It has a booster that can reach out several miles to pick up thousands of wireless systems and use them in parallel. The visual system is now in my glasses. A heads-up display gives me readings on data as it comes in."

Dennis continued, "The laser is one we'd considered when we were building the original MLA. The Army considered it too fragile for field use. The laser on each side is one of the last components sent to us by Xtreme Machines, which was one of our primary contractors."

Frank slid back in his chair and mumbled, "Xtreme Machines. Really? I don't believe it. Guess it really is a small world."

Dennis set the computer down. "You've dealt with that company before?"

"Not directly, but a friend of mind did. Lloyd Becker was my first partner in Denver. He was a great guy and super detective."

"What happened to him?"

"Well, he was working on that murder case involving the CEO of Xtreme Machines. I think his name was Curt Allen Towers. Anyway, Lloyd was doing some follow-up investigation when he was killed by a hit man who was part of the conspiracy against Towers. I heard about it a couple of months ago. I sure wish I'd gone back to see him before he was killed."

Frank paused, holding his emotions in check. "Now, getting back to your problem. If you've dismantled the old Medusa, why do you think someone is watching you?"

"I don't have a clue. You're the detective, don't you have any ideas?"

"Well, I do have a question or two. Is the new Medusa up and running?"

"The laser and DNA recognition program are running, but there are still a few bugs to work out."

"Hey, I hear that every time I put some new software on my computer, and it runs fine. Let's wait until the car's gone, go over, and take a look. Let's put my snake-head friend back to work. Guess I'd better come up with a new name for our gal. Is the guy still there?"

Dennis clicked the mouse on the workstation next to him. "Yep, and he seems more interested today than before. I'd guess that your arrival initiated more attention."

Frank leaned over and looked at the monitor. "Dennis, this is simple. He should know by now that he's been made, so if he's still here, then his boss wants him there no matter what. We need to go stir the pot. Grab Medusa and let's take a walk."

"Frank, what are you going to do?"

"I want to run the guy off unexpectedly, so we can check out the area where he's been stationed. One thing I can tell you about a stakeout is that no matter how careful you try to be, you

183

leave something behind inevitably. Let's go put our new girlfriend to work."

Dennis grabbed a compartmentalized backpack and started to gather all the Medusa parts. Fifteen minutes later, the two took one last look at the monitor to confirm the guy was still there.

As the two left through the front door, Frank stopped. "You know you need to lock the front door and set the security system. The guy out there may be trying to lead you away from the house so that a second man can get inside."

Dennis stopped, went back, and set the house security system. As the two walked through the front gate, the man's car engine started up and squealed as it made a sharp turn heading down the street.

When they reached the area, Frank started to do a thorough search of the area. He found no cigarette butts, no food trash, no signs that anyone was in the area. They found a few scraps of paper that looked several weeks old, but nothing recent. Dennis pulled the new Medusa out of his backpack and took the unit out of standby. He pressed the laser scanner option on the menu system and the display on his glasses indicated that everything was ready to go.

"Frank, I'll make a scan of the area next to the driver's side to see if there's any residual DNA in that area. It may take a few minutes, but if there's anything, Medusa should find it."

Frank stood back, watched the traffic on the street, and then checked the cars parked in both directions. If there was a second man, he wanted to know now. When he was comfortable it was clear, he turned back to Dennis.

"Is that thing going to work as well as the original Medusa?"

"Actually, it should work about the same as before, but she's one hundredth the size. We no longer need that massive power source to run the diagnostic system. Now that I can steal processing power from the network links, I have almost unlimited processing power.

"I have to ask this, Dennis, but what you're doing isn't legal is it? And how do you keep everyone from knowing that you're using their computer systems?"

Dennis kept scanning the area for microbiological samples. "It's illegal as hell, but right now it's the only way I can get the system to work. I can hide the use of the network systems by jumping from one system to the next every few seconds. Medusa keeps track of the links but turns them off and on randomly while accessing their processing power. A couple of years ago, it would have taken the processing power of thousands of computers to do what she needed. With the new Intel chips in computers today, that's been reduced to only a couple hundred."

"Wow, a couple hundred. Are there really that many available in the area?"

"Yes, and right now I am going to need all of them. I just got a flag on a small residue on a piece of metal foil in front of me."

Frank crouched down and looked at the foil wrapper. It was only half an inch across. He reached into his pocket, pulled out a small plastic bag, and pushed the metal foil into the bag with a stick. "It's not what I'd have done as a police detective, but what the hell. I'm in a new game now. Anything else on your display?"

"Nothing and I've gone over the area at least three times. I'm not even sure that the foil is from our suspect."

"Actually, I think it is because the foil is pretty clean. The foil was next to the edge of the road and with the rain we had a couple of days ago, there would have been splashed mud particles on it, but it's clean. You know it looks like the foil found on a medicine tablet packet. I bet anything the guy has an ulcer from sitting here for days. He probably took one of those antacid tablets wrapped in foil. So, what do we do now?"

Dennis reached down and put Medusa to sleep. "Medusa is configured differently now. The sensor system in my glasses is used to find DNA. There's a more sophisticated adapter in the lab that communicates with Medusa and does the molecular scanning of the DNA."

"Let's head back and see what fate is about to hand us."

The two said very little as they quickly headed back to the house and then down to the lab. Dennis took a set of tweezers and removed the foil from the bag. He carefully inserted it into the middle of a chamber that contained a dozen small lasers along the sides. He woke Medusa up and pressed the DNA analyze menu button. He sat back and looked at the security monitor while waiting for the results.

Frank walked over to the coffee pot and poured himself a cup. He looked back over to Dennis, who was fixated on the computer screen. "Do you want a cup?"

Dennis looked back over to Frank for just a second. "Sure, my cup is just to the right of the pot."

As Frank filled the second cup, he looked at the security monitors above and to the right of the coffee pot. The system was like those he saw at some of the more high-tech companies he'd been in the last few years. It looked like overkill for a personal residence. He set the cup down next to Dennis. "What's with all the high-tech security? I know you had to have some for the work you did, but what I see is on the corporate level. It had to cost a butt load."

Dennis pressed a couple of menu buttons before he looked up to Frank. "Most of the security was put in by my mother, and then upgraded over the years. When my father was murdered, we moved out right away, and she bought the house that was on this lot. She had it demolished, and a new one built from the ground up. The security firm that my dad had worked with designed the first system. Every few years, she would upgrade or replace the system with something newer. Most people don't even know we have such a system, and we try to keep a low profile. I used to think it was too much security, but lately I've been glad she put it in."

Frank took a sip from his cup and sat down next to Dennis. "Did you ever go back to your old house?"

"No, when I was little, my mother made sure that we never drove by the old place. She kept the house for years and had a management company maintain the property. No one lived in it for years. She finally sold the house to the management company who rented it out for about five years. I've lost track of it over the last few years, and I don't really know who owns it. A couple of years back, I started to drive over to see the house, but turned around when I got a couple blocks away. That night still haunts me. I've gone to a shrink a couple of times to try to unlock some of the repressed memories, but no luck. I'm not sure I'll ever remember what happened that night."

Frank was about to apologize for bringing up the subject when a beeping sound came from Dennis's workstation. Dennis reached over and pressed a couple of buttons.

"We have enough DNA information to run a search, but it'll take some time to run the comparisons."

Dennis moved to a new menu system that would scan through local and state records. When that was completed, the system would expand to national records until a match was found. "This is going to take some time. How about a sandwich? Mrs. Henson has the day off, so we're on our own."

"That's fine with me because I skipped breakfast, and my stomach is starting to growl. Besides, I need to check and see if I missed any calls. Mind if I go up and check now? By the time you come up, I should be done."

Dennis nodded affirmatively, and Frank headed toward the elevator. Twenty minutes later, the two were seated in the backyard wolfing down toasted ham and cheese sandwiches. As soon as they had settled, Tigger came over and tried to jump up on Frank's lap. He pulled a piece of ham out of his sandwich and set it on the ground next to the table. Tigger brushed against his leg a couple of times and then gobbled down the small, but tasty morsel. Dennis leaned over and looked down at Tigger.

"You really shouldn't do that, Frank. Mom hates it when people give Tigger scraps from the table. She's been trying to break him of the habit of begging for a couple of years now, and you've undone all her work."

Frank tossed down another small piece. "She hates me for most everything that I am or do, so we'll just add another item to her list."

"She doesn't have a list of things she hates about you. She hates the police and everything about them. You're just caught in the middle, but it really has nothing to do with you personally."

"I'm not sure about that Dennis. I think it's more than just hating the police. I think it's personal."

A small beep broke into the conversation. Dennis looked down at the remote display that was linked to the system in the lab. He panned through the results.

"This isn't good because there aren't any matches. Either the guy isn't in the system or his records are in more secure systems. I don't like to hack into the acronym organizations, but it looks like that's our next step. Medusa is good, but I always worry some new security software has been installed, and Medusa won't pick it up. I'll start with the FBI, the CIA, and then to Homeland Security. I already set up the system to start scanning in sixty seconds if I don't stop the search, so I'll let it continue."

Frank pulled out his phone, and checked to see if he had any new calls. He got up from the table and started to walk toward the back of the property. Tigger wandered right behind him. "I have a couple of calls to make, so give me a yell if anything comes up."

Frank looked down through the call list. Nothing. He went to the front page on his phone and pressed Debra's number. It rang just once, and she answered.

"Hi, Dad. What's going on with you today?"

"I'm over at Dennis's helping him out with a security problem. How are you doing?"

"I'm fine. I just finished clearing out everything at the D.A.'s office, and now I'm catching up on housework and paying bills. We need to talk about your offer for me to work in your new detective agency."

"Are you having second thoughts?"

"Yes and no. I do want to work with you, but I want to do more than manage the business. I still want to practice law. I can train someone to manage the office. I think a detective-lawyer combination would be better for your detective agency. I can make sure you don't cross any gray lines in the law."

"I would never do that."

"Yeah, right, Dad, you never bend the law. If that's the case, then you must go by another set of laws than the rest of us do."

"Well maybe I've done a little bending in my time, but you can keep me on the straight and narrow from now on. How do you feel about Dennis working as our forensic scientist?"

"I'm sure Dennis is very good at forensics, but doesn't it require a lot of expensive equipment?"

"In a normal forensic lab that would be true, but Dennis has it under control. If you need any test run, he can do it. Comparing evidence to a control item is a piece of cake. The bottom line is that he has a leg up on just about everyone when it comes to that subject. Why don't you come over here tomorrow afternoon, and he can show you his Batcave?"

There was a silence on the phone for a few seconds before Debra responded. "Batcave, Dad. What have you been drinking?"

Frank looked up at Dennis, who had a frown upon his face. He'd overheard the comment. Frank just grinned, and continued his conversation. "That's what I call his lab. You know comic books and me. Besides, I think it's time we got back together as a group and discuss our futures."

"Sounds good to me. How about 5?"

"Fine with me and you don't need to bring any food or drink, as we have it covered."

"Are you sure?"

"Absolutely, see you then and I love you."

"Love you too, Dad."

Frank pressed the end call icon, and put the phone back into his pocket. Dennis motioned that he had some new results.

"Looks like we have a hit on our mystery man. It appears he works for INSCOM, which is Army Intelligence and Security Command. He works directly for General Martin Harrison."

"Isn't that the guy in command of the MLA project you worked on?"

"The very same general. I'm not sure why he'd have someone watch me."

"Dennis, when I met you, you told me that the project was under the table. The general would have a lot to lose if you ever went public. I'm sure he wouldn't lose any sleep if something were to happen to you."

"What should we do?"

"First, let's try to figure out why he's watching you. I'm guessing it's because you showed up in the news, and he feels uncomfortable about you in the public's eye. He's probably worried you're going to mention his pet MLA project. The second reason is that he may have figured out that you still have a device. We were excited, but sloppy when we worked on those three cold cases. I think it will be just a matter of time before he has a team of people breaking into your house. We have to assume the worst and prepare ourselves. Is there any way you can rebuild the original Medusa?"

Chapter 25

The rented van parked next to the country bus stop, and Frank jumped out of the driver's side. Dennis began opening the side panel to expose the three and half foot high Medusa. The two each grabbed a side of the device and set it down next to the bus stop bench. Dennis scanned the surrounding area and then the diagnostic panel on the front of Medusa. There was lots of fast food trash, a tire, hubcap, and a bent bicycle wheel. Most of the items looked like they had been there for a long time.

"You know, Frank this is really a bad idea. Someone's going to see us, and wonder what we're doing."

Frank just nodded and continued to scan through the cold case file. He skimmed each page twice to make sure he covered everything.

"No one is going to see us, Dennis. Besides, this case has been bugging me ever since we started taking on these cold cases. This little girl was never found. The mother assumed that her daughter went down to the bus stop and got on the bus. It wasn't until late in the day that everyone realized she never got on the bus or went to school. Almost ten hours had been lost before a search was initiated. The CSI team went over this area with everything they had at their disposal. I just want to make sure that the team didn't miss something that would point us in the right direction."

Dennis continued the startup on the device and looked at the status panel. It was green all the way across. "I still think it's too risky. The parts in this thing are the ones I used to test the original system. They aren't as reliable as those in the other two units are. If any of the parts fail, I have nothing with which to replace them. Everything I put into researching the project is right here in front of me."

Frank closed the folder. "You worry too much, Dennis. You designed this thing. You can always build another one, right?"

"No, I can't. Some parts in this thing cost tens of millions of dollars. I couldn't even begin to rebuild the thing. Besides, many of the components were subcontracted out to Xtreme Machines, and they aren't about to hand over military parts to a project that's been canceled. No, Frank, if anything goes wrong, we're done taking shortcuts to solve cold cases. You'll have to resort to the old way you were doing it."

"Dennis, I get the whole picture. Do you think we can get one more solved case out of it?"

"I can try, but I'm not going to guarantee that it'll work very long."

Frank looked over Dennis's shoulder. "Just long enough to solve this case, please?"

Dennis continued to work the menus, and the snake-head sensors started to come out of the top of the device. Dennis was about to start the first diagnostic test when a warning light came on. The power meter was rising towards a critical point. Dennis turned and looked at Frank.

"I told you this wasn't going to work. The device is going into overload, and I can't stop it. We have less than thirty seconds."

Frank leaned over to the ditch running along the side of the road. He found what he was looking for. He grabbed Dennis by the arm and headed for the three-foot high culvert. They quickly got down on their hands and knees and crawled in as deep as they could. When they had reached the inside middle of the culvert, Frank turned around and looked at Dennis.

"You did great, Dennis. Now let's see if the rest of our plan works. I saw our guy way off on one of the hillsides. A reflection from the front of his binoculars gave him away. How much time?"

"Anytiiiiiiiii."

The rebuilt MLA device detonated like a small atomic bomb. The blast vaporized the device, and most of the van before the shock wave continued up and down the road. A very small mushroom cloud rose up from the center of the detonation. The blast wave passed by the edge of the culvert causing severe ringing in both Dennis' and Frank's ears. Frank motioned for Dennis to continue out the other end of the culvert. When they exited the culvert, they brushed the mud off their pants and shoes. Frank glanced back at the bus stop. The blast had dug a large hole in the road and removed any sign of the MLA device. There would be small pieces everywhere and that's what he was counting on.

"We need to get out of here, before someone reports the explosion. Let's cut across the field and pick up the road a mile over. There's a bus stop there, and we can get back without the local police stopping us."

Dennis was still pretty shaken. He was having a hard time hearing Frank. "Are you sure this is going to work? Maybe the guy didn't hear what we were saying?"

Frank increased the pace as the field reached an incline. "If he was part of the intelligence organizations, they would have a long-distance directional mike pointed at us. He heard everything, but the question was whether they believed it or not."

General Martin Harrison had just gone over his morning reports when his secure line started to flash. He turned the encryption device on and picked up the receiver. "General Harrison here, what do you have for me?"

"Sir, you were right. Dr. Andrews had another MLA device. He used the test device before building the two for the Army. Dr. Andrews and Detective Ridge were using the device to solve a cold case. The power unit on the device went out of control, and the device blew up. It took out the middle of the road and the transport vehicle. Dr. Andrews and the detective survived by crawling into a road culvert about fifty yards away."

He took a deep breath and continued. "The local sheriff is already on the scene, and they don't have a clue as to the source of the explosion. I used my fake FAA credentials to allow me access to the site. Most of the pieces they had collected were from an MLA device. The sheriff is assuming that a satellite fell out of orbit and crashed into the road. I think that'll work for us. I recognized the parts, but I don't think anyone else will connect the dots. From the conversation I overheard, Dr. Andrews used everything he had on this device."

"That's great news," said the general.

"General, my man at Dr. Andrews's house was able to bypass the security system to do a complete search of the house and the lab. Most of the research on the computers has to do with the lionfish invading the Atlantic Ocean. A few bits and pieces about three cold cases they solved using the MLA, but it was never mentioned in the report. It appears that you will no longer have to worry about Dr. Andrews. We'll monitor his movements for the next few days to confirm our assessment of the situation. Our recommendation is to do nothing further at this time."

The general leaned back in his chair to analyze this new information. "I agree that Dr. Andrews, and his detective friend have been in the news too much. Let's keep an eye on them for a couple more weeks. If things change, we may have to take more drastic measures."

The general disconnected and dialed a second number to Senator Bob Welding's private phone. "We need to talk."

As she drove to Dennis's house, Debra thought about the fact that she was completely in the dark as to where the evening was going to go. When she approached the gate, it opened and closed right behind her. As she pulled up to the front of the house, Frank came out and opened her door. He gave her a big hug and grabbed the bag she was carrying. When she entered the house, she detected the lovely aroma of a roast dinner. It was a heavenly smell that reminded her of the days when her mother was still around. Frank set her bag down, and Dennis offered her a glass of wine. The two men had been quiet and far too nice, so she knew something was up. She took a sip of the wine and took her first shot.

"So, what's with the two of you? You both look like you just came back from a big win at a poker game. Something's up, and I want to know what. It's more than just your new detective agency isn't it?"

Frank looked over to Dennis and then back to Debra.

"The truth is that we both have been keeping lots of secrets from you, and today one of them literally blew up in our faces. We survived, but that's really the middle of our story. You need to drink your glass of wine, and let us pour you another before we continue."

"Does this have something to do with the Jesse Carr shooting?"

"Yes and no. Jesse Carr was just the catalyst to a much bigger set of events."

"Come on, Dad, what gives? You know I have little or no patience. What the hell are you two up to?"

For the next fifteen minutes, Frank laid out the whole story of Medusa, the cold cases, and finally the most-recent events that had happened earlier in the day. The more he spoke, the quieter Debra became. Dennis was smart enough to stay out of the conversation, even when Frank had some of the science wrong. When Frank finished, she lifted her glass and chugged it all down.

"You know, Dad, this is not the conversation for a nice wine. I need a couple of beers. This isn't a bunch of bullshit is it? All this really happened? Neither one of you trusted me enough to tell me all this?"

She looked over to Dennis and continued. "I might expect this from someone I barely know, but my father? That's completely unacceptable. If you both are considering having me work with you in the detective agency, there can be no secrets. You both should know better."

The two men looked at each other, and nodded agreement. Dennis got up and headed toward the garden. Debra turned and looked at Frank. "So you're going to be first? How did you two decide this? A coin toss or what?"

Frank looked down and rubbed the back of his neck. "I know it was wrong not to tell you, but I really thought I was protecting you. If I'd told you everything, you would've had to turn me in, or resign."

"Maybe I wouldn't have, Dad."

"Honey, I know you pretty well. You would do the right thing, even though it jeopardized your family relationship. Do you honestly think you would have just let it pass? You would have gone by the book. Dennis really likes you; he just has a strange way of showing it. What he did to save your life, was one of the bravest things I've ever seen. He knew Carr could have shot him. Dennis was willing to risk his life for yours. He was protecting you the same way I did, by not telling you the truth. Now you can stay pissed at me as long as you want, but don't take it out on Dennis."

Frank stopped because Debra had tears in her eyes. She reached out and put her arms around him. "I understand why you did it, but I just think there could've been a better way. Now as for Dennis, I do have a few choice words for him. So if you don't mind, I'm going to have a little chat with him out in the garden."

Frank looked out to the garden. Dennis was trying to pick up Tigger, but the cat was not having it. Now Dennis had two souls mad at him. "I was sort of hoping you'd give Dennis a break."

She wiped the tears from her eyes. "So, you thought that pity plead for Dennis was going to save his sorry little ass? No way in hell. I'm going to read him the riot act, and you aren't going to stop me. So you stay right here, while I dish out his punishment."

Frank was confused. He was sure that Debra would cool down. Now she seemed more upset than ever. Dennis was on his own, because he couldn't save him on this one. He watched as she walked to the sliding door, opened it, and closed it part way. Tigger headed toward the gap in the door and was quickly rubbing back and forth against Frank's legs. Debra approached Dennis and stood right in his face like a drill sergeant would address his troops.

"I've said my piece with my dad, now it's your turn, Dennis."

Dennis looked like a kid who had been caught with his hand in the cookie jar. He was about to say something when Debra put her arms around him and brought her lips to his. The passion was strong and Dennis returned it once he realized his life was no longer in danger. Frank was in the process of picking up the cat when Debra had made her move. His jaw dropped in surprise, and he mumbled, "Tigger, she's just like her mother - totally unpredictable. That's the last thing I thought she would do."

Frank turned and walked into the kitchen to check the dinner. The way things were going in the garden, he might have to turn the heat down and delay dinner. He opened the microwave to check on the potatoes, and looked at the dining table to see what Dennis had put out so far. He looked through the cupboards and found the missing items to complete the place settings for three. As he finished he heard the sound of the slider opening. He looked up to see Dennis and Debra entering, hand in hand.

"So, are you two all right with each other now?"

Debra looked over to Dennis. "We're fine, Dad. I just wanted to scare you a little. You both are so easy."

197

Dennis pulled out a chair so she could sit down, and then looked at Frank. "Is everyone in your family like Debra? She scared the hell out of me."

Frank grinned. "Get used to it."

"I plan on it," Dennis said as he smiled at Debra.

Chapter 26

A week had passed, and the three members of The Ridge Detective Agency had spent long hours devising a business plan. Frank scheduled several appointments with possible clients and had already met with a few. The potential for their business was growing daily.

The biggest hurdle they had to overcome was Medusa. Debra refused to accept the methods that Dennis had used to gain access to databases via other wireless computer systems. Everything else had been resolved, but on this aspect, they had come to a stalemate.

Debra finally held up her hand and yelled at the two. "As I understand Medusa, she needs lots of processing power to extract DNA, and data to formulate a solution. I'm not the greatest with computers, but can't you buy some powerful systems and stack them together to form one big one?"

Dennis nodded his agreement to her idea.

She continued, "Let's say that they each cost two thousand dollars. Fifty computers would cost one hundred thousand dollars. I'd be willing to put up the money to buy them, so that we'd be legal."

Both Frank and Dennis were in shock, but for different reasons. Frank was the first to voice a reply. "Where in the hell did you get that much money? It took me forever to save that much and you've been working just a few years in the D.A.'s office. How's that possible?"

"I made good money, Dad. My salary was one hundred twenty-five thousand when I quit, and I was very good at saving and investing money. If we're going to make this work, the three of us need to contribute to the cause. The question is will fifty computers do the job to make us legal?"

Both Frank and Debra then glanced at Dennis, who had a blank look on his face. He was still processing all the variables.

"It could work," he said, "but before we do, we might consider another option. I need to give you some background on my idea first. I wasn't the only scientist the Army considered for the MLA project. A friend of mine, Dr. Kendall Dronager, was my college teammate at Cal Tech, where we worked together on computer applications. His part of the project was the designing of the computer system itself, while I was responsible for the performance applications. When we first started, we used 12 high-end computers to simulate what we wanted to accomplish. We linked them together and used them to run the various data analysis programs. He then built a single super computer that replaced the twelve machines we used for the initial tests."

Dennis paused briefly, and then continued. "After graduation, we both went our own ways. He continued to work on super computers, and I continued to work on programing applications for data analysis. The Army contacted him first about the MLA project, but he was in the process of developing a quantum computer system. It's a new system that manipulates atoms for data storage. The problem is that his system is very unstable when moved, and requires super cooled processors to work effectively. Since the Army wanted portability and compactness, it was rejected as a possible solution for the MLA.

"The Army found out that I'd worked with Kendall and contacted me about the project. I worked with Xtreme Machines to build many of the parts on the MLA device. I haven't talked with him lately, but he might be able to point us in the right direction. He still works at the college on a quantum computer research grant, so I'll give him a call. I think I'll need to go see him before we continue any further. "

Frank took a sip from his coffee, and set the cup down. "That sounds like a great idea. Why don't the two of you go? It would be good for the both of you to get away from here for a while. Take some time and enjoy the sights. I've plenty of work to do here."

Debra glared at her father. "Look Dad, I'm old enough to make my own decisions. You're not going to play matchmaker with me."

Dennis watched the two banter back and forth, before he put his two cents in. "So, you don't want to go with me to Los Angeles?"

Debra blushed. "No, Dennis, I didn't mean that. I do want to go; it's just being pushed by my father that I object to."

Frank grinned. "You two are something else. I can see it, but neither one of you can. You're a great couple, so why not just admit it?"

She recomposed herself. "Dad, drop it. This is between Dennis and me. Stop pushing me."

"I'm only doing what's obvious to me. Just forget I said anything. Your main objection to the way Medusa works is the computer system, so go with Dennis, and make sure you're happy with the solution. Besides, I have at least four appointments this week. One is even with Xtreme Machines. They want us to do some background checks and look at their computer security systems. When they hear that Dennis is part of our team, I'm sure we can get at least a limited contract. By the time you get back, we can put whatever solution you decide upon into place with Medusa."

Dennis had already started to pack some of the equipment and specifications he would need. "Sounds good to me, and I agree that Debra should come along. She has good insight on the obvious, and I tend to overlook it. Besides, I couldn't think of anyone's company I'd enjoy more than yours, Debra."

Debra said nothing as she knew it would only fuel her father's matchmaking.

Frank dumped the rest of his coffee in the sink and chuckled. "That's a first for Debra. She had no comeback, so there's hope for you yet, Dennis."

Chapter 27

During the first half of the trip to Los Angeles, Debra seemed to be giving Dennis the silent treatment. Finally, Dennis couldn't stand it anymore. "So, you're going to be mad at me the whole trip?"

"Look, Dennis, it's not you. This isn't the first time my dad has tried to pressure me into a romantic relationship, but sometimes he just goes too far. I love him dearly, but occasionally he really pisses me off."

"So, who before me?"

"Are you jealous? It was a long time ago, and he wasn't right for me."

"Who are we talking about, my college roommate?"

"It's not really important."

"It is to me."

"Yes, it was your roommate, Jeff. He was always into himself, constantly staring at the mirror to see how good he looked. He thought he was an actor, but that was just a joke."

"I found it refreshing, because he never bothered me much. He was always trying to be the big time actor. He thought that it would make him a babe magnet. He never brought you by our room, so I didn't meet you until after I met your father. I know you don't like some of the things your father does, but he's really a great guy."

"I know, and I love him dearly. He just pushes my buttons sometimes."

"Just ignore him when he does that."

"I'll try, but let's change the subject. We still don't know much about each other, so why not take advantage of this time together."

Dennis looked into her eyes. She was so beautiful. Why hadn't he seen it before? He knew the reason was his other love – Medusa. All of a sudden, Medusa was the last thing on his mind. Strong feelings he'd never experienced before were raging in full force. He wanted to reach over and kiss Debra, but she wanted to get to know him better. Dennis really didn't want to talk about his childhood, but knew he'd have to eventually.

"My childhood wasn't what you would call the norm. My mother started me into science education at age three. My alphabet was Atom, Biology, Crustacean, and so on. I had few friends because none of the other kids wanted to hang around with a straight-A student. I seriously considered purposely getting lower grades, so I'd have a friend or two, but Mom would have figured it out right away. Dad tried to step in and tone things down some, but he always lost the battle.

"Both of them were gone most of the time," he sighed. "Mom was teaching at the college, going on lecture tours, and working on research grants. Dad was a hotshot architect who designed more than one hundred large buildings across the United States. Many of the buildings downtown were his designs. His success in part was because he made sure that every structure he designed had the highest possible earthquake standards."

He hesitated, "My whole world was turned upside down at age six when he was murdered. The police never found the killer. I don't remember much about that night other than making the 911 call. I even tried going to a shrink to access my subconscious, but no usable memories about that night have surfaced."

Dennis stopped and saw she had tears running down her face. He reached over and grabbed a Kleenex.

"I'm sorry. Did I say something to upset you?"

"No, but I can relate to losing a parent. I don't know how you continued after such an experience."

"My mother was strong. She held and loved me when I was feeling down, and told me to buck up when she thought it was needed. She pulled me out of school for a year and home schooled me. When I entered school the next year, they bumped me up two grades. I graduated at age sixteen and had my first doctorate at twenty-four. I never dated much, and most that did date me, found me boring. I talked too much about the projects I was working on, and rarely about the real me. Look, I'm talking excessively."

"That's not true. I asked you to tell me about your childhood. I'm interested in your past."

Dennis hesitated a few seconds. This was new territory for him. He was putting his heart out on his sleeve. "Why did you kiss me in the garden? I thought you were going to chew me out, and well, ...I was so surprised. Don't get me wrong. It was wonderful, but I just wasn't sure how you felt about me."

"I'll be honest, Dennis, that up until a few weeks ago, I wasn't sure myself. I kissed you because I felt it was the right thing to do. Actually, I couldn't stop myself. Most of the guys I've dated had only one thing in mind - they wanted to get into my pants. You aren't one of those guys, and I feel you respect me. You listen to me, and don't try to impress me with your intelligence. I think you're a handsome man, and I feel very comfortable with you. I don't really know where our relationship is going yet. I know where my dad wants it to go, but I'd like to think that we can enjoy our future without any undue pressures."

"My roommate was one of those guys. When he wasn't exploiting his dates, he was looking at himself in the mirror. That's definitely not me."

"I respect that, Dennis. The key is respecting the girl first, and understanding what she wants from her date. Most men can't do that very well."

Dennis grinned. It was now his time for some fun. "So, you want me to get into your pants?"

Debra was flustered by his question, and blushed. "No, you didn't understand what I said."

"I understood perfectly. Is there a chance that maybe...uh, sometime maybe in the future?"

She felt boxed in. "You never know what the future may bring, Dennis. Let's take it one day at a time. Maybe the answer is yes, but let's change the subject. What does your mother do now? She seems to be gone all the time. Do you know why she hates my dad so much?"

Dennis looked out the window. They were just passing Santa Barbara. "Oh, I love a multi-part question. Mom has always had her head to the educational research grindstone. I rarely see her, and when I do, she talks endlessly about her projects. I know everyone thinks I'm a mama's boy because I live at home, but to be perfectly honest we seldom see each other. She needed someone to watch the house, and I needed somewhere to live. It's a strange family relationship, but it works. I love her very much, and she has the same feelings for me.

"As to why she hates your dad, I thought it was because he was a cop, but there's something more to it. I asked her a couple of times, and she immediately changed the subject. When I pushed, she told me that it was none of my business. So, the answer is that I don't have a clue. We're going to land in a few minutes. Let's check into the hotel, and then have a nice dinner. It's my turn to hear all about you.

"Oh, and one other thing..." He leaned over, put his arms around her, and kissed her - displaying some of his pent-up passion. She resisted slightly, but then gave in. The pilot broke it up with an announcement to buckle up.

Debra reached down and grabbed her seatbelt. "I was saved by the pilot. Guess that's a new one."

The two laughed as the jet touched down on the runway.

Dennis arranged for a taxi to take them directly to the hotel. He'd ordered two adjacent rooms, and everyone at the front desk was overly eager to help. They dropped their bags into their rooms, and Dennis led the way to the front of the hotel to grab another taxi. When they arrived at the restaurant, Debra could see from the outside presentation that it was going to be expensive. She stopped Dennis before they entered the restaurant.

205

"Dennis, I appreciate what you've done so far. You're going way beyond the norm, and we could go someplace less expensive."

"Nope, I already made reservations. I have several scientific friends who work down here, including the guy we're going to see tomorrow, so I come here often."

Dennis grabbed her arm, and the two were met by the headwaiter. He pointed toward the back of the restaurant.

"Dr. Andrews, we haven't seen you in some time. Your table is as you ordered, Sir."

Debra looked around at the crowd as they walked to the back of the restaurant. It was obvious that this was a place for the rich and famous to dine. When they reached the back, the waiter pulled back a sliding frosted glass door that opened up into a smaller room. Standing by their table for two was a couple more waiters. The lights were low, with only candlelight for ambiance. After the two were seated, wine was poured and all the waiters disappeared. She was still trying to take it all in. This was even more impressive than their first date.

"Dennis, you did all this for me?"

"There's no one else in the room."

"You know what I mean. We're supposed to be down here on a business trip. This is so much more."

"You don't like it?"

"No, I love it. The truth is I've never been treated this way by any man. It's a little too overwhelming, but marvelous."

"Relax and enjoy it tonight, because tomorrow we work. Remember our deal? I told you about myself, consequently, it's now your turn. We have the entire evening to ourselves, so take your time."

Debra took a sip from her glass. The wine was excellent, just like everything.

"My life was boring compared to yours. I really don't know where to start."

Dennis reached over and held her hand. "Start with school. Did you belong to clubs, or do sports? You know, school things."

"I was a loner. Being the cop's daughter isn't always a good thing when it comes to making friends. My parents were married in Denver, and my dad joined the Denver Police Department right out of the police academy. We lived there for fifteen years so most of my schooling was in Denver. I had one friend who was somewhat of a rebel, so we watched each other's back. Her dad had also been a cop, but was killed in the line of duty."

She paused and took a sip from her wine. "My most memorable times were with my dad's partner, Lloyd Becker. He was like an adopted uncle. I was mad when dad took a job with the Seattle Police Department, because I missed Uncle Lloyd. I got over it eventually, but it was some rough times."

She glanced over at Dennis to see if she had bored him yet. He just smiled, so she continued. "In college, I majored in criminal justice. Dad supported me all the way through college, in spirit and financially. I was hired right out of college into the D.A.'s office. When my mom got sick ten years ago, I almost lost dad too. He started drinking, staying out late, and raising hell at a couple of local bars. Captain Carson was the one who saved him. He got him to go to AA, and gave him some time off to clean up his act. He and the captain have been close friends ever since. There, I told you it was boring."

Before Debra could respond, the waiter brought in the main course. For the next three hours, the two talked about childhood friends, pranks they'd played, their first driving lesson, prom, and more until it was almost eleven and the restaurant was closing. Dennis had become mesmerized by her. Suddenly, everything in his mind was going very fast. He was starting to realize that she was "the one." This was a new experience for him, and he was struggling with it, yet loving it.

Dennis paid the bill, and the taxi took them back to the hotel. He checked for messages, and found one from Kendall reminding him of the appointment at ten the next morning. The two rode the elevator in silence, as they both knew there would be an awkward moment soon. Debra pulled out her room key and turned to Dennis.

"The evening was wonderful. I had such a good time. To be truthful, Dennis no one has ever treated me like this. I don't know how to thank you."

"I do."

Dennis pulled her close and kissed her as if they would never see each other again.

"Good night, Debra, sweet dreams. We can go down for breakfast together before we see Kendall."

"Good night."

Debra closed the door, and Dennis walked down to his room. He wasn't going to be getting much sleep tonight. His head was spinning from the wine, and Debra. He closed the door and stared at the wall.

Debra grabbed a quick shower, put on her nightgown, and picked up her Kindle. She needed to wind down, but a love story might not be the right solution. A few minutes had passed when she heard a knock at her door. She went over and looked through the peephole. It was Dennis. She unlocked the door, and talked through the crack in the door.

"Give me a couple of seconds," she said as she wrapped herself in a blanket. "Okay, come on in."

Dennis looked around the room and then at Debra. "Sorry, I never checked to see if everything was good with your room. It looks fine, but thought I should check."

She turned off the Kindle and set it on the nightstand. "That's not a very good line to get you into a gal's bedroom."

"That wasn't a line. I just wanted to make sure you were okay."

"I'm just having fun with you. Can you do me a favor, though?"

"Sure, what?"

"Please close the door behind you."

"Oh, I was planning on it when I left."

"You don't understand, Dennis. Walk into the room, close the door, and lock it."

Dennis hesitated, but did as he was asked. When he turned back around, he noticed that Debra had removed the blanket. He could see right through her nightgown, and he almost had a seizure.

She patted the bed and said, "Can you stay with me tonight?"

"Are you sure that's what you want?"

"I'm waiting."

"I didn't bring my pajamas. They're next door."

"Dennis."

"Yes?"

"You won't need your pajamas."

Chapter 28

Dennis awoke with a start. Debra felt so good nuzzled against him. She stirred and gave him a brief kiss. Dennis sat up and looked at the clock.

"It's almost 10 a.m. and we're going to be late for the meeting."

Her hands moved over his body. "What's more important, the meeting or this?"

At noon, Dennis reached up to turn on the showerhead. "I have to be truthful; I've never showered with anybody before now."

Debra put her arms around Dennis. "Are you complaining?"

"No, just thought you should know. I had no idea what I was missing. You know Kendall is really going to be pissed."

"Well, it's either him or me."

Kendall couldn't understand what happened to Dennis. He was normally a very punctual friend, but something important must have happened to prevent him from coming to the meeting. Kendall was about to leave the outside café table where he'd eaten his lunch when Dennis walked up with a beautiful woman on his arm.

"Dennis, I was about to chew you out for standing me up, but I can see that you had a very good reason."

Kendall put out his hand to Debra. "Hi, I'm Kendall Dronager. Dennis and I were lab partners in college, but I'm guessing he's already told you that. It's very nice to meet you."

Debra smiled as she shook his hand. "I'm Debra Ridge. I work with Dennis in a new detective agency that my father has formed."

Kendall scanned Debra with his eyes. "If I had someone who looked like you, I'd never get any work done."

Dennis pulled a chair out for her. "Don't get any ideas, Kendall. She's ...."

Debra finished the sentence. "His girlfriend too."

Kendall pointed to the other chair. "Sit down, Dennis, you lucky dog. I have to get back to the lab pretty soon, so what's going on that prompted you to make this special trip?"

Dennis looked around to see if anyone was listening in. No one was near the table.

"Remember the MLA project? Well, I worked on it until it blew up in their faces. They buried the project and eventually moved on to other projects that would waste even more tax dollars. After the project was killed, I combined forces with Debra and her father. I have the analysis part of the solution worked out, but lack an adequate way to process the data in a timely manner. We'd considered linking a lot of workstations together, but I wanted to see if you had a better solution before proceeding."

Kendall moved his head back and forth as though he didn't believe Dennis. "Wow, I can't believe this. Fate really saved my butt this time. I've had a grant from the university to develop a quantum computer system for a couple of years now. Unfortunately, the financial crisis has cut back severely on the budget. My grant is about to run out unless I can sell the super computer the university purchased for my previous grant. They left it up to me to find a buyer. It sounds like it would be perfect for you. The downside is that it's about the size of a refrigerator, and requires a super cooled environment to run efficiently. It's a typical parallel processing unit, and can do the work of a couple hundred computers in one-tenth the time."

Dennis was about to ask the next question, but Debra jumped in and asked, "How much?"

Kendall looked at the two and at then at Debra. "It cost a couple of million, but the college gave me a bottom dollar of five hundred thousand."

Debra picked up her coffee and said, "I'll give you two hundred fifty. Cash."

Kendall was in shock. His grant was about to be extended, but the college had to be convinced. He pulled out his phone and pressed one of the numbers. "Dr. Windall, this is Kendall. I have a buyer for the super computer - Two fifty, cash."

About twenty seconds of silence before Kendall continued. "No, Sir, I don't think that'll work. They're leaving in a couple of days. ...All right, I'll tell them."

Kendall set the phone down. "I don't think they thought the thing was going to sell at all. They jumped at your offer. You are now the proud owners of a super computer."

Dennis looked around again. The waiter was now on the other side of the table area. "We do have one other problem. We're sure we're being watched. A delivery of a large super computer might send up a couple of red flags. Do you have any ideas?"

Kendall opened his briefcase and pulled out a card. "Actually, I do. Many of the industrial corporations in the area use a great shipping company. They put the items to be shipped in common cartons for washers and dryers. The guys who deliver even wear clothing to match. I'd say that you are about to get a nice big refrigerator delivered in a couple of days. I can even talk the college into paying for the delivery. We have a deal then?"

Dennis looked over to Debra. She nodded and said, "Your grant has been extended, Kendall. Thanks for all the help. I'll have my accountant wire the funds to the college this afternoon or tomorrow at the latest. We're going to do a little sightseeing before heading back, so we should be back in Seattle in a couple of days. Thanks again, Kendall. You don't know how much this helps us."

Kendall got up. "It goes both ways. I don't have to worry about my grant for at least another year. I think I got the best deal."

Dennis shook his hand. "We both did."

On the way back to the hotel, Debra called her accountant and insured that the funds would be transferred by the next day. Once she'd hung up the phone, Dennis gave her a kiss.

"Thanks for all the help," he said. "I would have paid the half million. You just saved us all two hundred and fifty thousand. It's time we celebrate. Have you ever been to the San Diego Zoo?"

The two enjoyed an early dinner and went on a long walk along the harbor. Dennis canceled his room at the hotel and moved his stuff into her room. They spent the rest of the evening getting to know each other all over again.

The following day the two checked out of the hotel and flew down to San Diego. They spent most of the day enjoying everything the zoo had to offer. They checked into a hotel right along the beach, and the two consumed a quiet dinner watching a fiery red sunset. Near the end of the dinner, Dennis broached a subject that needed addressing before they returned home. He reached out and held her hand.

"How are we going to do this with your dad? He's going to know something's going on. I like your dad and don't want to lie to him, but I'm really not sure how he's going to take our new relationship."

Debra looked out as the sun was just about to disappear below the horizon. She then turned to him and said, "So, where do you think our relationship is right now?"

Dennis swallowed and almost choked. "We're a young couple who are very serious about each other."

Debra watched Dennis squirm. "And...?"

"I love you very much."

"Are you sure it's not just the sex?"

"Absolutely."

"So, sex has nothing to do with it?"

"You're not playing fair. I love you. Yes, the sex is great, but that's just part of it. I love you as a friend and a lover. It's that simple. You haven't said anything. So how do <u>you</u> feel?"

"Pretty much the same."

"Same what?"

"Okay, I love you too. Are you happy now?"

"Damn right I'm happy. I don't care what your dad says. I'm proud to be your boyfriend and lover."

"Then it's all settled. You won't say a word, and I'll break it to him."

"What? That isn't what I said."

"I know."

"I'm so confused."

"That's what I was hoping for."

Chapter 29

Frank had been working round the clock since his two partners had left for Los Angeles. Dennis had called him and told him about the super computer purchase, and that they were staying a day or two longer. Frank looked out the front window of his office, and smiled. He was happy for them and knew they were good for each other. He just never understood why it took them so long to get together. He was a little nervous as to how they would present their new relationship to him. Maybe they wouldn't say a thing, and keep him in the dark. That was fine with him, as he respected their privacy.

There was bad news brewing concerning yesterday's new case, and the fact that he'd' been keeping a secret from Dennis. He was about to make another call, when Dennis and Debra waltzed into the office. They looked so happy, and that's all that mattered. He got up and gave Debra a hug, then shook Dennis's hand.

"Good work guys. Looks like we're almost ready to move ahead. How long until the new computer is up and running?"

Dennis walked over and poured two cups of coffee. "I think I can get it up and running in a couple of weeks."

Frank pulled out a chair for Debra. "I don't want to push the issue, but your mother called the office early this morning. She's going to be back at the end of the month. I told her that you went on a business trip with Debra. She asked me to pass along a message that the lab needed to be up and running. She has a lot of lionfish data to process. She was actually nice to me, but I'm not sure what to make of it. I have a feeling that'll change once she gets here."

Dennis took a sip of his very strong coffee. He reached out and added some cream. "So, anything going on while we were gone?"

"Actually, there are two things we need to discuss. - one is personal, and one business. Which one do you want to hear first?"

"The personal first, I guess."

Frank took a deep breath and said, "Okay, here goes. I owe you an apology, Dennis. I've been keeping a secret from you, and we said we wouldn't do that anymore. You never asked about my new place. Why is that?"

Dennis added more cream because it was still too strong. "Frank, I think I know what you're going to say. You bought the house where my father was murdered, right?"

Debra glared at her dad. "You did what? You didn't tell me it was Dennis's old house. What were you thinking?"

Frank closed the folder he had been reviewing. "I know that I should have said something. Look, I needed a place to live and the house was on the market. Most importantly, I promised you that I'd look into Carl Andrew's murder. The captain let me look in the evidence box, but I needed more. Dennis, your dad was a distinguished architect. The house is great, but I have a feeling that there's more to his murder. When I looked through the crime scene photos, I noticed that many valuables were left in the bedroom. I don't think it was a simple robbery, as it seemed like the invaders were looking for something in particular. I have a feeling your dad hid something valuable enough to kill for. I don't think they found it because I think your dad hid it in a secret compartment in this house. When we find it, we just might find the killer. I've been looking at the blueprints searching for any extra space within the walls, but so far, nothing worthwhile. So, are you pissed at me? I'm sorry. I was only trying to help because you've grown on me."

Dennis got up and poured the oil-based coffee down the drain. "When you mentioned the area where you purchased your house, I suspected what you'd done. At first, I was angry, but the more I thought about it, I realized that you were only trying to help. Please, don't try to talk me into coming over though. I

216

don't know if I'll ever be able to make that giant step. What you say about the murder does make sense, but I don't see how you can do any more at this point. Let's table it for right now and concentrate on our new business. What's the other item you wanted to discuss?"

Frank looked over to Debra, and then to Dennis. "Neither one of you are going to like this one. I got a call yesterday from someone you both know. Dennis's old roommate, Jeff Windom is in a lot of trouble. He called me from jail. It seems that he has been keeping track of Debra, and knew about our new business. Anyway, he's up for assault and rape."

He continued, "The charges state that when he first tried to rape the girl, she fought him off. He beat her up and then continually raped her until she passed out. It seems he has no alibi and was in the same bar the night of the rape. There are few witnesses and very little evidence. It's just her word identifying Jeff. The bartender indicated that Jeff followed the girl out of the back door, and the rape happened a few minutes later. He contends he didn't do it, but I didn't know what to tell Jeff. I think he should get someone else to help him considering the fact that the three of you have a history."

Dennis and Debra were both in somewhat of a trance, with neither speaking.

Finally, she broke the silence. "I think our past can be put aside. We should take his case."

Dennis was not convinced. "Come on, doesn't the fact that he was stalking you provide reason enough not to defend him?"

"He wasn't stalking me, just keeping track."

"It sounds a whole lot like stalking to me. What do you think, Frank?"

"Before you decide, there's more you need to know. When Jeff was first picked up, he hired a local attorney who was just out of law school. The Assistant D.A. offered Jeff a good deal since the case was going to be difficult to prosecute without hard evidence. Jeff was about to go for it when he heard that Debra was now a defense attorney. He fired his attorney and called me. I checked with the Assistant D.A. after Jeff called, and found out that Jeff wasn't going to take the offer. Therefore, the Assistant D.A. turned it over to the Grand Jury. Jeff is sure that you can get him off. I'm not exactly sure what you should do, but I'm going to stay out of this one. It's between just the two of you to decide."

Dennis stood up and started to pace in front of the door. "I think it's a really bad idea. I know Jeff, and he likes to manipulate people to suit his needs. It sounds like he's guilty. I don't think it would be a good idea to lose our first case with a rapist."

Debra's face was starting to turn red with anger. "Are you sure that you're not against the case because we once dated?"

"Sounds like a good reason to me."

"Look, Dennis, I agree that Jeff is a jerk, but I can't see him raping and beating up a woman. No, we should take this case. I've seen cases like this before. When the only testimony is from the victim, the defense attorney can dig up something on the victim to convince the Grand Jury that there's reasonable doubt. So, Dad, tell us about the victim."

Frank really wished he hadn't opened this can of worms. The two had seemed so happy when they came in. Now they were looking at their first fight. He opened the folder and presented the data.

"Her name is Ginger Hallows. She works as a waitress in the day and as an actress at night. She has done a few commercials and wants to get a major part in a TV show or movie. She's been in the same bar as Jeff on several occasions. The police have yet to find anyone who saw them together. The only thing so far is testimony from the bartender and Ms. Hallows. She claims that they met in acting classes and reunited at the bar. That's all I have so far. Grand Jury is set to hear his case in a couple of days."

She reached out and took the folder from Frank. "It's settled then; we'll take the case."

Dennis closed his fists tightly until they started to turn white. "I don't agree. I think it's a really bad idea."

Debra started to scan down the papers inside the folder. "We started this agency to help people and companies with data analysis, detective work, and legal assistance. We can't turn down every case that involves someone we don't like. It doesn't work that way."

Dennis started for the door and said, "It does for me."

Before Debra or Frank could say anything, Dennis was gone. Debra was about to follow when Frank grabbed her arm. "Let him go. He'll come around. I may be going out on a limb, but I rather agree with Dennis. Your history with Jeff may cloud the issue."

Debra turned, walked out the door, and slammed it behind her. Frank sat in the empty room as the phone started to ring. "That went well. I really need to learn how to keep my mouth shut."

She sat fuming in her car and was afraid to drive. She was upset that her dad had sided with Dennis. Well, to hell with them. She started the car and headed for the county lockup where Jeff was being held.

When she arrived at the prisoner's holding area, she signed in. It was so nice being back in the game. She was on the other team, but still in the game. The guards and other prison personnel asked how she was doing. The closer she came to the interview area, the more she felt it was the right thing to do. She finally arrived in the interview area and waited for Jeff to be delivered. Jeff walked in handcuffed and sat down. A guard placed a cup of water in front of him and asked if Debra needed anything. She shook her head, and the guard left. It looked like Jeff had already been through hell. Debra opened the file that Frank had put together on the case.

"Look, Jeff, before you say one word, we need to set some ground rules. We may have had some history, but that's the past. I'm your lawyer, and that's all, nothing more. Do you understand and agree?"

Jeff took a sip from the glass. "We do have a history, and you can't just push that under the table. I liked you very much, and you still must have feelings for me or you wouldn't have come to my defense."

Debra stood up. "This is your last chance, Jeff. Our past is just that. You have a lot more pressing problems right now. Remember you're being charged with rape and assault."

"I didn't do it. I don't even know the girl. I don't understand why she picked me out."

She sat down and ran her finger down the page of the report. "The good news is that the only thing the D.A. has against you is her testimony. When I worked in the D.A.'s office that wasn't enough for a conviction. More times than I can count, the defense attorney could poke holes in the victim's testimony. However, right now, I have to ask you a question, and I must have the truth, or I won't defend you."

"Okay, what's the question?"

"Did you do it?"

"Absolutely not and I can't believe that you even asked me."

"Look, Jeff. The number-one reason defendants lose cases is that they lie to their attorney. What you tell me is privileged. So, I'm going to ask you one more time. Did you do it?"

"NO, NO, NO."

"Okay, tell me everything about that evening."

"You look very nice. I like your new hair style."

Debra closed the folder. "Okay, that's it. I'm out of here. Get yourself another lawyer."

"Wait. I'm sorry. We used to be friends. "

"You want to know the truth, Jeff? We were never friends. The only friend you have is yourself, and he's not that good of a friend right now. You had better get your act together, or you'll rot in here for the next ten years. One thing I do know for sure is that your handsome face will attract a lot of other men, and the consequences won't be pretty."

Jeff stood up from the table. "Okay, I understand. You have a thing with Nate now, but I was always better than he was. Please don't leave. I didn't rape that girl or touch a hair on her head. She's lying."

Debra was trying to decipher what Jeff had just said. "Who's Nate?"

Jeff sat back down and tried to grab her hand. "Dennis never told you. His middle name is Nathanial. We shortened it to Nate, and it became his nickname. All the guys at the fraternity called him Nate."

Debra pulled her hands far enough away that Jeff couldn't reach them. "Tell me about the evening."

"A lot of want-to-be actors and actresses go into this bar. Most of us have normal jobs and do part-time acting just waiting for the right role to come along. You never know when you might meet someone who can help you move up the ladder. Most everyone is there for the same reason. We all compare notes, but only to help ourselves. I did see the girl on the other end of the bar, but she was with another guy for most of the time. He's the guy who does a lot of the cleaning product commercials on the local TV station."

He took a drink and continued. "I tried to pick up a couple of girls, but my lines weren't working well, so I struck out, and went home. I watched some TV and went to bed. The police woke me in the middle of the night and arrested me. They read me my rights and asked me if I knew Ms. Hallows. I've seen enough cop shows to know that I shouldn't say anything without a lawyer present. The cop interviewing me wanted to know if I had anything to hide. He said that if I was innocent, I should tell them everything that happened that night, so they could clear up the situation. I kept my mouth shut and asked for a lawyer. They left me alone after that. I don't understand what's going on. I did nothing wrong."

Debra closed the folder and stood up. "Let me do some poking around and see what I can find out. Your bail hearing is set for this afternoon. Don't say anything to anyone. Do you understand?"

"Yes, I understand."

Frank hung up the phone. It was a busy morning with two more possible clients. He was going to have to get out soon and do some work. It was already apparent that they needed a receptionist to field the calls and relay messages. He was about to make another call when Debra came back into the office. She pulled up a chair and slid it across the floor. "I'm sorry I flew off the handle this morning. I know you and Dennis don't agree with me on this one, but now I need your help."

Frank closed the iPad that he had been using to collect notes. "Hey, I'm not against you. I only meant that I could also see Dennis's point of view. I wasn't saying he was correct, but that his comments had validity. I'd never question your decision. You know better what cases we should take or not. I'm sure that you're purely professional on this one. So, what do you want?"

"I need a complete background check on Ms. Hallows. I want to know everything about her. Arrest reports, boyfriends, her whereabouts for the last couple of weeks. Do what you do best and get me everything you can think of. I really can't stand Jeff, but he just isn't the type to do this. Something's wrong with this case. It's right in front of us, but we can't see it yet. Please find it, Dad."

"What about Dennis? You two seemed so happy when you first came in this morning. I seemed to have screwed that up. I should have just told Jeff we weren't interested. I know it's none of my business but what happened to you in LA? Is there something I should know?"

"What's going on between Dennis and me is private. You should know that."

"Sorry, I won't mention it again."

Frank tried to hold his smile in check. It was serious between them. Debra had never been so defensive about her relationships. Yep, it was really serious. From now on, Dennis was in for the roller-coaster ride of his life.

Frank opened his iPad again and made a couple of more notes. "So, what do you want me to say to Dennis if he calls?"

Debra said nothing as she turned and closed the door.

Dennis arrived home after driving around for more than an hour. He was so mad at Debra, and yet his stomach was tearing him apart. He wanted to call her and apologize, but he had nothing for which to apologize. He knew he was right about Jeff, but his heart was telling him that being right wasn't necessarily in his best interest.

Instead, he decided to bury himself in his work. The phone messages indicated a trucking company was scheduled to deliver a new refrigerator the next morning. That was great news. He could spend the rest of the day getting the lab ready. The pathway between the equipment elevator and the new computer's home would need to be cleared. He'd then set up the links between Medusa and the new super computer. Once that was completed, he'd have to link the rest of the lab computers into the same system so that his mother could process her lionfish data. She would be thrilled when she saw how fast the new system could process her raw data.

No matter how much Dennis concentrated on setting up the new system, his mind kept drifting back to Debra. When it did, his stomach turned upside down. This internal struggle was tearing him apart. He took a couple of pills to settle himself down, but it didn't seem to help. He was in the middle of running a diagnostic check on Medusa when his phone rang.

"Dr. Andrews, this is Detective Ortega calling from Los Angeles. Do you know a Dr. Kendall Dronager?"

"Yes, I do. We had a meeting with him a couple of days ago. Is there something wrong?"

"What was your meeting about?"

"It was both business and personal. What's going on and how did you find me?"

"Sir, Dr. Dronager was murdered last night in his lab. Did he have any enemies?"

Dennis turned off Medusa. Memories of his past started to surface. "None that I know of. He didn't have much of a social circle."

"Is there anything he was working on that someone would need to torture him?"

"Torture?"

"I can't tell you how, but someone was definitely trying to get some information out of him. Do you have any idea what?"

Dennis lied. His buying of the super computer might be a reason. "There's nothing that I can think of. My girlfriend and I had a short lunch with him. That was the only time I've seen him in the last six months. Do you have any leads in the case?"

"Do you work in law enforcement?"

"My job is a consultant doing mainly CSI stuff for the Ridge Detective Agency."

"Is that Frank Ridge?"

"Do you know him?"

"I worked in Denver for some time. He and Lloyd Becker were detectives when I worked there as a traffic officer. Is he around?"

"He's at the office. I can give you the number if you want."

"Thanks. I'll get back to you if I find out any more."

Dennis hung up the phone and pulled out a beer from the lab refrigerator. He started to think about the general, the senator, and the MLA project. He couldn't believe that they would kill Dr. Dronager just to find out what he was doing in Los Angeles. Fear that he hadn't known since he'd shot Jesse Carr began to surface and eat away at his stomach. He finished the beer, pulled out another, and mourned the loss of his friend.

Chapter 30

Senator Bob Welding scanned the morning papers and was about to put them down for another cup of coffee when a headline stopped him cold. He read the article several times before picking up his secure line to General Harrison.

"Before you say anything, Senator, it was never our intention to kill Dr. Dronager. My man was just supposed to search his lab, when Dr. Dronager surprised him. Things got out of hand, and my man shot him in the leg."

The senator looked to see if his office door was closed before he pressed the encrypt send button. "Look, I told you to look quietly into Dr. Andrews's activities and anyone with which he made contact. Not leave a trail of bodies. Do you realize that if a nosey reporter puts Dr. Andrews and Dr. Dronager together they might start looking into their shared projects? I can't have that with elections coming up. The party is looking at putting me in as a presidential candidate. If they connect me to the two doctors, I can kiss my political career good-bye. So, when does a gunshot wound to the leg kill someone?"

"My man was trying to impress me, and tried to torture the doctor into telling him the truth about his meeting with Dr. Andrews. Unfortunately, the second shot, meant for the arm, hit the heart and killed Dr. Dronager instantly. After all that, we're still not sure what the purpose of their meeting was. We did a check, and found out that the two have friendly meetings every six months. We now believe that Dr. Andrews was on such a visit and was taking his new girlfriend down to meet Dr. Dronager. I take full blame for the incident, and will make sure that none of it comes back on you. I'm in the process of going over all MLA records to make sure they're all destroyed. All any reporter will find will be bits and pieces of a puzzle that will never be completed."

The senator's temperament simmered down a bit by this new information. "So, you think Dr. Andrews isn't going to be a problem?"

"He has as much to lose as you do. I don't think the theft of billions of dollars' worth of government property would win him the Nobel Prize. He's wealthy, but could never recover from the release of that information. The bottom line is that if we go down, so will he. If he was considering blowing the whistle on us, he would have made some threat by now."

"All right for now, but stay away from Dr. Andrews," said the senator. "Just watch him from a distance and do nothing to harm him or his girlfriend. I may change my mind in the future, but let's put this to bed for a while. Do you understand?"

They both agreed and hung up. The general then called in his most trusted Black Ops member to rectify the situation. He hated apologizing for mistakes, and planned to rectify the situation as soon as possible. It would be just another body to bury...like so many before.

Frank Ridge picked up his newspaper and read a similar headline. He picked up the phone and called Dennis.

"Dennis, this is Frank. Hey, I just read about the murder of a Dr. Dronager. Isn't that the guy you met with in LA?"

Dennis had been expecting his call.

"Yes, it was. I got a call from a Detective Ortega in Los Angeles about the murder. He wanted to know how I knew Dr. Dronager, and why we were meeting with him. Ortega said he knew you in Denver when you partnered with Lloyd Becker. He indicated he might give you a call."

"I never got the call, Dennis, and I swear I didn't know a Detective Ortega. Are you sure about the name? He mentioned Lloyd too?"

"Do you think he wasn't a cop?"

"Good chance the man who called you, actually killed your Dr. Dronager and was trying to collect further information to report to his boss. If you get any more calls, redirect them to me. Do you want me to tell Debra?"

"Not right now, as I don't think she really wants to talk to me. She's still pissed about Jeff's case, but no, I'll handle telling her myself. She really liked Dr. Dronager, just like me."

After the called ended, Frank looked out the window and decided he needed to start interviewing for a receptionist.

Debra looked over the charges against Jeff. The very fact that the D.A. had made such a good offer convinced her that they didn't have enough evidence for a conviction. Jeff had forced the Grand Jury, and the D.A.'s office would probably be happy if the case was dropped. They were just going through the motions. Jeff's case will be on the docket tomorrow, so she had to prepare for every possible contingency. The only thing that stuck in the back of her mind was the way Jeff kept acting toward her. She'd made it clear that there was nothing between them, but she wasn't sure that Jeff listened. He seemed more interested in her than his own case. She'd have to jump over that hurdle later.

Dennis pressed the last connector into place and started up the cooling system for the new super computer. When the display was green, he powered up the computer itself. Dennis wasn't exactly sure what to expect. He'd seen this type of computer in operation, but was never around for the initial startup. It sounded like a 747 revving its engines. Once the system was green, a diagnostic display appeared. He pressed the "run" icon to see if Medusa would recognize her new partner. Thirty minutes later, the system was online and ready for use.

Dennis looked around the lab for a sample to try out with the new system. He ran into his mother's bedroom and looked for her hairbrush. He pulled off a few hairs hoping that one would have a root attached. He placed the hairs in the sample chamber and asked Medusa to analyze. He turned away assuming it would take a couple of minutes, but immediately heard a beep. He turned around to see "Match Found" at the bottom of an image of his mother. He smiled and began thinking of the marvelous potential of this powerful machine.

For the next two hours, he analyzed fingerprints, DNA samples, chemical powders, metal shavings, and every kind of numerical data he could find. Each analysis took less than a minute to provide results on the screen. His smile disappeared as his mind drifted toward Debra. Sometimes scientific problems were easier to understand than women were.

Chapter 31

The last twenty-four hours had been torture for Debra. She no longer had her heart in defending Jeff. He'd been a real pain in the ass, and her newfound love had been squashed by her decision to defend Jeff. She was feeling miserable, but was confident that the Grand Jury would see there was no case. She sat next to Jeff facing a dozen citizens who really had no idea what the legal system was about. The judge gave special instructions to the jury and proceeded with the reading of the charges. The next hours were opening remarks by the Assistant D.A., and then her opening.

Now it was time for the Assistant D.A. to present his case. Ginger Hallows walked into the courtroom and Jeff mumbled, "Shit, we're screwed." Debra looked back at Ms. Hallows. She was attired in a conservative dress that fell below her knees, and she acted very prim and proper. She had a bandage across the left side of her face even though the injuries should have healed by this time. She nodded towards the jury and smiled.

Debra turned towards Jeff and whispered. "This may be a bit of a setback, but I still think you are okay." The look on her face told Jeff otherwise. The Assistant D.A. started the questions about the alleged attack and rape. Ms. Hallows slowly told her story of how she had met Jeff and how he had come on to her. She then described the attack in extreme detail. She broke down several times, and the judge asked if she needed time to compose herself. Each time she asked to continue. The jury was mesmerized by her, and each objection made Debra look like the villain. She had been blindsided by a saint.

Her cross was a disaster. Every question Ms. Hallows tried to answer caused her to break down in tears. Debra had decided not to put Jeff on the stand, as he would surely do himself in. He kept smiling and combing his hair, trying to look his best for the jury. He was just making the jury hate him. She could put one of

Jeff's friends on the stand to testify that Jeff was talking to him on the phone at the time of the attack. His friend was as vain as Jeff was, and it only weakened his alibi. It was one of the shortest trials she'd ever conducted. When the jury adjourned in the middle of the afternoon, Debra knew that Jeff was doomed.

When she returned to the office, Frank was finishing a call with a client. He looked up at her depressed expression. "I guess I don't have to ask how it went. The look on your face tells me that things didn't work out as expected. Did Jeff screw it up?"

"He did, but that wasn't the biggest problem. The victim turned out to be a saint, or one of the best actresses I've seen in a long time. I was ready to throw Jeff in jail after listening to her. I didn't stand a chance. Jeff didn't help either by primping himself in court."

"He really did that? How did the jury look?"

"They resembled vultures ready to convict. Dad, I screwed up. I'm still in the prosecutor mode. I think there's a lot more to this case, and I should've been better prepared."

"Don't beat yourself up. You had no time to prepare, and to be perfectly honest, Jeff's wasn't the best case for you to start with. He strikes me as the guy who only thinks about number one. So, what are you going to do?"

Debra opened the small fridge and pulled out a beer. "I hope you don't mind, but I really need one. The Grand Jury will meet tomorrow to hand down their verdict on my case and another from the day before. It's a bit unusual, but the other case was missing some evidence, and the judge didn't want to waste a day. So, tomorrow I'll finish what I started, win, or lose."

"Whatever happens, I'm behind you. Have you heard from Dennis?"

"Not now Dad, I need to concentrate on the case, and I can't if I have to deal with Dennis. I'll talk to him tomorrow after the verdict is in."

"Are you sure that's a good idea?"

"Dad!"

"I get it, but I do have good news. I signed up three more clients, and I hired a receptionist. She'll be in tomorrow."

Debra took a sip from the beer. "What do you know about hiring a receptionist? How old is she? Is she out of school yet?"

Frank leaned back on his chair. "Boy, you really did have a bad day."

"Sorry, Dad. That was unfair to take it out on you. Let's start over. Who did you hire?"

"Well, you're not going to believe this, but I put a call into Dennis's house to ask him how the new computer system was working. While I was waiting for Dennis to come to the phone, I asked Mrs. Henson if she knew anyone who could work for us four hours a day. She wanted the job herself. She said that she now did very little around Dennis's house, and she needed some time away. What the hell, I thought. So, I hired her."

Debra choked on the beer. "Mrs. Henson? How does Dennis feel about it?"

"He seemed okay with it. In fact, he thought it was a good idea. She's been with the family for years, and he thinks the change will do her good. Are you alright with my decision?"

"Sure, Dad, but is she going to bug me about Dennis?"

He just threw up his hands in dismay.

She set the beer down and stormed out of the office. Frank turned and thought life had been so much easier when he was a cop.

Dennis had just finished shutting down the last computer system when he heard the intercom. He rushed upstairs to meet his mother taking off her coat. "Mom, what are you doing here?"

"I live here, Dennis. I just cut my trip short. I have all the data I need for the lionfish studies. What's going on here?"

Chapter 32

Debra looked at the Grand Jury and then over to Judge Benson. She was having a hard time reading their expressions. She'd been good at this when Assistant District Attorney, but now she really sucked as a defense attorney. What changed? It was still a courtroom, and the laws were the same as before. She lived, ate, and breathed the law, so why did it all seem different?

Then it hit her. The difference was Dennis. What the hell was going on with her? Her mind drifted from the case to the problem she was having with Dennis. She loved him and hated him at the same time. Wasn't there some old saying about love and hate? She was trying to remember it when the court proceedings started.

She looked around to see Ms. Hallows in the back of the courtroom. She was dressed differently, but still looked saintly and her bandage had been changed. Was it real or some kind of act? Debra looked over to Jeff. It must have finally hit him that he was going to lose. He held his head down as the jury's verdict to send the case to trial was given.

She had already decided that she would give Jeff his walking papers, and someone else could defend him at trial. Her heart wasn't in it anymore. She had to make some decisions about her future, and it wasn't going to include defending Jeff. She was sure he was guilty now, but she really didn't care anymore. She waited for the judge to accept the jury's decision and assign the case to a trial judge. The courtroom was deathly silent.

Judge Harold Benson had never seen a case like this one before. On the surface, it looked like any other assault and rape case. The problem was that fate had stepped in and created a new twist. His wife was a volunteer in a local theater group. On the previous evening, she'd been talking about the new play that they were producing and how the lead part was still up for grabs.

He stopped cold when she said that one of the actresses trying for the part was a Ms. Ginger Hallows. His wife went on to say that she overheard Ms. Hallows, and the show director get into a big fight. She said she was doing something in real life to prove she was the best actress for the part. Suddenly, everything made sense to the judge, and he knew what he had to do, something he'd never done before. He was going to overturn a Grand Jury decision. He cleared his throat lowered his gavel. Everyone looked up at his solemn face.

"Before we continue with this case, I find myself in a difficult position. I'm going to overturn the jury's decision to send this case to trial. I have to excuse myself from hearing this case because last night by accident, I became aware of critical information about this case. If the D.A.'s office wants to bring the case back to the Grand Jury, I can't be part of the process."

The judge started to stand up when Ms. Hallows stood up in the back of the courtroom.

"Judge, you can't do that. You're going to ruin everything. The jury believed me, and the case should go to trial."

The judge glared at Ms. Hallows. "So you can show your producer that you're the best actress for the part?"

Ms. Hallows sat down quickly. Everyone in the courtroom was clearly confused. Obviously, the judge and Ms. Hallows knew a lot more about the case than everyone else in the courtroom.

Debra was about to say something to the judge when Jeff burst out in explanation. "She did all this to ensure she got the part in the play. This was all about her proving her acting abilities."

Unfortunately, for Ms. Hallows everyone in the courtroom, including the jury heard his outburst. For the first time since the case had started, Debra thought they actually believed what Jeff had just said. The judge asked that Debra, and the Assistant D.A. come into his chambers. He explained in more detail why he'd overturned the decision and excused himself from future involvement in the case. He told the Assistant D.A. that it would be in their best interest to drop the case against Jeff and move on to more important cases. The Assistant D.A agreed, and Debra was on the front steps of the court building in fifteen minutes.

Jeff was waiting. "Debra, you were great. Thank you so much for saving me. Let's go celebrate. I know this great bar."

Debra glared at Jeff. "First, I didn't save you - the judge did. As far as celebrating, I'm not interested."

"Come on, Debra, let's start over. You took the time to be my attorney, so you must still have feelings for me."

"Jeff, let me make this very clear again - we're done. I have no feelings for you and never had in the past. You were just a convenient date, but nothing more."

"Hey, it's just a drink at a bar. I know you'll change your mind about me, because I've changed. You'll see."

"Oh, I see alright. You've changed. You're worse than you were before. You couldn't pay me enough to go to a bar with you. We're done Jeff; now get that through your head."

She turned and started to walk down the steps. Jeff grabbed her arm and pulled her back. He tried to kiss her, but a big arm stuck in between them. Jeff turned and looked at a large, burly security guard standing over him.

The guard looked at Debra to see if she was fine and then back to Jeff. "Where I come from, you don't strong-arm ladies when they tell you to get lost. If you don't want to end up in jail again, I suggest that you move along. If I see you try anything like that another time, I'll assume that you resisted arrest. I'd just love to see you do that, if you get my point."

Debra looked down at Jeff's shoes. He had peed his pants, and it was running into his shoes. Jeff turned and ran, dribbling as he went. He tried to flag a taxi, but none stopped. Frustrated, he continued running along the street and out of sight.

Debra turned to the security guard. "Thanks for your help."

"It's not a problem, Ma'am. Your father and I used to work in the same precinct a long time ago."

"Did my dad ask you to watch over me?"

"No, I haven't talked to him in more than a year. I just watch out for my friends and their family. We watch each other's backs, even when we no longer work together."

"Well, again thanks, but I wish you would've hit him."

"You know I really wanted to, but I know where that would have gotten me."

She shook his hand and said, "You're right. It was just wishful thinking."

Debra sat in her car for more than a half-hour before she started the engine. She had a lot on her mind. When she was in the D.A.'s office, the happiest times weren't in the courtroom, but rather in the office preparing for cases. She loved the law with its legal research, preparation, and organizing cases. She loved to be in command of people and putting it all together. With so much that had happened in the last few months, she'd made the mistake of replacing her position as Assistant D.A. with that of a defense attorney. It was all clear to her now. She started the car and headed back to the office to talk to her dad.

Frank was busy working on his iPad, but immediately stopped when Debra walked into the office. He looked very upset. She pulled up a chair and noticed a huge bouquet of flowers sitting on a nearby table.

"Dad, what's going on?"

"I heard about your case today. That was a weird turn of events but not as strange as what happened in the last thirty minutes. You need to promise me that you'll stay calm when I tell you what happened."

Debra focused on the flowers. "Are they from Jeff?"

"Yes, they're from Jeff, but Dennis saw them."

"Did they get into a fight?"

"No, sit quiet and let me explain. About twenty minutes ago, those flowers came, along with a card, but I never looked at it. Dennis came in not long after the flowers arrived, and saw them. He picked up the card, read it, and stormed out of the office before I could say a word. I had to know what the hell was going on, so I read the card, and I understand why he left. You need to read the card."

Debra walked over and looked at the bottom of the card. It read, *With all my love, Jeff.* She went to the top of the card and started to read. *Thanks for saving my life today. I knew we could work things out between us. I never knew you had such strong feelings for me. I know you need to talk to Dennis about us, and I know you'll be gentle with him. In the meantime, I've taped my apartment key to the back of the card. I'm looking forward to seeing you tonight.*

She turned the card over. Her face turned red, and her anger was at a boiling point. She grabbed the flower vase and hurled it against the wall.

Frank walked over to the now dead vase. "I'm not sure you should take it out on the flowers. They had nothing to do with this. They grew up and looked pretty, just like you."

"Dad, I'm not in the mood for your dry humor."

"Sorry, Honey. When I saw the card, I knew you were going to be pissed. Do you want me to go over and talk to Jeff, because I can be very persuasive?"

"Please, stay out of it. I'll take care of Jeff."

"That's what I am afraid of."

Dennis came in the front door of his mother's house and slammed the door hard enough to loosen the hinges. He was about to head down to the lab when the phone rang. He let it ring a couple of times before deciding that no one else was going to answer it. The voice sounded familiar.

"Hey, Nate, this is Jeff. I'm just giving you a call about Debra. She'll eventually call you about this, but I thought I'd get a head start."

Dennis pushed the record call button on the answering machine next to the phone. "What the hell do you want, Jeff?"

"Hey old buddy, I just wanted to make sure there were no hard feelings."

"What are you talking about?"

"Come on, Nate, Debra and I are an item again. Didn't she tell you yet? I'm so sorry. I was supposed to let her tell you. Well, now that you know, I expect you to be a gentleman and respect my relationship with Debra."

Dennis slammed the phone down so hard it fell to the floor.

It started to ring again. Dennis was about to pull the cord out of the wall, but decided to confront Jeff. He picked it up and pressed the talk button. "Jeff, I don't know what you think you're doing, but quit calling me."

"This is Debra. Did Jeff call you?"

"Yes. You want to hear what he said? Hang on a second and I'll play it for you."

Dennis pressed the playback button on his phone machine. When the message was over, he hung up on Debra and walked away.

Debra was in shock. Her world was falling apart and all because she had this grandiose idea of the law. Now she had picked up a stalker. She walked into her bathroom and pulled a tissue to dry her tears. As she dabbed her eyes, she noticed some subtle changes in her bathroom. She was obsessive about where things were placed, and it drove her mom and dad crazy when she was growing up. She was sure things had been moved, and she didn't do it. The tissue box was moved. Several items in the medicine cabinet were also in a new position. Most obvious was that the hand lotion had drops of lotion on the bottom lip of the pump. She always made sure that none of the bottles had any excess on the caps or on the sides. The more she looked around, she realized someone had been all over her bathroom. There were even several fingerprints on the mirror.

She went into her bedroom. Her dresser had been opened, and someone had gone through her underwear drawer. As she worked her way through her clothes, she felt dampness. She pulled out a pair of panties and found they were wet in the crotch. She smelled the dampness. It was semen. She went into the kitchen, dropped the panties into a plastic bag, and sealed it. She sat and cried for the next half hour.

When she got her composure, she called her dad. "Hi, we need to talk at your house. Can you lock up and go home right now?"

"What's going on?"

"I'm too mad to talk right now. I need some cool off time. Just go home and I'll be there shortly."

Frank knew this was very serious. He hadn't ever heard her talk or act this way. Something bad was happening, and his guess was that it involved Jeff. He checked his calendar, turned off the coffee pot, and looked around one last time. An old phrase came to mind, "Out of the frying pan and into the fire."

Debra was waiting when Frank arrived. She said nothing as he unlocked the door. He reached up to the key rack and hung his car keys. He then pulled another set off the nearby hook and handed them to Debra. "Here is my house key. Any time you need to stay, you are welcome. I have two extra bedrooms already set up for guests."

"I think I'm going to need it right now."

"What's going on, Honey?"

"You know how obsessive I am in the bathroom."

"How could I ever forget?"

"I don't know if I should be telling you this, but I have no one else to talk to."

"I'm here for you."

"When I got home, I found out someone had broken into my apartment and gone through my things. I found a window in my bedroom that had been jimmied. That's how he got in."

"When you say he, I'm assuming it was Jeff?"

"That would be my guess."

"I can run all the fingerprints in the room. That should narrow it down to him."

"I can do one better, but I really don't want to show you. You're my father, and this isn't something you normally show your dad."

"Let's make a deal. Right now, I'm a detective, not your dad. Talk to me like you would if I was still on the force."

"Fair enough, but I don't want you to go out of this house with guns blazing."

"Look, you may think I'm a loose cannon, but I can take it."

"I hope so, because this was in my dresser." She pulled out the plastic bag with the undies. "I can tell you right now, that they're soaked with semen. We don't know whose it is yet, so don't go off the deep end."

Frank thought he could be prepared for anything, but this was almost unbelievable. He wanted to go out and beat the bastard to a pulp. He knew if he did, Debra would never talk to him again. "You're right, I didn't expect this. I want to go out and kill the bastard, but I'll let you tell me the plan."

"For one thing, we can't have Dennis use Medusa to check the DNA."

"I haven't even considered it. I still have some contacts in one of the private DNA labs, and they owe me a couple of free tests. They're very discrete about their results."

"There's one more thing, Dad. I think he used my hand cream. I assumed it was on his face, but now I'm not so sure. Anyway, I used some scotch tape and some makeup dust to pull a print off the mirror."

"Boy, aren't we a team? Before I left the office, I got a set of Jeff's fingerprints. I have the fingerprint program and scanner installed on my laptop."

240

"You have a laptop now? Are you really my father, or did some alien take over your body?"

"Hey I can learn new tricks. Let's just see what we got. We can use the semen as backup evidence. You know that even if we can prove it was Jeff, he'll just get his hand slapped and not do any time."

"Remember, I was the Assistant D.A. I just want to do this right. Let's take it one step at a time. Confirm it was him, and then we'll plan on what we do next."

Fifteen minutes later, Frank had all the proof he needed. "For sure it was Jeff. I know what I want to do to the bastard, but I'll abide by your wishes."

"Can you put hidden cameras in my house? I want a record of him doing whatever he does in my apartment. I'll clean all the fingerprints off and reset the place. I'm not sure I can stay there anymore."

"Move into my place. There's plenty of room and I'll help you move your things."

"No, leave my things. I'll buy some new clothes, and will eventually burn the rest."

Frank went to the kitchen and came back with a beer for her. "You kick back and relax. I have some errands to run and don't worry, I'll leave Jeff alone. I just want to drop off your nasty plastic bag for DNA analysis and then go set up some cameras in your place."

"Thanks, Dad. I think I'll watch the news and then get some rest. Just make sure you leave Jeff alone. I don't want to have to bail you out of jail. Promise?"

"That's not a problem."

Frank grabbed his keys and glanced back. Debra was sitting in his lounge chair, a beer in hand, and was watching one of the local news stations. He had a lot to do, but first he had to stop by the DNA lab. Luckily, the technician who owed him the favor was on duty. Frank pulled out the plastic bag.

"Hey, Otis. Glad you're here so you can help me on this one. Is there any way you can put a rush on this?"

"Hey, Frank. Long time no see. I don't even want to know where you got this, but yes, I'll run it right away. Are a couple of days soon enough?"

"Sure. I've got one other question. Can you tell me something that will guarantee you'll itch uncontrollably?"

"We run tests all the time for allergies and that kind of thing. We actually have many people who come in here looking for solutions as to what is causing a rash or making them itch. Most want solutions; they're not looking to cause it. Why do you want to know?"

"Can this be on the QT?"

"Sure, Frank."

"What can I get that will mix with hand lotion and make someone who uses it itch like crazy?"

"Is this illegal?"

"No, of course not, Otis."

"I'm guessing it has something to do with what's in the bag?"

"You're pretty sharp, Otis. So, are you going to help me or not?"

"Mosquitos inject protein and a few other chemicals to make people itch. We do a lot of testing with people who are allergic to mosquito bites. We have all the components right here. Go get a cup of coffee and come back in fifteen minutes."

One hour later, Frank stood in the middle of Debra's bathroom. He'd already set four cameras and was going to install four more before he left. Right now, he had one other task to perform. He took the cap of the hand lotion off and squirted the bottle of mosquito proteins and chemicals into the bottle. He shook it around and set it back on the counter. Otis had told him that a very small amount would result in an extreme reaction. Frank ignored his recommendation and had transferred the entire contents. He smiled. He'd have to remind Debra not to touch the bottle, but he was sure she'd throw it away anyway. When everything was in place, he wiped the place clean, and reset the window that had been the entry point before. Now, all they had to do was wait.

Dennis sat in the lab staring at Medusa wondering where his life was going. A noise behind him startled him, and he almost fell out of his chair.

His mother was standing in the doorway holding her laptop. "I like what you've done to the lab. I don't even want to know about the super computer. I do like it though. I used one while I was in Europe, but never thought I'd have one in my own lab. I'm not sure I want to know how much it cost, but what I do want to know is what's going on with you? Don't tell me it has something to do with the lab, because I have a feeling it's about Debra."

"I really don't want to talk about it."

"I may be a crazy scientist, but I'll always be your mother first, and I love you."

This statement set Dennis back on his heels. She wasn't talking like a scientist, but a real mother. "Mom, it's complicated."

His mother set her computer down on a nearby table. "I love complicated. Let's go out to the garden and talk."

"I'm fine. I'll work it out."

"Garden. Now!"

Dennis couldn't understand what was going on. His mother wasn't herself. He was going to the garden if for no other reason than to find out what was going on with her.

When they reached the picnic table, she patted the seat. "Talk, Dennis. What's going on?"

For the next fifteen minutes, Dennis told his mother about his getting closer to Debra. Then he told her about the fight about Jeff that split up the two.

She said nothing for almost thirty seconds, as though she was formulating some new project. "Have you slept with her?"

"Mom, I'm not talking to you about my sex life."

"Well that answered my question. Now I want to tell you a story that will eventually have some bearing on your problem. This will take some time, so be patient. Remember when you asked me if something was bothering me when I returned from the last trip? I told you I didn't want to talk about it then, but now's the time.

"I met this really nice European history professor while I was in France. I'd seen him a couple of times before when he lectured in Seattle, but we never connected. We really hit it off when we met again in Europe, and traveled together for several weeks. We returned to Paris as he had several lectures to present, and then everything fell apart. On the surface, it appeared that he was involved with one of his students. I even caught him with one of the twenty-year-old coeds in his room. I was devastated and swore off men. It wasn't until I returned to Seattle that I found out the truth."

She paused to let him think about what she'd said. "I told a friend of mine what had happened, and she set me straight. It seems there was a group of three sweet young coeds who created a sex game. The object was to seduce as many of the male faculty as possible. One would be the seducer, while the other two would set up conditions to make it work. They would alternate positions, but the results were still the same. It takes putting a notch on the bedpost to a new level. The three knew that none of the faculty would report them, as many were married or had tenure and couldn't afford their reputations tarnished."

She took a deep breath before continuing. "The professor I was involved with was set up by those three. He'd refused advances by two of the girls because he was involved with me. They had a contingency plan to remove opposition like myself. The remaining girl made an excuse to stop by the professor's room. She wore no bra, and carried her panties in her purse.

244

The other one called my room saying she worked at the front desk, and I had a message to go to the professor's room. As I approached the room, the girl inside opened her blouse to expose her breasts, and threw her panties on the floor as she left. I met her exiting the room, attempting to button her blouse. I wasn't sure what to expect, but when I knocked at the door, I was greeted by a very surprised professor. When I saw the panties on the floor, I turned and left."

"I'm so sorry, Mom. I had no idea, but I knew something had happened."

"He called me several times trying to explain that he'd been set up. I ignored him and flew home. That's why I was so upset when I came home. I was disappointed because of the way I acted throughout the entire episode. The moral of the story is that nothing is ever as it seems, especially when it comes to love."

"Is there anything you can do about the girls? What about the professor?"

"There's nothing to do right now about the girls. The professor moved on and is in a relationship with a woman who trusts him, which is a lot more than I did. I'm going to give you some advice, which you can take or leave. Jeff wants Debra back, and he'll play dirty to get you out of her life. Close your eyes and picture Jeff and Debra standing in front of you. Knowing everything you know about the two, who would you trust if your life depended on it? Make sure you base your decision on what you feel in your heart."

Dennis opened his eyes after ten seconds. "I'm so screwed, Mom."

"You might have to grovel to get her back. Dennis, how much do you care about her?"

"Until now, I wasn't sure, but I love her with all my heart, and I want her to be my wife."

"I hope your groveling works, because I really like her. I think she's perfect for you."

"Frank said the same thing."

"Really? I would've thought he'd be against you two."

"No, he's actually been pushing us together."

"Wow, the world is full of surprises. Go make it up to her, Dennis."

Chapter 33

When Frank arrived at the office, Dennis was waiting, looking like a whipped dog. Frank opened the door and headed toward the coffee maker. "Dennis, it'll only take a couple of minutes to get the brewer going, and you look like you need it. What's up?"

"Frank, I really screwed it up with Debra, and I need to fix it."

"It sure took long enough for you to come to that conclusion. So, what changed your mind?"

"My mother did, although she doesn't give me much of a chance of fixing this."

"You know for once I agree with her. You really blew it, Dennis. Let me tell you a story that will raise the hairs on the back of your neck."

When Frank was done, Dennis was a nervous wreck. "It's all my fault. I should have done a better job warning you about Jeff. I knew he was crazy, but not like this. What can we do?"

"You have only one task. Take care of Debra, and make it up to her. Do you have any plans on how to do that?"

"I think flowers are out of the question."

Frank started to pour two cups of coffee. "Acres of flowers wouldn't be enough. Whatever you do, it'll raise the bar for what men will have to do to fix their screw ups. You might consider going online and researching it."

"I'm not going to fix the problem by going online. This has to be done from the heart."

Frank smiled. "That's a good start. Why don't you consider your possible solutions while I go over to Debra's apartment? She's at my house right now, so I know you won't go to see her. Just give me a couple of hours. If you need to leave, make sure to lock up. Most of my appointments are done for the week. Are you all right?"

247

"Sure, Frank. Go ahead, I'll be fine."

Frank packed up his break-in bag. Thirty minutes later, he was collecting the cameras. Jeff had been back, and he had used the hand lotion. Frank was afraid to check the underwear drawer, but his detective instincts overcame his resistance. He put on gloves, started searching the drawers, and found another set of panties containing semen. He wanted to go out and beat the crap out of Jeff, but that would come later. When he'd finished, he poured the hand lotion down the drain, collected the empty container, locked up, and headed back to his house. When he got home, he found Debra curled up on the couch. She jumped up when he came into the house.

"Have you been to my apartment?"

"Yep, and he was there again. He used the hand lotion and left another nasty in your dresser. This guy is a real wacko. I'm going to look at the videos from the master download drive right now. Let me wade through them, and I'll let you know what I find."

Debra got up from the couch and walked behind Frank. "Sorry, Dad, I'm going to watch with you. He was in my apartment, and I need to see what he was doing."

"It's not going to be pretty."

The first couple of camera views from the living room showed Jeff looking through music CDs and playing one. Frank stopped the video. "I can't believe he puts on music while he does his perverted acts. He's really sick."

Frank continued the video at the bathroom sink. Jeff picked every item up, fondled them, and then looked at himself in the mirror. He'd look at his left profile and after that his right. He reached down, took a large squirt from the hand lotion bottle, and smeared it all over his face, arms, and neck. He rubbed it around several times and then reached into his pants.

He stopped the video. "I can't really let you continue to watch this. There's no sense torturing both of us. I refuse to

248

look at it any more until you leave. Go watch some TV and enjoy a beer."

"Look, Dad, I can handle it."

"Why should you have to? That's why I'm here. Now I insist, otherwise I'll erase everything."

"You've made your point, but let me know if there's anything I should be aware of."

"I will, but please go."

As soon as Debra left the room, Frank closed the door. He pressed the play button, and the screen filled with Jeff fondling himself. Frank just remembered what he added to the hand lotion and smiled when he realized everywhere that it was being applied. By the time Frank got to the bedroom camera, it was obvious that Jeff would be scratching in a lot more places than his face. How was he going to tell Debra what he'd done? Then he remembered they agreed not to keep any secrets. This wasn't going to be easy."

Frank came out of his office with a somber look on his face.

Debra set her beer down. "So, how bad is it?"

"It's pretty much the same as before. He looked through everything in your drawers and used your hand lotion on most of his body, including his genitals. I'm sorry, but there's no easy way to say he masturbated into your panties."

"I'm going to have to burn down my apartment. I swear I'm going to kill that son of a bitch."

"Honey, that may not be necessary. I added a little something to your hand lotion, and it might tend to slow Jeff down a bit. Well, actually quite a lot, maybe even a trip to the ER."

Frank then explained the compound he added into the hand lotion. "We need to clean out your apartment and burn everything you don't want. I have a contact at one of the major hospitals. I'll have them check to see if anyone shows up with a skin problem. The important thing is that it'll take his mind off you, and he'll know that we're on to him. That should be enough for now, but I'm going to keep a close eye on him."

Debra grabbed Frank and gave him a hug. "Normally, I'd have been really pissed at you for doing what you did, but it makes me feel a little better. I just hope you have a good alarm system on this house."

"You're kidding, right? I have one of the best. Don't worry because he'll never make it inside this house. So, what about Dennis? He's at the office right now, and I told him about Jeff. I've never seen a guy hurting so much. He knows he really screwed up, but doesn't know what he can do to fix it."

"I'm not sure I want him to fix it."

"Oh, really? I don't believe that because you two have something special. He really messed up, but he's willing to do anything to make it up."

"Well, Dad, here's the way I see it. He'll have to do something for me that proves beyond a shadow of doubt that he loves and trusts me."

"He's lost, Honey. What can he do?"

"I don't know." She shook her head. "I just don't know."

Frank packed up his break-in kit and picked up his keys. "Honey, why don't you take the rest of the day off? Even take a couple of days if you want because the work at the office is light. Next week, we have plenty on our plate, so I'll need you ready to keep us out of legal issues. Oh, there's one more thing, and you're not going to like it. I'm going to tell Dennis everything that has happened today."

"No, Dad, leave him out of it."

"Sorry, but we agreed not to keep any secrets, and this counts as a secret."

Debra turned off the TV. "Just don't invite him back here."

Frank stopped at the door. "I think you forget. Dennis's father was murdered in this house. He told me in no uncertain terms, that he would never set foot in this house. It has too many bad memories for him. I've a feeling that you would have to drug him to the point of unconsciousness to get him inside this house. So, you don't have to worry about him showing up."

Frank closed the door and let the seed grow. He'd found a solution to their problem. Half an hour later, Frank arrived at the office only to find that Dennis had gone through all the coffee. He was wired. "What happened, Frank?"

"First, no more coffee for you, Dennis. You're going to have a heart attack if you drink more. You need to settle down because Jeff was in her apartment again. Let's say that Debra's idea to burn everything might just be a good idea."

Frank then described his visit to the private DNA analysis company and the extra hand lotion agents he'd picked up. It wasn't a perfect solution, but it would certainly slow down Jeff's antics.

Frank sat down directly in front of Dennis. "Now about your other problem. I think I have a solution, but you're definitely not going to like it. You'll have to work quickly to make it work."

Debra had just fallen asleep on the couch when the doorbell rang. She ignored it, but it rang again thirty seconds later. Finally, she got up and looked through the peephole. "Go away, Dennis. Leave me alone," she shouted through the closed door.

"I wish I could, Debra. You mean everything to me. I love you, and I can't stop. I know you loved me too, if even for just a short time. I know I don't deserve another chance, but please, I'm begging. I don't know what to do, but I'm not going to leave until you let me in so we can talk this out."

Then there was dead silence. Dennis sat down on the front porch and started looking around. He could barely remember how the house looked, but slowly, memories were returning. He got up and started to walk around the house.

Debra was about to settle back on the couch when it hit her. She jumped up and looked out one of the side windows.

Dennis was on his knees looking into his old bedroom window and there were tears in his eyes. He'd proven how much he loved her by conquering his greatest fear. This was a genuine effort on his part. Deep down, part of her wanted to run out and hold him close, while another part was still pissed at him. Watching him was tearing her apart seeing that he was obviously committed to her.

What the hell was wrong with her? She ran out the door, reached down, and pulled him into her arms. "Dennis, I do love you, and I don't want to fight. I just want to love you."

Just a block down the street, Frank sat in his car casually sipping a cold drink, watching them. He said to himself, "It's about time you two".

Chapter 34

Four weeks had passed since Jeff's final intrusion into Debra's apartment. Frank and Dennis helped move her belongings to Frank's house. The remaining items, mostly clothes and personal items were bagged up and set out with the trash.

Business at the Ridge Detective Agency had doubled. Frank would visit potential clients, Dennis would perform all the lab work, and Debra processed all the legal paperwork. They were a great team, and things were getting better day by day. One of the new policies set up by Debra, was a morning briefing. Mrs. Henson would staff the phones while the three were in their meeting.

Frank, who was last on the briefing schedule, opened a folder and said, "I have some news on Jeff. I know we'd all like to forget about that jerk, but he's still out there, and he could go back to his old ways. Here's what I've learned from one of my hospital contacts. It seems that two days after his last break in, he appeared in the ER with a severe rash over most of his face, arms, chest, and genitals. He told the doctor that someone had played a sick joke on him. It took almost two weeks to get the rash under control, and he still had bandages all over his face when he was finally discharged."

Debra broke in, "Good job, Dad."

Frank continued, "I did some checking and found out that he moved out of his apartment and has since dropped off the map. I checked with his theater group and found the last piece of the puzzle. It appears that Ms. Ginger Hallows and Jeff staged this fake rape scheme together. She played the rape victim, and he had the leading role as the rapist. Once the producer found out these two staged the plot to enhance their acting resumes, they were both banned from the theater. The producer hasn't heard from either one since, and I haven't been able to track their whereabouts either. We need to be aware that this whole thing may come back and bite us in the ass. I'll keep everyone posted on any new developments as they arise."

Debra and Dennis said nothing. Frank knew it was still a sore spot, but he didn't want them to stick their heads in the sand. The three got up from the table, and Debra headed for her desk. Dennis picked up a box of samples to process at his lab. He leaned over her desk and gave her a long kiss. "I'll be back for lunch. Love you."

Frank leaned back in his chair and realized one of these days he was going to incline too far, and he'd end up on the floor. He was so impressed with how Debra and Dennis had worked things out. They'd gone out on only a couple of dates each week. Dennis had been a perfect gentleman, which was no surprise to Frank. Rarely did he drop Debra off later than midnight. Frank knew that their relationship would evolve to the next level soon, if it already hadn't. He was about to call one of the new clients when Debra sat down in front of his desk.

Debra squirmed in her chair before she spit it out. "I need to talk to you about Dennis."

Frank set the phone down. "What did he do now?"

"Nothing bad. I want to talk to you about something that makes me very uncomfortable."

"Do you want to hear the birds and bees lecture again?"

"Dad, can't be you be serious?"

"Sorry, go ahead."

"I want Dennis to stay in my room with me on certain nights."

"Hey, I'm a modern-day father. I understand, and have a great set of earplugs."

"Dad!"

"Sorry, I just couldn't resist having a bit of fun with this. You seem uncomfortable, and I'm enjoying it so much. I sadly realize you're not my little girl anymore, and that you can do whatever you want. I'm just happy for the both of you. What you do in private is none of my concern. Your mom and I had our arguments, but we always went by that old rule that you never go to bed mad at each other. It worked for us, and it can for you too. Just remember that you're the result of one of your mom and my makeup sessions."

Debra didn't respond. She knew that she'd opened a door for her father to poke some fun, and the only way to close it was to leave.

Debra sat down at her desk and looked at the calendar for the day. She kept thinking about the discussion she'd just had with her father. She loved him so much, but he could be such a pain in the ass. She was trying to be so diplomatic and all he could do was make a joke of it. She had needs, and finding some quiet time with Dennis was difficult. They made love at Dennis's house several times, but she wanted the option of having her way with him in her own bed. Her dad was being too easy about all this. She sensed he was up to something. She had work to do, so tried to put it out of her mind.

Suddenly, she had an idea and punched in Dennis's number on her phone. "Hey, I talked to Dad, and he's fine with you staying with me at the house."

"Did he make a joke about it?"

"You're scaring me, Dennis. You're getting to know him better than I do. Listen, I have a new idea for lunch."

"What do you have in mind?"

"How about I have <u>you</u> for lunch at my house."

"Really?"

"You don't want to?"

"You're kidding. I'll be there for lunch and dessert."

"It's a date. Love you."

Debra hung up the phone and smiled. Then she realized that Mrs. Henson was standing in front of her desk with a pile of papers in her hand. "How much of that did you hear?"

"Enough, but don't worry sweetie, your secret is safe with me."

"I feel so embarrassed."

255

"Don't worry, I never heard a word."

"Really?"

"No, just keep telling yourself that I didn't. Before you leave for "lunch," you have to go through this pile of papers."

The rest of the day went smoothly. Debra came back from lunch with a smile on her face. Dennis returned about four and closed Frank's door. "We need to talk about a new client."

Frank was expecting a follow up about the new living arrangements, but this was something else. "What's on your mind?"

"I have a new client who wants you to do a background check on three college girls. The client needs video, audio, and everything you can get on the three."

"Who's the client, Dennis?"

"I can't tell you, Frank."

"I'm not doing anything unless you tell me about the client. We're talking about college girls. We could get into a lot of trouble doing a full background on them."

"It's my mother."

"Fine, I'll do it."

"First you refuse, and then as soon as I tell you it's my mother, you're fine without any hesitation. I thought the two of you hated each other."

"She hates me. I don't hate her. I have a great deal of respect for her."

Dennis's whole concept of his mother vs. Frank had just gone down in flames. "I thought you didn't like her."

"I'm not sure where you got that idea. I read the reports about the murder, and the cops screwed the case up big time. She has every right to be pissed and hate cops. I can live with it, Dennis. Why do you want all this background on the three?"

"To be honest, Frank, I'd rather not say until you have done the background check. I want you to be very objective. Don't share this conversation with anyone outside the company. Make no copies of the audio or video - originals only."

"Sure, but it sounds a little cloak and dagger."

"Wait until you do the background checks, and then you may change your tune."

"Can I run this by Debra for legal?"

"Not yet. Do some background first just to make sure we have something to discuss."

"Okay, I'm on it."

Senator Bob Welding looked over his weekly reports. They looked good, and he was still on the short list for his party's presidential choice. He just had to keep all his skeletons buried. The general did a good job keeping the MLA project hidden. No one who worked on the project knew that he had any connections to the general.

He hadn't heard from the general in weeks, so it was time to see if there were any problems on the horizon. He picked up his encrypted phone and punched a long series of numbers. Several rings later, the general came on the line.

"Senator, how's your campaign going?"

"The list is shorter now, which makes it more imperative that the MLA stays buried."

"You worry too much. Dr. Andrews is now part of a small detective agency with that detective who knew about the MLA. They seem to have moved on. They're not stupid and realized they would be in our crosshairs if they said anything. We can't kill them all, so let's let it quietly go away. I did find out that Dr. Andrew's trip to see Dr. Dronager was more than just a friendly meeting. He bought an old outdated super computer from the college to replace the MLA he blew up. He seems content with the replacement, so let's just leave it alone for the time being. If we have to go in, it'll be very messy, and you may not recover from it. My recommendation is to do nothing."

"I agree, but if anything changes, let me know before you take any action."

"Senator, I know what I'm doing. I'll lose as much as you if this thing gets out."

The general hung up before the senator could say any more. He now wished that he could have just killed them all. It would have been so much easier.

Jeff Windom was still licking his wounds, and his life had gone from bad to worse. He knew who'd done this to him. The hospital could never find out exactly what was in the lotion he put on his skin. Of course, he couldn't tell them he'd broken into an apartment and used the lotion.

He sat in his car and focused his powerful binoculars on the front of the Ridge Detective Agency. He was sure that Frank had been the one to put something in the lotion. They'd all pay for what they'd done to him. He couldn't act for months, unless the character part was someone with a scarred face. He was going to get even, but he would wait until the time was right. He smirked and opened the glove compartment exposing the .38 special. He was no longer playing. He was serious now.

Chapter 35
(Three Months Later)

Frank looked into the oven to see how the roast was doing. He turned around to see why it was so quiet in the dining room. Dennis and Debra were in a lip lock again. He smiled. Everything had worked out, well, at least, most of it had. Frank still avoided going over to Dennis's house too often. It was better that way. Frank and Dennis's mother had made peace enough to be sociable, but that was the limit of their friendliness.

He grabbed the salad bowl, wooden salad forks and headed to the living room. The two broke apart when Frank came into the room. He set the bowl on the table.

"You know you two should get a room. Oh, that's right you have one. When are you two going to get married?"

Debra stared at Frank. "Who told you?"

"You just did."

Debra turned red. "Dennis asked me last night at dinner, and I said yes. We want to have the wedding in Dennis's garden in a small ceremony in the fall."

"Why wait so long? That's several months away."

"Are you trying to get rid of me, Dad?"

"Well, yeah I am. It's nice having my daughter stay at my house, but you need your own life."

Dennis waved his hand in the air. "Hey guys, I'm in the room. You're talking like I'm invisible."

Debra and Frank started laughing. Dennis looked at the two. "What's so funny?"

Dennis was very quiet during most of the meal. He interjected comments every now and then, but Frank started to notice the silence. "Dennis, what's on your mind?"

"We have one problem with the wedding."

Debra set her glass of wine down. "You never said anything to me."

"Well, the problem is this thing between my mother and Frank."

Frank jumped in. "Dennis, there's nothing going on between your mother and I."

"That's not what I meant. I was talking about the fact that she doesn't like having you around."

"Don't you think she would make an exception for your wedding? I think you underestimate her."

Debra squeezed Dennis's hand. "He's right. You and I'll talk to her, and it'll be fine."

Dennis's lowered his head as if in prayer. "I hope you're right. I want our wedding to be perfect."

Frank awoke to a loud banging on his front door. By the time he got his bathrobe on and was in the living room, Debra and Dennis were not far behind. Frank looked through a side window to see a police car, and an unmarked car were in front. He recognized the two detectives from his old squad. He opened the door. "Detective Sloan and Detective Ronan. What can I do for you?"

Sloan took the lead. "Where were you last night?"

"I was right here with my daughter and her fiancé. What's going on detectives?"

"You need to come with us, Frank. We need to talk downtown."

"Hey guys, I know how this works. Before I do anything you need to tell me what's going on."

Sloan looked back at Ronan and then Frank. "Captain Carson was murdered last night. The gun that was used was one of your guns. It was one that should have been in the evidence room. The captain was tortured, shot in each hand, each foot, and then they worked their way up. It looks like whatever information they wanted, they didn't get. Everyone in the department is going crazy. Your name keeps coming up. Now can we go?"

Frank turned to Debra. "I have to go with them. It's procedure. Find me a good lawyer, just in case I need one. I know you're a terrific lawyer, but I also know it's not a good idea to defend a family member. You can be the liaison for me. Don't worry, they're going to look at everything, and everyone connected with the captain. It's procedure, and I'll be fine."

In the back of Frank's mind, he knew that wasn't necessarily the case. He knew that when one of your own is murdered, the detectives tend to go overboard. Frank said nothing going downtown. When he arrived, he was put in room #1. It became obvious when they came into the squad room that Sloan had been assigned as acting captain. That wasn't good because Sloan hated Frank, and let everyone know it. Frank looked at the one-way mirror and thought that Sloan was there watching him sweat. Finally, Sloan came into the room with a folder. He opened it up and scanned down the first couple of pages. Frank knew Sloan wasn't reading the papers. It was part of a textbook interrogation process.

Sloan closed the folder. "Tell me again what you did last night?"

Frank smiled at Sloan. "My lawyer isn't here yet."

"You don't need a lawyer. You just need to tell us what you were doing last night."

Frank was about to respond when there was a knock at the door. It opened, and a man in very expensive suit and large briefcase came into the room. "I'm Frank's lawyer, J. R. Lenson. Any questions you have for Frank have to go through me first. Frank, have they read you your rights yet?"

Sloan turned and walked out of the room. "You're free to go, but we're keeping our eyes on you. If we find out that you had anything to do with this, we'll throw the book at you. You'll make a mistake someday, and we'll be there to arrest you."

Once Sloan was gone, Frank put his hand out to shake Lenson's hand. "Thank you. You got here quickly. I was only here a few minutes, before you showed up. How's that possible?"

261

Lenson picked up his briefcase. "Your daughter is very persuasive. You must be very proud of her."

"I'm very proud. So, what do we do now?"

"Well, my guess is that this was just round one. We don't want to stick our heads in the sand. We need to know why the captain was murdered. I have some contacts higher up, and I'll have them poke around and see what pops up."

Senator Welding was fuming. The morning papers were full of articles on the murder of Captain Mark Carson. It wouldn't have been a big deal except the captain was a close friend of Frank Ridge, and Frank knew about the MLA. The bigger problem was that the captain had been tortured. The general was supposed to let him know when he was going to act. The only thing that came to mind was that the captain was about to say something, and the general had to take quick action. Whatever the reason, it was disconcerting because the party chairman had called yesterday asking about his political platform.

He picked up his secure phone and punched in the numbers. The general picked up the line on the first ring.

"Senator, before you say anything, we had nothing to do with the murder. I've already contacted all my operatives, and none of them knows anything. Someone else outside our group murdered the captain"

"Are you absolutely sure that none of your men were trying to impress you again?"

"Senator, I am absolutely sure that we didn't do it. The captain had to have had many enemies. You just assumed it was us."

"But the torture was your signature mark."

"Torture is not uncommon. What if Captain Carson had taken some money on the side and hadn't paid it back? He could've had a big gambling debt, and someone was trying to make a statement. There're a dozen reasons for someone to torture the man. It could have been a copycat murder to throw everyone off. Believe me when I say, we're clean on this one. Let the police follow the leads."

He continued, "There is one more interesting piece of news. The police dragged Frank Ridge in for questioning about the murder. We could add fuel to the fire and frame him for the murder. That would get rid of one of our problems."

"No, that would be a mistake. We don't want Frank in the news. Newspaper people follow all leads, and they may follow Frank and find Dennis Andrews too. I don't like that idea at all. Let's just see where things go. If there's a leak in the dike, we can plug it. Are we clear on this?"

The general hesitated. He wanted to assert some of his power. "I understand, Senator."

Frank arrived back at the Ridge Detective Agency midday and found Dennis and Debra sitting in his office.

She jumped up and ran over to her dad. "I'm so sorry about Mark. I know how close the two of you were. I really liked him, Dad. Why would someone torture and kill him?"

Frank sat down in his chair and leaned forward on his desk. "I don't have a clue. All cops have enemies, but this was more. The captain had something that someone wanted, and they took extreme measures to try to get it out of him. We need to close the office down for a few days. I need to go see the captain's wife because she's going to need some help with arrangements."

Chapter 36

Frank sat in light drizzle listening as the police chaplain spoke brave words about Captain Carson's devotion to family, his job, and to his colleagues. Debra sat next to him holding his hand and helping him nurse a broken heart. Frank was surprised by Dennis's absence, especially when he knew how important the captain was in his life.

The chaplain was about ten minutes into his sermon when Frank caught movement out the corner of his eye. Dennis was walking in with his mother on his arm. Frank was in shock because Dennis's mother hated cops, yet she was here to honor one. She wore a lovely dark outfit, very fitting for a funeral. They took seats to the side of the group, and Dennis nodded to Frank.

He looked at Debra. "You knew about this?"

"Yes, Dad, she called me. She sends her heartfelt condolences to you. She wanted to tell you herself, but I wasn't sure you were ready to talk with her."

"I would've talked to her, so next time, don't assume anything."

The rain let up by the end of the service, and Frank was on his way back to his car when Detective Sloan stopped him. "Frank, we know you had something to do with his death. It's only a matter of time before we find out."

"This isn't the time or place for this conversation, Detective."

"Mark my words; it's just a matter of time before we get you."

Frank really wanted to take a shot at Sloan, but he knew that is exactly what Sloan wanted. Instead, Frank just turned and walked away. Sloan tried to grab his shoulder, but Frank anticipated his move and dodged it. Frank got into his car and left the funeral.

Debra walked over to Dennis and his mother. She reached out to shake his mother's hand.

Instead, his mother reached out and hugged her. "How's your father doing?"

Debra was in shock. This wasn't the standoffish woman she knew. "He's struggling with the loss, but is doing fine."

"Let me know if I can do anything to help."

With that, she left Dennis and Debra standing on the curb.

Debra turned to Dennis. "What was that all about?"

"Hey, I told you that she wasn't the same woman since she returned."

"If I didn't know any better, I'd say that the iceberg between your mother and my dad is melting."

Frank grabbed three beers out of the fridge and came into the living room. He handed two to Debra and Dennis and kept the third.

Debra set her beer down. "Dad, I thought you didn't drink anymore?"

"That's true, but I want to toast my friend, and it wouldn't be right if we didn't do it with his favorite beverage. Don't worry, Honey, I'm not falling off the wagon. Let's toast to Captain Mark Carson - one of the good ones. He was one of the best friends I ever had."

The three toasted and took a big drink from their bottles. Frank then set his bottle down and pushed it over to Debra. "I don't want to tempt myself."

He took a deep breath and said, "I want to run some ideas by the two of you. Mark's murder seems very strange to me. Whoever killed him wanted the detectives to look at me for the murder. Using my gun from the evidence locker isn't enough to hold me. Whatever the reason, there's some connection between us. What do we have in common that someone doesn't want anyone to find out about?"

Dennis took a sip from his beer. "I think I know. The two of you worked in the same department, but that's not reason enough. I think the evidence box he gave you must contain something that someone doesn't want exposed to the public."

Frank thought about the conversation he'd with the captain about the evidence box. "Did I get him killed by asking for that evidence box?"

Debra reached over and touched Frank's shoulder. "You did nothing wrong. You were just trying to help a friend solve a murder. There's no way you could've known it might get him killed. We're not even sure that's the reason."

Frank got up and poured himself a glass of orange juice. "You know I made copies of all the documents and photographed all the evidence. I also took partial samples of some of the DNA evidence. It was a cold case, so no one was ever going to do anything. That has to be the reason as it's the tightest connection between the captain and me."

Dennis finished his beer and set it on the table. "Do you have the copies and samples here? I can take them back to the lab and run some tests."

"You don't have to do that. I have a private company that can run the tests."

"No, Frank, I want to do it. I think the captain's murder is linked to my dad's. Besides we really can't trust anyone right now, so we need to keep all of our investigations in-house."

Frank took a sip of his juice. "We need to run our own parallel investigation on both murders. Dennis, I have a question for you that may sound a little strange. At first, I assumed that your dad had a secret hiding spot in this house. I've measured everything and compared it to the blueprints, and find no discrepancies. Even so, I strongly believe that the answer is still in the house. Dennis, think back. Do you remember your dad doing any repair work just before he was murdered?"

"Sorry, Frank, but nothing comes to mind. What if I brought Medusa to the house? I can connect through your

266

Internet service and transmit the data back to my lab to the super computer for analysis. If we remove all the furniture from each room, I can scan for any minute changes to the walls. What do you think?"

"That's a great idea, but we still need to focus on our clients, or we'll be out of business. This investigation needs to be considered as a pro bono case, so when we have extra time we'll work it. All agreed?"

The question never even had to be asked.

Chapter 37

Another week passed keeping Frank and the kids busy working on the security for a new aeronautics research center. He worked on debugging security problems and completed background investigations on several of the researchers. Debra reviewed the legal aspects of employees signing non-disclosure documents, and Dennis preformed various security tests on the company's firewall. At one million dollars, this contract was one of their most lucrative.

In his spare time, Frank prepared extensive backgrounds on the three college coeds. The audio bugs were easy to install, but the video had pushed his abilities to the limit. He now understood why Dennis wanted the backgrounds. These girls were incredible, and something had to be done to stop them. They were destroying many solid relationships at the college, all for the sake of stupid sex games.

He'd heard nothing about Jeff and hoped that the pervert would be hit by a truck. Debra showed him the balance sheet for the month. More than enough to cover all expenses, including his lawyer, with a nice chunk of change still left over. Even though the economy was down, they were one of the few detective agencies in the black. He decided to stop looking for new clients, and concentrate on servicing their current ones. Debra recommended they farm out some of their DNA tests that weren't urgent to a private lab. At first, Dennis objected, but Debra reminded him that Medusa needed to remain a secret, and completing his testing in record time might send up a red flag. So, Dennis dropped off random DNA samples, just so they could remain under the radar.

Frank heard loud voices in the front office moments before Detective Sloan opened his door. Frank closed his iPad and turned off his computer monitor.

"What is it now Sloan? You just can't let it go, can you?"

"What's it with you, Frank? Do you think you're the local Godfather?"

"What the hell are you talking about, Sloan?"

"Have you heard of a Ms. Ginger Hallows? Well, she turned up dead last night with a .38 in her left temple. The way I understand it, she was a big problem in your daughter's last case, so it looks like murder runs in your family. We're taking her in for questioning."

He jumped up and ran into the front office. Detective Ronan was putting Debra in handcuffs. He ran toward her but she verbally stopped him.

"Don't do anything, Dad. Just call J.R. Lenson, and he'll know what to do."

Frank wanted to get into it with the two detectives, but again knew that's what they hoped. He looked over to Mrs. Henson and saw she already had the phone in hand and was calling Lenson. As soon as the detectives left, he called Dennis and told him to meet him at the station.

Thirty minutes later, Frank was pacing in the waiting area of the station when he spotted Lenson exiting the interrogation room.

He reached out to shake Frank's hand. "Your daughter is one tough cookie. I wish all my clients were like her. She did everything correctly."

Frank pulled him to the side. "So, where do we stand?"

"Well, they do have some circumstantial evidence. It's weak, but it might put Debra at the scene. It seems that the detectives found a large earring at the murder scene. It had one clear fingerprint on the surface, and it was a match to Debra. She said there was an explanation, but that I needed to talk to you first."

"There is, but it may take some time to explain, and we need to do it in private. Are they going to release her?"

"It looks like it. Right now, she's what they consider as a '"person of interest." They want to build a tight case before they officially arrest her for murder. So, does your explanation cancel the earring threat?"

"Absolutely."

"That's what I want to hear."

Dennis arrived five minutes later and was a basket case. Frank tried to settle him down by explaining what they knew so far, and told Dennis to be patient. Debra finally came out of the interrogation room and rode home with Dennis while Frank followed in his car. When he got home, he could see that they were in a heated discussion. The gist of the conversation was that Dennis wanted to divulge everything about Jeff, while she wanted to release information as needed. Clearly, Dennis's decision was emotional, while Debra was trying to be rational. Frank knew he had to stop their arguing.

"Stop it you two, because we have to work together. We have a ton of evidence that points to Jeff. We need to review the video tapes and see if we have Jeff taking the earring. If so, then Debra is off the hook. If not, we'll have to use the rest of the evidence to convince the police that he's the one they should be arresting. Arguing isn't going to do any good. You two get dinner ready while I look at the video."

Dennis got up from the couch. "I can help with the video."

"Sorry Dennis, but you're the last person I want to look at the video. Your judgment would be fogged. I've already viewed them once, and I know what to expect. I just need to take a closer look."

Dennis shook his head. "I agree with you, Frank, but there's something you don't understand. We can use Medusa to analyze the video. I'll tell her what we're looking for and have her enhance and search every section until she finds it. The video moves fast, and you may go right by it. Believe me when I say, I don't want to watch the video."

Debra reached out and touched Frank's arm. "I don't want Dennis to watch the video any more than you do, but it might just be our best chance."

270

The three agreed that Dennis should run the videos over to the lab after dinner. Frank got up to go to the kitchen and saw a car he recognized across the street. He pulled back the curtain and saw it was Detective Sloan watching the house through binoculars.

Chapter 38

Debra sat in the waiting area outside Lenson's office. Lenson came out and ushered her in, gesturing for her to sit down.

"So, Frank called me and told me that you were bringing what every defense lawyer wants in a case, ironclad proof."

"Well, I hope so. First, I need to tell you a story about the suspect we think killed the girl. Then I'll show you the evidence that points to him as the number-one suspect. It took longer to scan through the videos, but we have a still frame of this guy taking the earring and putting it in his pocket. He was in an acting scam with the woman who was murdered. You can look through the evidence, and see what you think. I have it organized, point by point."

Lenson picked it up and started to scan through the folder. Debra thumbed through a magazine and waited patiently. Thirty minutes later, Lenson closed the folder.

"Most cases I work on take a lot of work, but it looks like you did it all for me. I'm going directly to the Assistant D.A. and share what we have. When the Assistant D.A. sees the evidence, it'll force the detectives to stop in their tracks and look at Jeff. Where's Jeff, by the way? It says nothing about where he can be found."

Debra threw down the magazine and stood up. "We lost track of him after he left the hospital. He had some severe scars, so we think he's hiding out somewhere."

"I have to be honest, Debra, everything is solid except what you did to Jeff. I understand completely, but the police and or the jury in a trial might see it differently."

"Hey, he broke into my apartment. We didn't force him to put on the lotion. He did it of his own accord. It would be no different from someone breaking into a home and getting hurt in the process. I think we're good on this point. Besides, when you show the videos of how he got the rash, most jurors will sympathize with what we did."

"I agree, but I wanted to point out our weakest link. I'm pretty sure that the Assistant D.A. will immediately have the detectives back off and leave you all alone."

A day later, Mrs. Henson forwarded a call to Debra. Frank came into her office when he heard it was from Lenson. She didn't say much, but listened intently, before hanging up.

She smiled, "The Assistant D.A. agrees with Lenson that the detectives are barking up the wrong tree. The Assistant D.A. then called the detectives and told them I was no longer a 'person of interest'."

Frank moved to the side of the desk and gave her a big hug. "Honey, I wish that were true, but I think Sloan is going to keep coming at us. He's relentless and won't give up."

"If he does, I'll have Lenson go after him. He's a shark with lots of teeth. He costs a bunch, but is worth every bit. I think we need to put this behind us, and get back to business."

Everyone had returned to their offices when Sloan pushed his way into Debra's office. "You think you can get away with murder just because you have a fancy ass lawyer. I won't give up. I'll be there every time you stop to get gas. Don't worry because I'll be waiting every day outside your house and office. You may think you've won this one, but you haven't. You're not above the law. Mark my words; I'll get you."

Frank heard Sloan's voice and rushed back to Debra's office. Sloan was already on his way out. He was about to follow him when she held up her hand and smiled.

Frank turned around and looked at her. "What the hell was that?"

"That was your friend Sloan. He was just venting a threat. It was great."

"I don't understand. How's that great?"

"Well, Lenson told me to install a voice-activated system in my office. That way if something like this happened, we would have more proof than one's word against another. I had it installed early this morning. Let me play it back for you."

Debra pressed the play button, and the entire conversation with Sloan was replayed. She stopped the player. "I'll pass this on to Lenson, and he'll let the Assistant D.A. know that we'll be suing the police if they continue this harassment."

The three celebrated by closing the office early and heading home. Dennis had to make a trip back to his house to check on some tests that Medusa was running. Frank and Debra sat in the backyard enjoying the afternoon sun throwing its long shadows across the lawn. Debra had her beer, and Frank enjoyed a beer stein of orange juice.

Suddenly, they heard screeching tires in the front of the house. He ran toward the door as Sloan pushed his way in and shoved a search warrant in his face. Sloan had found a judge somewhere who'd bought his conspiracy theory. Debra ran up, scanned through the search warrant, and proclaimed it valid. Several officers with boxes came into the house and started to pull paperwork, computer disks, and all of Frank's guns.

Frank reached his limit and blocked Sloan from entering his bedroom. Sloan started to push Frank to the floor. He came in with an upper-right hook and sent Sloan flying across the room. Two officers quickly put cuffs on Frank and hauled him out to the police cruiser. Immediately Debra was on the phone to Lenson and Dennis. It was all over in less than thirty minutes.

Debra locked up as soon as the last one left, and headed down to the precinct. This Sloan was really starting to piss her off. She needed to be more aggressive. When she got to the precinct, Lenson and Frank were standing out front talking to the Assistant D.A.

As she approached, the Assistant D.A. started to explain. "I'm really sorry this happened. I already talked with the judge who signed the search warrant. He's now convinced that Sloan is on a witch hunt. Sloan has been suspended until internal affairs can do a thorough investigation. All of your stuff will be returned immediately, and again my apologies."

Debra absorbed this information a minute before responding. "I appreciate what you are saying, but we warned you, and you didn't take us seriously. You had an out-of-control detective, and yet you let him continue working. I'm sorry, but we'll be filing a lawsuit against your office and the police department for harassment. Let me play you a tape."

She pulled out a tape and played the recording from earlier. "If I were you, I'd talk to your people about a financial settlement. It seems to be the only way this will stop."

Debra couldn't believe her own words. She was going for the throat of the very people she used to work with. If she ever had any doubts, whether quitting the D.A.'s office had been the right move, they were long gone.

Lenson leaned in towards the Assistant D.A. "Normally, I would've recommended that Debra accept your apology and move on, but I love a slam dunk."

The Assistant D.A. didn't say a word. The look on her face told it all. The D.A. would get into this mess, heads would roll, and a settlement would be made. Sloan would be shipped out to a different precinct, or offered an early retirement package. He was now an embarrassment to the department, and they'd quickly wash their hands of him.

When the three returned to the house, they made short work replacing the materials to their original places. Frank stood back and looked at the replaced items. "You know we should have left everything in their boxes. We could have brought Medusa over and started to scan the house."

Debra was still straightening the last few items. "I think we've done enough for today. We have the weekend in front of us. Let's bring Medusa over on Saturday, and if we work together, we can quickly scan the whole house."

Dennis put his arm around Debra. "I'm exhausted. Let's call it for tonight."

Frank laughed. "I think we're all in agreement. What a day!"

Chapter 39

Frank and Dennis moved out the last piece of furniture from the living room before setting Medusa in the middle. Debra was in her bedroom putting everything back in place after they had finished scanning that room.

She walked back into the living room. "So, how're we doing?"

Dennis looked down at Medusa and confirmed the system was set. "Let's go because she's ready to scan." He programmed in a 30-second countdown, and they headed out the sliding door.

Frank opened the picnic basket and announced, "It's time to eat. Honey, you were right about working together. This is going much faster than I thought it would. Dennis, how long before we know what she's found?"

Dennis took a bite from one of the turkey sandwiches, and then set it down to answer. "Medusa should have the 3D images in about half an hour. The surface scans will take a little longer. If nothing shows up, we may have to rescan the rooms using a higher setting on the sensors."

Frank was about to hand a sandwich to Debra, but Dennis beat him to it. Frank nodded, and grabbed his own sandwich. "So, Dennis how does this work with the scans?"

Dennis took a bite and washed it down with a cold pop. "Medusa first does a distant scan to see if there're any variations on the wall's surface. When that's completed, she then does a density examination on each wall. She sends out high-frequency scans, which return to sensors that she can measure. A variation in density caused by changes to the Sheetrock material will be apparent. If my dad did anything to the structure of the house after it was built, I'll know what it was."

Frank took another bite out of his sandwich. "What if he hired someone else to work on the house?"

"Mom told me that he did all the repairs around the house. He was accomplished at all aspects of construction, which is why he was such an excellent architect. He knew everything about building from the ground up. He didn't trust anyone else to work on the house, so everything you see here, he built. It took him four times as long as a normal builder, but he did it right the first time."

Frank turned to Debra. "So, how is the wedding plan going?"

Debra wasn't prepared for this question, and almost choked on the question. "Well, we just started. If you are asking because of Dennis's mom, we'll talk to her next Wednesday night. With all that's been going on, the planning is on the back burner. I've only just said yes to Dennis, and you're already walking me down the aisle."

"I'm looking forward to doing that. I just want you to know that I'm proud of you two."

"We know you're a proud father, and I know you're in a hurry to get me married. I know how you think, Dad, so don't even go down that path."

"What path are you talking about?"

Dennis set his sandwich down. "What are you two talking about?"

He turned to Dennis. "Grandkids, Dennis."

Dennis started to turn red in the face then he got up and went into the house.

Debra looked over to her dad. "Did you really have to do that? We haven't talked about kids yet."

"Sorry, do you think he wants kids?"

"I don't know yet. We've talked about a lot of things, but believe it or not, we've had our minds on other things."

"Let's call a truce and go see what Dennis found out."

The two walked in as Dennis was pulling up the data from the super computer back in his lab. Dennis hooked a thirty-inch monitor up to Medusa. Frank and Debra crowded around while

Dennis navigated through the results on the screen. The first drawing was of Dennis's old bedroom. It showed a large patch about midway up the wall.

Dennis pointed at the screen. "I forgot about that one. When I was five, I was jumping up and down on my bed and hit the wall with a large truck I had in my hands. Mom was very mad at me, but my dad just laughed and got some Sheetrock repair material. Let's keep looking."

Dennis went from room to room and saw no obvious changes to the walls. When he got to his parents old bedroom, which was now Frank's, there was a discrepancy in the middle of the wall. The area appeared clear of wiring or plumbing and measured approximately three by three inches."

He zoomed in tighter on the area. "Look right there, this could be it."

Frank leaned in to see what Dennis was viewing. "Could it be a repair from moving the bed, and it hitting the wall, or if hanging a picture got out-of-hand?"

Dennis turned to Frank. "Normally, I'd agree, but my dad knew exactly where every stud was located. He took pictures of each interior wall, every wire, and all the plumbing before the insulation, and Sheetrock was installed. If he needed to hang a picture, he would pull out the documented wall images, and he would know exactly where to put the nail."

Frank shook his head. "All that just to hang a picture?"

"Hey, my dad was a perfectionist, what can I say? This tells me that this deviation wasn't a repair. According to Medusa, the discrepancy starts at eight feet, three inches from the corner and four feet down from the ceiling. Do you have a Sheetrock knife?"

Frank ran out to the garage and came back with a knife. Dennis started to measure and marked the area on the wall. In less than five minutes, they were ready to cut. Dennis stood back as Frank started to cut one inch outside the original modification to the wall. Once he made the final cut, he pushed a small screwdriver into the upper edge and pried out the square. He then took a flashlight and pointed it into the opening. He didn't see any insulation, but he did find papers sealed in a plastic bag taped to the back wall. He reached in and slowly removed the package.

Frank opened the package and slid out a large stack of blueprints. "Dennis, can you think of any reason why your father would hide blueprints in the wall?"

"It's a common practice for builders to hide all kinds of things in the wall. Some people take pictures of the building as it is being constructed, and put copies of the pictures in the wall like a time capsule."

He took a minute to review the contents of the package. "These look like blueprints of some of the buildings he designed. I'm not sure why he would hide them. I'm going to scan them for Medusa to analyze. It may take some time, but I should know something in a day or two. Maybe he left some small clue on one of them."

Frank put pieces of tape on the piece he removed and then put it back in the wall. "Hey, I know a little about wall repairing, so I can fix this."

Dennis put his hand on Frank's wrist. "No, Frank, I want to do the repair. I need to get in tune with this house, and this is one way for me to do it."

General Martin Harrison was getting very worried. Just when things with Dr. Andrews seemed to have settled down, something new flared up. He knew that the senator wouldn't like the publicity that Andrews and his partners were getting. Debra Ridge was now in the news, as part of a murder investigation. Eventually, the senator would tire of having Dr. Andrews and his little band of friends being in the limelight. It was only a matter of time. He needed to start working on his permanent exit plan. To hell with the senator.

Just then, the phone rang, and he saw it was the senator. He ignored the call and instead contacted his closest and most trusted Black Ops. He needed him for this one last job because it required his expertise and discretion.

Chapter 40

Dennis was as nervous as a hen because tonight he and Debra would talk to his mother about the wedding. Debra was so mad at him when she found out that he hadn't even told her he proposed. He had Mrs. Henson make his mother's favorite meal of roast beef and mixed vegetables. They started serving wine early.

He and Debra had a heated conversation last night because she couldn't understand how he could save her life from a killer, but not be honest with his mother. Tonight was his night to prove to her that he wasn't a "mama's boy."

His mother took a small sip and set her glass down. "So Dennis, what's going on with you two tonight. Are you going to tell me that you're getting married?"

He had just taken a large drink from his glass and choked on his wine. "Did someone tell you?"

"Dennis, the last time you were this nervous was on your first date. Besides, you look at Debra with love and respect. What took you so long?"

"Are you and Frank working together on this?"

"What does he have to do with this?"

"Well, he said exactly the same thing."

"Frank and I never see or talk to each other, and that's how I'd like to keep it."

"That would be a problem, Mom. He'll be at the wedding and walking Debra down the aisle."

"You're worried that I'm going to make a scene because Frank's there? Dennis, you must think very little of me. Debra is his daughter. Of course, he's going to walk her down the aisle. I'd never rain on her special day."

Debra relaxed, hoping the worst part was over. "Thank you, Mrs. Andrews. I love your son very much."

Dennis's mother reached over and squeezed Debra's hand. "No one has called me Mrs. Andrews in years. I miss that. Dear, I like you and feel you'll be very good for my son."

Dennis needed to change the subject and address the second issue of the evening. Debra told him he needed to come clean with his mother about what Frank had done and what they had found out so far.

"Mom, we have one other thing to talk about, and it involves Frank."

"Is this really necessary?"

"Debra and I think so. Frank bought our old house."

"He did what? What the hell was he thinking?"

"He was trying to help me."

"How could buying our house help you?"

"He's trying to solve dad's murder."

"It's a little late for that."

Dennis took another sip of wine. "He wasn't part of the original investigation, and he thinks that they screwed up the case. He's trying to make it right."

"What does he get from this?"

"Nothing, but he's a man known for doing the right thing."

"The police should've done the right thing when your father was murdered."

Dennis was starting to get very irritated with his mother. "Look, he's trying to help. We found something in the walls that dad hid."

"What're you talking about?"

"Dad hid blueprint copies of some of the buildings he built. Did you ever see him working on the wall in the bedroom? A hole about three inches square."

"No, but I did a few trips just before he was murdered. He could've done it then. How does this help solve the murder?"

"Do you remember the funeral you just went to for Frank's boss? He was Frank's closest friend, and we think he was killed because he helped him look into dad's murder. Before you start

283

getting upset about him working the case, remember he just lost his best friend doing it. He's trying even harder now to find the killers of his friend and dad."

Mrs. Andrews became silent and relaxed. "I didn't realize, and I'm sorry I got carried away. Dennis, I don't understand how you could go back into that house. I couldn't even get within blocks of the house before you got upset. That's one of the reasons I sold it and built this house."

Debra had been patient while Dennis and his mother worked things out. "I think you have to blame me for that one. I was really pissed at him for not trusting me. He proved just how much he loved me by coming into the house and overcoming his fears."

"So, when you're gone overnight, you're staying at our old house?"

The two kids nodded.

"Don't worry; I'll be good at the wedding. I won't antagonize Frank."

Mrs. Henson came in for the sixth time in the past half hour. "Are the three of you finished yet? I'd like to serve dinner, and I don't want to have to reheat it again. I can't believe all the intelligence in this room, and yet you can't work out a simple marriage. The two of you want to get married, why make it so complicated?" She put her hands on her hips, turned and stormed from the room.

Senator Bob Welding had been working late that evening setting up a strategy for his upcoming political campaign. His secure phone stated to ring, and the senator checked the number. It was the general.

"You are finally calling me back, General?"

"Senator, how's the campaign going?"

"It could be better if I didn't have to worry about dead projects."

"Unfortunately, the dead can come back to haunt you."

"What are you talking about, General?"

"Our Dr. Andrews is getting way too much publicity, and it's only going to get worse. It seems the Ridge Detective Agency is doing a gangbuster business, and Dr. Andrews seems to be the key. Many of the clients they're doing business for are the same military contractors I deal with. It's only a matter of time before the MLA project surfaces again. We have to take him out and minimize the collateral damage. I've a team put together who can break into their house, kill them, and make it look like a burglary."

"Is there any other way we can fix this without killing Dr. Andrews?"

"Not if you really want to live in the White House. Dr. Andrews needs to be long gone before you hit the campaign trail."

"Then precede, General, if there are no other choices. Just make sure the police believe it is a burglary."

"It will take a few days to put in place, but rest assured I'll make it happen. Good-bye, Senator"

Chapter 41

Normally, Dennis worked in the lab by himself, but today he was sharing the lab with his mother. She was in one corner working on her lionfish studies, and he and Debra were working on the blueprints across the lab. All the assignments for the agency had been done and delivered for the week. Mrs. Henson was manning the office phones for the rest of the day, and then was headed fifty miles north to visit her sister for the weekend.

Dennis had looked at the blueprints more than a dozen times and still found nothing. Medusa was looking for any further deviations in the drawings, but no luck yet. Debra had convinced him to stop for the day, so he was shutting down the systems when several security alarms started to go off. Dennis pulled up a security screen and saw a black-hooded man spraying paint over the camera lens. Second and a third cameras were then blinded. The cameras were too far apart for one person to disable them. Dennis looked over to his mother.

"Mom! Shut your system down now. Debra, we don't have much time. It looks like several men are breaking into the house."

"Call the police," Debra cried.

"I will but that'll be too late. We have to go now."

"Where? There's no way out except through the guys upstairs."

"Not true," came a yell from Mrs. Andrews. "We can use the safe room."

Debra looked over to Mrs. Andrews, who was pressing a code into a keypad previously hidden on the wall. Seconds later, a door appeared out of thin air.

"Dennis! What the hell is going on?"

"Medusa, are all recording devices on? Dennis grabbed Medusa and yanked out all cables that were attached to the side of the device. "Sorry, I should have told you, but mom and I swore not to tell anyone. That way, no one could be forced to tell about the safe room."

"Dennis, I'm scared. What's going on?"

"We had a secure room built on the outside of the lab. It's an escape route in case the security systems detected an intrusion. My mother insisted on it when she built this house. She never wanted a repeat of my dad's murder. No more time for talk, we need to go. Don't worry about the systems in the lab, as they'll take care of themselves. Medusa, how many men are there?"

Five men was the answer. Dennis looked one last time at the security screen. "Medusa, start the countdown on fire control systems."

Dennis grabbed Debra and dragged her across the room. His mother was waiting on the other side of the escape door. As soon as the two were through, she closed the door and looked up at a monitor. "They're coming down into the lab. I'm going to seal us off." She looked up at the screen as the men in dark outfits entered the lab.

"Don't worry, Debra. This is what's called a safe room. Some people refer to it as a panic room. Wealthy people have it as a security measure. When intruders break into a house, a family can hide in this room until the police arrive. The walls are two feet of reinforced concrete, and the six locking pins in the door would take twelve hours to cut through with the best cutters. I don't know who these guys are, but I have more than two dozen cameras in the room recording HD video and sound. Once they enter the room, their exit will be blocked, and the fire control system will pump in halogen gas. If there's no fire, then the gas is pumped out, but the intruders will be unconscious long enough for the police to arrest them."

Dennis took one last look at the screen. "Shit."

Debra looked up at the screen to see what Dennis viewed. "What...?"

"Frank. We need to warn Frank because he may also be a target."

Dennis grabbed the dedicated phone on the wall and punched in a number. Three rings and Frank picked up the phone.

"Frank Ridge here. Can I help you?"

"This is Dennis. Several men in black outfits are breaking into the lab. Debra, my mother and I are in a safe room. We've called the police, but whoever these people are, they may be after you too. Frank, your best chance is to come to the house. There'll be lots of police here in the next few minutes. Go, Frank and good luck."

He hung up, grabbed his gun, and ran out the front door looking for anyone gunning for him. The coast was clear, so he jumped in his car and roared toward the lab.

The five men moved through the lab quickly, looking for an escape route. The sounds from the room were hard to hear, but Dennis did catch the leader tell his other men to kill them. They watched as the gas sprayed into the room. Slowly, each man started to stagger as they inhaled the gas. The leader of the group was still looking for something. He raised his gun and started firing at a control panel in the corner of the room. Dennis took a quick look and realized the group leader had shot up the fire control system. The command to pump out the gas had now been disabled. The leader effectively killed himself and all his men.

Dennis worked feverishly to override the system. Nothing seemed to work until he pressed the system reset and manually turned off fire control. He then released the lock on the elevators, but it was too late for the five intruders.

Dennis pressed a button to rotate the camera so it viewed the front of the house. One of the systems on the outside hadn't been disabled. Several police officers and detectives were trying to get into the house. Once Dennis was sure they were safe, he pressed one last button, which slowly opened the door.

Dennis yelled out the opening. "This is a safe room. We're the owners of this house. We're coming out - there are two women and one man. We all have our hands up."

Dennis walked out first followed by the two women. As soon as it was obvious to the police that the three were hiding from the intruders, they were allowed to go upstairs.

Frank was frantically waiting. Debra ran up and threw her arms around him. "Dad, they were going to kill us."

"Who did this?"

Dennis looked at various detectives and cops moving about and said, "I'm not sure, but we'll know after they're gone."

The three sat in the upstairs living room waiting for the detectives to interview each of them about the break in. When the last detective was gone, Dennis walked to the front door and locked it. Frank had just finished cleaning off several of the cameras so that they would be operational again. Mrs. Andrews had just finished off another glass of wine and was getting very drunk. Frank stayed on the other side of the room, way away from her. When Dennis was sure that the security system was functional, he turned it back on. Frank looked at the tape across the elevator. They wouldn't be able to go into the lab for at least a day. The CSI team had taken some preliminary samples and pictures, but they'd be back early the next morning.

"Dennis, who were those guys?"

"My guess is someone from my past. General Martin Harrison would be my first choice. I think we've become too visible in the public eye, and that makes him very nervous. Just to be sure, we need to check through all the video and voice recordings."

Frank looked over to the tape on the elevator. "How're you going to do that? We really can't go into the lab yet."

"I have Medusa right here. We don't have to be in the lab because I can turn on the super computer remotely. The internal camera took video images of their faces when the police took their hoods off. I'll start running facial comparisons and background checks on the men. I'll also do some voice comparisons to see if we can isolate their employers. We need to get a good night's sleep and see what Medusa has for us in the morning. I'll call Mrs. Henson and tell her to stay at her sister's house for a few more days."

Frank looked across the room. "We may have another small problem. It looks like your mother had a little too much to drink."

Dennis walked over to his mother. She was barely conscious, and slurring her words.

"Can you two help me?"

Frank backed off a couple of steps. "No, not me, no way. You two do it."

Debra gave Frank a glare. "Really?"

Frank moved over and grabbed one side. Mrs. Andrews turned her head at Frank.

In a very broken and slurred voice she said, "Hi, Frank. Did you come over to see me tonight?"

Frank turned his head away. She smelled like a brewery. They finally got her into her room and on her bed. Dennis and Frank left, leaving Debra to getting her into bed. Frank was sweating as they sat back down.

Dennis looked back down the hall. "Thanks, Frank. I know that was something you really didn't want to do, but it was a big help. She won't remember a thing in the morning. I've never seen her this drunk. I think this thing tonight scared the hell out of her. I can't believe those people were coming to kill us. Are we that much of a threat to someone?"

Debra came into the room. "She'll be fine, but will probably have a big hangover in the morning. I wouldn't expect to see her until tomorrow afternoon. Thanks, Dad, for helping. You're a good sport. Dennis, are we going to be safe here tonight?"

"We should be fine. All the systems are in the green. Frank, are you going home?"

"Nope, I'll be staying right here in the living room with my friend." Frank patted the gun in his shoulder holster.

Debra walked down the hall and pulled out some blankets and a pillow.

"You should be fine with these. Thanks for staying. I was going to ask you to stay, but I should've known that I didn't need to ask."

"It's not a problem, Honey. See you in the morning."

General Harrison was in shock. His best five men were gone. What was worse was that he found out from a newscast. The rest of his men in his Black Ops group he didn't know as well, and he wasn't about to entrust them with another operation. He knew when to fold. He had plenty of money in the Caymans, so he planned to turn in his resignation and leave town. He had a retirement home he bought under another name in Montana that would become his safe haven. It had over a thousand acres, and the house was dead center in the middle. He'd stockpiled adequate supplies to last a couple of years. At least, long enough for the dust to settle and for him to come up with a new plan.

His biggest problem now was the senator. By now, he must be going crazy with concern. Although he thought it strange that he hadn't had any calls from him, but maybe that was a good sign. He looked around his office and gave his secretary his resignation in a sealed envelope to be delivered to headquarters the next day. That would allow just enough time for him to disappear and take up his new identity.

Thirty minutes later, the general pulled up to his modest home in south Seattle. He hadn't planned to stay there long, so he never put much money into the place. He had a realtor lined up with full authorization to sell the place upon his word. As he got out of the car, he could hear dogs and kids playing off in the distance. He'd never come home this early so all the sounds were new to him. His wife had divorced him years ago, so there was no one to greet him.

He unlocked the door and approached the security panel. He had thirty seconds to enter in his password in order to disarm the system. Once it was entered correctly, it would flash an *"all clr"* message. When he entered the last digit, a new message came up that said *"you dead."* He was panic stricken, but now realized why the senator hadn't called. That was his last thought before the house lifted fifteen feet off the ground and was blown into thousands of pieces, scattering in all directions. Car alarms all over the neighborhood started to blare, and every dog for ten blocks howled.

Chapter 42

Frank awoke to the smell of coffee. Standing in the kitchen was Mrs. Andrews pouring several cups. He was about to get up and leave when Debra and Dennis came around the kitchen corner. They'd been just out of his view. Debra handed Frank a cup. Mrs. Andrews headed back to her bedroom without saying a word.

Dennis leaned over to Frank. "She doesn't remember last night at all. I think she's going back to bed."

"She didn't say anything about me?"

"No, why should she?"

"Forget it. So, where do we stand with the audio and video that Medusa was working on?"

"She has most everything we need, but there's something more important we need to show you."

Dennis clicked on the large-screen TV, which was already tuned to a newscast. A reporter was standing in front of what was left of a house. The reporter kept going on about a possible gas explosion or a bomb, but the fire department was still investigating. Then it hit Frank when the reporter mentioned that it was General Martin Harrison that was killed in his home. The reporter continued to explain who the general was and continued into his military background. Dennis flipped to two other stations. The same thing was on each with different spins on the story.

Frank turned to Dennis. "So it was the general's men last night, and his boss decided to cut their losses. Didn't you tell me that the general worked directly for a senator?"

"Yes, Senator Bob Welding."

"Do you think that the senator had the general taken out?"

Dennis turned off the TV. "That would be my guess. I never had much to do with the senator. I worked mainly with the general and he in turn passed on information to the senator. I know the senator has many connections with the FBI, CSI, and

NSA to name a few. I'm sure that he used someone from one of those agencies to take the general out. They all consider losing those men last night a big embarrassment to the intelligence community. The general may be off our back but now a much bigger predator is after us. I looked at the breakdown of information that Medusa extracted from the video last night. Those five guys were part of a Black Ops group in the military who were court martialed. My biggest fear is that the CSI guys coming to process the scene will connect the general to these dirty military men. That wouldn't be good for us besides the problem we may have with the senator coming after us."

Dennis was about to continue when the phone rang. It was an assistant to the senator asking the three of them for a meeting at 1 p.m.

Frank responded immediately. "It has to be a trap."

Dennis started toward the kitchen to get another cup of coffee.

"Come on, Frank, he's not going to do anything in his office. My guess is that he wants some kind of truce, or he wants to know what he's up against with us. We need to work fast. The senator made a big mistake by calling and alerting us."

Frank was scratching his face. He needed a shave and a shower. "You've lost me and I want to continue this conversation, but first I really need a favor. I need to clean up, and I don't want to go back to my house right now. I also don't want to make the same mistake as the last time I took a shower here."

This piece of information got Debra's attention. "What mistake are you talking about?"

Frank realized he'd opened a big door. "It was no big deal, so just forget it."

Dennis looked toward Debra and grinned. "My mother came home to find a naked man in one of the bedrooms."

Debra was trying to grasp this completely new development. "Really, Dad. She saw you naked?"

Dennis smirked. "In all his glory."

Frank didn't say a thing. He just headed toward Dennis's bathroom and slammed the door.

Debra leaned over to Dennis. "We need to talk more about this later."

Senator Welding was in a panic. On the surface, everything looked perfect for him. Everyone in the party was behind him as a candidate for president. He would have to knock half-dozen others out in the primaries, but right now, he was the front-runner. The problem was his connection with the general. When he thought back about the MLA project, he realized that his newest solution should have been done a long time ago. With the general gone, the only link to the MLA was Dennis Andrews and his friends. He stayed up all night running through all the possibilities. Dr. Andrews was like a forest fire. You put out one part, and another pops up. The only idea he could come up with was to confront Dr. Andrews and his two partners. He had to know where he stood before blowing millions of dollars on a campaign that was going nowhere.

He had two choices. He would work something out with Dr. Andrews, or take the money and run, just like the general was planning to do. Dr. Andrews was due to arrive any second, and the senator checked one last time to make sure all the electronic detection systems were functioning. His secretary called and told him that the three were outside. He walked to his door and ushered them in.

"Can I get you anything to drink?"

Dennis motioned for Frank and Debra to sit down. He was going to stand for a few moments.

"Senator, I don't want to beat around the bush. Is this meeting about the MLA and the general's untimely death?"

"Just so you know, any electronic devices you may have on you will be blocked or fried. Yes, I asked you here to talk about our common interests, which now have been reduced down to one. I know that all three of you know about the MLA. That's fine with me, but you have to understand that not all military projects work out the way they were intended. The MLA was one of those projects. The general in command made many decisions that I never approved. I should have stopped him when I realized he'd gone too far. I can't believe he tried to have you killed, but that's not why I asked you here. I want to know what you plan on doing with your knowledge of the MLA project. Remember you did sign a non-disclosure statement."

Dennis looked back at Debra and Frank. They had already rehearsed several scenarios they thought the senator might present.

"Senator, you can justify what you've done by putting it all on the general, but the truth is we don't care. We just want to be left alone. We have no plans on exposing the MLA project. You and I both know that we'd be grouped with you, and to be perfectly honest, we don't want to be connected to you in any way. As far as we're concerned, we don't know anything about a dead MLA project. If anyone asks us about it, we'll play dumb. Senator, we know that you have powerful resources with which we couldn't compete. So, call off the dogs, because you're wasting your time. Just in case you change your mind, I put all the incriminating data on the MLA project in a data cloud. It has to be reset every month. If anything happens to my friends, or me the cloud will send the data to some very important law enforcement agencies. If you don't know what a data cloud is, Google it. One last thing; don't count on our votes."

The Senator was about to make a comeback, but the three were out the door before he could compose himself. He was surprised at how the meeting went. He felt sure that Dr. Andrews was going to go for his throat, but instead he called a truce. He could live with their proposal. He'd have to call a couple of people and make sure that no further actions were taken.

As the three walked out the front door of the Federal building, Dennis stopped and looked at the other two.

"So, how do you think it went?"

Frank wanted to say something in the meeting, but they had agreed Dennis would be the spokesperson. "Do you really think he'll leave us alone? He has a lot to lose if we say anything."

Dennis knew Frank was right, but didn't want to fuel the fire.

"I think the senator has to focus on his election. He should be leaving us alone for quite some time. I think the data cloud will make him think twice about trying to go after us. I know he has some powerful resources that can break any encryption, but remember we're talking about Medusa."

Debra and Frank seemed satisfied with Dennis's response. By the time they'd returned to the house, the police were removing the tape.

Frank stopped at the door. "Hey, guys. You go on in, and I think I'll go back to my house. I need to take a moment to reflect on the direction we're headed. I think we're going a bit too fast, almost like a train wreck. There are dead bodies all around us. Even when I was on the force, I never saw so many bodies."

She reached out and held his hand. "We'll be fine, Dad. I think things did get going too fast, but you have to admit, much of what happened was fate, and we had no control. Make sure you call us when you get there."

Frank took off, and Debra and Dennis headed for the house. They found Dennis's mother sitting in the living room. Debra headed toward their bedroom, while Dennis confronted his mother.

"How are you doing today, Mom?"

"How am I doing? Five people come in our house and try to kill me. Your cop friend buys our old house, and I can't remember a damn thing about last night."

"Really, Mom, you don't remember a thing? Nothing about you and Frank? Wow, I didn't think you'd forget that."

Fear crossed her face. "What are you talking about, Dennis?"

"I'm just pulling your chain, Mom. You need to lighten up a bit. The safe room was your idea, and it saved our lives. You did well, except that you drank too much last night."

"Who put me to bed?"

"Debra."

"Good thing. Thank you Dennis, and thank Debra for me."

Frank arrived at his house thirty minutes later after driving around, trying to clear his mind. He almost got his daughter and business partner killed. He knew that it was partly because of Dennis's past, but it wouldn't have surfaced if he hadn't started the detective agency.

While Dennis was talking to the senator, all Frank could think about was all the other loose ends. Jeff was a big one, but they still had the three coeds, and Dennis's dad. Then there were all the new contracts with some very large powerful corporations. Maybe they were getting in too deep by playing with the big boys. It started to scare the hell out of him.

He opened the door to his house and headed for the refrigerator. He reached for the orange juice, but stopped and grabbed a beer instead. He pulled out his cell and called Debra to let her know that he was home safe. He hung up the phone and took a big swig from the bottle.

Chapter 43

Frank awoke to his house alarm signaling unauthorized entry. He wasn't drunk, but close. He was already regretting falling off the wagon. He was trying to focus on his surroundings but having trouble sitting up. He heard a crash and then footsteps. Why did he drink those beers? He struggled to find the light, knocking several items on his nightstand to the floor. He finally pulled the drawer open to get his gun, but was stopped when a pistol-whipped across his face. He fell to the floor, and the light came on. He looked up to see Sloan.

Sloan grabbed the gun out of the nightstand drawer. "You're not as fast as you used to be, Frank. Had a little too much to drink last night? Now just keep your mouth shut and listen. I need to know what you found out about Dennis Andrews' dad. If you don't tell me, Frank, it won't be good for your health."

Frank tried to sit up. Blood was pouring out of the large gash on his temple. "Screw you, Sloan. What the hell's going on with you?"

"That's not the right answer, Frank," he said and shot him in the lower leg.

Frank winced in pain. What was Sloan doing? Why all this sudden interest in Dennis? Whoever said gunshots don't hurt? The pain was intense and numbing his mind.

Sloan leaned down to Frank. "Let's try this again. What have you found out about the murder of Carl Andrews? You still have plenty of body parts left, and I don't have my answer. Now tell me what you've found out!"

"I don't know what you want. We haven't found anything to do with the murder. I was just looking into it as a favor for Dennis."

"Wrong answer again, Frank." Another shot was fired, and this time the bullet passed through Frank's left hand. The pain was even more intense, making it hard to concentrate. He struggled to keep his mind clear. He looked under the bed and saw a flash of silver. Then he remembered he'd stored his father's military saber under the bed. He was running out of time. Sloan was going to continue torturing him until he died, just as he did with the captain.

Sloan pushed the barrel of his gun against Frank's other leg. "I'm getting tired of this, Frank. Let's try again."

Sloan shifted his weight getting ready to put another round into Frank. Just then, Frank moved his wounded leg, trying to distract Sloan. Sloan's eyes shifted allowing just enough time for Frank to make his move. "You're going ..."

The military saber went through Sloan's heart, and he dropped like a rock. The gun discharged, and the bullet hit Frank in the fleshy edge of his right leg. Sloan had fallen directly on him, and now Frank was struggling to get the body off. He reached for his phone and dialed 911. He tried to talk, but passed out dropping the phone to the floor.

The light was bright and blurry. Frank tried to focus and recognized he wasn't at home. He heard familiar sounds, and realized he must be in a hospital. He looked to the side of the bed, and a blurry figure was sitting in a chair next to him. His vision started to clear when he heard a familiar voice calling for a nurse. By the time he could discern more detail, the nurse was the only person in the room. Seconds later, Debra and Dennis came into the room, followed by a doctor.

The doctor tested his vision and checked his wounds before turning to Debra. "You can't stay long because he needs rest. No more than two of you in the room at a time. I'll be back in an hour to check on him."

Debra shook his hand, and the doctor closed the door. "Dad, you really scared us. The bullet in your left leg hit an artery. You lost a lot of blood, which is why you passed out."

Frank tried to sit up. "I'm still groggy, but was Dennis's mother here earlier?"

"Yes, she was. She's been here with you for the last four hours, but she's gone home now."

"What about Sloan?"

"He's dead, Dad, and your house is now a crime scene. You'll be in here for several days, so I'll check on things for you. There're a couple of detectives outside who want to talk to you, so I decided to call Lenson. He told me you shouldn't answer any of their questions until he gets here. I told the detectives they couldn't come in until your lawyer arrived, and they weren't very happy. In fact, your doctor called hospital security to stop them. So, how do you feel?"

"I'm ashamed and feel really stupid. I was feeling sorry for myself last night and fell off the wagon. I'm really sorry, Debra. It slowed me down, and I couldn't react fast enough to stop Sloan. I feel like Sloan's gunshots punished me for taking that drink."

Frank took a sip of water then said, "I don't understand why he kept asking me about Dennis's dad. I'm also feeling confident that Sloan killed Mark."

Dennis moved closer to the bed. "We're missing something, Frank. Why all this increased interest in what we're doing on my dad's murder? I need to go back and re-evaluate the evidence and the blueprints you found. I'll put Medusa on it full-time. Don't worry about anything, except getting better."

Debra continued the thought. "The doctor told me that you'll be several weeks healing. I think you should stay at Dennis's house, because it has better security, and we can take care of you. I cleared it with Mrs. Andrews, and she said it was fine, as long as she didn't have to take care of you. We're also concerned that other dirty cops may pick up where Sloan left off. Just rest, Dad. Lenson will be here soon."

Just then, Lenson entered the room and whispered something to Debra. She motioned to Dennis, and the two of them left. Detective Morris entered the room and was about to ask a question, but Lenson beat him to the draw.

"Detective, I'm Frank Ridge's lawyer. Any questions you ask have to go through me. He'll only answer those questions that pertain to the murder attempt on his life."

The detective looked at a document in his hand. "Mr. Ridge, did you have a personal problem with Detective Sloan?"

His reply was simple. "Next question, please."

"Did you ask Detective Sloan to your house so that you could kill him under the guise of self-defense?"

Lenson stood up. "Detective, I don't know what you're thinking, but look at Frank. He was tortured and shot three times, just like Captain Carson. You seem to think that Frank lured Sloan in, allowed him to shoot him three times, just so he would have a reason to kill him. If that's where you're going, then this interview is over. If you have charges to file against Frank, let me see them. Otherwise, get the hell out of this room."

After the detective left, Debra and Dennis came back into the room. The doctor followed and told everyone to leave so he could rest. Debra asked if one person could stay if they let him sleep. The doctor agreed, so Debra would take the first four-hour shift and Dennis the second. It was going to be a long night.

Chapter 44

Mel Zubner had been a journalist all his life, and like many journalists, all his efforts went to the job. Not surprisingly, he had little time for a social life, and spent his time in government libraries trying to unearth clues that would lead him to his big breaking story. His last success was uncovering kickbacks by several high-ranking Air Force officers who had their hands in the back pockets of some military contractors.

His research had shown that the CEO of Brandon Industries had bribed some generals to achieve an advantage over his rival, Xtreme Machines. It had taken months of research, and he even lost his girlfriend in the process, but the result was a front-page story.

Now he was on a new mission. He had a source in the document section of the Army. The source hated his job, because he saw all the money the government wasted. He finally wanted to do something about it, so he hooked up with Zubner. When they needed to transfer information, they always met in the back of a hole-in-the-wall bar.

Tonight, his source seemed overly nervous. "Look, Mel, this one may be too hot. I really feel uncomfortable because it goes way up the ladder."

"Just tell me what you feel comfortable with, and we can go from there."

They were interrupted by a waitress, so they ordered a couple of beers. When she was gone, the informant continued.

"You know that general who was killed a couple of days ago? Well, a few months back, I processed documents that showed a lot of money being transferred to a special project called MLA. The general ran the project which was under the financial control of a Senator Bob Welding."

"Just how much money?"

"I saw at least five hundred million transferred."

"Is there any other person who could confirm this?"

"Not that I know of."

"I can't run a story with only one source, unless I have hard evidence."

"Would documentation of a wire transfer of funds be enough? It was for one hundred million."

"Wow, you have no idea what you've given me."

"I do understand, and it scares the hell out of me."

Frank awoke late in the afternoon, and found Debra sitting next to him. She handed him a glass of water with the straw and urged him to drink.

"How're you feeling?"

"Like a half-dozen trucks ran over me."

"Lenson stopped by an hour ago. I'm not sure what's going on, but it looks like the cops are trying to make you the bad guy and Sloan the innocent victim. Someone higher up is trying to bury you. Lenson keeps running into brick walls. He said he usually stays away from conspiracy theories, but right now, he's quickly becoming a convert. They're trying to prove that you invited Sloan into your house with the intention of killing him and then pleading self-defense. They claim that your police training allowed you to frame Sloan. The biggest problem for them is that the evidence supports your story, not theirs."

Frank took a sip from the cup. "Do they really think I shot myself three times, and before I passed out, I killed Sloan? Most of the detectives I've worked with in the department would have immediately shot holes in the framing idea. Generally, what you see in front of you is the truth. There usually isn't a hidden agenda. That's great, because now we have bad guys coming at us from two different directions."

"That's why you'll be staying at Dennis's place. I don't want to hear one word about Mrs. Andrews. She's agreed to let you stay there, and I think that's a big step, so don't screw it up."

"When can I leave here?"

"Just a couple more days, but don't worry, Dennis and I have it covered. We'll check on your house once the detectives are done, and make sure it is locked up tight. Mrs. Henson and I are taking care of the clients. A couple of them were concerned about doing business with us, but I appeased them and worked it out."

Debra stopped for a second and Frank reached out to hold her hand.

"You know what scares me the most? With all the bodies that keep falling all around us, we're damn lucky to still be alive. When you said you thought we were going too fast, I thought you were exaggerating. I now agree that it's like a freight train, and we're in its headlights."

He picked up the glass again. "Are you sure you can handle the office?"

"Dennis can do the lab work, and the two of us will work together on the background investigations you were running for that new software company. If we need help, we'll let you know because you can still use your laptop and iPad to do online research. Don't worry; we'll all get through this. Now rest."

Chapter 45

The senator was feeling good about the most recent polls showing him in the lead. The party chairman called him a few minutes ago to congratulate him. There was a political commentary show just about to start and the subject today was the candidates in his party. He grabbed the remote and turned on the TV. The commentator had one reporter who the senator knew, and a second whose name sounded familiar.

The commentator cleared up the mystery when he mentioned the reporter's story about Alex Brandon and the bribery charges against his company. He didn't like where this was going, because he'd worked with Alex Brandon before he died. Brandon knew where all the bodies were buried and had used the information to influence several high-ranking generals. General Harrison was one of them.

Luckily, the reporter's initial investigation somehow missed the general and his connection with the senator. The general had been good about covering his tracks, but it now looked like it might come back to haunt him. The questions zinged back and forth, but it was all about the upcoming primaries. The senator started to relax.

The commentator then asked the second reporter, Mel Zubner, if he had any closing comments. He said, "I do have some concerns about Senator Welding and his approval of several military contracts. The contracts were over five hundred million dollars, and they were issued without the approval of the armed force's committee. I've seen the documents and have an informant who can confirm it."

The commentator was in shock and was about to respond, but was trumped by a commercial for a new diet program. The show never returned and was replaced with a message stating, "We are having technical difficulties, please stand by."

The senator sat in shock and poured himself a brandy. He didn't see any way out. The genie had escaped the bottle and putting her back was almost impossible. He was about to make a call to a retired CIA agent who worked for Alex Brandon when a call came in from the party chair. His life, as he knew it, was over.

Frank was settling into his old room in Dennis's house. Debra and Mrs. Henson were great changing his bandages, bringing him food, and they even set up a bedside table for his laptop and iPad. He was surprised at how well Dennis and Debra had taken control of the business. Dennis even forwarded the business phones to Frank's cell phone. Frank had just completed a call to the software company they were trying to bring on board, when the phone rang again.

"Ridge Detective Agency, Frank speaking."

"Senator Welding here. We had an agreement. You broke that agreement when one of you decided to become Mel Zubner's informant. You put the MLA project on national TV. You need to stop, or you will be very sorry."

"Who's Mel Zubner?"

"You were warned, Frank. Now all of you will pay for what you did."

Debra came into the room. "Who was that, Dad?"

"Call Dennis up from the lab, and have him bring Medusa."

Minutes later, Dennis arrived. "What's going on?"

Frank leaned back on his pillow. "We just had a call from the senator. He thinks we spilled the beans about the MLA project to a reporter. Someone called Mel Zubner."

Dennis pulled up a chair. "He's the one who did the exposé on Alex Brandon and all his bribed officials. Zubner is good at finding conspiracies, so it makes sense that the senator assumed we told him. The problem is what do we do now? The senator sounds like he'll come after us with everything he has."

Debra leaned over and touched Dennis on the shoulder. "It's even worse than that because we still have someone trying to find out what we know about Carl Andrew's murder. We're open targets, and I'm getting really tired of people trying to kill us. We need a plan, and to be honest, I don't have a clue."

Dennis opened Medusa. "So far, I haven't found anything to do with my dad's murder in the documents or evidence, but that doesn't mean it's not there. It could be staring us in the face, so I'll keep working on it. In the meantime, Debra and I will put out any fires at the office. We'll drive together and keep our phones ready to speed dial 911. Frank, do you have any ideas how we can fight on two fronts?"

"You know retirement to a tropical island is sounding good about now. If I'd known that working on your dad's case would put us all in jeopardy, I'd have taken a much lower profile. Now the captain's dead, I'm laid up, and you're both moving targets. Although, I do have one idea, but you both aren't going to like it."

Debra looked over to Dennis to see his facial response. "Okay, Dad, what's your idea?"

"I know a couple of retired detectives who hire out as bodyguards. I trust them and we can employ them as your bodyguards for whenever you leave the house. They'd drive you to wherever you need to go, and then you'd be safe. We have the money, so let's use it to stay alive."

Dennis was about to object, but Debra stopped him.

"I agree. I don't like the idea, but I don't think we have a choice. So, who do we call?"

Frank opened his iPad. "I'll take care of it and work my way down my resource list until I find the best ones for us. Right now, you need to stay in the house. Going outside might not be safe."

Mrs. Henson came into the room with several envelopes in her hands. "I had the incoming mail for the agency delivered here. However, before you get into that, I have lunch ready."

Dennis turned to Mrs. Henson. "What about my mother? Will she be joining us for lunch?"

"No, she's eating in her room."

Frank grinned.

Chapter 46
(Three Days Later)

Tensnani Thorp looked at the contents of the envelope that contained information about his new targets. It showed some possible locations where the hit could easily be made. His life had been on a downhill slide now for five years, so maybe this job could change things around.

He had such great expectations for his career with the CIA. He was one of the best snipers they had, until one mistake changed everything. His ego had gotten in the way, and he took a risky shot. Instead of getting the bad guy, he killed the five-year-old girl being held as a hostage. She'd been the daughter of a very prominent DC politician, who'd made it his goal to ensure that his sniper career ended with that shot.

After his forced retirement, he was picked up by Ross Langer, a henchman for Alex Brandon. He was now working on the other side of the law. The money was good, so he let his morals go by the wayside. When Brandon Industries collapsed, he again was on his own.

When General Harrison came along, he was called back to work, and the money was even better. Now the general was dead, and he was working for a senator. He smirked thinking that he kept outlasting all his employers, but his pay kept increasing.

This time he had three targets. The biggest problem was that only two were mobile, and it looked like they'd picked up a pair of bodyguards. This was going to push his skills to the limit. One bodyguard was in the car with the two, and the other was following in a second car. His shots were going to be from a couple hundred yards, but shouldn't present any problem as the wind was light today. He'd mounted wireless cameras outside the target's house, so that he could tell when they were on the move. They randomized their routes, so he was just going to have to be patient. He looked in his scope and saw they were headed his way.

The chopper hovered at a couple thousand feet and was loaded with onboard tracking systems.

The technician looked at his monitor and pressed his mike. "Sir, I found him. He's on a hill, just above the road."

From a side street that intersected with the targets, a heavy-duty Humvee sped toward Dennis and Debra.

The sniper made his final adjustments to compensate for a slight wind. He slowly readied his trigger finger as the driver of the target's car came into view. He would have to fire, and then move slightly to the left to hit the second target. It was tricky, but he'd been trained for such conditions. In his peripheral view, he saw a car rushing in from the side. He pulled the trigger, but it was too late. The Humvee had hit the target's car and pushed it out of his crosshairs. He knew then he'd been spotted. He glanced up to see a sniper in a chopper with his scope zeroed in on his position. He assumed it was an impossible shot, but that was his last thought before his head exploded.

The technician in the chopper clicked his mike. "The threat has been neutralized."

Their car sat on the side of the road, and when its airbags deployed, they had hit both Dennis and the bodyguard in the face. Debra was thrown forward, and she hit the back of the driver's seat. Two men, armed with pistols, pulled open the door. The bodyguard tried to go for his gun, but the armed man pulled it from his hand. The second bodyguard's car had rammed into the back of the first car, and he'd hit the windshield. Another armed man took away his weapon and forced him out of the car. Moments later, a large black van came up alongside and Dennis and Debra were ushered inside. The two bodyguards were placed in a second car that followed close behind.

Fifteen minutes later, Dennis and Debra were sitting in a large room of a warehouse. The two armed men were standing guard. A door opened, and two men in expensive suits entered.

One held his hand out to shake Dennis's. "Sorry for all the excitement, but we really didn't have time to warn you. Just call me Sam, and I work for the CIA. The man with me is Special Agent George Tenson from the FBI. I know you have many questions, so I'll start, and then Mr. Tenson will finish."

He looked at the two before continuing. "The reason we ran you off the road is that a sniper was about to shoot you both. The bullets he was using were armor piercing and explode on contact. He shot, but the slug hit the front of our car and blew up the engine. This man is a rogue agent we've been tracking for months. We spotted him a couple of days ago, and realized you were his targets. The man is an embarrassment to our organizations, so we needed to eliminate him immediately. Now it may seem strange that both the CIA and the FBI are working together, but, Dr. Andrews, you are vitally important to both of our organizations. Mr. Tenson will now explain."

He held out his hand and shook both Dennis's and Debra's hand. "The truth is, Dr. Andrews, you're one of the most important assets our organizations have encountered. The MLA device you built is the closest thing to Artificial Intelligence we've ever seen. We had dozens of our best people try to recreate it, to no avail. It was unfortunate that you were sidetracked by General Harrison and involved in his own personal project. We think that Senator Welding was the brains behind the deception and misuse of funds, but we haven't been able to prove anything yet. Speaking of the senator, we haven't been able to locate him. Have you had any calls from him in the last couple of days?"

Dennis and Debra were still in shock. Dennis pulled her close and put his arm around her shoulder. "Debra's father talked to him a few days ago. He made threats to get back at us for a leak about the MLA. Frank told him that we hadn't created the leak, but that didn't seem to satisfy him."

The FBI agent looked over to his counterpart. "That's what we're afraid of. He's a bit of a loose cannon right now, because he's lost everything. We discovered the reporter dead this morning, and we think the sniper picked him off. We're going to find the senator, and when we do, he won't be a problem for you anymore. Right now, we need to talk about where we go from here."

Debra finally was able to stop trembling since the shooting. "One thing hasn't changed; the senator will still try to kill us."

The FBI agent hesitated and considered his response carefully. "I agree, and we'll have someone with you at all times until we get the senator, but we need to talk about what happened today. The CIA wouldn't like anyone to know they had a rogue agent, and we all want to keep the MLA a secret. We know you modified the MLA to be more portable, and that you have it in your lab. That's fine for now, but understand it's never allowed to leave the lab. We'll also expect you to turn it over to us in four weeks. We'll be keeping it in a secure location for the CIA and FBI to use jointly."

Dennis started to say something, but he was stopped. "Before you start yelling about it being your invention, we totally agree. We want to move you and the MLA device to our new lab so you can work for us. We'll wipe the slate clean and forget where you got the device. Take the four weeks to address your other problems and to decide if you want to work with us. Meanwhile, if anyone asks, nothing happened here today."

He smiled and continued. "I know you have plenty of questions, but save them for tomorrow, and I'll stop by. Your new bodyguards are ready to take you back to your house. You can tell Frank everything we've discussed. We've checked into his military background and trust him completely. Relax you two. It's going to work out for the best, just give it some time."

Dennis and Debra quietly sat in the back of the van and when they approached his home, the gate opened. Dennis wasn't sure how it happened, but then realized they were now in the hands of people who could do most anything. The two agents got out of the car and looked up to see a chopper circling in a wide loop. One of the agents spoke into a mike and then motioned for Debra and Dennis to head into the house. Dennis punched in the alarm code, and the four entered. Frank was standing with a crutch, under one arm and a Glock in his hand.

"Frank, they're FBI agents and our protective force for the next few days. You need to sit down on the couch because we've quite an incredible story to tell you."

Chapter 47

Dennis was surprised that his mother didn't put up more of an objection to FBI agents staying in the house for weeks. A second agent was stationed in a parked van on the outside of the property and remained in constant communication with his office. Mrs. Henson prepared extra meals for the very appreciative agents.

Frank was slowly getting better and was walking around the house using crutches. A home-health nurse stopped by every other day to check his dressings and see how he was healing. The prognosis was that Frank would make a full recovery.

The three talked it over and decided they needed to dissolve the Ridge Detective Agency. Debra worked with her dad to move their caseload to two other detective agencies Frank had recommended. Only two of the clients raised a stink about the switch, but Debra smoothed it over. In a week's time, the Ridge Detective Agency was nonexistent.

Frank had settled back into his bed when Debra came in his room.

Debra pulled up a chair next to his bed. "We need to talk about where we go from here, now that we've moved all the jobs to the other agencies. I'm so sorry, Dad. I was really hoping it was going to work out for all of us."

"It's not a problem, Honey. I was already considering a permanent retirement. I'm just not sure what I'll do because I don't really have any hobbies. When I'm feeling stronger, I'll consider doing some travel. You two will be fine. Dennis can go work for the acronyms, and you can do whatever you want. Do you have any ideas about that yet?"

"Actually, I do. Yesterday I had a long talk with Mrs. Andrews. You know, she's a nice lady. I don't know why you two don't get along. Anyway, we talked about Dennis and his new job potential, and then she asked me the same question. When I told her I was unsure, she suggested that I might consider being a guest lecturer at the college. She indicated she has connections with the right people, and the pay was very good. I'd have short hours, no late nights, and lots of summer vacations. I reviewed their curriculum, and it looks great. I talked it over with Dennis, and he was supportive of the idea. I think he's decided to take the position with the government, because he wants to continue the work he loves. I'm so sorry that The Ridge Detective Agency had such a short life, but Dennis and I agree that it was the right thing to do."

She took a deep sigh. "Dad, I'm worried about him right now because he's spending so much time in the lab. He's working on both his dad's murder and trying to get to the bottom of things with the senator. The last time I went down, he was trying to do a full background on the senator. When you get a little better can you talk to him?"

Frank puffed up his pillow before leaning back. "I agree that he's becoming somewhat obsessive. I can tell him to back off on the senator, but how do you tell someone to stop looking for the person who murdered their father? Don't worry, I'll talk to him, I promise."

Dennis exhausted just about every search engine option. Medusa cross-referenced every document and event in the senator's life. Dennis did find one interesting piece of information that the senator's first government job was in the CSI division. He'd become very interested in subject identification via fingerprints, blood types, DNA and other biological links. That explained why the MLA had become his pet project.

Dennis went through every document, purchase, and bill that the senator had paid before he got lucky and found a fee provided to a realtor in Montana. That seemed a bit strange, so he started to check through all the background records he'd collected. He found that the general had also made a payment to someone in Montana, but it was a lawyer. Dennis cross-referenced the real estate lawyer and found that the lawyer had purchased a large parcel for a client in Washington State.

After two more hours of digging, he could put it all together. The general had purchased a large parcel in Montana under a different name. It looked like the senator assumed that name when the general was killed. The newspapers were full of articles speculating about the senator's disappearance and the fact he dropped out of the race. No one seemed to know where he'd gone. There was even scuttlebutt about a kidnapping, and conspiracy theories were surfacing.

Dennis asked Medusa if she could hack into any of the satellites over Montana. In a few seconds, the images were on the screen. Dennis isolated the property in question, and could see a large house in the middle of a huge ranch. There were several gates into the property and near the house, he spotted the senator's car.

Dennis turned around to see if anyone was watching. Debra was still upstairs, and his mother was in the kitchen. He started to have Medusa search for Euryale, the last remaining MLA device, and she found it in an Army storage facility. Dennis smiled and thought, curiosity just might kill the cat.

Sergeant Thomas Spanner had been working the secure storage facility for the last five years. He was proud of what he was doing. His building housed some of the most top-secret inactive experimental devices and their related documents. Orders to bring items in or out came either through the message center or personally by an Army messenger.

He was just finishing his morning break when a new order came in via an Army messenger. This rarely happened, so he verified the sender had the required security clearance. Everything seemed in order. He sent out a conformation verification, and it came back with the correct codes. He then called one of his men and ordered him to bring the requested box to the shipping department. The box was quite large and weighed more than 200 pounds. He checked the manifest one more time and shook his head. He was never supposed to speculate on the box's contents, but he really wondered what the hell an MLA was.

Detective Ronan waited until he was off shift and far from the station. He pulled out his burn phone and made a call. "Sir, I haven't found anything yet. Before he died, it appears Sloan got nothing out of Frank. ...Yes Sir, I realize how important this is and what's at stake. Maybe there's nothing for you to worry about. He may not have hidden anything before he died. If he did, it may be lost for good because it's been such a long time. ...Yes, Sir, I can try, but they're not leaving their home. ...I don't think I can get a judge to do that. ...One of the guys who came out of the house looked like FBI. ...Yes, I'll try to find out. Good night, Sir."

Ronan was sweating like a pig. The man had asked a lot from him, but he knew a couple of good guys who could break in and keep their mouth shut about it. Frank Ridge wasn't staying at his house any longer, so all they had to do was bypass the alarm system. They needed to get back into the house one more time, even if it meant taking a few more risks.

Dennis finally gave up with the blueprints. If there was something there, he didn't know what it was. He needed a break. No, correct that, what he really needed was Debra, but this house was very crowded. The FBI agent was talking to Mrs. Henson when Dennis motioned for him to come over.

"Dr. Andrews, what can I do for you?"

"Debra and I need to get out of here. We're going crazy, so I have an idea for you to run by your boss. If you can get me to the private airport, we can fly to San Francisco for the night. You can assign someone down there to watch us. We just need to get away and have some private time. It might help me make my decision, whether to work for you guys."

318

The agent grinned, leaned over, and whispered. "That sounds like a good story to me. I'll tell him that your decision depends on it. How'll that be?"

"Thank you."

"That's not a problem. I've been there myself, and my wife would approve of your idea."

Dennis was now ready to put the second part of his plan in motion. Debra was in with Frank. He leaned in and said hi to Frank, and then motioned for Debra to come out.

She came out with a worried look on her face. "Is there a problem?"

"Well, in a way, but it's not something you broadcast. I'm arranging for us to go down to San Francisco tonight. You know dinner, dancing."

She added "... and some sex."

"Well, that would be nice too, but not a deal breaker. Just getting away with you for the night is all I need."

"That's the right answer, Dennis. I'll have to think about the sex option."

The FBI agent came up to Dennis. "You're all set. Two of our people will pick you up in two hours and take you to the airport. Don't worry because we'll be fine here. Although, I'm going to owe Frank a lot of money because he's really good at poker."

Two and half hours later, the Learjet was leveling off at twenty-five thousand feet. Dennis opened a bottle of wine and poured a glass for them. They toasted their parents and then set their glasses down. Dennis pressed his lips to hers and gently pushed her back on the couch. She put her arms around him and kissed him ardently. When they separated, she looked up toward the front cabin.

"Can she see us back here?"

"I told her that this was a private trip. She's married and understands completely. You need to relax."

He started to unbutton her blouse and then her bra. She grabbed his hand when it was moving down to other areas. "Dennis, are you that horny?"

"Yes, but that's not it. I love you, and I thought making love to you at twenty-five-thousand feet would be something we could remember when we're old and gray."

She grabbed his hand and moved it where they both wanted it to be. When the pilot announced they were about to land, the two had just finished getting dressed.

Debra kissed Dennis on the lips gently. "I still want dinner, dancing and the whole nine yards. I do have a question I've wanted to ask, but was afraid I'd sound like a gold digger."

"How much am I worth?"

"Was I that obvious?"

"No, but I've been waiting for you to ask ever since I asked you to marry me. If you count all my property, stocks, and royalties, it's about one hundred million. Mom has more, probably twice as much. Does that change things?"

"Well, yes and no. No, on our relationship, but when I shop for groceries, I might consider a little better brand than the generics."

The two laughed and relaxed more than they had in weeks.

They spent a long evening at a very plush Italian restaurant. They talked about their childhood, first dates, and what they had wanted to be when they grew up. When the waiter came with the bill, Dennis started to write when the blue ink pen quit halfway through the signature. The waiter apologized and reached for a second pen saying the ink was red. Dennis finished the signature and then stopped cold. Debra glanced at him with a worried look.

"What's wrong?"

"I can't be that stupid."

"Dennis, what are you talking about?"

"The blueprints. Some are signed in red ink, and some are in blue. Dad would never do that unless there was a good reason. I need to look at them as soon as we get back."

She reached across the table and touched his hand. "You promised me a night of dinner and dancing, and I promised sex. Put the blueprints out of your mind and let's skip the dancing."

"You didn't even have to ask."

Chapter 48

The two lovebirds didn't return until late the next day. When they arrived at the house, Dennis immediately ran down to the lab. Her dad was sitting in the living room talking to the FBI agent. Debra undid her coat, and Frank gave her a big hug.

"Are you two good?"

"Yes, Dad we're fine. Actually, great if you must know. A brainstorm came to Dennis when we were at dinner last night. He's testing his theory right now."

"I hope this brainstorm didn't screw up your evening. We both know that once Dennis gets focused on something, it's hard to get him to look at anything else."

"It wasn't a problem for me. Besides, I don't mind. If this gets us closer to who ordered Sloan to shoot you, then I'm all for it. How was your night?"

The FBI agent answered for Frank. "Your father cleaned me out. My wife's going to kill me. Other than that, it's been quiet. We haven't heard anything further regarding the senator yet. When Dennis left, he told me that we no longer had to worry about the senator. That seemed a bit strange, but I just figured it was wishful thinking."

Dennis laid all the blueprints out and found fourteen with blue signatures and a dozen in red. Then he looked at the signatures with a magnifier. His dad's signature was first, followed by the building inspector just below. The fourteen blueprints had a different building inspector's signature than the twelve where his dad had signed in red. There was no rule about the pen color for the signature, so it would have gone unnoticed until now. Dennis zoomed in on the signature and found it was very difficult to read. Dennis looked at them all until he found one where someone had typed the names under the signatures. His heart almost stopped when he recognized the name on the bottom. He took a deep breath and ran upstairs.

When he ran into the room, Frank and Debra knew Dennis had made a breakthrough.

Frank held up his hand. "Take a deep breath. We know you found something. Take your time."

Dennis held up the blueprint with the typed name on the bottom. "Dad was sending a message to whoever found the blueprints. Twelve of them are signed in red and fourteen in blue. Each set was inspected by a different inspector. The one I'm holding has a typed name of the building inspector. Anyone want to guess who it was?"

Even the FBI agent was speechless.

"The mayor of Seattle was a building inspector before he became a politician."

"And your father hated him," came from Mrs. Andrews in a loud voice.

Everyone turned to hear what Mrs. Andrews had to say. "In the back of my mind, I always suspected that Larry had something to do with all this. The problem is going to be proving why and how he killed my husband."

The FBI agent was quick to add to her assessment. "She's right. Just having his name on the bottom means nothing. If there were kickbacks for using poorer grade materials, it's going to be hard to discover."

Dennis smiled. "You don't know Medusa. She does a superb job analyzing DNA, but she's just as great at compiling data. Now that I know what I'm looking for, I can find the missing piece of the puzzle."

The agent stopped Dennis before he could continue. "If you do find something, make sure you turn it over to us. I'd love to tell my boss that we had found corruption that far up the food chain. Just make sure your evidence is solid because I don't want to be demoted to doing background checks on new recruits."

"Don't worry, I'd never consider going after the mayor without help. I'll have solid evidence before I do anything."

Mrs. Andrews leaned toward the FBI agent. "Make sure you castrate the bastard before you throw him in the slammer."

Dennis looked at his mother with a strange expression on his face. "Mom, I've never heard you talk that way."

"When it comes to your father, I'll say whatever needs to be said."

Dennis gave Debra a small kiss and headed back to the lab. She was happy that Dennis had a new direction, but sad that he was so focused on the problem.

She headed for the bedroom, but couldn't sleep because she kept reliving their trip to San Francisco. The more she thought about it, the more awake she became. She eventually must have dozed because she awoke around two when she felt Dennis slide next to her. She kissed him on the shoulder and asked, "Are you busy right now?"

"Are you kidding?"

"No, I have a job for you."

The next morning Dennis rushed downstairs to check on Medusa while everyone else was just trying to wake up with a cup of coffee. He came back with nothing in his hand and his head hanging low. He sat down and took a sip from his cup. Everyone stopped and looked at him.

Debra said what everyone was thinking. "What did you find?"

"Nothing yet, but Medusa has compiled a lot of data. We're talking about thousands of applications, permits, and building contractor's invoices. It's mountains of data, but she'll find a connection. We just have to be patient. If there's something there, she'll find it."

Chapter 49

Senator Bob Welding sat out on the front porch sipping a cup of his favorite coffee. He now understood why the general had picked this place. The mornings here were beautiful and the area was so remote, that no one bothered you. He really hated the idea of leaving the political arena. He could've stayed, fought any charges that surfaced, and survived to come back another day. Senators, representatives, and even presidents had done it, but he was a realist. Deep down, he knew that even if he'd won his party's nomination, he would still lose the election. It just wasn't in the cards.

The truth was he was tired of it all. His doctor had warned him that if he didn't slow down, he was going to drop dead someday soon. The senator looked out at the expanse of the property and realized there was no way that he could maintain it all. Thankfully, the general arranged for several Mexican workers to keep the place up in his absence. Best of all, even if they recognized him, they'd never say anything, because they had just as much to lose as he did.

He chuckled to himself as he reflected on last night's newscasts. Everyone was speculating about his disappearance. The most popular scenario was that he was buried in a piece of concrete along with Jimmy Hoffa. Other newscasters guessed that he was under protective custody. There were reporters at his home, and others in his office talking with his assistant. Victoria Bishop from Denver's D.A. office was handpicked by the federal prosecutor to look into his case. Her name sounded familiar; then he remembered that she had been in the middle of the Alex Brandon investigation. It's strange how everything became so interlaced.

He was about to take another sip from his coffee, when a dog ran up vying for his attention. Following behind was one of the workers the general had hired.

The man reached out to shake the senator's hand. "Señor, my nombre is Filipe Torres. I work today for you. You have things for me?"

The senator petted the dog and was about to give Filipe a list of chores when he heard a buzzer in the house. He told Filipe to wait while he checked the alarm. He looked at the video feed from the front gate a mile from the house and saw a government delivery truck.

He pressed the buzzer. "What can I do for you?"

"I have a package for you."

"I didn't order anything."

"It's for a General Martin Harrison. It's a big box and must weigh at least 200 pounds. I don't want to take this heavy thing back, so just sign for it and it's yours."

"You said it was for the general. Who shipped it?"

"The general himself put the order in a month ago. It took this long to get through the system."

"Does it say anything on the outside of the box?"

"The only thing I can see is a bunch of numbers followed by MLA2."

The senator was trying to understand why the general would've taken a risk and move the remaining MLA to his property. He thought about telling the deliveryman to take it back, but figured there'd be an investigation as to where it should ultimately go. They'd look for the delivery address, and then he'd have to leave this hideaway. He was quickly running out of options.

He clicked the mike again. "I'm sending one of my workers up to get the package in his truck. He can sign for me."

"I'm not sure I can do that, Sir. I need your signature."

"Fine, just take it back where it came from then."

"Oh, all right. Send your worker up, and I'll help him load it."

An hour later, Filipe and the senator manhandled the box into the barn adjacent to the house. Filipe asked if he should open the box, but the senator told him instead to work on the list of projects he'd been given. For the rest of the day, the senator sat on the front porch reflecting on his involvement with the MLA project. He loved his first job in the CSI division. By the time DNA analysis had become an accepted investigation tool, he'd entered politics. He worked to incorporate DNA into the military intelligence system, and although several projects came along, he couldn't back them.

Then Dennis Andrews entered the scene with his MLA project, which analyzed DNA differently. His machine was one of the first Artificial Intelligence devices the military had ever tried. Sure, there were smart bombs, but the brainpower of the MLA excelled. Then General Harrison had screwed it all up, and when the dust had settled, more than a dozen lives had been lost.

Once Filipe had left for the day, the senator couldn't stand it any longer and his curiosity got the better of him. He went into the barn, found a battery operated drill, and started removing the two dozen screws holding the shipping case together. He set the sides and top of the box against the barn wall, and stood back to admire the device. It looked the same as the one that had blown up at the test center with both offensive and defensive weapons installed, so he'd have to be careful.

He was about to put the container back together, but then stopped. He'd seen the previous unit demonstrated, but had never worked directly with the device. This peaked his curiosity. The senator remembered that one of the unit's problems occurred when everything was powered on at the same time. What harm would there be to see if the unit still worked as long as he was careful? With nothing else to do, he located the 220 outlet in the barn that was used for welding. It would be perfect for powering the MLA.

He opened a small panel on the front of the unit and located a detailed set of instructions. Sitting down on an old milking stool, he read through the information. It seemed simple enough. He went over and plugged in the power cord, and a green light indicated that it now had power.

He needed something to test, but then remembered he had cut himself earlier working in the kitchen. The blood on the band-aid would be perfect for the DNA test. He took his band-aid off and set it on the small diagnostic platform on the front of the unit. He hesitated for a second and then pressed the "On" button. A couple of minutes later, he had green lights across the board. He looked at the instructions to make sure that both weapon systems were turned off, and then pressed the DNA diagnostic function on the unit.

He'd been so wrapped up in the operational instructions that he never glanced at the maintenance manual. If he'd read it, he'd have seen that the unit needed a full maintenance cycle run every two months. Many of the parts on the power capacitor had short life spans and needed replacing. They weren't expensive, but were critical to the safe operation of the MLA device.

As one of the snake-like analysis arms came out of the top of the unit, a red warning light appeared. The senator saw that the power levels were quickly climbing like a timer on a bomb. He considered trying to stop the unit, but instead just ran. He was about twenty feet away when the barn and the house were vaporized in a blast that was heard for miles. A few seconds later, a small mushroom cloud appeared above the horizon. Curiosity had truly killed the cat.

Later that afternoon Dennis clicked on the news while waiting for the results from the data collected on the mayor. He was about to turn the set off, when a breaking story announced there was a large explosion at a remote ranch in Montana. A tourist traveling near the entrance to the ranch captured the mushroom cloud on video and sold it to a local news station. Regional law enforcement agencies said there was one known fatality, although the identity was uncertain, and an investigation was underway.

Dennis knew there'd been a big risk in what he'd done. There could've been innocent people in the area, but more than likely, they too were mixed up with the senator. This was one secret he wasn't going to be able to share with anyone. He decided he could live with the burden of what he'd done, because he was tired of people trying to kill his family and friends. It had to stop, so he'd taken the first move.

He was about to continue his analysis, when he was buzzed by the FBI agent in the house. He said he needed to talk to him, so Dennis told him to come down. When the agent opened the elevator door, Dennis could tell that something serious was on the agent's mind. The agent pulled up a rolling chair.

"Dennis, was that the senator in the explosion in Montana?"

"What makes you think I'd know?"

"Was it the senator?"

"Yes."

"Does anyone else know?"

"No, I'm the only one."

"Was it the other MLA device?"

"Yes, it was."

"Dennis, this is classified as Top Secret. You can't tell anyone - Debra, Frank, or your mother - absolutely no one. This Top Secret clearance will be your excuse for not telling them, so you're off the hook. Do you understand what I'm saying?"

"Yes, I do, but it'll be hard because Debra and I never keep secrets from each other."

"This is one you'll keep to yourself for the next fifty years. We're trying to put a lid on the MLA project, and thankfully this event has done that."

"I'm not sure it was the right thing to do. Even if I didn't pull the trigger, taking someone's life is not the way to solve problems. I'm beginning to regret my actions. If I had to do it over, I'm not sure I'd do it again."

"Dennis, relax, you did the right thing. Now let us clean up the residual mess. You had every right to protect your loved ones with any resource available. He'd have continued to hunt you down until you were dead."

Dennis shook the FBI's hand. "Are you going to release the fact that the senator was in the blast?"

"No, it will probably be an unsolved murder by a mugger who tried to dispose of the body by burning it. We'll come up with something. Just act surprised when Frank and Debra see it on the news."

"I really don't like doing this."

"I know, but we all have to carry around some baggage. Yours just got a bit heavier."

Chapter 50
(Two Days Later)

Dennis, Debra, Frank, and the FBI agent were sitting around the TV watching the stories about the senator's untimely death. Most of the newscasters were following the lead that the senator's car had broken down; he was mugged, and killed. The killer then took his car and the body out to a remote forest and burned it. The DNA results had confirmed that the charred remains were indeed the senator. The stations were now doing biographies of the man, and speculating on what he could've done if his political career hadn't been cut short.

Frank turned off the TV and turned to Dennis. "Do you consider me a good detective?"

"Yes, Frank, you're one of the best. You've great instincts about crime scenes."

"So, do you really want us to believe the BS the TV announcers are feeding us?"

"I'm not sure what you're talking about."

"Really, because two days ago there was a massive explosion in Montana. There's one dead, but no ID on the body. A couple of locals remember seeing the guy when he first arrived, and said he was about the same age and build as the senator. The explosion was the same as the one we set with the other MLA. Now, magically the senator dies at that same exact time, and he's directly tied to the MLA project. So, what's really going on?"

Dennis froze. He looked over to the FBI agent for help. He was about to say something when the agent held up his hand.

"Frank, you need to stop this line of interrogation. Dennis can't answer your questions because he's restricted by a Top-Secret order preventing him from saying anything about the senator, or the MLA device. I know that you and Debra want information, but you're going to have to trust the FBI and Dennis.

The incident is over and now you can move on with your lives. Dennis would like to forget the incident and so would the FBI. You don't need to explore this line of questioning ever again."

Frank was quiet for a few seconds. "You know, I forgot what I was talking about. Has anyone heard the Portland Trailblazer's score?"

Debra put her arm around Dennis. "We're with you in this, Dennis. The agent is right, we need to move on."

Dennis looked down at the floor. "I hope I can."

Detective Ronan felt his burn phone ring. He pulled it out and told the caller he'd call back in ten minutes.

Once he was back in the car, he returned the call. He listened for a moment before responding.

"Yes, Sir, he works for the company that installed the alarm, and he's one of the best. He found a hole in the wall and there were marks indicating that some kind of documents had been taped inside the wall. They're not in the house now, so I assume that he moved them to Dennis Andrews' house. ...No, Sir, there's no way we can get into that house because the FBI is still there. ...I really don't know if I can do that. It's too much in the open. ...Yes, Sir, if I see them leave, I'll follow and then get back to you."

Ronan was backed up against a wall. The mayor was about to go down, and he was going with him, unless he stopped Dennis Andrews. As much as he hated the idea, it was either Dennis or him, so he knew what he had to do.

Dennis had secured every possible document that linked his father and the mayor. He gave them to Medusa to crunch the data and come up with a hypothesis. Dennis jumped up from his desk once he had read the printed solution.

"Medusa, you're the best! You solved a cold case murder that will give my mother and me closure."

"Can you explain closure and how it affects humans?"

"It's when something comes to the end, and there's no more."

"I understand. You now need to tell Frank and Debra."

Dennis ran upstairs with the printout, and handed it to Frank.

"Take a look at this, Frank; I finally have the proof the FBI needs."

Frank looked down the list. It cross-referenced low bids and the use of substandard materials with payments to contractors and the building inspector. The mayor was smack-dab in the middle of it all. There was enough evidence to put away the mayor for years.

He looked up to Dennis. "How's it that your dad didn't know about this while it was going on?"

"I was worried about the same thing, but I found notes from the contractors and the building inspector saying the architect was unaware of what was going on. They'd arranged for the correct materials to be on hand when my dad made site inspections. He had twelve projects in progress at the same time, so he rarely went to the job site. He was usually just given photos of the site as construction progressed. He must have suspected the building inspector, and contractors were in cahoots, because he started using the red pen on the building plans of those he suspected of wrongdoing. He was murdered before any of them were completed."

Debra took the printout from Frank and scanned the front page. "Are those buildings safe?"

"That was my first concern. Five were never completed and torn down. Three were completed and then replaced. The last four are still there, but have many code violations that the owners are trying to fix."

Debra handed the documents to the FBI agent. He read the entire document while the three waited.

He folded it up. "This is perfect. Dennis, how would you like to go with us when we arrest the mayor? It should take a day for logistics, so we can do it tomorrow afternoon. Right now though, you need to come down to our local office with these documents, and we'll fill out the initial report."

"Are you going to guarantee you can protect my son through all this?" Dennis' mother had been in the doorway listening for the last ten minutes, and no one had noticed her. "Larry took my husband away. I don't want the same thing to happen to my son."

The FBI agent folded up the paperwork. "We'll be fine, Mrs. Andrews. This whole thing is about to come to an end."

Debra gave Dennis a kiss, and he and the agent exited the house. The agent on the outside moved inside the house and was immediately replaced by another agent assigned to guard the outer perimeter. The FBI agent and Dennis headed out and would take an indirect route, just in case they were being followed.

Detective Ronan had parked on a side road and was watching the hidden camera he'd positioned pointed at the house. He dialed the secure line to Mayor Larry Millstone.

"Sir, Dennis Andrews just left with the FBI agent. They had a manila envelope, and I think they're headed for the local branch of the FBI. ...Sir, I really don't know if that's possible, and the odds aren't on my side, but I understand what needs to be done."

Ronan turned off his phone and shoved it in his pocket. He knew some shortcuts, and if he drove fast, he might be able to beat them. He mulled over the new information the mayor had just given him. It seems that several of the crooked contractors called the mayor. Someone had been electronically snooping into their business and downloaded some very incriminating evidence.

Ronan knew this was a lost cause. If he didn't do as the mayor asked, he'd go right down with him. Sitting in prison with those he'd help put away wouldn't be good for his health. It seemed like no matter what he did, the results would be the same, so he sped up.

He arrived within a minute ahead of them and walked toward Dennis and the FBI agent as they approached the front entrance. One of the agents exiting the building saw Ronan reach under his coat and pull out a gun. The agent yelled "*gun*" and shot the weapon out of Ronan's outstretched hand. It discharged and fell to the ground. The FBI agent with Dennis ran over to Ronan and pointed his gun directly at his chest. Ronan was screaming in pain and before anyone could say another word, Ronan literally fell apart.

"Mayor Larry Millstone ordered me to do it. I'll testify against him. Please get me to a hospital."

As the other agent put handcuffs on Ronan, the FBI agent with Dennis grabbed him and ran inside the building. Another agent who appeared to be in command came up and shook Dennis's hand.

"I'm Darrel Quinten and I'm in charge here. Are you all right?"

Dennis shook the dust off his jacket. "I'm fine, but what about the mayor? He'll know now that you're on to him."

"We're pretty sure he already does, so this just pushes up our timeline. We need to quickly look at the documents and then run them by the legal department. You'll need to stay here and get debriefed, but we'll let you know when we're ready to go."

Dennis's phone sounded with Debra's ring tone. "Are you okay, Dennis? Dad and I just saw the newscast about the shooting. Are you sure you want to continue? There just doesn't seem to be an end to it all."

"I'm fine and it'll be over today. They're going over the documents right now, and then they plan to arrest the mayor. I'll call you when that happens. Please keep my mom in the loop."

"I will. I love you, so come back safe. You promised to marry me, and I'm holding you to it."

Three hours later, Dennis and several agents headed toward Mayor Larry Millstone's office. The evidence against him was overwhelming. Agents had gone to the mayor's house with a search warrant and found a gun hidden in the garage. It was a match to the weapon that had murdered Dennis's father. Dennis had assumed that the building inspector, who now was the mayor of this fine town, had hired someone to kill his dad. He now knew that the mayor himself had pulled the trigger.

The mayor told his secretary to cancel all his appointments, and that he didn't want to be bothered by anyone. There would be absolutely no calls. The secretary questioned his reason, but the mayor ushered her out and locked the door.

He walked to the window that faced the street and saw that FBI agents and the local authorities were everywhere. He figured that Detective Ronan had rolled over on him. He knew he'd never survive prison life, and shuddered when he imagined what the inmates would do to him. He needed to do something while he still had control over his life.

He looked out the window one more time, and then sat back down at his desk. There was a knock on the door, and a voice told him that the FBI was on the other side. He pulled out his old .38, put it in his mouth, and pulled the trigger. Seconds later, the agents broke the door down, only to find blood and brain matter splattered over the window. The first agent in the room stopped Dennis from entering the room.

"It looks like your work's done, Dr. Andrews. One of our agents will take you downtown for a statement and then take you home. Ronan has given us a list of all the other dirty cops, judges, and politicians. The list is huge, and it's going to be a field day for the media. The press will be relentless, so it might be a good idea for you to stay out of sight for a few days. You can relax now; it's really over."

Chapter 51
(Three weeks later)

It was Frank's first day without crutches or visible bandages. He'd been secretly working on a special project with an old friend who ran another detective agency. All the original tapes, recordings, and research material were in the box he held. Now it was time to bring it all to a head and make a visit to the college.

Debra asked where he was going, and he told her that it was a private matter. She started to push the issue, but then backed off and let him leave.

An hour later, Frank sat in the outer office of President Sharon Conners. He'd called ahead for an appointment using a problem with Dr. Sandra Alexander as an excuse. He still found it confusing using her professional name in public and her married name in private. When Frank was ushered into the president's office, he was offered something to drink. He refused and asked if this could be a private meeting. Conners looked over to her secretary.

"Please close the door, and no calls."

Once the door was closed, she continued. "What can I do for you, Detective? You said this had something to do with Dr. Alexander."

"It's rather about what I can do for you. Have you heard any rumors of a group of coeds having sex games at your college?"

"I hear rumors, but that's all they are. The suppositions have never been substantiated."

"Well, Dr. Conners, I'm here to tell you that it isn't a rumor, but it's a very delicate situation. Inside this box is everything you'll need to make a wise decision as to a course of action. The videos are very convincing, but I hope you have a strong stomach. These girls play for keeps."

Frank opened a small video player and started the first video. An hour later, the president was in shock watching these girls incriminate themselves. Her secretary called back that he had exceeded his time slot, and the president had urgent calls and meetings pending. The president yelled at the secretary not to bother them again.

"You have to understand, that I'm doing this as a favor for Dr. Alexander. She was exposed to this group, and it wasn't pretty. They hurt her badly. This isn't what higher education is about. You have the only copies of the collected evidence there in the box. I'm trusting you to do what you need with it to make matters right. I know that one of the girl's fathers is on the board of trustees, so that might present a problem for you."

President Conners got up and shook Frank's hand. "So, what are you, Dr. Alexander's protector?"

"Yes, I am, but please leave my name and hers out of whatever you decide to do."

338

Chapter 52
(Three weeks later)

Dennis was as nervous as he'd ever been before. He wanted everything to be perfect. Debra had insisted that they sleep in different bedrooms the night before the wedding. He respected her wishes and spent the night alone in the guest bedroom. He got very little sleep, but almost felt human after a long cold shower.

He heard Frank up walking around. His bandages had come off three weeks ago, and he seemed to be his old self again. The news about the senator and the mayor was now ancient news, and some other headline had stolen the limelight.

Frank knocked and entered his room to help him get ready for the big event. He sat Dennis down in a chair, as if he was going to interrogate him.

"Do you love my daughter?"

"Yes, with all my heart."

"Are you going to treat her like she's a princess?"

"Haven't I been doing that already?"

"Yeah, I thought so, but I just wanted to hear it from you."

"Whew, is that all you got, Frank? No threats that you'll kill me if I treat her wrong?"

"I thought that was understood."

Dennis turned white.

"Don't worry, Dennis, I'm just kidding. I know you'll treat her right. You two are a perfect match, just like Ann, and me. In fact, you two remind me of our first year together. Just don't be surprised if she does something you don't expect."

"She already does that, so you should've warned me sooner. Are you and my mom going to be all right? I know she has this hatred for you, but I don't understand it."

"Just keep your mind on the wedding, and let me worry about your mother. She's fine – we're fine. Oh, do you remember that problem you mentioned about the three college girls with the sex games? Relax, because it has been taken care of."

"She mentioned that to me last week. The president of the college called and told her that the three had been banned from the college grounds, and their transcripts would include mention of their little games. They were stripped of all their college credits, reducing them back to high school graduates. It's not much, but my mom seemed fine with the solution, so thanks, Frank."

"Just don't tell her I was responsible."

"Maybe she'd feel differently about you if she knew you helped?"

"Her feelings for me are not about to change Dennis, so just give it up."

"Thanks for being my best man."

"Don't know that I've ever heard of the best man being the father of the bride. It might be a wedding first."

"We don't care because it means so much to both of us."

Dennis looked at his watch. "We need to get moving because I have less than a half-hour of freedom left."

Frank gave Dennis a frown, and the two laughed as they exited the room.

Jeff Windom reached up and felt his scars. He was determined to get revenge. His original plan was to use the .38 he'd purchased from a drug dealer to shoot Dennis during the wedding. As the wedding approached though, he became more agitated with everyone associated with Debra. He no longer wanted to have anything to do with her, so he developed a new plan. He'd gone back to the drug dealer and he was more than happy to sell him a MAC-10 with two magazines. If he couldn't have Debra, then no one else could either. His plan was simple –

he'd walk up just before they said I do, and empty the magazine, killing the entire wedding party. No one would have enough time to stop him.

Fifteen minutes before the wedding procession the captain's son, Officer Tim Carson, came over to Frank.

"Sorry, but we need to talk. There's a minor problem outside, but I don't want to upset the wedding."

"Can't it wait?"

"Sorry, but no."

Frank followed the officer out of the front of the house, and he could see the flashing lights from several police cars at the end of the driveway. Officer Carson lifted the yellow crime-scene tape and ushered Frank through. Up ahead he saw a crumpled car door that had been struck by a large delivery truck. As they came around the side of the damaged car, Frank could see the victim was Jeff Windom. He'd been killed by a truck.

Carson explained the situation. "As far as we can tell, Windom bought an MAC-10 with two magazines. It looked like he planned to wipe out your wedding party. Because of all the cars parked for the wedding, he couldn't get his car very close to the curb. When he got out of the car, the gun strap caught on the door handle. This provided enough distraction that he didn't see the delivery truck, and was killed instantly. We'll try to clear this up as soon as possible, but your wedding party will have to take the other way out. Just tell them that a traffic accident caused the problem. There's probably no need to mention the gun."

Frank reached out and shook the officer's hand. "Thanks for the update. Sure wish your dad could have been here today."

"He's right here," he said pointing to his heart.

"Roger that, and thanks again."

Frank returned to a very worried daughter. She'd sent a couple of people looking for him.

"Where were you?"

341

"There was a traffic accident outside, but everything is fine now. Dennis is waiting, so let's go."

The processional music began and Frank proudly walked down the aisle with his daughter on his arm to meet her man. As the minister recited the vows, Frank thought about his deceased wife, Ann. She'd have liked Dennis as a son-in-law. When the vows were over Dennis gave Debra an endless kiss, causing the guests to cheer and laugh.

The reception itself was in the backyard and was catered by Seattle's best vendors. Dennis escorted his new wife out for the first dance and then shared her with Frank for the second. Dennis made the rounds catching up with some of his college friends, and Debra visited with people from the D.A.'s office. They eventually met up in front of one of the food tables, and Dennis glanced around the thinning crowd.

"Have you seen Frank?"

"No, I haven't seen my dad for the past half hour."

"I would expect that of my mother, but I can't believe your dad would leave the party. Mom hates social gatherings like this. I know she's hiding in her room. Maybe Frank is out front checking on the accident."

"I forgot all about that. You're probably right."

The party wound down to the point that the caterers started packing up. Debra left to look out front for Frank, but found the front lawn was empty. She met back with Dennis in the living room and shook her head indicating her lack of luck. Dennis decided he'd better make sure everything was all right with his mother. The last time she drank too much they had to put her to bed.

He walked down the hall with Debra close behind, and knocked on the door.

"Mom, we're just checking to see if you are all right."

There was no sound from the room. Dennis waited thirty seconds and then knocked again. Finally, the door opened a crack, and his mother looked out wearing a pink bathrobe that Dennis hadn't seen before.

"Are you okay, Mom? You left the party early."

"I'm fine. Do you need something?"

Dennis was about to answer when Frank came out of the bathroom.

"Hey sweetheart, let's go back to bed," he shouted, unaware that Dennis was at the door.

His mother slammed the door shut.

Dennis was in shock. Debra hadn't seen what he had, and she wanted to know what happened.

"What's going on, Dennis?"

"I just found your dad."

"Where?"

"In bed, with my mother."

"What?"

The door opened a small crack again, and Frank poked his head out.

"Can't we have some privacy? Go enjoy your own bed. Isn't that what newlyweds do? Can you please leave us alone?"

The door slammed again.

Chapter 53

The next morning was awkward for everyone. When Dennis and Debra came into the kitchen, Dennis's mother was sitting at the table sipping coffee. She was still in her bathrobe and so was Frank. He poured himself a cup as Dennis and Debra stood in the doorway, not quite sure what to make of the situation. Frank walked over to Dennis's mother and asked her if there was anything else she needed. She smiled coyly, and he gave her a kiss that couldn't ever be considered casual. He sat down and put his arm around her. He pointed to the coffee on the counter.

"You two look like you need a cup of coffee, and maybe a bit of an explanation."

Neither Debra nor Dennis said anything they just sat down.

"Sorry you found out about us the way you did," Frank continued. "In case you haven't figured it out, we're not mad at each other. We love each other very much."

Debra was finally able to produce some words. "How long has this been going on?"

"For several weeks now. Why?"

"It would have been nice to let us know."

"What would that have accomplished?"

"Dad, what's going on? Why all the deception?"

Dennis's mother fielded this question. "We didn't want to influence your relationship. We wanted you two to discover each other without any outside interference."

"You mean like our parents sleeping together?"

"Well, there's that."

Dennis was now getting into the conversation. "So, what are your plans? Are you just going to live together?"

His mother was quick to respond. "Really, you and Debra have been sleeping together for some time, and you weren't married. Besides, Frank and I are already married."

Dennis and Debra responded in unison, "What?"

"We went to Vegas a week ago."

Dennis looked down at his cup of coffee. "You know I might need to trade this cup in for something stronger, but it's kind of early. So, you two are really married?"

"Yep," said Frank as he took another sip of coffee. "Your mother is a wonderful woman, and we're looking forward to a great life together. She's going to quit lecturing, and I'm done with detective work. We want to experience the world one country at a time, until we've gone all the way around. Then we might even do it again. Now we have a question for you two. You've been very secretive about your honeymoon. So, where are you going?"

Dennis took a last sip from his coffee mug. "The truth is we're split on the destination. Debra wanted to go to Grand Cayman where there are some very comfortable resorts with lots of water sports. I wanted to go to a more remote location like Mexico. We've had so much going on with the wedding and everything else that we never made a firm decision. We had a tentative reservation in Cayman, but lost it when we couldn't make up our minds."

Frank leaned across the table. "So, you're having an argument already. It's only the second day you've been married, and you can't agree on one very important decision. I may be able to help you if you don't mind me meddling."

Debra looked to Dennis and then her father, unsure of what Frank had in mind. "Okay, Dad. What do you have in mind?"

"Well, I know this guy who has a very nice place. Very remote, but has top-of-the-line accommodations. To be honest, I knew that you hadn't decided on a place. So, I hope you don't mind, but I asked him if his place was available. That is if you're up for a little adventure."

Dennis reached over and put his arm around Debra. "I'm game. What about you, Honey?"

"I don't know what my dad is up to, but he would never screw up our honeymoon. I thought it would be nice to be around people, but now I'm leaning the other way. Is that what you had in mind, Dad?"

"I think I know what you two need, and this place is perfect. Just be ready at nine in the morning, and I'll arrange for the jet to take you there tomorrow."

Frank and his wife got up from the table and were about to leave, when Frank turned back.

"Dennis, I have to tell you. Even with all my years as a detective, you snuck one right by me."

"What's that?"

"Dennis Nathanial Andrews - DNA. I don't know how I missed it."

"You can thank mom for that one."

"Don't worry; I plan on thanking her many times."

The two old lovebirds left the room, and the new ones burst out laughing.

Chapter 54

Frank had told Dennis and Debra that where they were going was hot, humid, and had bugs. It was all very mysterious to Dennis and Debra, and they kept asking questions about the trip, but got no answers.

In the morning, the two couples said their good-byes. Dennis was sure he saw tears in his mother's eyes. He'd decided that Frank was going to be the best thing that happened to her.

They arrived at the airport and found their pilot preparing for takeoff. Dennis asked her about the flight, and she told them she was under orders not to say anything. She also told them that the blinds were to stay down until they reached their destination.

The newly married couple was exhausted from the wedding, and quickly fell asleep in each other's arms. Four and a half hours later, they were awakened by the pilot.

"Make sure you are buckled up because we're about to land. You can pull up the blinds now."

Dennis pulled up the blinds just before the wheels touched down. The runway was only large enough for the plane to land with little room to spare. There was no terminal, just a small hanger to the side of the runway. They could see an airplane mechanic working on a biplane and a couple of kids and dogs running about.

Dennis called up to his cousin. "Where are we?"

"That's not for me to say, Dennis. I'll let your host give you the details. Grab your stuff because it's time to go."

The door opened, and the pilot helped Dennis set the bags on the runway. She reached over and gave Dennis a hug and then Debra.

"Congratulations to the both of you. I'll be back in a couple of weeks. Enjoy your honeymoon."

She went back into the plane, to await her next set of passengers.

Dennis looked over at the biplane in the hanger and then to Debra. "Do you have any idea where we are? What have we gotten ourselves into?"

Before she could respond, a jeep exited out of the jungle. There was a man in the back seat and a man and woman in the front. The man driving looked familiar and Dennis was trying to place him.

The man jumped out of the jeep and walked over to Dennis extending his hand.

"Welcome to Mexico. "I'm Curt Towers, and this is my wife, Bonnie."

Then Dennis remembered where he'd seen the man. He'd been CEO of Xtreme Machines until he had been wrongly accused of rape and murder. He'd been framed by his competitor Alex Brandon, but eventually was cleared of all charges. Towers had turned his company over to department managers to run until his kids were old enough, and then disappeared. There'd been a lot of speculation as to where Towers had gone, but it looks like the mystery has been solved.

The other man got out of the jeep and walked over. Curt put his arm around the man's shoulder.

"This is my trusted caretaker, Phillip. He'll drive you to our house. Bonnie and I are taking the jet back to Denver so that we can visit my kids, and then return in a couple of weeks. Our place will be yours while we're gone. Phillip lives in his own place a quarter-mile from ours, but he'll drive you home and get you set up. Congratulations on your wedding. Enjoy our humble abode, and say hi to Frank when you get back to Seattle. Tell him he's welcome here anytime."

Dennis reached out and shook Curt's hand again. "Debra and I appreciate your generosity. What can you tell us about your place?"

Curt grinned and looked at Bonnie. "The road is awful, but we think what you'll find at the end is worth the ride."

Curt and Bonnie grabbed a couple of small bags from out of the jeep and headed toward the jet. Phillip grabbed the bags Dennis and Debra had brought, set them in the Jeep's back seat, and motioned for the two to get in. Before they had even started their ride, the jet had taken off.

Bumpy road was an understatement. Dennis and Debra both started to wonder if this was a big mistake or that Frank had played a practical joke on them. The potholes were deep and several of the bounces almost ejected Dennis. They finally arrived at a small building that didn't look elegant or large enough for someone so wealthy.

Phillip jumped out and grabbed their bags.

"Follow me and keep in mind, that appearances can be deceiving. This building is just a front to keep nosy people out of Curt and Bonnie's life."

Dennis and Debra followed Phillip through the door and down a hall. They exited through the back of the building and proceeded to a second smaller building that resembled a fancy outhouse. Phillip lifted the keypad cover and punched in a code. The door opened, and the three walked into a small elevator that took them down twenty feet. When the door opened again, Dennis was in shock. The room was huge and had curved portholes that looked out into underwater caves called cenotes.

Phillip pointed to a table next to the port.

"Sit down and enjoy the view while I get you some cold drinks."

Debra sat down and surveyed the room. This was technology at its max with a big-screen TV, fancy kitchen, and exercise room in the distance. The hallways looked like they were hundreds of feet long. She was in awe.

When Phillip returned with a bottle of wine and two glasses, he asked, "So, what do you think so far?"

She took a sip and asked, "Wow! So how did Curt and Bonnie know our parents?"

Phillip sat down and joined them.

"Frank was a partner with Curt's friend who was killed while trying to prove his innocence. Sharing this place with you for your honeymoon is just one way Curt can repay him for everything he did in a roundabout way."

"Wow, your' talking about my Uncle Lloyd," said Debra.

"Besides, from what I hear, you two have gone through hell the past few months. It's a little bit like what Curt went through with people coming at you from all directions, and nowhere to turn. Well, now you can relax. This place is secure and very green. It's run on solar power. The water is from collected rainwater, and the food is purchased from local villages. We provide them with seeds; they grow the food, and then we buy it back from them. It's a perfect solution for everyone."

He took a breath and continued. "If you need to go into town, just let me know. There're some great places to shop and many unique sites to see. I know you're tired, so let me fix you a quick bite to eat, and then I'll leave you alone."

During lunch, Phillip explained how the house was set up and where everything was located. Phillip then carried their bags to their room down the hall. The newlyweds followed, but stopped every few feet to admire the incredible underwater photography on the walls. When Phillip finally opened the heavy door, they walked into what looked like Captain Nemo's bedroom. The room was huge and there was a large glass dome with fish swimming by, and beams of light flickering down from the surface to the cave floor. The two just looked at each other and smiled.

Phillip turned to the two. "We have no time schedule here. Wake up when you feel like it. I won't be back to bother you, but if you need something, just dial 66 and either my machine or I'll answer. Remember that it will take me ten minutes to get here. The refrigerator and cupboards have been well stocked, and everything is fair game. Now if you don't mind, I've work to be done on my place. Congratulations and enjoy."

Phillip walked down the hall and was out of sight in a minute. The two newlyweds sat on the edge of the king-size bed and were in shock.

"This place is incredible, Dennis. Our parents made a great choice. Although that sounds strange doesn't it? Our parents...who are married. I can hardly believe it."

Dennis was mesmerized by the glass dome and all the fish life being displayed in their bedroom.

"You go ahead and shower first, and then I'll follow."

Debra didn't need to be told twice as Dennis was a shower hog. Minutes later, she emerged swathed in a large bath towel.

"You're not going to believe the shower. It has another small dome facing in another direction, so I watched fish as I showered. This place is incredible. Go; check it out as I'm not going to wait forever."

Dennis was also amazed by the shower, but cut his shower short when he realized he had a new wife waiting for him. He dried off and wrapped a towel around himself. He opened the door to discover the breathtaking view of his new bride lying on the bed without the towel.

Debra motioned for him to join her.

"Lose the towel, dude."

Dennis dropped his towel but then realized there were no blinds on the dome.

"Do you think someone can see us making love?"

"Do you really care?"

Book Three in the Acroname Series

S.O.S.

By Jack and Sue Drafahl

Available Soon in Paperback and Kindle

University professors, James and Stacy Sanders, find themselves caught up in the social networking world to such an extent that it affords them minimal time for themselves or their two children. A catastrophic disaster throws these two together on an uninhabited Pacific volcano, with little hope of being rescued. They quickly discover that teamwork and close communication are a priority, if they plan to survive.

They must rely upon their scuba diving skills, and their extensive knowledge in World War II history, to keep one step ahead of the of the forces of Mother Nature, and a relentless cold-blooded killer.

S.O.S. is loaded with twists and turns that keep you guessing on what's going to happen next. I liked the idea of bringing back some characters from D.N.A. and adding them to the mix. The realistic description of the island and the world disaster makes you feel like you're right there struggling with them. This is the best Acroname book so far. S. Adams

SOS is a hard to put down, enjoyable thriller set in the stunning location of the Solomon Islands. Having read three of the Acroname series books by Jack and Sue Drafahl, SOS is my favorite one to date. It has something for everyone with interesting characters, fast-paced action, good guys, bad guys, natural disasters, romance, humor, and scuba diving! SOS will keep you turning the pages to find out what happens next! Kellie Oldfield

Book One in the Acroname Series

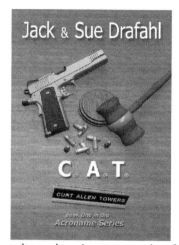

C.A.T.

By Jack and Sue Drafahl
Available in Paperback and Kindle

Curt Allen Towers (C.A.T.) owns a successful manufacturing company, specializing in miniaturized robotic devices. His life is turned upside down when he is accused of the rape and murder of a business associate. Curt struggles to prove his innocence, but finds there is a fine line between friend and foe. He must now rely on his gut feelings to judge a person and read them with his heart.

A fugitive from prison, he desperately runs for cover, evading one attempt after another on his life. Curt lives up to his nickname of CAT, but wonders if nine lives are enough? If you loved the TV action adventures of "The Fugitive" and "MacGyver," then you'll enjoy C. A. T.

This book is a great read - you won't want to put it down! It's full of action, and will have you cheering for CAT (Curt Allen Towers) as he dodges the bad guys . The book has it all - there are twists and turns, suspense, action-packed moments, intrigue, humor and romance. It will keep you interested right to the end! I'm looking forward to their next book. Highly recommended! Paul S.

Reading CAT provided the escape and the entertainment I was looking for. I tried to second-guess the twists and turns – to no avail. A real page-turning adventure. Michele Hall

I could not put the book down once I started reading it. Hope to read many more novels from these two!! Laure Dannewitz

What a plot! You just don't know what the authors will fire at you next! L.Moore

Book One in the Ship Series

Discovery

By Jack and Sue Drafahl

Available Soon in Paperback and Kindle

Jake MacDonald's life has hit rock bottom. He's lost his job, and his wife and two children have lost their faith in him. It seems that everything that could go wrong has happened, and he now has nowhere to turn. In a final effort to salvage his financial problems, Jake turned from banking to lobster fishing off Santa Barbara Island. While scuba diving, he discovers an underwater cave that extends deep beneath the island shoreline. As he swims into the cave looking for fish and lobster, he finds an alien artifact. This discovery makes a drastic transformation to his life, and changes the history of planet Earth in a way no one could have ever imagined.

Discovery is the first book in the *Ship* series that draws suppositions from the future science of NASA, and asks the question, "Are we really alone?" Jake MacDonald uses the artifact he discovered to help answer that question, while attempting to unify his family. His ability to think outside the box allows him to turn his life around, and explore beyond the bounds of Earth's atmosphere.

Ship is a view from inner space to outer space on a journey of Discovery. It's about a new journey...about those who chose to go, and those that ultimately give life a new meaning. Jack and Sue Drafahl have created a view that few have ever imagined - a moment in time beyond our view...tomorrow. Ernie Brooks

Jack and Sue Drafahl are a husband and wife writing team. Over the past forty years, they have written over 800 articles in sixteen national publications from *Petersen's Photographic* to *Skin Diver Magazine*.

They have also authored seven non-fiction technical books for Amherst Media on various aspects of photography, both topside and underwater.

In 2006, they changed the course of their writing to include fiction. They have written two book series: (the *Acroname* series and the *Ship* series) that currently include twelve novels than span the gamut of genres from Action/Adventure to Science Fiction.

They both received their scuba diving certification in the early '70s, and have logged over ten thousand dives in almost every ocean on earth. Jack and Sue were awarded Divers of the Year from Beneath the Sea in 1996, and were given the Accolade Award for their conservation efforts. Sue is an inaugural member of the Women Divers Hall of Fame (2000) and is an Honorary Trustee. They are members of the Pacific Northwest Writers Association.

Jack and Sue make their home on the Oregon coast. In addition to their book writing, they enjoy leading underwater photo expeditions around the globe.

Send any comments or errors you may find to: novels@earthseapublishing.com.

http://www.JackandSueDrafahl.com
http://www.EarthSeaPublishing.com

43560583R10201

Made in the USA
Middletown, DE
26 April 2019